Praise for Lu

WillowTree Press, LLC

LUCINDA'S WEB

Dorothy Morrison

E. M. A. Mysteries

Lucinda's Web
A WillowTree Press Book
E. M. A. Mysteries is an imprint of WillowTree Press

PRINTING HISTORY
WillowTree Press First Trade Paper Edition/October 2008

For information, contact WillowTree Press, LLC at http://www.willowtreepress.com

ISBN–13: 978-097945332-8
ISBN–10: 097945332-1

Cover Design Copyright © by Johnathan Minton

Author Photo by Kelly L. Varner

10 9 8 7 6 5 4 3 2 1

PRINTED IN THE U.S.A.

For
Murv

My friend, confidant, and traveling buddy extraordinaire, whose unwavering support, encouragement, and absolute refusal to let me fall on my face gave me the courage to move ahead with this project, and without whom this book simply would not be. (I'm so glad you're a part of my life—and it's not just because I'm clumsy!)

ACKNOWLEDGEMENTS

Spinning a good tale is a lot of fun, and it's something I've always enjoyed. But spinning one on paper is much different than weaving one in person. To put such to paper requires a lot of folks working behind the scenes—each adding his or her own personal strands and making solid connections in the framework—before an author's idea can be spun into the story she envisioned. And it's to these people that I owe a great debt of gratitude:

To my mother, Laura Belle, for sharing the stories of our ancestors and instilling in me a love of history; and to my father, Ed, for providing first-hand information of what it's like to be a law enforcement officer in a small town, and for teaching me the joys of spinning a good tale. I only wish you'd both lived to see this novel published.

To Lilah, Ellen, Eunice, Ardelia, Erb, Carl, and all the other wonderful African-American folks who played an integral role in my early childhood, and each of whom—even posthumously—breathed life into many of the characters in this book and live on through them.

To Mark—my husband and the love of my life—for always being there for me, for believing in me, and for loving me just the way I am (even when my messes spill out far beyond the confines of my office). I love you beyond measure, and still can't believe my luck at having found you! And to Sadie, whose ability to keep me company and help me write is truly a rare treasure.

To my dear friend, M. R. Sellars, not only for allowing me to pick his brain about fabrics, fibers, and plantations crops—Yes, folks…he really is quite the expert on those topics!—but for his belief in my abilities, his friendship over the years, and for just being the wonderful person he is.

To Gay Lowe for life-long friendship, encouragement, and advice—both writing and otherwise—and for being an integral part of what eventually became this novel.

To Dameon Wilburn and Stephanie Rose Bird, for sharing their knowledge of both fixing tricks and breaking them, and for assistance with the African-American dialects of the Old South.

To Judika Illes, for sharing her knowledge of parcel location and helping me to figure out how to locate and dismantle one over a hundred years old.

To Jill Kiefner, for sharing her medical knowledge of sedatives and pointing me toward the one that would produce the side-effects necessary to the story-line of this book.

To Lady Miriam of The Voodoo Spiritual Temple in New Orleans, for her wise advice and for reminding me that "folks in the 1800's just didn't do things for the same reasons that they do now."

To Cindy Kyte and Lexi Kavanaugh, for reading the first few chapters of this book and encouraging me to finish it.

To my sister, Mary Anne, as well as to Z Harrell, Linn Lipford, and Samantha Beaty, not only for reading the first draft and offering opinions and advice, but for believing in it enough to work a little "publication magic" of their own. You're the best!

To Kathy Epps, for her amazing ability to edit, find solutions when I had none, and make me look so good in print. You truly are a Goddess!

And finally, to the fabulous folks at WillowTree Press, for taking a chance on both me and *Lucinda's Web*. Mere words cannot express my appreciation!

"The soul should always stand ajar, ready to welcome the ecstatic experience."

–Emily Dickinson–

PROLOGUE

Sikeston, Missouri–1994

It's hard to say how it all began, but I guess the house is as good a starting place as any. It was the only house I could find on such short notice. Oh, there were others all right, but something was wrong with every single one of them: bad neighborhood, high rent or non-availability. Not that this was a prize winner of any sort. The floors had fallen from the center and every stick of furniture I owned had to be leveled with scraps of cardboard torn from moving boxes. A previous remodeling job had left light switches in inconvenient spots, and the wiring was so old that I had to take care not to use too many appliances lest every fuse in the house be blown. The biggest problem, though, was that the house was so small there was no place to put anything. Other than that, it was absolutely wonderful.

I wanted to cry. It had been a bad month—so bad in fact, that I wished the Gods had just seen fit to remove the entire block from the year. Unfortunately, they hadn't, and I was forced to swallow every tasteless morsel it had to serve. It was the end of life as I knew it.

First, there was the surgery, which by itself would have been no big deal. Then the landlord called to say that he wanted to take possession of the house I'd lived in for the past two years—and he wanted me out as soon as I was released from the hospital. I said I couldn't do it. He said my medical difficulties weren't his problem. The house was his and he wanted it back. Not as soon as it was convenient for me, but by the end of the month. Period.

I wanted to ask whether his mother had forgotten to teach him any manners. I bit my tongue instead. Not that I was afraid of him or anything. A person in my position had nothing to lose. There are just those times in life when you can feel your mother watching you from two thousand miles away, and you don't want to be caught misbehaving. This was one of those times.

The search for a house on such short notice was enough to test the patience of the Ancients. And before it was done, I felt a lot like the very pregnant Virgin Mary. I checked the local papers. Nothing. I called every landlord in Sikeston. No vacancies. The cosmos may as well have put up a sign that said "No Room at the Inn."

Fortunately for Christians everywhere, I wasn't the Virgin Mary and—thank heaven—wasn't pregnant. If I had been, the Christ-child would've been born under very different circumstances, and the biblical authors would've been forced to scrap their first draft. I'd have seen to it. I'd never been the patient sort, and I didn't have time for this shit. I was nearly forty years old, and I'd be damned if I was going to live in a barn. Besides, I had a book to finish.

Now hitting one brick wall after another has a way of fueling the temper. And after a while, I wasn't just mad—I was thoroughly pissed off. I screamed. I yelled. I shook my fist at the sky. I threw a tantrum to rival that of any five-year-old child.

"What the hell are You doing up there?!" I spat. Gone to lunch and stayed for dessert? Decided to take a nap? Well, wake Your Divine asses up! I need help down here!"

The neighbor's dog looked at me like I'd lost my mind. I had.

"It's me! Remember *me*?! Your favorite child? What's the deal with You, anyway? Is this Your idea of a 'growth experience?' Well, if it is, go help someone *else* grow! I've grown *plenty*!"

I threw myself on the ground and waited. There wasn't any answer. Not that I'd really expected one; in fact, I'd have probably fainted on the spot if I'd heard so much as a peep.

There was nothing left to do but go inside and pack. Those inconsiderate bastards had ruined my summer, taken my home and made me miserable—but they sure as hell weren't going to get my stuff in the bargain! What a mess! No matter what I might have done in this lifetime, I sure as hell didn't deserve this.

I spent the next week crying a lot, sleeping a little, and cramming my life's accumulation into a dwindling supply of boxes. I made countless phone calls, daily trips to the newspaper stand, and delivered tirades that would've won Academy Awards had they been on film. One morning though, my best soliloquy was interrupted by the jangle of the phone. Life changed again.

"Tess? This is Sylvia."

What did she want? I hardly even knew the woman.

"Hi, Sylvia. How are you?"

"Fine. Couldn't be better. Listen, I just called to see if you were still house hunting. My uncle bought a house to rent and I thought..."

"I'll take it! What's his number?"

"Don't you *even* want to know where it *is*?" I could tell by the rising pitch of her voice that she thought I was crazy. Well, maybe I was—just a little.

"No."

"Well, okay. I don't think he's closed on it yet, but I thought it might work out for both of you."

She gave me the number and hung up. That's when it occurred to me that maybe Somebody up there really did get Their messages. I had, after all, just been saved by a complete stranger!

Sylvia's uncle was a nice old man and just the type you'd expect to be someone's uncle. He was delighted to rent me the house, but just as I thought everything was going beautifully, my world turned to shit again. Did I know the house was right across the street from the cemetery? Interesting. Did I realize the property wasn't in a good part of town? Locks. I'd need lots of them. Oh, by the way, the present occupants couldn't possibly move until the first week in July. Was that a problem? Hell yes it was, but hardly as bad as the barn I'd envisioned. Amazing how priorities change—especially when the alternative is impending homelessness.

That afternoon, I formed such a firm relationship with the telephone that I thought it might actually have to be surgically removed from my ear. I called the movers, the phone company and everybody else that mattered. I filled out change of address cards. I called the office of every single magazine company that sent their wares to my door. I finally finished with all the arrangements late that night. That's when I remembered to call my mother.

"What do you *mean*, you're moving again?!"

Mama'd never been able to understand this moving business. I could almost hear the thoughts running through her head. *You're forty years old and should be settled by now. Rent? Why don't you buy? You don't have enough money to buy? Why not? Haven't you saved anything?*

Thankful that she didn't say any of the things she was thinking, I finished the conversation and called it a night.

The bed felt good. It was the only thing I'd ever owned that made me feel rich. The fluffy down comforter and the sheets embellished with Battenburg lace and embroidered cutwork could make any pauper feel like a queen. I patted them fondly. *No barn for you, my pretties!* Snuggling down into them, I thought about my family and the stock I was made of. Kings and knights, poets and patriots, doctors and ministers. Important folks, all of them. I wondered if they'd ever accepted possession of a house without looking it over first. Probably not. I grinned at the thought of my royal Scottish ancestors and the vision of them in my kettle of stew.

"What?! Old run down castle smack dab amongst the peasantry thieves? In need of locks aplenty? Excellent view of the graveyard? Why, m'good laddie, 'tis a bargain indeed! I'll take it!"

I laughed out loud, playing the king's conversation over in my head. It was the first time I'd laughed since I'd gotten the news. Feeling better, I snuggled down into the comforter and drifted happily off to sleep.

Had I known what moving day would bring though, I wouldn't have been so happy—in fact, I probably wouldn't have slept at all—because the only thing worse than the house search itself proved to be the actual move. The truck I'd reserved two weeks earlier—and confirmed twice—had been cancelled inadvertently by the careless touch of some disembodied finger on a keyboard, and there wasn't another to be had within a hundred mile radius. To make matters worse, most of my moving help managed to back out at the last minute.

But that wasn't all. I got to the house only to discover that I had no electricity. Instead of transferring the service into my name as requested, some idiot at the electric company had simply turned it off. Not only was it a hundred and two in the shade, but there was no air-conditioning, no way to turn on a fan; I was forced to swelter in that hell hole until something could be done about it on Monday morning.

The whole ordeal was a nightmare—doomed from the very beginning—and there was nothing I could do about it. Except, of course, to follow things through. It looked like I'd been called. And the cemetery across the street was the culprit.

The activity there was unrivaled by any other. Waves of confusion, displeasure and perplexity emanated from inside. At first, I'd chalked it up to the Great Earthquake—the one that had changed the course of the Mississippi River in the early 1800's—for a tremor that powerful had probably disengaged more than just a few residents from their respective headstones and left their spirits bewildered and confused. However true that might have been though, the fact remained that no other cemetery in Sikeston shared that same sense of foreboding and chaos. No, it was something else—something secretive, dastardly, evil and black—and it all centered around the plot of graves privately encased in a disheveled wrought iron fence.

CHAPTER 1

"Where is it?" The silvery voice belonged to Chloe.

"Over yonder." I pointed toward the other side of the cemetery. "Inside that wrought iron fence!"

The gravestone with the shrouded urn had grabbed my attention the very first time I saw it. It had called out—beckoning me closer—as if it had some deep, dark secret to tell. Being the picture of practicality though, I'd brushed the summons aside as if it were a nagging fly, and I'd gotten busy with the everyday business of unpacking, grocery shopping and laundry.

Not that I didn't know better. I did. I knew full well there were no coincidences in life and that something there needed attention. My attention. I'd taught Chloe and countless others to deal immediately with just this sort of thing. I was a Wiccan high priestess—a modern day Witch—and as such, I felt personally responsible for investigating that sort of stuff. But I hadn't been able to make myself enter that cemetery. Not until today anyway. I just hoped it wasn't too late.

Chloe stopped short, and the resulting collision jolted me right back into reality. We fell to the ground in a tangle of arms and legs, and our laughter rang out through the silence.

"What's *wrong*, Tess?" Remnants of laughter still echoed in her voice. "Mountain goat get in your way, oh plodding one?" With a twinkling wink of her azure eyes, Chloe struggled to her feet and gave me her hand.

"Oh, Chloe...I am *so* sorry! Are you all *right*?"

"Yeah, I'm fine, but what about *you*? What wave of the ether have you been surfing since we left?" The hand she'd run through her golden hair now rested on her hip, and she assumed her best stance of mock seriousness. "Did you hear a single word I said, Ms. Logan? I've been talking to you ever since we left the house."

"My most humble apologies, Ms. Dawson," I replied with a flourish as I burst into laughter again. "Now then. What were you saying?"

"Nothing important, really. Just that I'd done a little research on my own and didn't come up with anything."

"Research on what?"

"The name on the headstone. I checked the Sikeston histories and couldn't find his name. Not that I'm *surprised*," she said with a shrug of her shoulders. "I just thought it might help if you had a place to start. Of course, *nothing* is ever *that* simple!"

"Tell me something I *don't* know!" I said, shaking my head. "I called the courthouse to check on death certificates and burial records yesterday and hit a brick wall too. Evidently, the cemetery was privately owned up until 1907, and no one kept records until after it was sold to the city. I swear, Chloe...that clerk was about as dumb as a box of rocks!" I rolled my eyes and chuckled. "Said he couldn't *imagine* where I might find any *pertinent* information about the folks buried here in the 1800's."

"So, who owned the land?"

"Anybody's guess. Apparently, there was a lot of shoddy record-keeping. But get *this*! He couldn't even find the bill of sale on his microfiche. Good Gods...where *do* they *find* these folks?!"

We were still laughing when we finally reached the cast iron fence of the plot in question.

I rounded the corner and pushed on the gate.

"What's the *matter*?" breathed Chloe.

"Damned thing's rusted shut. Maybe that's why I never bothered to check this out. Can't get in this place even if you *want* to!" I grumbled. I put my weight against the gate and fiddled with the rusty latch. "Just a little more, now...there!"

The gate swung open. I took a deep breath, squared my shoulders and calling to Chloe over my shoulder, marched right inside like I owned the place.

I stood there looking at the grave that had peaked my interest. Finally, I walked over and touched the headstone, then bent down to test the grass beneath. There was nothing—no peculiar energy, no startling psychic flashes, no ghostly soliloquies floating through the ether. There was nothing. Nothing at all.

Yet, something did stop me from leaving the plot and heading toward the house. What could it be, I wondered as I glanced at the other graves there. What was the big deal? Something was definitely out of kilter. Something I just couldn't put my finger on. But what?

"It's not this one," I said. "Got any ideas?"

I turned to face Chloe, but she was still outside the fence looking in.

"Get *in* here! I could use a little help, you know."

"Can't," said Chloe, her eyes filling up with tears of emotion.

"Why *not*, for Goddess' sake?"

"This place is only for *real* Witches...and you know I'm just a *'Wish'* until I'm initiated!" There was a half-hearted chuckle and then a tear fell from her eye. "Try the stone next to his." The chuckle had died and her tone was serious. "I have a funny feeling about that one."

I'd learned long ago that dismissing any advice Chloe had to offer—no matter how silly it seemed at the onset—was an exercise in sheer stupidity. The woman's brain was constantly bombarded by psychic flashes, and though difficult to sort out at times, they all meant something. That being the case, I looked at the tiny white stone with the hands clasped together on the front and instinctively reached over to touch them. *What the hell was this?!*

"Chloe! *Chloe!* Get *over* here!"

The August sun danced on Chloe's blonde hair as she started toward the gate. She took a few steps and then stopped dead in her tracks as if some unseen hand held her at bay.

"I *can't*!"

"Sure you can,"

"No, I *can't!*" came the irritated response. "It's not that I don't *want* to—it's just that I'm being *prevented*!" She sighed deeply. "I guess this must be *your* thing. You'll just have to get through it without me."

We looked at each other for a minute, and I finally realized that Chloe wasn't kidding. It wasn't the first time something like this had happened with us; in fact, it had happened so often over the years that neither of us even thought it strange anymore.

Resignedly, Chloe stayed where she was. Finally, she asked what was wrong.

"The hands on the stone are warm, but the rest of the marble is like ice."

"What else?"

"It belongs to a female with the same last name, but I can't decide whether it's the man's daughter, wife or mother because..."

"Check the dates, silly!"

"That's what I've been trying to tell you, Ms.'Wish.' There aren't any."

"What do you *mean*, there aren't any?!" Chloe shielded her eyes against the sun and peered at the marker.

"Just what I said. No birth date. No death date. Nothing!"

"There *has* to be one *somewhere*. Look on both sides."

"Already did, Sherlock. There's an inscription here too, but it's so faded I can't make it out."

Reading the inscription was a real exercise in patience. I moved closer to the stone, but the words wouldn't focus. I moved farther back, but that didn't help either. Finally, I tried tracing the words letter by letter with my fingers.

"'These were'...something...something...'last words,' and then the last line reads: 'I think I shall go to heaven.' Damn it, I'm missing some words in the first line and having trouble with the second."

After playing with the lettering for a few more minutes, I decided to go home to get paper for a rubbing. It was the sensible thing to do. And I, after all, was a sensible person. Something though—a force beyond all comprehension and without any measure of rhyme or reason—held me glued to the spot. And that something insisted that I just keep working right where I was. Fortunately, its insistence not only paid off but did the job in spades.

"Wait...I've got it! Oh, Chloe! Here's what it says:

These were amongst the last words of she who really lies beneath this stone: I think I shall go to heaven.'"

The message seared through my core, and one look at Chloe's tear-stained face proved its impact on her as well.

"Oh, Gods, Chloe! You don't suppose the person listed on this headstone isn't really the person in this grave, *do* you?!"

"I don't know," came the slow response, "but I guess it's possible."

Trying to shake off the uneasy feeling that threatened to envelope me, I allowed practicality to take over once more.

"Tell you what...let's check out the rest of the cemetery before we jump to any ridiculous conclusions. Maybe that inscription was pretty common for the time period. There's no reason to let our imaginations run away with us."

"Good idea." Chloe exhaled slowly and ran her hand through her hair. "Wanna split up or canvass the area together?"

"Why don't we split up? That way we can cover more ground. I think I'll leave the gate open though. What d'ya think?"

"How should *I* know? After all, I'm just a..."

"Wish!" we chimed together, and the uneasy moment was broken by another round of giggles and laughter.

We spent the rest of the morning exploring the grounds, with Chloe canvassing the south side and me taking the north. When we finally caught up with each other at the west entrance, neither of us had found anything that even remotely resembled the epitaph in question.

"I was afraid of that. What d'ya say we get out of this heat. I've got sweat dripping from places I didn't even know I had!"

The phone was ringing when we reached the house. I raced toward the sound, unceremoniously plowing through the stack of unpacked boxes in the middle of the living room floor. Full speed ahead, I leapt down the hall, lunged across the bed, and managed a breathless hello.

Chloe was already in the kitchen measuring scoops of coffee. No matter whether the phone call was good news or bad, she was sure that Tess would want coffee. The woman drank the stuff like health nuts drank water. She wondered what Tess would be like if she didn't get at least two pots a day. Probably as still and sedate as the cemetery residents across the street, she thought with a grin. With the picture of a sedate Tess still roving through her mind's eye, she chuckled, poured a mug full of the steaming stuff and started down the hall.

"Well, what did she say?" Chloe asked.

I was still on the phone but motioned her inside and patted the bed. "Yes, I understand and that's no problem. I'll be looking for it in the mail." I said my thank-you's and goodbye's and hung up the phone.

Chloe looked at me expectantly. I didn't say a word.

"Well?!"

"I think we need to break out the Bailey's because," I said with a sigh, "...we've got something to celebrate, my friend. I've got a *book contract*!"

We hugged and screamed and danced around the room. Then we threw ourselves across the bed and screamed some more. In fact, had it not been for the silver strands in our hair, we might have been mistaken for a couple of teenaged girls who'd just managed to snag front row seats for their very first concert. We weren't teenaged girls though. And I, for one, was damned glad of it. Teenaged girls were cute, but they couldn't afford good coffee—or Bailey's—and today, I intended to have my fill of both.

As we climbed over the mountain of half-unpacked boxes and headed for the kitchen, I wondered if I really needed all that stuff. There was no place to put anything—the house was already bursting at the seams—and I didn't have any idea what to do with it all. Hauling the whole mess outside and striking a match certainly seemed like the best solution. But even so, I quickly changed my mind. With my luck, I'd probably torch something I really needed. And it only took the thought of spending weeks trying to reconstruct something important to push that thought aside. Besides, maybe being a packrat wasn't so bad. Of course, I changed my mind about that too—just as soon as I tripped over a box of books and stubbed my toe on a cast iron door stop.

"*Fuck ME!!*" I screamed the obscenity at the top of my lungs.

"Are you all *right*?!"

"I will be as soon as I quit hurting. Holy *shit*!" I hobbled the rest of the way into the kitchen where, fortunately, all the stuff *was* unpacked and *did* fit. Best of all, I knew where I'd put the Bailey's. So with steaming mugs of coffee laced with Irish cream, we plopped down at the table.

Chloe stared at me, her eyes twinkling. She was waiting for me to say something, but I just grinned from ear to ear instead. She hated it when I did that and held her ground. Well, at least until she couldn't stand it any longer.

"So?" She threw up her hands in complete exasperation.

"So, what?"

"So, what changed their minds?"

"I'm not sure. But apparently, the gal who said I couldn't write—you know, the one who insisted that I was an illiterate nitwit—is no longer with them. Honestly, Chloe," I chuckled, "I almost had to shove a pillow in my mouth to keep from laughing out loud when I heard that!"

"Must've been the fact that her favorite word was 'yuck.' Or maybe that she never managed to learn the definition of 'augment'!"

Our giggles changed quickly into chuckles and snorts and then finally dissolved into full blown laughter. We laughed so hard, in fact, that I thought we might actually wet our pants.

You see, the woman in question had read my manuscript nearly a year before, and had not only raked my work over the coals but had taken some very personal potshots at me. She'd likened me to a Victorian lady at a tea party. *Yuck! Someone needs to take you down a notch.* She'd told me to stop pretending that my readers were my students. *Yuck! Have you lost your mind?* And just when I thought she'd delivered the final blow—*Yuck! You'll never be published until you learn to adhere strictly to the rules set forth by the Chicago Manual of Style!*— she upped the ante. She informed me that I must forever and irrevocably strike the word, "augment," from my vocabulary. The reason was simple of course. That word was so advanced, my readers would be forced to grab the nearest dictionary and look it up! [Yep, there was a "yuck" by that comment too.]

Of course, I'd been as mad as a wet hen. So much so in fact, that I'd plopped right down and written a rebuttal to her ridiculous review report. Yes, I reminded her that "yuck" was not a proper word—not a preferred one in any English dictionary that I'd ever seen, anyway—and that since she'd chosen to use that idiom on a constant basis, I simply could not take her seriously. But it was probably my response to the "augment" criticism that really got her goat. I reminded her in no uncertain terms that the word "augment" was found in every fifth grade vocabulary list in the continental United States. And that being the case, it might behoove her to go back to school.

In the final analysis though, I'd gotten nothing at all for my trouble. Except, of course, my manuscript—all boxed up and delivered to my front door by the UPS man—along with a nasty little rejection letter and pride so wounded I thought it might never heal.

But that was yesterday, and today was an entirely different story. The Goddess was alive and well, all right. She was tap-dancing to beat the band—and right in the acquisitions department of my brand new publishing house!

"...so do you think we need a reservation?"

"Hunh?"

"Haven't you been listening at *all*?!"

"To what?"

Chloe rolled her eyes heavenward, ran her fingers through her hair and expelled a heavy sigh.

"I said that a celebration's in order. So why don't Brian and I take you out for supper? How about Lambert's around seven? Our treat. And...do you think I should call for a reservation?"

"But I don't have anything to wear."

"It's Lambert's, silly. A tee-shirt and shorts will get it. Besides, I don't feel like cooking and you haven't been to the grocery store. You have to eat and..."

I couldn't stand whining. And Chloe'd started to do just that.

"Okay! *Okay!*" I put up my hands in mock surrender and started to laugh. "But if I'm going to meet ya'll at seven, I've got to cleaned up in short order. It's already five forty-five."

"Cool! I'm out of here. See you at seven!"

Commonly known as "The Home of Throwed Rolls"—a term that really galled the part of me who'd minored in English—Lambert's Restaurant was a nationally famous eatery. It really had nothing to do with the quality of the food, which was passable. Instead, the claim to fame came from an absurd practice of sorts: Their wait staff literally threw hot yeast rolls at the folks seated in the dining room. Even more absurd—to me at least—was the fact that their customers not only came from miles around to have that food thrown at them but actually paid for the privilege. It just went to prove what I'd said all along. People, as a rule, were a stupid sort. And tonight, I thought as I turned left on Malone, I was on the way to join the ranks of idiocy. My only consolation was that I wasn't going to pay for it.

Lambert's didn't take reservations on Friday night, and by the time I turned into the parking lot, the line was already half-way down the porch. But that was all right with me. It was a beautiful night, and for the first time I could remember, there was no reason to hurry. I locked the Jeep and scanned the waiting line. Sure enough, I spotted Brian towering over the crowd.

I liked Brian Dawson. He was a big man—nearly six-foot-six—with a voice as gruff as they came, but he was the most charming, gentle man I'd ever met. He was also absolutely full of it. I couldn't imagine having a party without Brian there to get things started. Or to keep them going.

"Hi, Handsome! How the hell are you?"

"Hey, Gorgeous!" He hugged my neck and twirled me around, then he held me out at arm's length. "I understand congratulations are in order. Good going, Gal! So, tell all. How the hell did this happen?"

I decided to play it straight—just to see if I could.

"Well, I wrote fifty thousand words, printed it out and bought five bucks worth of stamps. Then..." I collapsed into giggles. Obviously, playing it straight was not my forte.

"Still the Queen of Bullshit, aren't you?!" Brian chuckled, then burst into full blown laughter. "You know exactly what I mean, Tess. What the hell happened at the publishing house? I thought they hated that book."

"So did I. But apparently, they've had a change of heart *and* a change in personnel. Yep...looks like the woman who gave me such a hard time doesn't work there any more. And I'd bet nickels to donuts she got her ass canned for stepping on the wrong toes."

"Wouldn't have had anything to do with *your* toes? Or some sort of nose-twitching or wand-waving or anything like that, would it?" He'd put on his most serious face, but the twinkle in his eyes gave him away.

"I can't *believe* you'd think that," I retorted with mock indignation. "You've cut me deep, Brian. *Deep*, I say. Straight to the bone!" Our laughter rang out over the crowd.

"So, where's Chloe?"

"She had some last minute errands to run. Doesn't she always?" he said as he glanced at his watch. "So I came ahead. She's going to meet us here. When*ever* she's *done*."

By the way he delivered the last statement, I could tell I'd broached a sore subject. I wondered at his aggravation though. After all, this was typical Chloe. Time just didn't affect her the way it did other folks. It was a known fact that she was late for everything; so much so, that I usually insisted she arrive an hour before expected—just to make sure she didn't keep me waiting. Hell, the woman would miss her own funeral if I hadn't already selected six of her most punctual friends to tote her in. But if *I* knew that much about Chloe, I had to wonder at Brian, who—even after nearly twenty years of marriage to the woman—didn't seem to have a clue. Still, I'd opened this can of worms, and it was up to me to see what I could do to close it.

"Well, all I can say is that she'd better hurry. Otherwise, she's not going to get anything to eat. Besides," I teased, "I might just steal you away while I've got the chance!" My last remark did the trick, and Brian's laughter rang out over the crowd again.

Chloe's timing was impeccable. She breezed in just as we were being seated, and I was damned glad of it. Had she been any later, I'd have had my hands full. For all of Brian's good points, he wasn't the most patient man in the world. By the time she'd arrived, he'd already glanced at his watch four or five times. Spending an entire evening defending Chloe's complete lack of regard for time wasn't high on my priority list of fun things to do. Neither was running constant interference so the two of them would play nice. And I knew I'd have had to do one or the other if she'd been any later.

Everything seemed to be fine now. Chloe'd had the good sense to present him with tons of apologies, several kisses and that adoring smile of hers, the latter of which I was sure could melt *any* heart—and Brian's didn't stand a chance.

"Where the hell have you been? And what's up? You look like the cat who swallowed the canary."

"Just running errands," she said with a grin. "No big deal." I knew better though. Chloe'd been up to something all right, and from the look in her eyes, I could tell she was more than just a little tickled about it.

"And what sort of errands might those be? What could you have possibly been doing that was..." My words were cut short by a roll zipping toward my head. That's right. A roll. The guy on the throwing end was obviously in sore need of pitching practice, and if it hadn't been for Brian's quick hand, the damned thing would've smacked me right between the eyes.

I was fit to be tied. This was the first time in forever that I'd really had something to celebrate, and now I couldn't even have a pleasant conversation without having food thrown at me. Something was wrong with that picture. Bad wrong. Of course, it was my own damned fault. If I hadn't agreed to come here in the first place, I wouldn't be dealing with this shit. Instead, I'd be having that quiet, happy little celebratory dinner I'd envisioned.

Unfortunately, personal irritation loomed larger than any sense of reason. There would be no more food tossed at me tonight. I didn't give a tinker's damn about their practices or why they were famous. This was a party, damn it. My party. And surely—even at Lambert's, The Home Of Throwed Rolls—I could party as I pleased.

The roll-thrower was twice my size, but I didn't care. I cocked an eyebrow, pointed at the roll in Brian's hand then gave my finger a healthy shake in his direction. I don't know what that guy thought I was going to do to him, but the look on his face was priceless. It was a cross between sheer mortification and pure terror—that same sort of look kids get when they've just been caught misbehaving and their mamas offer to paddle them 'til they can't sit down. And I was so shocked that a simple finger-wagging would have that effect on *anyone*—much less someone *his* size—that in spite of my aggravation, I couldn't do anything but giggle.

"You shake a mighty mean finger there, Lady," Brian said with a wink. "Nearly scared that kid half-to-death. Bet he'd shit if he knew there was a Witch attached to the other end of that thing!"

I could tell that Chloe was amused too. But more than anything else, it was the fact that the episode had put a stop to my game of forty questions. She thought she was off the hook. And I decided to let her think that. At least, until we finished supper.

The chicken and dumplings was scrumptious—almost as good as Mama used to make—and the rest of the meal went off without a hitch. Best of all, every single roll that graced our table was placed firmly in its plate instead of sailed through the air. Supper went so well, in fact, that I even entertained the idea of a return visit. But not too soon. First, I'd have to learn to truly enjoy having food thrown in my direction. Based on tonight's reaction, I wasn't quite ready.

"So...why don't we finish out the evening with some Irish coffee?" Chloe asked as we walked out to the parking lot. "I've got all the fixin's in the car, but I think we ought to do it at your house, Tess. You've got real coffee there and a three-minute pot. If we have it at our house, it'll take half the night for the damned stuff to brew. And if you have to wait for it, I know what's going to happen."

"What?!"

"You're going to get grumpy. And," she said with a giggle, "I think we've had plenty of that for one night!"

"Me? Grumpy?" I gave them my most innocent look but couldn't help laughing at how right she was. "Sounds good," I said with a grin as I unlocked the car and slid in. "See you in a few minutes."

I knew something was wrong when I pulled in the driveway. The house was dark. And I knew I hadn't left it that way. I distinctly remembered leaving the kitchen and porch lights on, and now everything was black as pitch. I fumbled through my purse for my gun, but it wasn't there.

"Shit," I muttered. I thought about my father and all his years as a police officer. I thought about all the weapons training I'd had at his hand. And then I thought about the one thing he'd tried to drill through my skull. In fact, I could almost hear his voice chiding me from the dead:

A gun's not worth a damn if you leave it where somebody can use it on you.

"Yeah, Daddy. I know. But it's too damned late to worry about that now, isn't it?" I muttered under my breath.

I slid from the Jeep and edged toward the back of the house. The element of surprise was the only weapon I had left. And if someone really was in there, the last thing I wanted to do was prance right through the front door and offer myself for the taking. It just wasn't high on my priority list of fun things to do.

I crouched below the window and peered up just in time to see it. The neon glow of a lit cigarette. The asshole inside hadn't come to rob me. He was waiting for me with calm, calculated patience. And he'd had the balls to light up and enjoy a smoke while he did it.

This wasn't good at all. My heart beat so hard I thought it might bounce right out of my chest. Up until that point, I'd actually prayed that I was being silly and that the light bulbs had just burned out.

I crouched lower to the ground and made my way back to the driveway, willing myself to think. Willing myself to stop shaking. Willing myself to overcome the fear that threatened to overtake my better judgment. My mind screamed for help. And this time, someone heard. For just at that moment, Brian and Chloe pulled into the drive.

"What the hell are you doing on your hands and knees?" Chloe asked as she slid out of the car. "Drop your keys?" A chuckle escaped her lips.

The finger I held to my lips to hush her didn't do any good. Hell, it didn't even slow her down.

"Bri', get the flashlight, and let's see if we can help her..."

Fortunately, the finger I drew across my throat stopped her in mid-sentence. I pointed toward the house.

Brian laughed so loud I thought he might wake the dead across the street. I was horrified at his behavior because he, of all people, should've known better. Much better. Brian Dawson, after all, was a deputy sheriff—and I just couldn't believe that even with all that experience under his belt, he could still be such a screw-up.

"Oh, *SHIT*!" He was laughing so hard he could barely speak. "Calm down, Tess. It's just a *surprise* party!"

"It damned sure is," I whispered hoarsely. "There's somebody inside and he's got the balls to be..."

"No, Darlin'. A *real* one! We thought it would be fun, but I guess we should've warned you. I didn't dream you'd think that somebody'd broken in." He grinned that apologetic grin of his. The one that could melt ice.

I looked at him uncertainly. Then I lifted my eyebrow, crossed my arms and shot them my best go-to-hell glare. "How *could* you?! You both know I *hate* surprises—and yet, you couldn't leave well enough alone. You *do* realize, don't you, that if I'd had my gun, those people would be dead right now, and we'd be having this conversation from the comfort of a cell in the city jail?"

"Don't be pissed, Tess. We just wanted to do something nice for you. So, let us. Okay? C'mon now. Just give me your keys and I'll let us in. Otherwise, these folks will still be here at dawn, and you'll really be pissed."

Sure enough, a shout of "*SURPRISE!*" rang out through the night the second he opened the door. I'd never felt so stupid in my life, so glad I'd been unarmed or so happy to have company. It was good to have people around just in case my greatest fear was realized, and I was, indeed, losing my mind.

Chloe had outdone herself. The house was awash in yellow roses, and the table held urns of Irish coffee, six kinds of dessert and truffles from Godiva. Congratulatory gifts were scattered here and there, and a big banner read, "Best Witches, Tess! You've arrived!" Best of all, the partially unpacked boxes had simply disappeared into thin air. And even if I hadn't had anything else to celebrate, that, in and of itself, was enough to give me good reason.

The party was a huge success—everyone had a great time—but I was really glad to see the last person walk out the door. For even though it had been a truly wonderful evening, I was tired. Dead tired. And all I wanted to do was crawl into bed.

I made my way through the house switching off lights, but just as the living room settled into darkness, I spied something from the corner of my eye. It was a flash of light. And it was coming from the cemetery.

I knelt on the loveseat to get a better look through the picture window but let out my breath just as quickly as I'd sucked it in. All I saw were a couple of people out there with flashlights—people, I suspected, that were doing nothing more than scoring a joint or two. And while that might be cause for alarm anywhere else in the country, such wasn't the case in this neighborhood. This was a place where small-time drug deals were a matter of course. I was just thankful that the local hoodlums had seen fit to do their business amongst the dead instead of right in the middle of my front yard.

With that in mind, I locked the front door and went to bed.

The little girl stood at the window looking out into the garden, hardly able to believe what she was seeing. There they were...Mama and Daddy...wrapped up in each other's arms...again! She was prettier than Mama, smarter than Mama and could do a much better job of running things than Mama. That much was clear. She'd already made it look like Mama was crazy, hiding things so she couldn't find them and getting her into trouble with Daddy.

She glanced toward her closet and grinned. That's where she'd hidden the ledger. And Daddy'd sure been mad when Mama couldn't find that! He'd screamed and yelled and said they were ruined. She'd thought he'd throw her out then. But he hadn't.

She'd even bruised herself up real good—that sure had hurt—and blamed it on Mama. But Daddy hadn't believed her. He'd just said she had an active imagination and needed to be more careful.

"I'll get rid of Mama if it's the last thing I do," she said to the yellow tabby kitten that jumped on the bed. "And then, Daddy'll see just how smart and pretty I am. He'll see that we don't need Mama at all!"

The kitten blinked at her and yawned. It was Daddy's cat and Mama didn't like it much. She said she only put up with it on account of him. She said it made her sneeze...

The child's eyes lit up and moving toward the bed, she picked up a pillow. "Well," she said smiling at the cat and holding the pillow on top of his torso, *"you won't make her sneeze anymore...will you?!"*

The terrified kitten yowled and hissed and struggled to get away, but the child was quicker. She jumped on the pillow in sheer delight, shifting her body until she sat squarely in the center. And then placing her chubby little fingers around the kitten's neck, she twisted slowly...slowly...slowly...until the sound of cracking bones brought a tiny giggle up from her throat. A giggle that blossomed quickly into full blown laughter.

CHAPTER 2

I felt like I hadn't slept a wink. Part of the night had been taken up with tossing and turning. The rest had been plagued with fragmented dreams. And if that weren't bad enough, just about the time I finally dozed off into peacefulness, I was rudely awakened by a clap of thunder loud enough to shake the house. Except it wasn't thunder. A quick look out the window revealed nothing but a clear, starry autumn sky. And then, it was back to bed for more of the same. I felt just like I'd been run over by a Mack truck.

The coffee pot by my bed was already doing its thing, and the aroma of its rich contents made my nostrils flare. That meant it was sometime around six, and time to get up. Still, I couldn't open my eyes. All I wanted to do was snuggle down into the comforter and pull the covers over my head.

Instead, I fumbled around for the handle of the pot and forced an eye open just long enough to judge the distance from my mug. Then I poured while I counted to five, figuring the measure was just about right for a full shot, and set the pot back on the warmer.

Damn, I was tired. In fact, I couldn't remember ever being so exhausted. And yet, I couldn't just spend the day in bed. I had tons of stuff to research, calls to return and about twelve dozen other things that needed attention. I also had to find out what Chloe had done with all my stuff. So with that in mind, I propped myself up against the pillows, lit a cigarette, grabbed my coffee and set about clearing the fuzz from my head.

The dreams had been more than just a little disconcerting. In fact, they'd been downright frightening. One had to do with the gravesite in the cemetery. It started with the tombstone cracking in half—right between the clasped hands—and falling to the ground. Then the earth below split open and four women dressed as if they'd lived during the Civil War stepped out. The first two seemed to be upper middle-class ladies who were about thirty and fifty respectively, and the women of color who followed were close to the same ages. Each took different escape routes, moving in separate directions, until finally they stood at the four corners of the fenced plot.

And that's when things really got eerie. They all started talking at once. Each speaking in monotone. Each saying something different. Each voice growing louder and louder to deliver its own personal message. But no matter how hard I tried, I just couldn't make out the words.

Then that dream faded into another, which focused solely upon one of the women as a small child. A nasty youngster, she was so jealous of her father's attention that she was willing to go to any lengths to have it all. And that, she did. It started with childish pranks like moving things in the house to make her mother think she was crazy and escalated to causing herself personal harm so her father would think she'd been beaten. The final straw was when she slowly strangled her father's cat and blamed her mother for the deed.

Of course, that was just about the time that the thunder—or whatever it was—had brought me straight out of bed. And that was a real blessing, for dream or no dream, I simply couldn't bear to watch anymore of that evil insanity.

I sighed heavily, filled my cup for the third time and sauntered into the bathroom to complete my morning ritual. I'd just started brushing my teeth when the doorbell rang. It had to be Chloe because no one else on the planet would dare to show up on my doorstep at that hour. No one in their right mind, anyway. And I was beginning to wonder about hers.

I started to finish the task at hand before answering the door but thought better of it. After all, anyone with the audacity to ring my doorbell at that hour deserved exactly what they got. With that in mind, I whipped open the door with the toothbrush still jutting from my mouth.

"What the hell are you doing here?" I mumbled between brush and suds. "Do you have any idea what time it is? The whole world's still in bed, and..."

"Don't be ridiculous! The whole world's been up for hours," Chloe said with a grin as she tossed my newspaper on the couch and breezed past me toward the coffee pot. "Except, of course," she added with a chuckle, "for the select few fortunate enough to live in *Tess'* world!"

As much as I loved Chloe, I was more than a little peeved. She knew that I wasn't a morning person. She knew that it took me awhile to wake up. And she knew that I liked to do it by myself at my own leisure. That being the case, I decided not to get dressed or do anything about my hair. Instead, I finished brushing my teeth, wiped down the counter and grabbed the newspaper. Then I marched into the kitchen to give her what for.

She already had coffee and was settled in at the kitchen table with a cigarette in one hand and a pen in the other. To make matters worse, she was busily scribbling notes across a legal pad, and I knew that could only mean trouble. I had too much stuff to do today to put up with her whims, and I intended to tell her so.

"So...what *are* you doing here at this ungodly hour? I certainly hope this is important! I've got a ton of stuff to do today, and..."

"Ungodly, my ass! *We've*," the word was punctuated heavily, "got tons to do today. And if we don't get started, we won't even make a dent." She pointed at the notepad in front of her.

"Do I *dare* to ask what *that* is?" I was getting more annoyed by the second.

"It's a list, silly. I've been up half the night thinking about that tombstone and whose it might be. So I've jotted down a few things along with where we might get some answers. And yes, it's important. Especially after what happened in the cemetery last night!"

I felt the blood drain from my face. "What?! Something happened in the cemetery? What the hell are you talking about?"

"Just your average case of vandalism—it was probably the hoods up the road—but your favorite tombstone got knocked over and..."

I didn't wait for her to finish the sentence. I was already throwing on clothes, grabbing shoes and heading for the door.

"Aren't you even going to brush your *hair*?" It was more of a wail than a question.

"Not today. I seriously doubt that anyone gives a rat's ass what I look like this early in the morning," I retorted. "Especially not the resident dead!"

Chloe beat me to the door and tried to bar the way. "Now, wait just a *god-damned minute*!"

I couldn't believe my ears. She'd actually screamed at me. "There's nothing you can do about it on your own. And it's too early to call the parks department. They won't be open for at least a couple of hours, and..."

"No, Chloe." My voice had hit that cold, calculated, calm tone, which meant that I was just before committing murder with my bare hands. "*You* wait just a god-damned minute! Get away from that fucking door and leave me alone. I've got just one nerve left. And you're standing on it." The last sentence was delivered through clenched teeth.

"What the hell's gotten into you?!"

"You have, Ms. Dawson. First, you come barging in here at the crack of dawn when you know damned good and well that I don't like company as soon as I open my eyes. Then you plop yourself down at the table and—as if I don't have enough to do already—intend to present me with a fucking to-do list as long as my arm. And now, you've got the balls to try to prevent me from leaving my own house. I've had it, Chloe. Get the hell out of my way!"

I reached past her, grabbed the door knob and was out the door before she could answer.

It took me less than two minutes to reach the gravesite and even less time to figure out what had happened. Still, I couldn't believe my eyes.

The wrought iron fencing was twisted and bent and partially resting on the ground. The gravestone had been knocked over and was, indeed, cracked down the center—right between the hands. Fortunately for my wildly beating heart though, the grave itself was intact. Otherwise, I'd have probably just died of cardiac arrest right on the spot.

"Fucking white trash *ass*holes!"

"*White* trash? How do you know?" Chloe'd arrived just in time to hear the utterance and now had her hand on my shoulder. I was too upset to shrug it off. Besides, it was her way of showing comfort, and I was in dire need of some just then.

"Just an expression. My father used to say that only white trash didn't take care of their dead. Fact is, he used to maintain the sites around our plot once the other families had died off. And as far as I'm concerned, anyone—regardless of race, creed or station in life—who'd do this sort of thing is exactly that. White trash. At least, in my book anyway."

I wanted to cry. I couldn't imagine anyone doing such a thing. Not even on a dare. My eyes welled up with tears, and I did my best to blink them back.

"How could anyone *do* this, Chloe? Just back a truck over a gravesite? And to what *pur*pose? It's despicable. Disgusting. And something I'll never be able to understand."

My best wasn't good enough, and a tear rolled down my cheek.

"Well," she said as she rummaged around in her pocket for a tissue, "there's nothing you can do about it right now, Darlin'. So dry your eyes and let's go home. We'll call Parks and Recreation just as soon as they open. And then you can..."

"Call them, my ass!" I snapped. "We're going over there. And I don't intend to leave that office until I get some satisfaction!"

I turned on my heel and marched toward the house. I was more than just a little pissed off. I was furious. Livid. And determined that this sort of shit would never happen again. At least, not as long as *I* lived in that neighborhood.

Chloe, who was a good head shorter than I, was having trouble keeping up. By the time I reached the door, she was literally gasping for air.

"Look, Tess," she panted, "I know you're upset, but don't you think that a call might do more good than..."

"No, I don't. The bad thing about telephones is that people can hang up on you if they don't like the tone of the conversation," I said as I emptied the kitchen ashtray and wiped it clean. I straightened the papers she'd left on the table, then grabbed the bottle of spray cleaner and wiped up the mess she'd made with her coffee that morning. I just couldn't understand how one person could destroy a house—and all in less than fifteen minutes. At least, I didn't have to live with her, I thought. "I want them to look me in the eye when they tell me there's nothing they can do," I went on. "In the meantime, I'm going to call the police department and file a report." I made a point of putting the spray bottle back on the shelf and hoped she noticed.

"Okay. But at least have one more cup of coffee before you dial. You won't get anywhere if you bite their heads off like you did mine this morning. You're much more effective when you're calm, and they don't love you like..." Her voice broke into a whimper.

I looked up just in time to see the first tears fall. If they were designed to make me feel guilty, they definitely did the trick. Except that Chloe wasn't that way. She didn't do guilt and didn't expect anyone else to either. Still, I'd been a jerk. A total ass. And I knew for a fact that only Chloe would've put up with the shit I'd dished out earlier and still even bother to speak to me. Yet, she was still there and loved me in spite of myself.

"Oh, *honey*," I said as I put my arms around her, "I am *so* sorry! Please don't cry. I'm really not mad at you. It's just that I hardly slept at all last night. I got up in a bad mood, and you arrived just in time to catch the brunt of it. You're the best friend I've ever had. And I really don't know what I'd do without you." I held her out in front of me and wiped her tears with my hand. "*Friends*?!"

"Friends! But only if you promise not to yell at me like that again. Especially not before seven in the morning," she said with an innocent look.

I put on my sternest face and raised an eyebrow for good measure. "Don't push it, Ms. Sweetness and Light," I teased her. "You're treading on thin ice. Now, I think we have some work to do!"

The rest of the morning went off like clockwork. The Sikeston police had not only responded positively to my report but had dispatched someone right away. In fact, two officers arrived before I could even hang up. I visited with them for a few minutes, took them over to the gravesite then left them to their own devices.

The visit to the Parks and Recreation Department had gone well too. There was none of the crap I'd expected. The receptionist had shown us in to the director's office right away, and he'd made phone calls to his clean up crews and cemetery caretaker while we were there.

The only hitch at all had to do with the state of the grave marker itself. It seemed that there was no family left to notify of the damage—they'd all died years ago—and as a result, there was no one left to pay for the repairs. Since I just couldn't bear the idea of the marker being left split in half and propped up against the fence, I agreed to foot the bill myself. I filled out the paperwork to remove the marker for repairs and left the office armed with a list of monument companies to call for estimates.

"So, should we stop for a bite to eat? Or are you hungry yet?"

"Only if we can go to Dumplin's," Chloe said with a grin. "They have this to-die-for chicken salad sandwich on homemade bread, and their potato salad is scrumptious too."

Chloe's choice was definitely a good one, for Dumplin's probably had the best lunch menu in town. The only problem was that it was more of a tea-room, which catered to urban professionals, and neither of us was exactly dressed for the occasion. Not wanting to stick out like a sore thumb——I absolutely hated looking out of place anywhere—I opted for a compromise.

"Tell you what," I said as I turned down Center Street toward the restaurant, "Let's place our orders to go. I'll pick up the tab, and then we can look at your to-do list at home while we eat. We'll still get those great sandwiches, and..."

"You just don't want to go to Dumplin's in jeans!"

"Guilty as charged," I said with a chuckle. "And if we go now, we can get in and out before the lunch crowd arrives." I parked the car, turned off the ignition and started to get out.

"But I wanted to eat *here*," she whined. "I wanted to sit down and have someone *serve* my..."

"Oh, come on, Chloe! If we sit around all day, we'll never get to your list. Besides, I've got a ton of other things to do too. And I just don't have time to fool around today." I was trying my damnedest not to get pissed again, but her whining was really getting on my nerves.

"How about this? We'll take the stuff home and I'll serve you myself. Real plates, real napkins and everything. Okay?!"

I didn't wait for an answer because I knew what would happen. She'd whine some more. I'd get mad. And before it was said and done, we'd wind up in another squabble. Only this time, it would probably last all day. And I just wasn't going there. Instead, I marched right up to the restaurant door and held it open for her.

"Are you coming or not?"

She sighed heavily but grabbed her purse and got out of the car. And that's exactly what I'd been banking on.

This was definitely going to be a day of compromises, all right. And I had no one to blame but myself. When would I learn not to be such a jerk? It never failed to bite me in the ass. This time though, it hit me a little higher. For by the time our order arrived, my little episode had lifted thirty-two dollars and sixty-seven cents right out of my wallet. I wasn't the least bit happy about that but put on my best smile anyway.

"Ready?"

"Not quite. Luke Benson is over there," she gestured toward the publisher of the local newspaper, "and I just want to say hello. Besides, you need to meet him."

"Not now, Chloe! We can tend to introductions later, *okay*?!" I grabbed her elbow with my free hand and ushered her firmly toward the door.

The ride home was a quiet one. In fact, the only words uttered at all came from the radio in the form of song lyrics. But that was probably for the best. There'd be plenty of time for talking later. When that time came, I intended to put an end to this nonsense. I wasn't sure what had gotten into Chloe—she'd never tried to manipulate my every action before—but whatever it was needed to stop. And damned fast.

With that in mind, I put on a pot of coffee and set the table, complete with the good china and silver. I even got out the silver coffee service for good measure. By the time I was done, it looked like we'd invited royalty for lunch. I hoped she was satisfied.

"So, let's see that to-do list," I said as I sat down and filled her coffee cup. I was still aggravated but tried to keep my voice light.

"It can wait. Let's just have a nice lunch and talk about something else, okay?" She bit into her sandwich and looked at me expectantly.

What the hell was she *doing*? It wasn't like her to test my patience. Especially not when it was already hanging by a thread! Still, I decided to bite my tongue and try to be pleasant. Maybe something was bothering her, and she really needed to talk. So I gave her an opening.

"What do you want to talk about?"

"Oh, I don't know! The weather. The state of the economy. Anything will do." She smiled that wide-eyed, innocent smile—the one she always reserved for getting her way when nothing else would work. Only this time, I wasn't going to play. The time had come to straighten this shit out, and this time, it was going to be straightened out in short order.

"Look, Chloe," I managed with a calm tone that surprised even me, "I'm not sure what's gotten into you, but it needs to stop. I know I was a real ass this morning. I know I hurt your feelings. And I'm really sorry about that. But I've already apologized—quite profusely, I might add—and you accepted that apology. I thought everything was fine..."

"*Did* you?" she asked as she shot me a glare.

"Yes, I did. But now you're playing this to the hilt. It's just not like you. You're treating me as if I were Brian. And I'm not going to play that game. I am *not*," I punctuated the last word as if it were a sentence of its own, "going to pay for this for the rest of the day—and certainly not for the rest of my life. Especially not when you're at fault too and knew better than to barge in here before seven in the morning. Now, what the hell's going on with you?!"

"I don't *know*," she wailed as she lit a cigarette, "but you're acting squirrelly too. You've never been so bossy before. You've never been so mean to me. And you've never—not ever!—just pushed me aside like yesterday's newspaper.

"Not only that," she went on, "you're cleaning and polishing and scrubbing like there's no tomorrow. Just look at this silver. I bet it hasn't been polished like this in years! And look at this *place*! You're wiping down counters, wiping down cabinets, and if one speck of dust dares to light somewhere, you're wiping it up too. That's just not like you. You don't give a rat's ass if stuff is out of order or not. You don't give a tinker's damn about mess. Or at least, you didn't. Not until you moved into *this* house!"

"That's not true! I just moved in and I'm trying to get things straightened out so I can..."

"Bull shit," Chloe enunciated each word as if it were a stand–alone sentence. "Just *look* at yourself! I haven't even put this cigarette out, and you're already trying to empty the ashtray!"

Holy shit! She was right. I jerked my hand back like it had been burned. What the hell was wrong with me? What the hell was wrong with *us*?

"Okay, Chloe. You're right. Something's definitely wrong here, but I'm not sure what. I do know one thing though. We need to calm down and call a truce. Then we need to sit down and figure out exactly what's going on."

The words were no sooner out of my mouth than a thud sounded from the living room. "No need to worry," I said as I headed toward the noise. "This has been going on ever since I got here. It's just the house spirit."

"Good Goddess!" exclaimed Chloe. "That's *it*!"

"That's what?!" I called over my shoulder as I picked up the pillar candle that had fallen from its shelf.

"The house spirit, silly! That's what's causing all this shit."

"C'mon, Chloe," I said with a grin. I pulled my chair up to the table again, grabbed my sandwich and took a bite. I knew she was jerking my chain, and I shot her a glance just to be sure. She wasn't though. The look on her face was anything but playful. In fact, it was almost somber. "You can't be *serious*!"

"Oh yeah, I am. Serious as a heart attack. Remember what you told me about house spirits?"

"What?"

"That they're not always spirits of the deceased. That sometimes they're a culmination of the energies of those who have lived in a house. And I think that's what we've got here."

"So?"

"Just think about it, Tess. According to your landlord, those little old ladies lived here for more than seventy years. They never married. They were set in their ways. And I'm willing to bet you that they were bitchy and bossy and had nothing better to do than scrub and clean."

"Okay. That explains *my* attitude, but..." I paused to find the right words. The last thing I wanted to do was start another fight with Chloe, but there just wasn't a diplomatic way to say what was needed. Fortunately, she came to my rescue.

"What about *mine*?" she chuckled. "That's easy. I'm also willing to bet that every time someone visited here, it was just like being invited to high tea. That every person who walked through that front door entered with a better-than-thou attitude. That they had no consideration for anyone but themselves. And I'm also willing to bet that this kitchen was the source of more gossip and conniving than you could shake a stick at!"

Of course, she was right. And it was something I'd never even considered. Living in a house for that long was bound to breed energy. Enough of it to create a thought form. One that was not only strong enough to live and breathe and cause mischief but strong enough to impose itself upon the psyches of anyone else who dared to enter its domain.

"So," Chloe continued, "what do we do now? How do we get rid of this thing?"

"We can't."

"What do you *mean*, we can't?! We *have* to put things right again. We sure as hell can't go on like *this*! And the only way I can see to accomplish that is to banish this thing from..."

"There's a better way," I said with a grin, "and even though it's a little unconventional, I think it'll work. Now then. Where did you stash the liquor box?"

"You want a drink *now*?!" She looked at me like I'd lost my mind.

"Of course not!" I said between giggles. "I just need the bourbon and scotch—it's all part of the plan—and whatever you do, don't let me empty any more ashtrays. We're going to need every cigarette ash we can get our hands on."

The look on her face was priceless—it was obvious that she couldn't believe her ears—but instead of questioning me any further, she just put her plate in the sink and scurried off to locate the booze. While she was doing that, I got busy on the phone. What I needed was kids— lots of them—so I called everyone I knew who fit the bill, at least within a five mile radius.

By the time Chloe had unpacked the liquor cabinet, I had everything else under control. A white seven-day candle sat in the middle of the kitchen table, accompanied by a paint brush and some incense. Two small bowls rested there too: one filled with a mixture of scotch, bourbon, and water, and another full of cigarette ashes. Every window in the house was raised, and the doors were propped open with unpacked boxes. All I needed was the kids, and they'd be here in less than an hour.

"Do you really think this'll work?" Chloe raised an eyebrow and looked askance at the table. I could tell that she was more than just a little apprehensive about this. Even after all the time we'd spent together, she still relied more on ceremonial magic than my personally styled off-the-cuff kitchen witchery.

"Can't miss! Besides, what's the worst that could happen?"

"Your spirit becomes more of a problem," she said with a grin. "It becomes a cigarette-smoking lush that burns down the house—with you in it!"

"Don't you worry about that," I retorted. "Even *this* spirit isn't *that* ballsy! In fact, the worst problem I'm looking at here is that my house is going to reek like a bar room before this is over. And I'm going to have to buy three cases of air freshener to fix it!" I said with a laugh.

"Okay," she said, as she glanced at the clock, "but we probably need to get started. The kids will be here any minute."

We took a few minutes to ground and center, then I lit the incense and candlewick. "As I create light, let light come back to me," I intoned. I nodded at Chloe, and she picked up the bowl and brush and headed for the living room.

"Spirit of the house, come forth" I called, "I honor you this day. Don't be shy—just come on out—so you and I can play. I'm not upset, but things have changed and new rules now apply. This is *my* life. This is *my* house. Things must be rectified."

I could hear Chloe in the background as she asperged the house with liquor, and I couldn't help but grin at her incantation. In fact, it was all I could do to keep from laughing out loud as I heard her say, "By design of alcohol, I purge this house now once and all of everything that is not Tess—and sterilize all other mess!"

It took a second or two to regain my composure—in fact, I had to shut her out completely—but I took a deep breath and went on.

"You may stay or you may go. It's really up to you. But if you choose to stay, my friend, here's what you need to do. Adjust yourself unto my life. It's mine—not yours or theirs. Do not impose your will on me; do not impose their cares. And I shall keep this candle lit should you decide to stay, to honor you and all you do until I go away."

Chloe had already worked her way back to the kitchen, and by the time I uttered the last word, she'd finished with the liquor. I glanced at the clock and nodded urgently toward the other bowl. We only had a few minutes before the kids arrived, and we had to get this done. She grabbed the bowl and hurried out, sprinkling ashes as she went.

"By smoke and ash of cigarette," I heard her say, "this house now Tess does claim. Get with the program. Understand. Your lifestyle has now changed."

The atmosphere was already starting to change, but it wasn't at all what I'd expected. Instead of lightening the mood, things suddenly became dark and heavy. In fact, the energy was almost suicidal. Shit! I hadn't intended to push the spirit over the edge. I'd just wanted it to get with the program. I had to do something—and fast—before everything spun right out of control.

I desperately probed my mind for a solution. *For the love of the Gods, Tess, THINK! You know that you're good at thinking on your feet. If you don't do something—and goddamned quick—you'll never ever be able to live in this house!* Then suddenly, I had it.

"Do you under*stand*, my friend?" I continued, "I don't want you to go. But neither do I want for you to live here filled with woe. So, let's be friends and live together happily from this day. Chin up now. No need to sulk. I'd *love* for you to stay!"

Fortunately, that did the trick. That awful heaviness left. The dark mood went with it. And the suicidal shit? That was a thing of the past also. Everything was beginning to return to normal. And not a moment too soon either. I barely had time to breathe a sigh of relief before the doorbell sounded.

There were my kids—about forty of them—and they were all standing on my front porch. Time for phase two, I thought with a grin. I put on my best smile and went to the door.

"Okay, kids...listen up. We're going to play a little game. And here's what I want you to do." I glanced over my shoulder to check on Chloe's progress while I spouted the rules. And once I was sure that she was done, I finished up with, "No losers in this game, kids. Ice cream for everybody when we're done—but the loudest of the bunch gets *two* scoops. Now come on in and do your stuff!"

They rushed past me screaming at the tops of their lungs. I had never—not in my entire life—witnessed such a ruckus! They ran in and out of the house and back again. Yelling out the windows. Hollering out the doors. They bellowed, they shrieked, they howled and they roared. They made noises I'd never heard before and wasn't likely to ever hear again. And all the while, they swung their arms forward as if to push something out of the way. The energy was so pure and so strong, it was nearly overpowering. So much so, that I remember wishing I could bottle it for sale.

I glanced at my watch. They'd been at it for nearly twenty minutes and that was just about right. It was time for the grand finale. And with that thought, I blew the old police whistle that hung around my neck.

The kids stopped dead in their tracks. The noise did too. It was so quiet, in fact, you could have heard dust hit its mark. Satisfied, I gave the whistle another trill.

Then from the silence came a single giggle. Then another. And another. Until finally, the whole house was filled with one gigantic and united belly laugh—a laugh so delightful and so heartfelt that it couldn't bring *anything* but out and out joy.

Joining in the laughter, I knew my troubles were over. At least those concerning the house spirit. All I had to worry about now was small by comparison. It was nothing but the ice cream bill. And I thought I could handle that.

CHAPTER 3

"*Bullshit!*"

I banged down the phone and grabbed my purse and keys. I'd been trying to get in touch with Luke Benson for two days now but couldn't seem to get past his receptionist. I was sick to death of hearing that "Mr. Benson just stepped out," that "Mr. Benson is interviewing" and that "Mr. Benson can't be disturbed." Hell, if Chloe hadn't mentioned seeing him at Dumplin's, I'd have thought that "Mr. Benson" was only a figment of the imagination and that the local newspaper was really being run by some disembodied head much akin to the Wizard of Oz!

Yeah, I should've taken Chloe up on that introduction and just forgotten about how bad I'd looked. But it was too late to worry about that now. I *would* wangle an introduction, and it *would* happen today—even if I had to camp out in front of his office, I thought as I started the car and pulled out of the drive.

Who the hell did he think he was, anyway? He hadn't made the slightest effort to return any of my calls. Not that I knew if Little Hitler had even bothered with the messages. But that didn't matter. What did matter is that he had an office and a telephone. And if he was any sort of a businessman at all, he'd know how to use them. Moreover, had he been *in* his office *by* the phone, I wouldn't have had to waste *my* time dealing with the front desk Gestapo at all. I was still stewing when I pulled into the parking lot.

I checked my makeup in the rearview mirror, took a deep breath, and willed myself to calm down. Marching into the Sikeston Press Herald in a rabid fury wasn't going to get me anywhere—except maybe, arrested. I certainly didn't want to go there. Besides, I was probably being more than just a little unreasonable. Deep down, I was certain that Luke Benson *was* a busy man and *did* have tons to do. It was just that I wasn't used to not getting what I wanted when I wanted it. The older I got, the more it bothered me. So with that in mind, I took a deep breath, wrapped myself in an aura of professionalism, made my way up the walk and prepared to meet Little Hitler—right up close and personal.

Luke Benson leaned back in his chair, propped his feet on the desk and inhaled deeply. Nasty habit, he thought, as he exhaled three perfectly formed smoke rings. Problem is, that's what everybody else keeps telling him. Now, if he really thought it was, that might be a different story. He might actually do something about it. Like maybe even quit, he mused, as he watched one of the rings settle around the toe of his brown leather loafer.

He'd been in the office since before five o'clock this morning— same as every morning for the past two weeks—and there still weren't enough hours in the day for everything that needed his attention. Damn Roxanne and her sick mother! He'd needed a secretary in the worst way, and Roxanne had been the best. She'd not only been able to juggle forty things at once but been able to do it effortlessly while standing on her head and whistling Dixie. Maybe he should have offered her more money to stay. Maybe he should have begged. Pleaded. Gotten on his knees and groveled. But none of it would have made a damned bit of difference. Illness was a fact of life. And so was parental responsibility, he thought as he stubbed out his cigarette and pulled another from the pack.

What he really needed now was a miracle. A Secretarial Goddess to march right through that front door and fix everything. Someone to keep his appointments straight, handle that never-ending flow of messages that streamed across his desk and deal with complaints from the rural route customers.

And as long as he was dreaming, maybe this Goddess could even deal with the Sikeston Charities Guild and that high-fallutin' Miss Ada Thompson who ran it. He was sick to death of her insistence on coverage for ice cream socials and tea parties—events designed solely to defray college expenses for those whose families could well afford to put any six kids through Yale—when there were homeless people living in cardboard boxes on the outskirts of town. Of course, the plight of the homeless didn't bother Miss Ada a bit—except for the fact that they were *unsightly*. She just wanted them run out of town so no one would have to look at them. How anybody could be so obtuse and still manage to breathe the same air as normal folks was beyond him.

He crushed out his cigarette disgustedly, grabbed his cup and headed for the coffee pot. So, how many pots did that make today? Three? Four? He'd lost count but guessed it didn't really matter. He'd never heard of death by coffee, regardless of how much was ingested.

Now, if he could just keep from bouncing off the walls, he'd be doing fine.

Must be oldies hour again at the radio station, he thought with a grin as the first few bars of "Mr. Sandman" wafted from the overhead speakers. Yeah, that's what he needed, all right: a dream. A made-to-order dream. Before he knew it, he was singing along silently to the personal version running through his head.

> *"Mr. Sandman, pick up some steam*
> *Bring me a Goddess—a clerical dream*
> *With typing fingers and the genteel finesse*
> *To handle problems and whip through this me-ess!*
> *Mr. Sandman..."*

And there he stood—still lost in his own world of dreams and Secretarial Goddesses—when Tess came waltzing through the front door.

Well, wasn't this a fine way to run an office! No Little Hitler at the front desk. No Gestapo to meet you, greet you or send you on your way. No one at all. Unless of course, you could count the dreamy-eyed idiot leaning against the door facing on the other side of the room. And that one? Well, he'd have to be deaf as well as blind since he hadn't so much as looked in my direction. Still, I thought I'd take a chance. After all, what did I have to lose?

"Excuse me," I said, sauntering in his direction.

The poor guy nearly jumped out of his skin, but at least, I had his attention. That'll teach him to keep his mind on his business, I thought. I did my best to keep a straight face, but the look on his was so befuddled that I couldn't help cracking a smile.

"I am so sorry," the idiot offered. "What can I do for you?"

"Well, I'm actually looking for Luke Benson. Is he in?"

"Who wants to know?" Now the idiot had taken a different stance. Peering down at me from over the tops of his wire-rimmed aviator frames, he was actually trying intimidation. Something that obviously didn't sit well with me, especially after the morning I'd had.

"And just what sort of question is *that*?!" I'd promised myself that I wasn't going to get pissed, but my new-found calm was quickly flying out the window. "Is he screening his visitors today? Just like he's been screening his calls for the last few days? Well, let me tell *you* something, sir..."

"Now hold on there just a minute..."

"No! *You* hold on there, buddy. I will not be pushed aside like.."

The sudden realization that we were not only literally standing toe to toe but that I was standing on the very tips of mine to get right in his face, stopped me short. The whole thing was so ridiculous that I burst into laughter.

"Sorry," I said as I set my heels back on the floor. "Perhaps we could start again?"

"Perhaps," he said with a twinkle in his amber eyes. "Coffee?"

"Absolutely."

"Cream and..."

"Completely unnecessary, but thank you. I'm a purist when it comes to coffee."

"Well now, a woman who knows her own mind as well as mine. You wouldn't happen to be a secretary, would you?"

"Once," I said as I followed him to the coffee pot, "a very long time ago. But I'm not looking for work. In fact..."

"Pity," he said, filling our cups. "I was beginning to think you were a dream come true."

"Excuse me?" I took the cup and looked at him.

"Oh, never mind. What did you say your business with Luke was?"

He was studying me. My face. My body language. My reactions. The whole ball of wax. I quickly came to the realization that I was right in the middle of a personal game of cat and mouse, and I was the one with the shorter legs.

"I didn't...Mr. Benson," I retorted.

His laugh was free and easy, with no trace of embarrassment at being caught. In fact, he didn't even have the common courtesy to blush.

"Guilty as charged. Now then, if you'll just tell me your name and have a seat," he said as he gestured toward the empty chair in his office, "I'll see what I can do to help you."

"It's Tess. Tess Logan. The same Tess Logan who's been trying to reach you by phone for the last couple of days."

"Well, Ms. Logan—the same Ms. Logan who's been ringing my

phone off the wall," he said with a smug grin as he fished for a cigarette, "What can I do for the fine ladies of the Sikeston Charities Guild?"

"Excuse me?" I was beginning to think my first assessment had been right on. This guy was, indeed, an idiot. And one of the worst kind.

"You're not with the Charities Guild?" Now he looked embarrassed. And even though I didn't get the joke, I'd somehow managed to unsettle him with nothing more than two words. The ball was back in my court, and I was enjoying it immensely.

"No," I said with an arch of my eyebrow. "I'm actually researching a Barnes family that lived in Sikeston during the Civil War, and I thought you might be able to help me." I tossed the file across his desk and waited while he thumbed through it.

"Well, I'm not familiar with these folks, but I do have some connections who may be," he said as he scribbled down a phone number and handed it to me. "Give this guy a call. He's the area's unofficial historian. Fair warning though. You'll probably want to have five gallons of coffee, a carton of cigarettes and an endless supply of pencils and paper by the phone. It's common knowledge that once he starts talking, he never shuts up," he said with a chuckle.

I looked at the Post-it note and grinned. "Silas Shrum," I mused. "Name sounds like it came straight out of a fairy-tale."

"Well, for God's sake, don't tell him that," he said with a wink. "Silas takes himself *very* seriously." He handed me the folder, lit a cigarette and inhaled deeply. "By the way, it might be a good idea for you to leave your phone number. Just in case I think of anyone else who could help you."

"No problem," I said as I handed him my business card. "I could certainly use a few more days of synchronicity at work!"

"What did you say?" He was wearing that deer in the headlights look.

"Synchronicity at work. I said I could use a few more days of that."

He leaned across the desk, propped his chin on his hands and looked me right in the eye. "And I suppose you actually know what that word means?"

A burn of color crawled across my cheeks, and for a moment, I thought I might actually catch on fire. I couldn't believe my ears or his audacity. That pompous little twirp! Just who the hell did he think he was?!

"As a matter of fact, I do," I said through clenched teeth as I got to my feet and leaned right in his face. "And now, I have a question for *you*, Mr. Benson. Were you born a pompous ass? Or is that a practiced art?"

Now then, I thought, as I watched his jaw drop ten feet. If you're going to run with the big dogs, Buddy, make sure you know how to play the game.

His mouth was still agape when I wished him a lovely day and sailed out the door.

"What a *jack*ass!" I screamed as I stomped through the house. "I can't believe he had the audacity to..."

"Well, at least you got a phone number. That's got to be worth something." Chloe was being Chloe and doing her best to calm me down.

"Look, Chloe, I love you. But just this once, please don't make me try to see reason, okay? I just want to be mad for a while. Besides...the sonuvabitch deserves it! And I'm not entirely certain that one little phone number could ever be worth all the bullshit I had to trudge through to get it!" I waved the Post-it note in the air then tossed it on the table. "That holier-than-thou asshole! How dare he even pretend that I'm stupid!"

"Sounds to me like you're forging quite a relationship with our illustrious newspaper publisher," Chloe chuckled.

"Yeah, right!" I exhaled a stream of smoke and drummed my nails on the kitchen counter.

"But you have to admit he's cute."

"Cute?! What the hell are you thinking? Are your hormones on overdrive this morning? The only thing cute about that idiotic jerk was the look on his face when I cut him off at the knees."

"Oh, come on, Tess. The only time I *ever* see you this pissed at some guy is just before you fall head over heels!" Chloe was right. Intimate relationships had never been easy for me. I couldn't remember any ever having started out with hearts and flowers or that light and fluffy romance that's supposed to make you spontaneously break into song. No, every single one of mine had started out with a real bang—the sort of bang that generally heralds a war rather than a love affair.

And as much as I hated to admit it, Chloe was right on the other count too. Luke Benson—regardless of his arrogant, self-serving nature—was, indeed, cute. He had that distinctive look of what Aunt Mary had termed "the black Irish," with those hazel-amber eyes set into a freckled face, framed by the darkest brown hair I'd ever seen. Still, I wasn't going to give Chloe the satisfaction of being right. Not right now anyway.

"In case you didn't hear me the first time, let me spell it out for you. He's a cocky, arrogant, self-serving bastard! That's why I'm pissed. I could strangle him with my bare hands! I could just..."

"Whatever. But you know what they say. Anger is just the flip side of passion. And if Luke Benson can drive you this close to the brink of insanity with just a few words, can you even imagine how good the sex might be?!"

Sometimes, the Universe steps in and saves you from having to answer questions you'd rather not. And this time, the rescue came by way of the ringing telephone, which Chloe picked up immediately. That was the great thing about having a friend like Chloe. She not only knew when to unleash you upon the world to stir things up but when the world was much safer left to its own devices.

What the hell had just happened? Luke rubbed his chin and stared at his empty office. He'd thought everything was going along just fine. In fact, he'd really been enjoying the banter with Tess Logan. What wasn't to enjoy? She was smart, sassy and had a quick wit. Her independent nature was intriguing. And the fact that it was all tied up into one nice, neat attractive package didn't hurt either.

What was it with women anyway? He'd gotten her phone number and had even entertained the thought of inviting her to dinner. Then—wham!—she'd let him have it right between the eyes.

"Hey, Luke!" The disembodied voice belonged to his twin sister, Liza, the front-desk receptionist. "Could you give me a hand with the stuff in the car? There was a sale at the office supply store, and I nearly bought the place out."

"Sure thing, Liza. And I'm glad you're back. I need to talk to you about something."

"Women from the Charities Guild giving you a hard time?" she quipped as she rounded the corner, but one look at his face told a different story.

"Gosh, Luke, what's wrong? You look like you lost your best friend."

"Woman trouble."

"You've got to be kidding," she said as she tossed a box into an empty chair and began sorting through the stuff inside. "You don't even go out. In fact, you haven't been close enough to a woman in years to..."

"Well, one came to me. And just before I could ask her out, she called me a pompous ass, turned on her heel and walked right out the door. She may as well have spat in my face."

"What the hell did you *do*?"

"Well, that's just it. I'm not sure," Luke said, "I was hoping that maybe *you* could tell *me*!"

"Okay, we'll just worry about the stuff in the car later," she said as she grabbed a chair. "Just sit down and tell me everything."

Liza listened while Luke talked and went through his morning pack of smokes. And by the time he got to the punch line, it was all she could do to keep from smacking him.

"Holy shit! You did *what*?! And you can't figure out why she was *pissed*?!"

"All I did was..."

"Say she was stupid, Luke!"

"No, I didn't. I was just amazed that anyone in this two-bit town even *knew* that word. And she didn't just *know* it, she used it in a sentence!"

"And you had the balls to ask her if she knew what it meant. Just how stupid are you? Lucky I wasn't on the receiving end of that shit, or I'd have hit you so hard..."

"...That by the time I quit rolling, my clothes would've been out of style," Luke finished with a roll of his eyes and a chuckle. "So...what do I do now?"

"Well, groveling at her feet might be good," said Liza with a grin, "as well as kissing her ass up and down Main Street. But I guess it all depends on how much you really want that date. In any case, you're going to have to apologize—and do it profusely—or she'll never even speak to you again. How about giving her a call?"

"Geeze...I don't know, Sis. I really don't think..."

"Do you want that date or not?" she quipped, grabbing her keys and starting for the door. "Now help me get the stuff out of the car before the plastic wrappers melt right into the legal pads."

"Logan residence, Chloe Dawson speaking."

I scanned Chloe's face for some idea of who was on the line. And when I saw her eyes light up and the smile crease her lips, I figured that my luck might just be changing. At least, it wasn't somebody trying to sell me something. And with the way things had been going lately, that in itself was good news.

"...just fine, thank you. Hold on a second, please."

This must be really good, I thought as she handed me the receiver. Chloe was, after all, grinning from ear to ear.

"Hello?"

"Hi, Tess. This is Luke Benson."

For the second time in less than an hour, I couldn't believe my ears. How much nerve did this guy possess? How dare he call me—especially after what he'd done! Had he no manners at all?!

And what about Chloe? She damned sure knew better than this. What sort of fucking friend was she anyway, to subject me to this sort of shit? I shot her a dirty look, but the only response I got was a muffled giggle.

"Tess? Are you there?"

"Yeah," I responded rather tersely. "What do you want, Mr. Benson? Some further discussion of my personal vocabulary?"

"Well, I certainly don't think that's in order. In fact..."

"Look, I don't like you very much right now. And I really don't feel like making small talk with you. So...if you'll just state your business, we can get this over and done with."

"Oh, geeze!" he sighed heavily. "I knew this wasn't going to go well—this sort of thing never seems to go well for me—and you're obviously not going to make this easy..."

"If this morning is any indication, *everything*," I said as I clearly enunciated all four syllables in the last word, "is easy for you, Mr. Benson. If it enters your head, it just rolls off your tongue. How difficult is that? Especially for someone who makes his living with words? So, how about just spitting them out?"

I was being a real bitch, and it just wasn't like me—particularly when someone was as nervous as he seemed to be. But try as I might to do otherwise, I just couldn't help myself.

"Look, Tess...I am *so* sorry about this morning. I don't know what got into me, and I'd do anything to take it back. Could we just start over? *Please*?!"

I let out my breath slowly. The man actually sounded like a wounded, grief-stricken child, and as much as that touched my heart, I'd been that route with men before. Once you accepted poor behavior, you never got any better. And I was worth more than that. I'd promised myself long ago that no one would ever again treat me like my ex had, and it damned sure wasn't going to start now.

"...and you're the most intelligent woman I've ever met. So please, Tess. Let me make it up to you. How about over dinner?"

Good Gods, I thought as the words sank in. Dinner? He had to be kidding. Bad enough that his crap had already ruined my appetite for lunch, but dinner too? I didn't think so.

"When pigs fly on gossamer wings, Mr. Benson!" I retorted. "Now then, are you going to ask whether I know what *that* word means too?" I paused just for effect. "No? Good. Then I believe this conversation is over. Have a good day."

I put the receiver back on the hook without waiting for a response then strolled into the kitchen to refill my coffee cup. I lit a cigarette and stared defiantly at Chloe.

"What?!" She shrugged her shoulders and put on her most innocent look.

"What the hell do you mean, 'what?!' You knew better than that! What the hell is wrong with you? Have you lost your fucking mind?" I spat at her in a stage whisper. I was right on the edge of losing control and doing my best to keep my voice down. The last thing I needed now was for her to burst into tears, and that was something that seemed to happen lately when I yelled at her.

"What the hell is wrong with *you*?" she countered. "The man calls to apologize—something he obviously needed to do—and how do you respond? You fucking hang up on him! What sort of shit is *that*?!"

"The sort that needs my food digested in peace and quiet," I said, throwing my arms in the air and pacing through the kitchen. "After all this, he had the unmitigated gall to actually invite me to dinner."

"Well after all this, don't you think he actually owes you something?" Chloe chuckled. "And a nice dinner at his expense might just be a good starting point, don't you think?" she said with a twinkle in her eye.

"No," I countered with a half grin. "I'm old enough to choose who I eat with. And I've gotta tell you, Chloe...he's simply not on the list."

Luke stared at the receiver in his hand for a good while and just listened to the dial tone. He still couldn't believe she'd hung up on him. And even after he'd jumped through his ass apologizing—something that had never been easy for him. He wanted to scream. Yell. Maybe even kick something. But instead, he just placed the receiver back on the cradle, lit a cigarette and walked out to the front desk.

"How did it go?" Liza asked with a smile. "All set for dinner?"

"You and your great ideas!" Luke grumbled as he swatted his sister on the head with a file folder. "Next time, just keep 'em to yourself, okay?"

"Please tell me that you didn't insult her again—and that you actually *did* apologize."

"No, I didn't—insult her, that is. And I definitely apologized. I even went so far as to tell her that she was the most intelligent woman I'd ever met."

"And?"

"She told me that she'd have dinner with me when—geeze, I still can't believe this one—pigs flew on gossamer wings!"

Liza swallowed back a chuckle. But the look on his face coupled with the punch line was just too much. Before she knew it, she was beside herself with laughter.

"Well, you've got to admit she's got balls, Luke," she said, trying to get herself back under control. "But I guess now the question is, can you make it happen?"

"Make what happen?"

"The 'gossamer wing' thing. Can you make pigs fly on them?" she asked with a wink.

"What the hell are you talking about?" He was looking at her like she'd lost her mind.

"Well," she said, arching her eyebrow, "if you're going to have dinner with her—and it looks like nothing else will satisfy you at this point—then you're going to have to do it on her terms.

"Besides...I have an idea. A quick call to Phil over at the Flower Basket might just do the trick."

"The Flower Basket? I'm sending her *flowers*?" He couldn't believe what she was suggesting.

"Yes, dear brother, you are. If you have to eat crow, then at least dine with class. Take that route and you might even find it's a tastier dish than you originally thought."

Luke shrugged his shoulders. "Okay. I'll bite." He had, after all, nothing to lose. Still, the idea of sending flowers to a woman he'd just met a few hours ago seemed more than just a little over the top. Especially since he usually reserved flowers for really special occasions—things like birthdays and awards and such. And oh, all right, then...fucking up—which he'd not only managed to do but had apparently done in spades.

But making pigs fly? And on gossamer wings? Just how the hell was Liza going to make *that* happen?

"So...what exactly did you have in mind?"

I ground out my cigarette in the ashtray and thought about how good it felt to be alone in my own space. As much as I loved Chloe, sometimes I just needed to be by myself. This was one of those times. Besides, I had tons to do. For one thing, I needed to work on the book. Editing wasn't fun, but it was necessary, and there was plenty of that to be done before I could send in the final draft. And since I had another book on the back burner as well, it might be a good time to work up an outline.

But first things first. Everything went better with coffee, and getting to work called for a fresh pot. Since it was closer to my office than the bedroom, I set up the coffeemaker in the kitchen. In a matter of seconds, the house was filling with that wonderful aroma that never failed to bring me to my senses. About two more minutes, I thought, grabbing my cup from the table, and all will be right with the world.

A wadded up scrap of paper fell to the floor. When I picked it up, I saw that it was the Post-it note with Silas Shrum's phone number scrawled across the top. Well, I mused as I straightened the small sheet, at least Chloe was right about one thing. I had gotten a phone number out of this morning's ruckus, and it was more than I'd had before. Since this was as good a time to call as any, I might as well give it a shot. Remembering what Luke had had to say about him though, I waited to fill my cup and grabbed a fresh pack of cigarettes before reaching for the phone. No sense in putting myself through caffeine or nicotine withdrawal, I thought with a chuckle. At least not if I could help it.

Of course, it's a fact of life that advanced preparations are seldom necessary when in place, and such was the case with the phone call. So, I left a message on the historian's answering machine and hoped he'd call me back. I was just itching to see what I could find out about the folks buried in that cemetery plot—especially the owner of that peculiar tombstone—and at this point, Silas Shrum looked like my best bet.

Still, there wasn't any point in wasting the rest of the day just waiting around for a phone call, so I sat down at my desk and started picking through the manuscript. There were only a few more chapters to edit, and with any luck, I figured I could get through it in a few hours. But before I could really get settled into the first chapter, there was one more interruption. And this time, it was the doorbell.

For the love of the Gods, I thought, as I stomped to the door. What *now*?! Didn't people stay home anymore? I certainly hoped it wasn't the crazy woman who lived next door—the pregnant one who'd decided I should take up mid-wifing and had offered to be my first patient—because there was no way I felt like dealing with that sort of insanity. In any case, I steeled myself for whatever might greet me and whipped open the door.

It was my turn for the deer in the headlights stare. For there on my front porch stood Mickey, the delivery man from the Flower Basket. And he was holding the most enormous basket of yellow pink-tipped roses I'd ever seen.

"Must've been a really good girl today, Tess," he chuckled.

"Good Gods, Mickey," I breathed. "Who on earth did these come from?"

"Don't have a clue, m'dear," he said, "but I'm willing to bet there's not a single Talisman rose left in the entire state!"

I wished him a good day, set the basket on the coffee table and reached for the envelope. Before I could even rip it open, something else caught my eye. There, nestled in among the flowers, were three little pigs bobbing about on tiny metal springs. Attached to the back of each was a single pair of sheer, sparkling iridescent fairy wings.

"Holy shit," I murmured as a round of the giggles burst forth. "Pigs flying—and on gossamer wings! How funny is *that*?!" I was still laughing when I tore into the envelope, but instead of a card, there was a hand-written note, which read:

> *Please forgive this pompous ass. (I obviously need no more practice in that department and wouldn't blame you if you never spoke to me again.) But as I've met your terms, I would very much appreciate it if you'd reconsider my dinner invitation.*
>
> *Should you be so inclined, please call the number below, and a car will pick you up at seven. If you are not, then please accept my sincere and grateful appreciation for brightening my morning.*
> *Humbly,*
> *Luke*

Stunned, I sat down on the couch and stared at the note. Holy shit! This man was absolutely full of surprises. No one had ever gone to so much trouble for me, or done so with such elegance. By the Gods, he'd even made it his business to find out that these roses were my absolute favorites and had managed them even though they weren't easy to come by. And just look at those pigs! This must've cost him a small fortune, I thought leaning over and inhaling the heady perfume.

Could I have been that wrong about Luke Benson? Dyed-in-the-wool jackasses certainly didn't behave this way. Or did they? Well, there was only one way to find out. I reached for the phone and began to dial.

CHAPTER 4

"So, how did it go?" Chloe looked at me expectantly from her perch on the kitchen counter. And from the Cheshire cat grin on her face, I could tell that she was fishing for details. Every last juicy one of them.

"Okay." I replied nonchalantly, then filled my cup and lit a cigarette.

"Just o*kay*?!*" She leaned forward to peer at me as if I'd suddenly morphed into some sort of alien life form.

"Yeah." My reply was punctuated with an arch of my right eyebrow, a punctuation she knew meant to leave it at that. But the smile that pled to be unleashed strained against my lips, and the tiniest trace of it escaped despite my efforts. I shoved the cigarette in my mouth as camouflage and hoped she didn't notice.

"Oh, come *ON*, Tess," Chloe pressed without missing a beat. "A man sends you three dozen Talisman roses—complete with flying pigs, I might add—and sends a chauffer-driven white limo to fetch you for dinner. And all you can say is, 'okay?!'" She rolled her eyes heavenward, jumped down off the counter and repositioned herself into a chair right in front of me. "For the love of the Gods, Girl...even if you wanted to kill him before the night was out, you know damned good and well that things had to be better than okay!"

The look on her face was so akin to that of an old-maid school teacher—you know the one...it's the look that makes you draw back your knuckles for fear of connecting with the wooden ruler—that I couldn't help but laugh.

"Wipe that look off your face, Darlin'," I said between giggles. "It doesn't suit you at all. In fact, it's very unbecoming!"

"Then let's hear it—all of it—and don't leave out anything!" she exclaimed.

She was positively bubbling over with excitement; so much so, in fact, that if I hadn't known better, I'd have thought she'd been the one whisked off to dinner. I'd never seen her quite so giddy.

"Oh, all right," I said with a wink as I topped off my cup. "To start with, Luke Benson really did his homework..."

"Don't tell me he took you to the Royal N'Orleans? He did, didn't he! Criminee, Tess! That's the most romantic restaurant in Cape

Girardeau—maybe in all of Missouri—and the décor is fabulous. It looks just like...”

“One of the best restaurants in the French Quarter,” I said. “Yes, I know, Chloe. Now...am I telling this story—or are you?”

“Sorry,” she said with a sigh. “But just one more thing before you go on.” She hemmed and hawed like she was trying to broach a really delicate subject then finally put her hands on my shoulders and blurted, “Were you dressed okay? It’s a really fancy place, and I know how you get when you’re not dressed right.” The concern in her voice was so genuine that I almost felt guilty about teasing her. But not enough to make me throw on the brakes. In fact, I was having so much fun at her expense that I just sailed right on, full tilt boogie.

“Did your newspaper arrive on time today?”

She nodded in response but shot me a blank stare.

“Well, that’s your answer, Ms. Dawson. Obviously, the publisher of the Sikeston Press Herald isn’t a dead man, yet!” I managed with a nearly straight face. “Of course, I was dressed okay, you ninny! I got the address when I called the limo service. You certainly don’t think I’d leave something like *that* to chance. *Do* you?” I chuckled.

“Did you wear the black slinky backless number? The one split up the thigh with the rhinestone straps that crisscross up the back?”

“Yep...”

“My Gods! His eyes must’ve popped right out of his head!”

“His eyes are fine, Chloe,” I said with a grin, “but if you don’t let me get on with this story, it’s going to last longer than the date did.” She pretended to zip her lip and looked at me with twinkling eyes. “We had a nice bottle of Merlot with our Châteaubriand, and crème brûlée for dessert,” I hurried along, “And then we went for a walk along the Mississippi River and had a Bailey’s nightcap. End of story.” I finished with a wave of my hand, lit another cigarette and inhaled deeply.

“Not so fast there, Ms. Logan! Are you going to see him again?”

“I don’t know. It’s not that I wouldn’t like to, Chloe. It’s just that I may have screwed things up,” I said as I exhaled a heavy breath.

“What do you mean, screwed things up? How could you possibly...I mean, after everything was so perfect...I mean...for the love of the Gods, Tess!” she stammered.

“Well, remember how pissed I was that I couldn’t get through to Luke on the phone...”

“Yeah. That bitch at the front desk wouldn’t let you through...”

"And remember how we nicknamed her Little Hitler?"

"Yeah."

"Well, it turns out that the bitch in question is none other than Luke Benson's twin sister, Liza."

"Oh shit, Tess, you *didn't*!"

"Yeah...I did. I made mention of Little Hitler—by name, no less—right in the middle of our after dinner coffee. And the look on Luke's face was enough to curdle the cream."

"But he still took you for a moonlit walk instead of cutting the date short—and he didn't have to. And he still offered you a nightcap. He didn't have to do that either." She sounded as if she were going through a mental checklist. "Goodnight kiss?" she asked.

"Peck on the cheek."

"So, maybe he really wasn't that upset."

"Of course, I apologized up one side and down the other—and he made a quick surface recovery by laughing it off—but you know what they say, Chloe. Blood is thicker than water. And that definitely seems to be true of twins. So...I guess I'll just have to see if he calls."

"Oh, he'll call. I don't think you have to worry about that," she said, patting my knee.

I drummed my nails on the table and stared out the window. Leave it to me to screw things up, I thought. And this time, I'd done it up right. I hadn't just stuck my foot in my mouth. I'd stuck it so far down my throat, it had damned near tickled my bellybutton.

Rob Malloy, the deejay at the radio station, was doing the oldies thing again this morning. And for the second time in less than twenty-four hours, Luke wondered if the guy was roaming around inside his head. He'd not only opened his show with *The Hollies'* "Long Cool Woman" but seemed to be playing it every hour on the hour. Not that Luke minded. It was just a little weird, that's all.

Luke glanced at his watch. 8:59 a.m. He watched as the second hand ticked off its increments—5...4...3...2...1...—and laughed out loud as the opening bars sounded through the speakers.

It had never been one of his favorite songs. In fact, he'd never even known all the words. Well, not before this morning anyway. But

Rob had changed all that, and now Luke was singing along as if he'd written the song himself.

Talk about synchronicity at work, he thought, stepping to the beat and dancing around the office. The song lyrics could actually have been written about Tess, as they told the tale of a five–foot–nine woman dressed in black with enough sex appeal to mess with some guy's ability to reason. And aside from the fact that she'd made him weak in the knees rather than screwed with his head, that song described her perfectly.

He was still singing and dancing when Liza walked in. She couldn't believe what she was seeing. There he was—her tight, buttoned up brother with no sense of humor—cutting loose like he was a fifteen-year-old child. Jesus God...he hadn't even acted like this when he *was* fifteen! This was just too good, she thought as she wished for a video camera and burst into laughter. To capture him on tape like this—completely and utterly oblivious to the rest of the world—would have made for a priceless treasure indeed. In fact, it might even have made great blackmail material for the day when he had kids, she thought with a wry grin. Now wouldn't that be something?

"Just what the hell are you doing?!" she asked with a chuckle as she turned down the volume on the radio. "Brushing up for karaoke night? It sounds like a party in here."

"And top of the morning to you too, Sister dear," he replied, grabbing her hands and swinging her around the room.

"What's gotten into you, Luke? I've never seen you act like this. Not in all our forty years." She searched his face and got nothing but a silly grin in response. "Ahhh..." she said, remembering. "Dinner went well, huh?"

"Oh...I'd say better than well."

"Get laid?" she asked with a grin. Liza enjoyed making him blush, and he didn't disappoint her.

"I can't believe you said that," he retorted, feigning disdain. "That cuts me, Liza...that cuts me deep...that cuts me..."

"Yeah, yeah, yeah," she said, serving up the punch line with a roll of her eyes, "right to the bone." She couldn't help but chuckle when Luke accommodated her by grabbing the make-believe knife in his chest and staggering around the room.

"Okay, funny guy. Grab your smokes and let's hear it. Play by play. And if you dare to leave out any of the good parts, I'll tickle you 'til you can't catch your breath!"

"Geeze, Liza...now you're threatening torture! Maybe you really *are* Little Hitler!" he said with a chuckle and fished a cigarette from his pack.

"Excuse me?"

"Little Hitler. That's what Tess called you. Of course, she had no idea that you were my sister—and that even made it funnier." He did his best not to double over in laughter but lost the battle.

"She called me *what*?!"

"Little Hitler," he said as he tried to catch his breath enough to connect flame to tobacco. But he lost that battle too and finally just gave up, putting the cigarette aside. "How funny is that?!"

"Not too. In fact, I'm not sure I like it at all." From her tone of voice, Luke could tell that his sister was more than a little annoyed. Two more seconds, he calculated as he watched her index finger working its way up and down in a rhythm all its own. Yep...there it was: full blown tap mode. A sure sign that she was well on the way to being pissed.

"So, just what the hell did I ever do to *her*?" Liza quipped. "I've never even so much as met the woman. I've never..."

"Oh, good God, Liza," Luke countered good-naturedly, "give it a rest. It only means that she couldn't get past you when she was trying to reach me the other day. It only means that you're the very best receptionist in all of Sikeston. It only means that..."

"You should give me a raise!" she said with a chuckle as she reached for his neck with both hands and pretended to strangle him.

"Yes, I should," he said. "And I intend to do just that. Effective immediately."

"You're kidding, right?"

"Not at all, Sis. In fact, I see a dollar an hour in your future," he teased.

"Don't screw with me, Luke." She tossed her head in the air and looked away for effect. "You know damned good and well I'm on salary."

"Well, then...how about fifty bucks a week? Little Hitler!"

"I'm starting to feel better already. In fact, I'm beginning to think the new moniker isn't so bad. Hmmmm...Little Hitler," she mused as she contorted her face into an evil look. "Has sort of a nice ring to it, don'cha think?" She wiggled her eyebrows up and down and flexed her fingers to tickle his ribs.

Luke jumped back out of her reach and laughed heartily. "Now hold on there, LH! I'd hate to have you prosecuted for criminal torture," he teased, "especially before you could spend that raise."

"Yeah, *that* would be torture!" she said with a grin. "But enough of this. What about the date?"

"I think 'incredible' pretty much covers it," he said with a wink. He smiled softly and thought back to the night before. It had been perfect, all right. The night was beautiful, the lady, gorgeous, and the conversation, delightful. What else could he have asked for?

"And?"

"And, what?!"

"You needn't think you're going to get out of this that easily," she said, "especially not when you haven't even been the slightest bit interested in anyone for years. So, let's hear it!"

"She's stunning. She's well-educated. She's an author with a new book contract. And if I had my way, I'd just blow off work this morning and spend the rest of the day looking at her," he said dreamily.

"All right, already. Enough about Tess," she exclaimed. "What did you do? Where did you go? Details, Luke! Details!"

"Okay...white limousine, Royal N'Orleans, walk along the Mississippi River, Bailey's nightcap," he said happily, checking them off on his fingers for his sister's benefit.

"Wow!" Liza was blown away. "What happened to flowers being over the top? What happened to *that*?!"

"Nothing. Just changed my mind...that's all," he said with a smile.

Liza took a deep breath and exhaled heavily. Something was wrong with this picture. Well, it was if it included her brother anyway. He wasn't just tight with his money—he literally squeaked—and to see him running through it like water on a woman he just met was more than a little disturbing. It was downright frightening.

But that wasn't all. Luke hadn't lit one single cigarette since she'd walked through the door. And from the looks of the ashtrays, he hadn't smoked all morning. A very interesting development—especially for someone who'd smoked like a bad exhaust pipe for the last twenty years. She was beginning to feel like she'd just stepped into an alternate universe where life as she knew had ceased to exist.

"Who *are* you?" she demanded playfully. "And what have you done with my *brother*?"

"Oh, come on, Sis! Don't you like the new me? You've been

after me for years about being so..."

"Tight. Yeah, I know," she said. "But don't you think you're getting in a little deep here? I mean, you just only met this woman and..."

"Get used to it, m'dear," he said with a chuckle. "If this is getting in too deep, I very well may decide to drown. Hell, Liza, I may even decide to propose before the day's out!"

The smile on his face was genuine and went all the way up to his eyes. She'd never seen him so happy. And even though he *had* to be teasing, something about the way he'd delivered that last sentence unsettled her.

"I certainly hope not," she said lightly, "about proposing today, I mean. We've got a lot of things to..."

"Listen, Sis," he said excitedly as he turned up the radio. "It's coming on again!"

And sure enough, there it was: the ten o'clock rendition of "Long Cool Woman," compliments of Rob Malloy.

Chloe Dawson sat at her kitchen table, sipping coffee and looking through the want ads. The last thing she wanted to do was get a job. There was plenty to do at the house, she thought as she lit a cigarette and savored the menthol that cooled her throat. Damn Brian anyway. She enjoyed staying at home. She enjoyed her morning coffee klatches with Tess. And, yes...she enjoyed spending money. Way too much money, according to the Gospel of Brian, the author of which had stated only this morning that she couldn't spend another cent until she managed to bring in a few of her own.

Horseshit, she thought as she topped off her cup. When the hell is it going to be her turn? She saved the money so they could get married. She saved the money for the down payment on the house. She saved the money for almost every fucking thing they've got. And now? She's the one who can't spend anymore! What kind of crap is that?!

Still, there wasn't a lot she could do about it—not without money anyway—so she settled back in at the table and peered at the classifieds. The section was positively littered with fast food and babysitting ads, but she certainly wasn't going there. The last thing she wanted to be at the end of the day was greasy, pukey or shitty! But just for fun, she decided to cross through the listings as if she'd called. That way, Brian couldn't say a word when she said there was nothing to be had. It was a good plan, and she was sticking to it.

"Son of a bitch!" she breathed. She'd been half-way down the page when she saw it, and if she hadn't stopped crossing through ads to take a drag on her cigarette, she might have missed it entirely. The conditions were great—no puke, no shit, no grease—and the salary, above average. It wasn't just right up her alley, it was custom-made for her. Besides, this job might just kill two birds with one stone. Yep...there was something to be said for synchronicity after all, she thought as she grabbed the phone and began to dial.

"Chloe Dawson calling for Luke Benson, please," she said as she lit a fresh smoke.

"Damn it, Liza! The last thing I wanted to do today was interview," Luke grumbled. The tone of his voice hadn't quite reached the yell pitch yet—it was somewhere between a growl and a whine—but was definitely not happy.

"Oh, come on, Luke," his sister coaxed. "Just do the interview and hire her. How long will that take? You know she's more than qualified. And besides that, you like her."

"You don't even know her. Suppose you don't like her."

"Doesn't matter. I'd work with Attila the Hun at this point—if it meant less work for me! Come on, Luke. Just interview her. *Please*?!"

"Oh, all right!" His voice was still terse but was starting to soften. "Have her come by about..."

"Too late for that. She'll be here in fifteen minutes," she said. "And, Luke?"

"Yeah?"

"Have I told you lately how wonderful you are?" she asked sweetly.

"Yeah, yeah, yeah," he replied and lit his first cigarette of the day.

Chloe was on cloud nine. She squealed her wheels as she rounded the corner, zipped into Tess' driveway and tossed the bottle of Asti into her purse. Then she did a little freeform jig all the way up the walk. By the Gods, she had a job! No more bullshit from Brian. No more crap about the money. Life was good and about to be better, she thought as she danced through the screen door and let it slam behind her.

"Wooohoooo!!" she yelled through the house. "Tess! Hey, Tess!"

What on earth was wrong with Chloe? She was making enough noise to wake the neighborhood dead. I raced down the hall and nearly collided with her in the living room. "What's the matter? Are you all right?" I panted, trying to catch my breath.

"Just heavenly!" She yanked the bottle from its hiding place and laughed her silvery laugh. "Grab the corkscrew and wine glasses, friend of all friends. I just landed the job of the century—and it's celebration time!"

"No shit?!"

"No shit!" she exclaimed, grabbing me by the hand, skipping toward the kitchen and trying to shove the bottle at me, all at the same time.

"Well?"

"Wine first!"

What fun to see her so happy, I thought as I opened the bottle and grabbed the glasses. Hard to believe, though, that a job was responsible for Chloe's new-found excitement. She'd never wanted to go back to work. And yet, here she was, positively delirious at the prospect of re-entering the work force. There had to be more to this story—a lot more—and I intended to find out exactly what it was.

I filled the glasses and handed her one. "Okay," I said with a smile. "Spill it!"

"Let's have a toast first!"

"Oh, all right. But then you have to tell me everything. Okay?"

She nodded in agreement and held her glass high. "To Luke Benson," she declared breathlessly, "and his wonderful taste in women!"

"*What*?!"

"Come on, Tess," she pleaded. "Just drink...and then, I'll explain!"

The look on her face was so wistfully child-like, there was nothing I could do but shrug my shoulders and shake my head in agreement. "To Luke Benson," I said with a chuckle as our glasses clinked together.

"Damn, that's good!" Chloe drained her glass and motioned toward the bottle on the counter.

"Keep that up and we're going to need a case of this stuff!" I teased, as I filled her glass again and looked at her expectantly.

"Okay. Here's the deal," she said between sips. "I'm going to work for Luke Benson. And I'm starting first thing Monday morning."

"You're kidding!" I was incredulous. "How the hell did that happen?!"

"He ran an ad and I answered it." She pulled a fresh pack of cigarettes from her purse and tore off the wrapper before going on. "Good pay plus benefits, and best of all," she said, pausing to light up, "my hours are ten to five, so that means..."

"That you'll still have time to stop here for coffee on the way to work!" Now I was grinning from ear to ear too. "Oh, Chloe...that's fabulous!"

"And I'll also be able to run interference for you with Luke," she added with glee.

My smile faded as I felt the blood drain from my face. Of all the fucking nerve. It was hard for me to believe that anyone—even someone as pushy as Chloe—would even dream of going there.

"You'll do nothing of the fucking sort, Chloe Dawson!" I said between clenched teeth. "What goes on between Luke and me—if anything more goes on that is—is strictly between the two of us. And you'd better get that through that thick skull of yours," I ranted. "There will be no butting in. No kibitzing from the sidelines. No meddling whatsoever. Or I swear..."

She laughed, refusing to allow my apparent aggravation to even slightly dampen her spirits. "Oh, chill out, Tess! It was just a thought. That's all."

"Well, wipe that thought right out of your little pea brain," I said. "Okay?"

"Okay."

I still wasn't sure I'd gotten through to her, but there wasn't much else I could say on the matter. At least, not at this point. I'd just have to bide my time, see what happened, and reel her in if necessary. For now, it was probably best to change the subject, and my attitude.

"So, since you don't have to go to work until Monday, what do you say we have a real celebration," I offered cheerfully as I refilled our glasses. "Maybe dinner here tomorrow night? Around seven?"

Her eyes lit up again. "That'd be great! How about your world-famous beef stroganoff and that scrumptious chocolate cheese pie I love so much?" She took a sip from her glass and beamed up at me.

"Done deal," I said with a grin. "Why don't you call Brian right now and make sure he's free? That way, I can hit the grocery store tonight and not have to fool with that tomorrow. It'll be one less thing on my to-do list."

"Gotcha," she said and reached for the phone.

"Well, will you look at this," Luke said to no one in particular. He had Chloe's resume in hand and had decided to actually look it over before tagging it for an employee file. The interview had been nothing more than a formality—Liza had all but insisted that he hire the woman—so there was no real need to check her references. Besides, he knew Chloe on a personal level, and that was good enough for him.

Still, one reference she'd listed more than intrigued him. It gave him the excuse he was looking for. Yes, indeed, he thought as he picked up the phone, Chloe Dawson had become indispensable already.

The phone rang just as I was seeing Chloe out of the driveway, but I still managed to pick it up on the second ring.

"Tess Logan," I answered.

"Hi, Tess. It's Luke." The smile in his voice came through loud and clear, and a sense of relief washed over me. Apparently, I hadn't screwed up as much as I'd thought.

"Hi, there," I said, glad that he couldn't see the silly grin on my face. "And how is my favorite newspaper publisher this afternoon?"

"Just peachy," he chuckled.

"Glad to hear it. What can I do for you?"

"Well...I hired Chloe Dawson today, and you're on the top of her reference list. So I thought I should talk to you about her."

"Really," I said, trying to keep the laughter from my voice. "Isn't that normally done *before* hiring someone?"

"Yeah," he admitted, "but Liza really wanted me to hire her on the spot. And I couldn't exactly check her references right in front of her now, could I?"

"Well, I guess not," I said with a grin. "But I really don't think you've got anything to worry about. She's got a terrific work ethic and great organizational skills, to say nothing of being fiercely loyal. So, I'd say congratulations are in order, Luke. You've just hired yourself one hell of a secretary."

"You have no idea how glad I am to hear that!"

"Terrific." I was still undecided whether I should take the conversation a step further or not. Oh what the hell, I thought. Worst case scenario is that he says no. So I gathered my courage and said, "Speaking of Chloe, I'm having a little celebration dinner for her over at my place tomorrow night. And unless you have a policy against socializing with employees..." I could hardly believe I was giving him an out, even if it was just to soften the blow if he refused. "...I'd love for you to join us."

There...I'd gotten it out, I thought as I willed my heart to slow its pace. And I'd know in a matter of seconds whether he really wanted to see me again or not. Thankfully, he never missed a beat.

"I'd love to come," he said casually, "provided, of course, that I can bring the wine. So, what's it going to be? Red, white or something in-between?"

"Red," I said. "So, we'll see you around seven?"

"I'll be there."

"Great! And Luke...it's really casual, so dress comfortably.'

"Somehow, I knew it would be," he chuckled. "See you then, Tess."

After placing the phone in the cradle, Luke danced around the room and gave himself a big thumbs up. He'd be there all right—and with bells on. Even Jesus Christ himself couldn't keep him away.

I slipped between the covers and closed my eyes. It had been quite a day all right. Chloe had gotten a job, I'd finished the editing process, and things were progressing with Luke. Well, I wasn't sure progressing was exactly the right word, but at least things weren't over and done before they'd really gotten started. And after I'd fucked up with his sister, that was something. Chloe's celebration dinner would tell the tale, and then I'd know whether pursuing this relationship was in the cards. And if it wasn't? Well, I'd just pull a Scarlett O'Hara and worry about that tomorrow.

At least the grocery shopping was done. And that, in itself, was quite a feat, I thought as I went through the checklist in my head. I'd gotten a nice Johannesburg Riesling to go with the fruit, veggie and stuffed mushroom hors d'oeuvre trays and a case of Budweiser, just in case the guys were in a more casual mood. The fixings for the beef stroganoff, the broccoli-cheddar side dish and the chocolate pie were in place. The only things left were the flowers, and I probably didn't need those anyway, I thought with a yawn.

Hooking up with Silas Shrum was the only thing I hadn't managed, but that was okay. Maybe he was out of town or something. Maybe he didn't return calls to folks he didn't know. Or maybe, he was just an eccentric old nut. Regardless of which it was though, it really didn't matter. With everything else going on, I hadn't had any real time to visit with him anyway.

All in all, it had been a pretty good day, I thought as I snuggled down into the bed, yawned again and felt the first stages of sleep take over.

She gently stroked his hair and let the nail of her index finger slide across his cheek as he slept. Then she slipped from between the covers and went to the bedroom window. The full moon was up, and she stood there for a moment, basking in its silvery rays as they bathed her naked body and cast shadows on her caramel colored skin.

She held her hand up to the light, smugly considering the strand of copper hair under her fingernail and smiled. Won't be long now, she thought, glancing over her shoulder at the sleeping man. No suh, not long a'tall. Freedom was one thing—she remembered well the day he'd given it to her—but marryin' was another. And no matter what the law allowed, she thought as she tossed her calico dress over her shoulders and gave him one last look, he'd be doin' some marryin' a'right. An' he'd be marryin' her!

She stole down the stairs, carefully stepping over the creaky spot, and then out the door to her cabin. Everything was ready and waiting. All she need is dis, she thought as she knotted the hair strand around her fingernail and used her teeth to bite it off. She let it drop into the palm of her hand and muttered something over it before slipping it into the red felt bag laid out in front of her.

Looking in the bag, she checked its contents. The knotted red thread, three times the length of his penis and soaked in his semen was there. So were the coins, the rosebud and the tiny hot pepper. All she needed was a bit of this and that from the jars on the table. She quickly made her selections and added the herbs. Then she closed the bag, knotted it securely and went back out into the moonlit night.

She was awash in the moonlight as she stood in the crossroads with legs apart, the bag held high over her head. She swayed side to side, her voice low but firm in her demands that the gates be opened. Chanting softly at first, then rising in volume, the invocation issued from her mouth as she swung the bag in a circular motion overhead several times before her body went rigid and formed a human X.

Working her magic, she was oblivious to everything else around her—even the man with the copper colored curls who silently crept up behind her. His face was set with a venom and fury and hatred beyond all verbal expression. And as he raised both arms over his head—and the axe hit its mark—his scream spewed forth like blood...

Holy fuck! The dream had brought me straight out of the bed. But even as I sat there in a cold sweat trying to calm the pounding in my chest, the details were beginning to fade. Damn it, Tess—hang on to them, I told myself and reached for the legal pad on the nightstand. But try as I might, it was no use. They all slipped away—irreversibly and irrevocably—into the black of night. All except for one, that is, I thought with a shudder.

That man—that vicious, venomous, murdering monster—looked exactly like Luke Benson.

CHAPTER 5

I tossed and turned, but sleep never came. Every time I closed my eyes, I was met with the image from my dream: the face of that vicious man who, except for the color of his hair, looked just like Luke. I tried to shake it off and remind myself that it was just a dream, but past experience prevented that. Most of my dreams were precognitive—and thus far, they'd never been off target. Still, the time period was all wrong. This guy was dressed as if he'd lived a hundred years ago or better, and it just didn't fit.

I glanced at the clock and sighed. Four a.m. I'd been lying here awake for nearly two hours, I thought as I reached for a cigarette and lit up. Part of the problem, of course, had to do with another piece of my past—a piece that had involved a violent ex-husband. And since I'd been more than just a little lucky to escape with my life, those experiences seemed to color anything else even remotely violent that crept into my current existence.

I thought back to all the near misses I'd had with him. There was the time he'd offered to throw acid in my face. The time he'd threatened to kill me because he didn't like his dinner and had gone on to shoot up the wall around me. But all that was small potatoes compared to the night he'd stuck the barrel of his .45 in my mouth and held me there for eight hours. Looking back, it was hard to believe I'd ever put up with that crap. And yet, I knew I had.

I lit a fresh smoke from the one already in my hand, crushed out the old butt in the ashtray and reached for the button on the coffee pot. No sense in lying here for another two hours, I thought as I sat up and exhaled a stream of smoke through my nose. Nope. No sense at all.

Now, sitting in bed and sipping coffee has a way of kick starting the brain, and by the time I poured the second cup, mine was into overdrive. I considered Luke, the guy in the dream, and what the two had to do with each other. And except for the fact that they shared the same face, I couldn't find a common denominator. Nothing seemed to fit. And yet, I was sure it did somehow. Otherwise, there wouldn't be any reason for the uneasy feeling that kept crawling up and down my spine.

I set my cup on the nightstand and headed for the bathroom to brush my teeth. So, what was the deal? Could it be a warning of some sort? Maybe that Luke had a violent streak? Surely not. Well, he

certainly needed to learn to engage his brain before opening his mouth—
that much was obvious. But *violence*? It didn't seem possible.

Still, it might not hurt to be just a bit cautious where he was
concerned. Okay, a lot cautious, I thought as I uncapped the toothpaste
and squeezed some out on my brush.

By the time the whirlwind that was Chloe whipped through the
front door, I'd already done a day's work. The laundry was finished and
put away. The meat was marinating, the crab stuffing was ready for the
mushrooms, and I was just putting the finishing touches on the pie when
she sailed into the kitchen. I greeted her with a "'Mornin', Darlin',"
motioned her toward the coffee pot and turned to put the pie-filling bowl
in the sink.

"What do you think you're *doing*?!" she screeched as she
snatched it out of my hand.

"I was just going to..."

"You're going to nothing of the sort," she said, hugging the bowl
to her chest with one hand and grabbing a spatula from the canister with
the other. "I haven't had breakfast yet, and this will do just fine." She
went to work on the bowl, looking just like a pleased child who'd snuck
up to the cookie jar and liberated its contents while Mama's back was
turned. "Now, where are the beaters?"

"Too late," I said with a chuckle.

"Damn!" She gave the bowl one last scrape, stuffed the spatula
in her mouth and peered into the sink to make sure I wasn't holding out
on her. "Story of my life," she said, expelling a heavy breath and picking
up her cup.

"So...what's on your agenda today?"

"Thought I'd do a little shopping." She leaned in close and
grinned a conspiratorial grin. "I've got this new job, you know...and I
don't have a thing to wear!" Her eyebrows shot up, her mouth flew open
and her hands hit her cheeks in a great impersonation of Macaulay
Culkin in "Home Alone."

"You know Brian's going to have your ass for that," I retorted
but couldn't help but smile at her antics.

"What he doesn't know won't hurt him," she said. "Besides, I'll be back from Cape long before he gets home. Wanna go?"

"Always have an accomplice, hunh?!" I laughed.

"Well, we all know that Brian *never* gets mad at *you*, Princess Perfect," she said. "And if you were any kind of friend, you'd come along to make sure he didn't get mad at me either." She was tossing out the bait all right, but I wasn't biting.

"Oh, puh-*leeze*!" I said with a chuckle. "I may be your friend, but I'm in no mood to catch a bullet today—especially not one aimed by an expert marksman! Besides...I'm having a very important dinner over here tonight, Ms. Dawson. Or have you forgotten?"

"Of course not," she said as she put her cup in the sink. "I'll be here right on time."

"Yeah, right," I said with a roll of my eyes. "I'll be expecting you at six o'clock sharp—and don't be late, okay?"

"Thought it was at seven." she said, looking more than a little puzzled.

"Changed my mind," I said with a smile. "Since tomorrow's a work day and all, it just seemed more accommodating to those who have to get up in the morning." It wasn't really a lie; at least the part about being accommodating wasn't. What Chloe would never know though, was that I was more worried about accommodating her than anyone else. As pissed off as Brian would be if she pulled her usual and made them an hour late, he'd have to stand in line if she ruined this dinner party. In fact, there was a good possibility that our relationship might not survive it—especially if my anger got the best of me. Since I didn't deal well with folks being late, it was just best to avoid the problem altogether if I could. And with Chloe, that meant using the only tactic that had never failed us. I was keeping my fingers crossed that it didn't fail us this time either.

"Okay, I'll be here," she called over her shoulder as she headed for the car. "And if dinner's really good," she added with a wink, "maybe I'll bring my stash over tomorrow so you can take a peek."

She got in the car and buckled her seatbelt, then stuck her head out the window for one last plea. "Sure you don't wanna go? Come on...it'll be fun!"

"No way," I said, emphasizing the words with a shake of my head.

"Oh, all right," she said with a heavy sigh. "But this shopping trip is going to be a doozy—the mother of all shopping trips—and you're going to be really sorry you missed it!"

The hell I would, I thought as she pulled out of the drive. Her fixation with spending money was exactly why she'd been forced to get a job. But more important, it was a major source of her problems with Brian. Her last "doozy of a shopping trip" had damned near caused their divorce—and there was no way I was going to be a party to any more of that. I didn't give a damn what was on sale. Not even a five carat diamond for a penny could interest me. Well, okay...maybe it would. But not if I had Chloe in tow, I thought with a chuckle.

I went back into the house, poured a fresh cup of coffee and started to work on the hors d'oeuvre trays. I thought about the dream some more while I stuffed the mushrooms. Damn! I'd so wanted to tell Chloe about it—I usually told her everything—but in this case, I just couldn't. I had no clue how she might react—she was the most impressionable person I knew—and I certainly didn't want her to have any preconceived ideas about her new boss. Especially if those ideas weren't warranted.

Just as important though, I didn't want to have to listen to how he might not be trustworthy, how I might be repeating the same old pattern with my choices in men, or how I never seemed to be happy unless I was inviting some sort of bullshit into my life. This time, things would be different. There wouldn't be any bullshit at all, and I was starting by putting her need to interfere at the top of the list.

I put the pans in the oven and set the timer. Then I topped off my cup, lit a cigarette and headed for the couch. Gods, I was tired, I thought as I sat down and propped my feet on the coffee table. I leaned back, closed my eyes and did my best to think about nothing.

Funny how the very idea of thinking of nothing works. Just as soon as that thought enters the head, a million others seem to follow suit in a full-blown parade, and my head was no exception. I spent the next five minutes trying to block them all or at least, send them packing. And just about the time I'd almost reached success, the scream of the timer rudely yanked me back into the real world.

Maybe I was going about this all wrong, I thought as I headed for the kitchen. Maybe instead of trying to clear my mind of the dream and whatever it entailed, I should simply try to remember. I knew that a woman had been murdered. A black woman. A woman who, during that time period, had probably been enslaved. But who was she? And what did she have to do with me—or Luke?

I retrieved the pans from the oven, grabbed the vegetables from the fridge and glanced at the clock. While there wouldn't be time for a nap, there was still plenty left for a long, hot, bubbly soak in the tub. And with that to look forward to—there was little I enjoyed more, and I could almost feel its soothing warmth already—the dream and its related questions quickly faded from the viewfinder of my mind. In fact, by the time I'd finished the veggie trays, they'd taken the route of distant memory.

Everything was ready by the time Chloe and Brian walked through the door. All except for the pasta, that is. There just wasn't any point in cooking that until just before we sat down to eat—or at least, not before I saw the whites of Chloe's eyes. Fortunately, she'd surprised me. The Dawson's had arrived a whopping fifteen minutes early. Brian was in a good mood, Chloe's ass was still intact, and for the moment, all seemed right with their world. I, for one, was damned glad of it. Playing referee to the third world war had never been high on my list of fun things to do, and the last thing I'd wanted was give it a shot during dinner.

Luke's timing had also been impeccable. He'd gotten there at seven straight up and had not only arrived as promised with a delightful bottle of Bordeaux, but an added surprise: a pound of Irish cream dessert coffee. I had to admit that I was liking this man more and more. He instinctively seemed to know the way to my heart, and the fact that he'd gone out of his way to be charming didn't hurt either.

Dinner hadn't just gone well; it was a smashing success. It was one of those made to order nights where the personalities of the guests not only complemented each other but interacted as effortlessly as threads in a tapestry. Brian and Luke had more in common than I'd thought and spent a good part of the evening reminiscing about some old cases never solved by the sheriff's department. Luke and Chloe had gotten on well too.

In fact, the only tense moment of the entire evening had come when Chloe almost outed her little shopping spree with a promise to reward my cooking with a sneak peek at all her new goodies. Fortunately for all of us, she hadn't been too specific, and I was able to wipe the look of horror from Brian's face by bringing up the new items she'd added to her river rock collection. Then just for good measure, I'd delivered a swift kick to her shin under the table.

Since Brian was on mornings and had to be at work by six, things broke up around nine. But just as I was seeing them to the door, Luke served up one more surprise: He insisted upon helping me clean up. And that was definitely an offer I couldn't refuse.

"You really didn't have to do this, you know," I said as he handed me the last rinsed dish, and I slipped it into the dishwasher.

"Oh, but I did," he said with a grin. "My mother would roll over in her grave at the thought of my making a mess in someone else's house and not staying to clean it up."

"And keeping Mama from bumping her knees is worth getting dishpan hands?" I asked with a smile of my own that couldn't be seen as anything but flirtatious. Oh, what the hell, I thought. I was a big girl, and I wanted to see just how far this might go.

"Well," he said, tapping out a cigarette and lighting up, "I have to admit to an ulterior motive."

"That sounds ominous." I said lightly as I fished out my own smoke and his lighter rose to meet it.

"Depends on how you look at it." He placed his hands on my shoulders and searched my eyes. "Otherwise, I wouldn't have had a single minute alone with you tonight." His eyes still locked on mine, he leaned in closer. So close, in fact, that I could feel his breath on my skin. My heart pounded, my shoulders tingled at his touch, and as he pulled me even closer, I thought I might actually melt. My fingers found his neck and slipped gently down the line of his jaw. That long, hot, steamy kiss—the one that turns you inside out and leaves you in a puddle on the floor—was inevitable.

Or it would have been if not for one important factor: The nasty little caution light in my mind's eye picked that exact moment to blink on and off like there was no tomorrow. And there was nothing I could do to shut it down.

"So," I said, looking up at him with a teasing grin and reluctantly breaking the tension, "maybe we should just re-name you."

The look on his face was questioning, but he recovered quickly. "And what should my new name *be*?" he asked with a grin.

"Oh...Big Bad Wolf comes to mind!" I chuckled and so did he.

"Well, my ex-wife certainly called me worse," he said, still laughing.

The joke had done the trick, and we opted for peach brandy nightcaps that we took into the living room. I kicked off my shoes and folding a leg under me, plopped down on the couch. Luke sat down beside me, and after a toast to a lovely evening, we each had a sip of the luscious fire in our snifters.

"So...how long were you married?" Old relationships weren't a subject I'd normally have pried into. But since he'd opened the subject himself, I decided it was fair game. Besides, it was always easier to broach sticky subjects *before* the heart got tangled up with someone else's. After that, neither the questions nor the answers seemed to flow as easily.

"Ten years. We were high school sweethearts," he replied, pausing for a sip of brandy. "Fortunately, there weren't any kids, so things were pretty easy to dissolve."

"So, what happened?" I was just waiting for him to go on a tangent about his ex-wife being a bitch. In fact, I was actually baiting him to reach out and grab for the poor-baby routine. It had been my experience that divorced men always seemed to take that route. And I'd already decided that when he did, his chances with me were over and done.

"Mostly it was just a matter of growing apart," he said pleasantly. "I was trying to re-build the newspaper—my father had let it go to hell in a handbasket—and she was trying to start a business of her own. Suddenly, we were working different hours and had different agendas. We just never had any time to spend together." He paused to light my cigarette before continuing.

"It's not like we didn't try—or that there's anything wrong with separate agendas," he explained. "It's just that we suddenly realized there was no common ground at all. And a marriage without common ground is little more than a roommate situation." After a sip from his snifter, he lit a cigarette of his own. "So, what about you?" he asked with a grin.

"Married for sixteen and divorced for six," I replied. "And...I'm probably the last of the truly happy single women in the world," I said with a wink.

"He was from the old school—you know, the one that believes women should be subservient—and spent a lot of time trying to make me fit that mold. So, a good amount of his anger came from the fact that I just wouldn't conform. The icing on the cake though," I said as I took a drag from my cigarette, "came when I changed religions. And he just couldn't deal with that."

His eyebrows shot up in surprise. "You're kidding. A change of religion caused the breakup?"

"Well, not entirely. But it sure as hell had a lot to do with it." I wondered if I should tell him or not. But as it was another of my "weeding out" factors, I decided that I might as well get it over with. "You see, Luke," I continued, "I'm a Witch."

I watched him closely in an effort to gauge his response. No change in body language. No change of facial expression. Not even so much as the slightest muscle twitch. In fact, he never missed a beat.

His eyes twinkled. "Not surprised. So, does this mean you're Wiccan?"

"Yeah." I said, trying to keep my voice even. To say that I was shocked beyond belief was an understatement. I'd never gotten such an accepting reaction—not in response to that admission, anyway—and it was all I could do to keep from hugging him in delight. I grabbed my snifter instead and gulped down the last sip. "So," I asked lightly, "does that mean you actually know what Wiccans *are*?!"

His warm, light laughter filled the room. Then he took my hands in his, locked his eyes on mine for the second time that night, and said pointedly, "Well, I'll be damned. Now we're going to discuss *my* personal vocabulary?" His eyebrows moved upward to form a crease across his forehead, and the look on his face reflected a mixture of hurt and surprise. Still, his lips curved with the slightest trace of amusement. How could they not? There's nothing more entertaining than watching someone fall flat on her ass when tripping over the very thing she finds so objectionable in other people. This time I'd done it up right. And he'd had a front row seat.

"So," he asked, "shall I spout off a definition?" His tone of voice was more than reproachful. It was downright sarcastic.

Holy *shit*, I thought to myself. My face flushed with horror, and the heat of embarrassment crept up my neck. That'll teach you to be such a self-righteous bitch! Could you have fucked up any worse? Of all the things you could have said—and you had to go *there*?! Just how stupid *are* you?!

"N-no...I...I..." Damn it! Now I was stuttering. It was something I hadn't done in years, and this was no time to start. Even worse, my eyes had started to tear up. I felt just like a small child who'd been thoroughly chastised for some slight indiscretion. But this time it wasn't slight. I took a deep breath, reminded myself that I was a grown-up and willed myself to calm down.

This was bad all right, but it wasn't the end of the world. Not by a long shot, I told myself as I blinked back the tears. I'd pulled myself out of far worse messes, and if I played this just right, there was still a chance of landing on my feet. And if I didn't? Well, I'd worry about that later.

So with that in mind, I put on my most pitiful poker face and looked him directly in the eye. "Well, Ollie," I said in my best Stan Laurel impersonation, "'tis certainly a fine mess I've gotten us into."

To say that Luke was taken aback was putting it mildly. He wanted to be mad—that was a given, and I could see it all over his face—but the line I'd just delivered had quickly replaced any hints of anger with sheer disbelief. Then after a few seconds, I got what I was after. The grin he tried so hard to suppress finally broke loose. And when he was laughing so hard he could hardly talk, I knew I was home free.

"I can't believe you said that," he said, smiling and shaking his head. "I can't believe..."

"No, no," I interrupted. It was all I could do to keep a straight face at this point. But I managed, albeit with a twinkle in my eye. "This is where you're supposed to slap me around with your cane. Go on...do it! You'll be surprised at how much better you'll feel." I chuckled.

"But I don't *have* a cane," he whined in mock seriousness.

"Can't help you there, Buddy," I said with a wink. "Seriously though, Luke...I'm so sorry. I didn't..."

"Forget it," he said good-naturedly. "We all screw up..."

"But after I made such a big deal of this and all..."

I never had a chance to finish. For just at that moment, Luke covered my mouth with his in a series of those light, feathery kisses that have a way of giving birth to goose bumps. Gently tracing the outline of my mouth with his tongue, he let it suckle and probe my bottom lip before reaching my tongue in a demand for attention. His fingers were enjoying an investigation all their own—lightly slipping across my neck, my collar bone and finally reaching my breast—igniting white hot sparks of desire in their wake. By the time he pulled me down on top of him, I was already drowning in the passion of his kisses, the heat of his body and the hunger of his touch. But feeling his hardness press against me—a hardness that yearned to be enjoyed, savored and released—ignited something within me I'd never known: a fire so hot that nothing—not dreams, nor warnings, nor that ever-blinking caution light—could squelch its raging flames. Its passion licked and teased and was quickly beginning to scorch every nerve ending in my body. And as I felt its wet, searing heat flood my core and take my breath away, one thing was certain. The raging fires we'd kindled in each other weren't just burning out of control—they were well on their way to taking us both to the point of no return. And there wasn't one damned thing that either one of us could do about it.

Luke woke with a start. He'd never had such a weird dream—at least, not one that was vivid enough to make his heart race or bring shortness of breath. Slow deep breaths, he reminded himself, were the key to getting this under control. So with a concerted effort to flush everything else from his mind, he brought the process of focused breathing to the forefront, filling his lungs with air and exhaling as fully as possible.

Still, remnants of the dream plagued his memory. He'd killed his sister...only she wasn't his sister. She was a black woman who'd not only poisoned his wife but had been trying to cast some sort of spell on him.

How weird was that?!

Nonetheless, he needed to shake it off. It was only a dream and probably nothing more than the product of too much brandy shared with his newly found Witch. He wrapped his arm around Tess' waist and smiled.

He really couldn't remember when he'd ever felt so good or been so happy. He wanted to sing and dance and laugh out loud. He wanted to turn cartwheels down Main Street. Hell, he wanted to do all the silly things he'd missed out on as a child. But most of all, he thought as he drew Tess close, he wanted to stay right here and never leave.

He propped himself up on an elbow to get a look at the clock. It was already seven—he should've been in the office over an hour ago—

but today, he didn't care. It was just one day. And he deserved that after all the thousands he'd spent at the office without so much as one day of vacation. Life seemed to have turned the corner, and maybe it was time for him to follow suit.

Damn, she was beautiful, he thought as he watched Tess sleep. She lay on her side with her back to him, her naked body a delicious mix of curves and angles that stretched nearly the full length of the bed. The morning sun danced across her olive skin and created glorious sparks of red in the mass of long dark curls splayed across her pillow. It cast its spell of pink light on her face, making her seem more ethereal than human—almost like some heavenly goddess who'd mistakenly landed on Earth and stopped to take a nap before finding her way home. She was more than beautiful, he decided as he eased back down in the bed beside her. She was nothing less than a work of art. A luscious creation whose essence Rembrandt himself couldn't have even begun to capture.

His fingers slid lightly over her silky skin, outlining the curve of her waist and hip, then slipped around her body to draw her closer. His fingers trailed down her neck and shoulder, slowly traveling downward to trace the slope of her breast. Her nipple stiffened under his touch as she stirred in her sleep with a moan and backed up against the rigid hardness that awaited her.

"'Mornin', Handsome," I murmured.

"Didn't mean to wake you," he lied, grinning a devilish grin and still caressing the nipple beneath his fingers.

"Of course you did. But if this is your normal wake-up call, Mr. Benson," I said lightly, reaching back with a stroke of my fingers and feeling him grow even harder in my hand, "you can wake me up any time."

Smiling, I rolled over on my back, gasping as his tongue replaced his fingers and sent sparks of electricity flying through my body. And just when I thought I couldn't bear any more, its searing journey continued slowly down across my stomach, the bones of my hips and the muscles of my thighs. Panting with desire, I reached for him— the need to feel him fill me and quench the flames that threatened to burn me alive over-riding everything else in the universe.

"No hands," he murmured, pushing mine away and separating the petals of my core with his tongue. My body writhed and trembled under his hands as he opened me wider, licking, sucking, probing and devouring every spot within its reach. And only when I screamed his name and shuddered in the convulsions of orgasm, did he finally slide within.

Why the hell was the door locked? This wasn't like Tess. Not like Tess at all, thought Chloe as she stood on the front porch and scanned the neighborhood. The Jeep was in the driveway, and everything seemed okay—at least on the surface. But if life with Brian had taught her anything, it was that things weren't always as they appeared. And that meant that what things looked like on the surface seldom really mattered. Not in the big scheme of things anyway.

She tossed her shopping bags on the porch and walked to the end of the street to take a look in the cemetery. No sign of her there, but she really didn't expect there to be. It was just shy of eight o'clock, and while Tess was always up by now, she wasn't usually dressed.

Chloe made her way back up the street and around the back of the house. Could something have happened to her? Everything was fine last night when they'd left. She recounted the events of the previous evening in her head. Yes, everything had gone off like clockwork. The only surprise had come from Luke when he'd decided to help clean up. And surely a man who'd spent so much money on her friend—and an entire evening just staring at her with adoring eyes—couldn't be the culprit. Could he?

Concern grew by leaps and bounds at the discovery that the back door was locked too. Then she noticed that the blinds weren't open either. Something was definitely wrong. Bad wrong. The one thing Tess detested beyond everything else was a dark house. And there was no way the blinds would still be drawn if there wasn't.

Okay, Chloe, she told herself as she settled in beside her bags on the porch, just calm down. The mind is a strange entity—yours especially—and it doesn't take much to work it into a real tizzy. So...just look at the facts, she thought expelling a heavy sigh, and let's see where they take us.

Tess was expecting her. That was a given since they'd already made arrangements to meet that morning. She'd have left a note if she wasn't going to be there—no way she'd have gone anywhere without doing that—so it only stood to reason that Tess was at home. And all Chloe had to do was knock on the door to find out. End of problem.

Still, she had a sneaking suspicion that she shouldn't do that. Not right now anyway. But try as she might, she couldn't come up with any good reason not to. All the facts pointed toward that as the solution. So why couldn't she make herself take that route?

"Facts be damned," she finally said out loud. Nothing was wrong with Tess. She'd just slept late was all, and Tess certainly had a right to do that, Chloe reasoned as she gathered her bags and got in the car. She'd just run over to the Quik-Stop and grab a cup of coffee. Surely Tess would be up by the time she got back.

She pulled out of the drive and a smile creased her lips as she turned up the radio. Rob Malloy was playing "Witchy Woman."

Liza tried Luke's number for the umpteenth time that morning. Just where the hell was he? He was always in the office by five-thirty—six at the absolute latest—and it was quickly edging up on eight. Oh sure, sometimes he locked up the office to run an errand, but that wasn't the case today. No...he hadn't been there yet. The coffee wasn't made, the ashtrays weren't overflowing and she hadn't been met with the never-ending pile of messages that always demanded her attention.

Damn him for worrying her like this! And damn him, too, for leaving the fucking radio turned on full blast, she raged as she reached over and flipped it off. She'd already heard "Witchy Woman" three times this morning, and she damned sure didn't need to hear it again—especially not at the volume of the *Eagles* being in the same room with her. What the hell was Rob Malloy thinking anyway? Didn't he have any other records at that fucking station?

She stomped over to the coffeemaker—it wasn't finished brewing yet, but she poured herself a cup anyway—then made her way to Luke's office to check his day planner. Well, at least he didn't have any appointments today. But if he had, she thought sarcastically, he'd have expected her to handle them. *That* was typical Luke. Always expecting someone else to do the dirty work.

But this *wasn't* typical Luke, she thought with a sigh as she sat down at his desk. He'd never pulled this shit before. Not in all the years since their parents had died. He'd always been here six days a week, and sometimes even on Sunday. Yeah, she could say a lot of things about her brother, but lazy wasn't one of them. He was the prime workaholic. In fact, he probably wrote the book on it.

She drummed her fingers on the desk in exasperation, then picked up the phone and tried his number again. Of course, there wouldn't be any answer. Why even bother, she thought as she idly thumbed through his day planner. Wait...what was this? Hanging up with one hand, she flipped the page back to yesterday with the other. There was a seven o'clock entry for Tess Logan. And he'd made a note to bring Bordeaux and dessert coffee.

It was eight-thirty when Chloe pulled back into the driveway at 103 Daniels Street, and for all practical purposes, it looked like nothing had changed. The blinds were still drawn, and the front door still wasn't standing open in welcome. Okay, she thought as she got out of her car and made her way to the porch, this is it. No more fooling around, no more worrying about feeling silly, no more trying to convince herself that there was no reason to knock on that door. She wasn't just going to knock, she was going to knock so hard that Tess thought the whole fucking world was coming to an end.

And that's exactly what she did. She knocked and banged with all she had—completely unsatisfied until the door shook, the windows rattled and the pictures threatened to fall from the walls.

"What the hell is *that*?!" The startled question came from Luke, who grabbed a towel and started from the bathroom.

"Oh, *shit!* It's *Chloe*," I returned in a stage whisper, a look of horror creeping across my face. "I'm really sorry, Luke! I forgot all about her coming over this morning. Shit, shit, *shit!* Since you parked in the alley though, I can probably hold her off long enough for you to get out the back..."

"Not to worry," he said with a chuckle as he finished drying my back. "Things are what they are. Grab a towel and answer the door. Otherwise, she might just kick it in!"

"But you may not want her to know that you spent..."

"Don't be ridiculous! I'm way past the age of worrying over what anyone else thinks—even your best friend. And just wait until she gets a load of me here!" he said amusedly. He was still laughing as he strode down the hall to get dressed.

"*COMING!*" I screamed at the top of my lungs, hoping that Chloe could hear me over all the ruckus. But by the time I got the towel wrapped around me, she'd already started in on the doorbell. So much for my voice carrying, I thought as I raced toward the door.

"Are you *okay?!*" Chloe screeched as I whipped open the door. I'd never seen her look so panic-stricken. Her hair was in complete disarray, her eyes were wild, and beads of sweat had already formed on her brow. Still, the whole thing was so funny that I couldn't help but tease her a little.

"Never better" came the casual reply. "I was having *sex*," I whispered in her ear. "And, Chloe...you were *right*...it was *fabulous!*"

The look on her face was priceless. But it was nothing compared to the one I got when she heard Luke singing "Witchy Woman" from the back of the house.

CHAPTER 6

"So, Chloe," Luke said as he refilled our coffee cups, "you want to start work today? I could really use some help on a special assignment."

"Well...I don't know," she whined. If she hadn't already had enough to digest this morning, now he wanted her to go to *work*? Maybe Tess had been right all along, she thought. Maybe he really *was* a jackass. Still, he was her new boss, so she weighed her words carefully. "I still have some loose ends to tie up first," she started. "Besides, I'm not dressed to go to..."

"Not a problem...about not being dressed, I mean," he said, breaking eggs into the cast iron skillet and pausing to add more bread to the toaster. "I just need you to whip by the office and tell Liza I won't be in today, then head for the library. After breakfast of course," he added as he divided the contents of the skillet onto the three plates in front of him.

"The library?"

"Yeah," he said with a grin, "and last time I was there, they hadn't instituted a dress code." When this brought a smile from Chloe, he knew he had a shot. All he had to do now was dangle the carrot in front of her. "Of course, you'll get paid for the whole day...even if it only takes you a few hours."

He studied her face from his spot at the stove. She was interested all right. If she'd just take the bait, he wouldn't have to fool with Liza this morning. And knowing the sort of mood his sister was likely to be in with him just now, it was the last thing he wanted to do.

"Okay," Chloe said resignedly. "I'll bite. What do you need from the library?"

"Just copies of any census records from the mid-1800's through early 1900's that mention Dr. Jonah Barnes," he said as he placed the plates on the table and sat down. "And of course, anything else you might find on him or his family in the Sikeston histories."

"You're kidding, right?" Chloe quipped as she set her plate in the sink. "You're going to *pay* me to work on Tess' project?!" Maybe, she thought, he wasn't such a jerk after all.

"Absolutely. If we all work together," he replied, "we might actually make some headway with this. So...what do you say?"

"I'm on it!" She flashed him that million dollar smile, then grabbed her keys and bags quick enough to make my head spin.

Luke called his thanks as she headed out the door, but they fell on deaf ears. Chloe being Chloe was already thinking about how she was going to spend that extra cash.

I sipped my coffee and watched Luke wipe down the stove. The way he'd fallen into the role of taking charge—fixing breakfast, engineering a plan for the Barnes research and even cleaning up the kitchen—was amazing. How could it be otherwise though? *He* was amazing. But as thrilled as I was with all of that, it was also a little scary. I had the feeling that left to his own devices, he could also be a control freak. And I didn't like the thought of that one bit.

I lit a cigarette and considered the situation a bit further. Maybe I was over-reacting. Besides...how could he control me if I didn't let him? And since the thought of *anyone* controlling me ever again was positively laughable, I reasoned that there was really nothing to worry about.

"So...what are your plans for the day?" Luke asked as he finished loading the dishwasher.

"Hadn't really thought about it. But since you sent Chloe out to research census records for me...Gods, Luke, I still can't believe you did that...maybe I should get on the stick and work on the project some too. In fact," I said, smiling at him and rolling the excess ashes from my cigarette into the ashtray in front of me, "it's probably a good day to try Silas Shrum again."

He grinned. "I'm already one step ahead of you, Gorgeous. Silas is expecting us this afternoon. Unless, of course, you've got something else you'd rather do."

"Well, aren't *you* just full of surprises?!" I couldn't help but laugh at how everything was suddenly falling into place.

He shrugged. "Wasn't all that long ago that you ordered a few days of synchronicity at work. And I thought that when a Witch ordered something, it was supposed to happen in short order." His eyes sparkled as he framed my face in his hands. "Even if it took a little outside help!"

"There's that word again," I said with amusement as I tousled his hair. "The one that always gets us in trouble. Maybe we should just strike it from our vocabularies all together."

"Not a chance," he teased. "Besides...if I use it enough and in all the right places, I may just get that honorary Witch certificate."

"Yeah, right," I said, still grinning at him.

"Well, let's not be too hasty." His face took the form of mock seriousness. "I still have one more surprise up my sleeve. A surprise that may, indeed, be worthy of that certificate."

"And what would *that* be, pray tell?!"

"Oh...just the most extraordinary lunch on the planet. That is, of course," he added, "unless you have other plans."

To say that he was pleased with himself was an understatement. He was grinning from ear to ear and positively ecstatic over whatever he'd cooked up. In fact, I thought he might break into a little jig right on the spot.

"Okay," I said, pretending to be cautious. "And just what is this 'extraordinary lunch'—should I be willing to accept your invitation—going to cost me?"

He broke into laughter and scooped me into his arms. "Oh, you'll pay, all right, Ms. Logan! As a matter of fact," he said between kisses, "I've already begun to collect payment."

It took less than five minutes with Liza for Chloe to figure out why Luke had so generously offered to pay her for the day, and it didn't have one single thing to do with Tess' project. Liza wasn't just in a foul mood—she had managed to wrap herself in the mother of them all. And once she'd discovered that Luke was not only all right but had spent the morning playing short order cook, any worries she might have had flew right out the window. Now, she wasn't just angry. She was downright livid pissed.

Chloe had never seen anybody so mad. Fact is, she nearly expected to see Liza spin around and plaster herself to the ceiling like some old cartoon character. But when that didn't happen, she just listened to her rant and rave and carry on, inserted "uh-huh's" and "uh-uh's" in the appropriate places, and made no mention whatsoever of getting paid for the day. There was no need, after all, to add fuel to the fire. That was something she could take up with Luke later, she thought as she waited for Liza to wind down. Fortunately, that only took about twenty minutes, and the second it happened, Chloe made a bee-line for the door and headed for the next place on her agenda: the library.

Even though it was story-time—and the place was filled with noisy kids—the building was quiet by comparison to the newspaper office. But after the ruckus she'd just been party to, Chloe thought with a chuckle as she made her way to the local history section, *any* place would've been quieter!

Within twenty minutes or so, she'd turned up several census records that listed Jonah Barnes. And just as suspected, he'd been married to the woman who supposedly claimed the strange gravesite next to his: Lucinda. They'd had one child, and three slaves.

But the real question still remained: Who was Lucinda? There wasn't a birth date or a death date. Hell, there wasn't even a maiden name. All the census records actually showed was her age, and she was twenty-nine at her last appearance in the listings. There was no mention after that. So, Chloe reasoned, she must've died before the data was collected for the next report.

She dutifully made copies of her findings, then pulled all the local history books from the shelves and stacked them on the table. Flipping through these was going to take the better part of the day, she thought, and it made her wonder why the library didn't have a computer. It would've been so much easier if she could've just typed in Jonah's name and come up with a list of books that mentioned him. Wishing wasn't going to help at this point, so she resigned herself to the task at hand with a heavy sigh and flipped to the index in the first book on the stack.

The first two volumes had no listing, but the third had some fairly interesting information. It seemed that Jonah's father had been the very first Methodist minister to live in Missouri and that he and his wife had moved there from Kentucky. Not that this had anything to do with what she was really looking for, Chloe thought as she made a note to copy it, but Tess would find it more than a little interesting. Reverend Barnes was, after all, solely responsible for the construction of the first church this side of the Mississippi River, and that was a place to which her friend had always been drawn.

The next volume proved much more fruitful. It spoke of Jonah's seminary education and how he'd managed to become a doctor.

Apparently, he'd been sent to the seminary on his fourteenth birthday and had lived there until he was seventeen. Hell of a birthday present, Chloe thought disgustedly. Well, maybe it was, she thought as she pondered it further. Even though the histories didn't say so, she got the distinct impression that Daddy was a self-righteous jerk of the first degree. And if that was the case, then maybe life in the seminary—even for a youngster—was much better than that at home, she mused.

But the really interesting part had to do with Jonah's medical degree. It seemed that the area doctor was also a judge and had been offered the position of Lieutenant Governor. The only problem was that he couldn't leave the area without a physician. So...he'd taken Jonah under his wing and taught him enough to get his degree—something that the young Mr. Barnes had managed to accomplish by the age of twenty.

Oh, shit, thought Chloe, here they come! It wasn't like psychic flashes weren't common enough in her world, but she just didn't have time for them now. Not when she had at least another twenty volumes to look through. Not *now,* she prayed. Please, not now! But it was too late. The images raced to the forefront and, using her mind as a movie screen, soared right into three-dimensional Technicolor.

> *God, he was hungry, he thought as he climbed from the window. He hadn't been this hungry in the seminary, not even during the weeks on end when the fare was merely bread and water and only came once a day. Why was his father doing this? Didn't he know that being a doctor was important too? Didn't he realize that someone had to heal the body as well as the soul?*
>
> *His body ached also, but it was likely to ache worse before the end of the day. Especially if his father caught him at Doc Chaumette's place again. He tried to mentally prepare himself for the inevitable lash of the bullwhip—he'd been able to reconcile it within himself as a part of seminary life—but it just wasn't the same when it came from the hand of someone who was supposed to love you.*
>
> *Thank God for Doc Chaumette, he thought as he stole through the woods. He was the only person who'd ever been the least bit kind to him. And now he was paying for medical school. The reasons didn't matter. It was his one chance to finally escape the self-righteous*

indignities of a man who thought service to God meant forcing undue suffering upon his own family.

If he could just find another place to live during his training, life might finally be worth living. A grin worked at the corners of his mouth as the Chaumette place came into view. Maybe there was a way after all, he thought.

Chloe shook her head to clear it. For the love of the Gods...she certainly hadn't expected this. Not over some old history book anyway—and not in the public library! Was there no way to keep this stuff from coming through?

Maybe a breath of fresh air would help, she thought, marking her spot in the book and heading outside. She fumbled through her purse, found her cigarettes and lit one. It was going to take some time to digest this, all right. Especially the fact that Jonah Barnes—the one *she* had seen, anyway—looked exactly like Luke Benson.

"So, where are we going?" I asked casually. Luke was taking the Benton exit off I-55 North, and I couldn't imagine a lunch spot—much less the perfect one—even remotely close to that area. It wasn't that Benton wasn't a nice little place, but if you blinked twice, you'd miss it entirely. Besides, it was out in the middle of nowhere.

"It's a surprise!" he exclaimed, happily zipping up the country road and chuckling to himself.

It was obvious that he was more than just a little pleased with himself over whatever he had in store. I secretly hoped that I was just as pleased. It wasn't that he didn't have good taste—it was just that he didn't know me that well. And it had been my experience that men who found themselves in that position usually didn't have a clue of what I saw as perfect. There was no way he could know that I didn't like...

"Not to worry," he added, interrupting the thoughts I hadn't dared to express in my out-loud voice and making a left on Route N. "You'll love it!"

The countryside *was* beautiful, and I tried to focus on that instead of my apprehension. The branches of ancient oaks and catalpas stretched across the road to form a natural canopy from which clusters of purple and white wisteria trailed in full bloom. Rays of golden sunlight peeked through here and there, giving the impression that they'd been painted in place by some cosmic artist. I'd never seen anything quite so awe-inspiring, quite so lovely, or...well, for that matter...quite so perfect. I was so enthralled, in fact, I didn't even realize we'd reached our destination until Luke killed the engine and got out.

"What *is* this place?" I asked in wonder as he opened my door.

"Just the most gorgeous slice of paradise in all of Missouri," he replied, offering his hand with a flourish then adding, "Except for you, of course!

"Welcome to The River Ridge Winery!"

Chloe sat at the table and eyed the stack of useless books she'd already perused. For someone as important as a guy who'd spent most of his life as the area doctor, there sure wasn't much information.

She sighed heavily and looked at the clock on the wall. Almost three, she thought as she gathered the books and headed for the shelves. With any luck at all, she might actually get through the last four volumes within the hour and still manage to get home before Brian did. Not that it really mattered though. He already knew she was working and had even offered to pick up dinner. Still, it would be nice to have just one peaceful evening at home—an evening without having to listen to digs about her complete disregard for time.

Resigned to the task at hand, Chloe settled in at the table again and opened the next book. There was a small snippet about Jonah having owned a general store, but other than that, it wasn't much help. Still, she set it aside for the copy machine.

It wasn't until she got to the last volume that she finally hit pay dirt. Well, sort of, anyway. There was actually a mention of Lucinda in connection with her marriage to Jonah Barnes. And while it didn't note her maiden name or their wedding date, it did provide information nearly as important. It confirmed that Jonah Barnes had married a Mrs. Lucinda McGee.

Well, fancy that, Chloe thought as she looked at the page. That meant that Lucinda was probably a Civil War widow. What's more, since McGee was still a common name in the area, it probably wouldn't take much to get the information Tess was looking for.

Now, she was getting somewhere, she thought happily as she copied the pages. And since she still had time to spare, she retrieved the history books to check for the McGee surname and went back to her place at the table.

Oddly enough, there wasn't a lot of information. In fact, there was even less than there had been on Jonah—and that wasn't saying much. The only name Chloe could find in any of the indexes was Sarah Nell McGee, and she doubted there was any connection. But just for grins, it wouldn't hurt to give it a shot. That way, she could honestly say that she'd exhausted all possibilities.

She turned to the page and scanned its contents. Where was it? It had to be here...the index said it was. Or did it? She went back to the index and checked the page number. Yeah, she was on the right page, all right. Maybe her eyes were just tired, she thought, and gave them a quick rub.

Grabbing a piece of paper, placing it horizontally below the first line of print and moving it down as she went, Chloe painstakingly scanned the page line by line. And she found it about three-quarters of the way down.

No time to read it now, she thought, glancing at the clock. Plenty of time to do that later. She hurried to the copy machine, placed the open book on top and hit the button. Then she gathered her copies, placed the book in the return cart and checked the time again. A quarter to five. Still time to beat Brian home, she thought happily as she headed out the door.

It was, indeed, the most romantic lunch date I'd ever had. Luke had ordered ahead, reserving a picnic basket filled with assorted cheeses, fruit and bread. He'd also ordered a bottle of Serendipity; and since the word, itself, means a pleasant surprise discovered quite by accident— something that definitely applied to us—it was more than appropriate. And if that wasn't enough, he'd reserved a rowboat to get us across the river to his idea of the perfect picnic area: a secluded little spot sprinkled with Queen Anne's lace, daisies and black-eyed Susans.

It was like going back in time a hundred years or so, I thought as we spread the blanket and set out the food. A time when life was much more simple, and no one lived by the tick of the second hand. In that setting in fact, I could almost see myself in the clothes of an earlier century, with cream-colored lace up to my neck and a wide-brimmed picture hat adorned with ribbons and the roses I loved so much.

I could tell there was something on Luke's mind, but I didn't want to spoil things by pressing. I figured he'd tell me whenever the time was right.

The right time came on the way to visit Silas. And the something in question was the dream he'd had about Liza.

"Well, it was only a dream," I said lightly. There was no point in letting him know that fingers of apprehension were working their way up and down my spine and making my skin crawl. But from the sidelong glance he shot me, I knew that my response didn't even remotely resemble the one he'd expected—or wanted.

"So, other than the fact that you dreamed about killing your sister, what's bothering you so much?" I asked calmly, trying another tactic.

"Like that's not *enough*?!" he spat.

Instead of chancing further frustration, I opted to say nothing. I looked at him expectantly and waited for him to go on. Fortunately, he didn't let me down.

"Geeze, Tess..." he started. "Aren't you hearing one damn thing I've said? Liza wasn't Liza. She was some slave woman. And I wasn't me either—but I was. Only in the dream, I had curly red hair. And to top it all off, I know the exact spot it took place. Except that the setting was at least a hundred years ago, and..."

Holy shit! Luke and I had somehow managed to share the same dream! And if I'd thought those fingers of apprehension had been doing their thing before, I'd had another think coming. They now gripped me so tightly I could barely breathe. But with that realization, another surfaced. And that one not only prompted the hairs on the back of my neck to stand on end but rows of goose bumps to burst forth on my arms and legs.

Liza wasn't just the slave woman in the dream we'd shared. She was also the younger of the slaves from my first dream. The dream in which the four women had stepped from the grave.

"You know the exact *place?!*" Even though I tried to keep my voice even, the effort failed miserably. I'd damned near shouted the last word in astonishment.

"Yeah," he said flatly, as he maneuvered the car into Silas's driveway. "It's in the clearing that separates the two cemeteries behind my house. The same house that's been in our family since the 1800's."

While the visit to Silas Shrum had been a complete bust—at least as far as compiling the information I'd had in mind went—I had to admit that he was very entertaining. Even his appearance fit that bill. His white hair was long, wild and looked like it hadn't been combed in months. His fingernails were unkempt. And his clothes were in such disrepair that I just knew he'd slept in them for a week or better. He couldn't have looked more like a modern-day Einstein—or acted like one—if he'd tried.

It wasn't that he didn't know anything about Jonah Barnes. It was just that the little he did know—things like who his parents were, how he got his medical degree and owning the general store—wasn't very helpful. I was more interested in the woman who lay next to him in the cemetery. And every time I brought her up, he just shrugged his shoulders and went on to some other tidbit of useless information.

Even so, he'd entertained us with several great stories related to the Great Earthquake of 1812, the most amusing of which was that of its only fatality, which had occurred at a saloon in the town of New Madrid. It seemed that a drunken woman had wandered out on the porch to check on all the racket and was struck by a falling eave support. Had she just stayed inside and kept on drinking, he'd said, who knew how long she'd have lived. Thus, it was his theory that whiskey didn't kill—earthquakes did. And it was the very same point of debate he used with everyone who tried to meddle in his life-long affair with Jack Daniels.

As amusing as all that was though, I was glad to get back in the car and have Luke to myself. I wanted to question him about the clearing behind his house and ask him to take me there. I was dying to see the place, check out its energy and gather my own impressions. And up until now, I hadn't had a chance to talk to him about it.

"I'm sorry he wasn't much help," Luke said, as he pulled out of the drive. He looked genuinely sorry. Almost pitiful, in fact. It was almost as if he thought this was some sort of battle, and he'd expected to just ride in on a white horse and save the day.

"Good Gods, Luke," I said, searching his face. "It's really not that big a deal. It's just one possibility exhausted—that's all—and there are definitely a good number of others. Besides," I added flirtatiously, trying to lighten his mood, "if we hadn't gone to see Silas, I wouldn't have had any excuse to spend the rest of the day with such a handsome, sexy man!"

He laughed out loud then put on his most serious face. "And that handsome, sexy man you're speaking of...would that be me? Or," he asked with a wink, "Silas?"

"Oh, I don't know," I teased as we headed south on I-55. "That Silas is a live wire. And that hair! A girl could really get lost in *those* tresses!" I was laughing so hard I could barely get the words out.

His face lit up immediately, and a mischievous smile worked at the corners of his mouth. "So, fair lady," he said, "where to now? Care to get a bite to eat?"

"Good Gods, Luke," I exclaimed. "If you keep feeding me like this, I won't be able to get through my front door!"

"Like you couldn't afford to put on a few pounds," he chortled, exiting the interstate and turning right on Highway 61. "How about we get a burger and go from there? I know this great little place, and the burgers are..." He finished the sentence with a wistful sigh.

"Really?" I'd known he was up to something but hadn't been able to figure it out until he'd turned into the Market Place parking lot. "And we'd find those to-die-for burgers *here*?! At the *grocery store*?!"

"Of course not, Gorgeous," he replied, the mischief in his grin worked its way up to his eyes. "We'll find them at *my* place...once the master chef stops in here to pick up a few things!"

Well, well...synchronicity, I thought happily, that word by which its very name had caused such a ruckus, was still at work. And this time, it seemed to be working in my favor.

The McGee plantation. I had never seen anything quite so magnificent. An architect's dream, the wings of the house jutted from the main structure to give it a sprawling, living effect. A wraparound porch trimmed with gingerbread carvings seemed to hold out its arms in welcome. French doors opened onto scattered balconies, just begging visitors to take in their expansive view. But the turrets, with their decorative lightning rods, were the adornments that impressed me most. Each different, they almost appeared to be carefully selected hats beneath which the house itself lived and breathed.

It definitely had presence, all right. But it was more than that: It almost seemed an entity unto itself. And as I stood there watching it watch me, I had the distinct impression that it had been waiting for something—waiting for something for nearly a hundred years—and that the something for which it had waited so patiently was me. In fact, I could almost hear "Welcome home!" whispered on the breeze.

"My compliments to the chef," I said between bites of my burger. "This really *is* to die for..."

"You think I'd *lie* about something like *food*?" he quipped. "Well, maybe I would," he said thoughtfully, "if I thought it might tempt my favorite Witch to come home with me..."

"*Favorite* Witch?!" I shot back with a chuckle. "Unless I'm mistaken, Mr. Benson...I'm the *only* Witch you know!"

He arched his eyebrow. "What is it you're trying to say, Ms. Logan? Would it be that I don't know what I'm talking about?" His tone was playful and he was obviously enjoying the banter. "You know, that's dangerously close to saying that I'm stupid!"

I laughed at his response. "Well, I don't suppose we should go there. I think we've both learned a valuable lesson about that," I said with a wink.

"So, on a more serious note...how did you wind up with this glorious place?"

"It's been handed down through the family forever," he replied, "and it always goes to the eldest son. And since I'm the *only* son, I wound up with it when my parents died."

"And who owned it before the McGee's?" I asked. I still had the feeling that I might somehow be connected to the house itself, but I didn't want to say that. At least, not just yet.

"Don't know who owned the property, but the house was built

by my thrice great-grandfather, Jack. Story goes that he built it for his wife, Etta, as a peace offering for his constant philanderings. But God only knows why," he said with a grin. "They say she was mean as a snake and had no saving graces whatsoever."

"Maybe she held the purse strings," I said thoughtfully. "Or maybe she actually brought the McGee fortune into the marriage."

"Well, one thing's for sure," he said with a chuckle. "It certainly wasn't for the sex. If that had been worthwhile, he'd never have had to build this house in the first place!"

"Hmmm...in that case, perhaps great-great-great-granddad deserves a toast," I said with mock seriousness as I raised my glass. "To Jack McGee...without whose wandering parts and sexual escapades...Luke would surely be homeless!"

That brought some hearty laughter from both of us. But as soon as we could compose ourselves again, we clinked our glasses together and drank to old Jack.

"Maybe," Luke said with a grin, "we should drink to Etta too. If she hadn't been so mean, I might very well be living in a shack. In fact..."

Etta McGee, I thought. Now, why did that name sound so familiar? And why did its very utterance cause that shivering chill to crawl up and down my spine?

It was so good to be inside, she thought, shaking the hood back from her thick auburn curls. Even if inside was only a slave cabin. It was just awful out there with all the sleet and rain and thunder and lightning. The little girl took off her wet coat, spread it on the wood pile behind the stove and looked around the cabin. Her eyes rested on some calico pouches tucked between the bottles and jars of herbs on a shelf high above her head. And pointing at them with a chubby finger, she asked the old slave woman what they were.

"Dey's mojo bags, Chile. Dey makes magic" came the response.

"But what are they for? Can they make things disappear? Or make rabbits hop out of a hat?" the little girl asked, her eyes sparkling with delight.

The old woman chuckled. "Not lak you thank. Dey's jes' fo' dis an' dat. Ain't gone t'be conjurin' no rabbits. Not less'n I be need'n um fo' yo' supper. Sho ain't."

"But what then, Mattie? What can they do?"

"Done already tol' you, Chile. Dis an' dat. An' dey's not fo' chillun. Dey's fo' grown folk. So you leave 'em be, you heah?"

The little girl sighed at the unfairness of it all. Those bags were so pretty, and she wanted one in the worst way. And what did Mattie mean, they were for grown folks? She, Sarah Nell McGee, was almost five and a half already—and that was nearly grown. Well...wasn't it? Still, it might not hurt to humor Mattie. At least, for a while.

She'd get one of those bags, all right, she thought with a dimpled smile. Even if she had to go against everything Mama had taught her. And that meant even if she had to swipe one.

The shock of the dream brought Chloe straight out of a deep sleep. Surely it couldn't be, she thought as she sat up in bed and willed her heart rate to slow. Sarah Nell McGee was the name on the last pages she'd copied this afternoon—the pages she hadn't bothered to read—the very same pages she'd thought held no connection whatsoever to the Barnes project.

Well, maybe there was no connection to the Barnes project—that much might be true—but there sure as hell was a connection to her. For try as she might, she couldn't erase the image of that little girl from her mind's eye. While she didn't share her coloring, the child in her dream shared something vastly more important. Sarah Nell McGee and she shared the very same face.

Grabbing her cigarettes from the nightstand, Chloe headed down the hall to the kitchen. She lit up and set the cigarette in the ashtray then rifled frantically through the sheaf of papers on the table. Where was it? For the love of the Gods! We weren't going to play this game *again*, were we? The same damned thing had happened at the library this afternoon during the name search, and she didn't have time for this shit. Not right now anyway.

There it was, she thought with relief as she retrieved the page from the floor. Her heart still beating wildly, she took a drag from her cigarette. Then she sat down and began to read:

Sarah Nell McGee [AKA Nellie], daughter of Will and Lucinda, married Bartholomew Benson on June 21, 1876. They had five children: Lucian, Lucinda, William, Mathilda, and Zachariah [see Volume 24], and lived on the McGee plantation, which Nellie inherited upon the death of her mother. Bartholomew died on May 1, 1901. Nellie lived on the plantation until her death in October 31, 1944, and bequeathed the house to her eldest son, Lucian [see Volume 24 and Volume 26]. Both Nellie and Bartholomew are buried on the property.

Oh my, Chloe thought, running her fingers through her hair and her mind going a mile a minute. There wasn't just a connection here; it was the mother of all connections! And it didn't just have a bearing on the Barnes project but also brought Luke Benson into the picture. Lucian was, after all, Luke's grandfather—the very same man who had started the newspaper. What's more, Luke himself still lived on the plantation.

Excitement getting the best of her, she picked up the phone to call Tess. But one look at the clock stopped her cold. It was only 5:45, and she knew death was imminent if she woke her friend at that hour. She'd just have to wait for a while, she thought as she put on a pot of coffee.

Just how cool was *this?!* Cool on *all* counts, she thought with a smile. Not only had she made a ton of progress in uncovering Tess' mystery but had connected with one of her very own past-life experiences. Even better, she might actually get to visit the grave of a previous self! And how many people could say *that?!*

CHAPTER 7

*I*t was their wedding night.
  Facing him, she slipped the gown from her shoulders and let it fall to the floor. My God! She was the most beautiful woman he'd ever seen; in fact, she was exquisite. In perfect contrast to alabaster skin, her long dark hair fell in loose waves across her shoulders, its tendrils curling around dusky rose nipples that begged to be suckled. He grew hard as his eyes slowly explored her body. They traveled downward as he savored the view, taking in the nip of her waist, the slope of her hips and the soft, delicate patch of hair that rose between her thighs.

  He rose from the bed and wrapping his fingers in her hair, slowly worked the tip of his tongue across her lips, down her neck and shoulders, then down between her breasts, leaving trails of white, hot pleasure in its wake. The fingers of one hand slid over her nipples, and she gasped as he drew one into his mouth and brought it to hardness, while the fingers of the other slid slowly downward to encircle her navel, downward to caress her stomach, then even farther still, until a single finger reached its destination and slid into the hot, wet crevice that awaited it.

  Throbbing with pleasure, he pulled her toward the bed.

  She looked at him with seductive eyes and smiled. "Not yet" was all she said as she pressed her body to his and slid slowly to the floor to take him in her mouth.

  "But I..." he gasped.

  "Not yet," she repeated. Her tongue slid slowly up and down the shaft, savoring the pulsating hardness in her mouth and the spasms of his body. Finally she released him, and allowing the tip of her tongue alone to explore and tease each curve and crevice from base to tip, the throbbing gift he offered grew harder still. And just when he thought he couldn't take any more—it was pleasure so excruciating, he actually thought he might die of it—she gently pushed him back on the bed and straddled him.

  Holding him in her hand and shamelessly opening herself with her fingers, she slowly rubbed him against her, teasing him unmercifully with her wetness and bringing him right to the edge of ecstasy once more.

  "Now," she said, still holding him in her hand, as she opened

herself even farther and guided him at last into the tunnel of fluid heat he
so desperately craved.

  Luke woke flushed and short of breath. "Holy fuck," he muttered. "What the hell brought *that* on?!" Still panting, he focused on slow breaths and tried to recover from the sexual frenzy he'd witnessed in the dream.

  Good luck, he thought as he raised up on one elbow and fumbled around for his cigarettes. Finally locating them on the nightstand, he put one in his mouth and lit it. He watched tendrils of smoke weave their way through the darkness of the room and tried to remember any non-sexual remnants of the dream.

  It wouldn't do to focus on the sex now anyway, he thought with a grin as he looked over at a sleeping Tess. Otherwise, he might not get anything else done at all. And no matter what else happened—even if hell froze over—he *had* to go to work today. Liza would kill him if he didn't show since that would mean she'd have to handle his appointments all by herself. In any case, he'd bought himself some time. He'd called the office last night and left a message saying he'd be late—and once she heard that, everything would be fine.

  But back to the business at hand. He crushed out what was left of his cigarette and made a concerted effort to put his thoughts back on track. The bedroom from the dream was his. And while some of the furniture was different, the bed was his too. He'd always had an affinity for mahogany, and he'd fallen in love with the intricately carved swirls and flourishes of this piece as soon as he'd laid eyes on it. He'd had it hauled down from the attic immediately and spent the better part of the day cleaning it up.

  He lit another cigarette and racked his brain, trying to remember the origins of the bed. And as he sorted through a plethora of distant memories—memories pertaining to the house and the family history—he seemed to recall that the bed had not only belonged to his great-great-grandmother but had been stored away in the attic after her death, never to be used again. Then another memory surfaced and surprised him as well. This room—the very one he'd selected when he'd taken ownership—had been hers too. Well, he thought with a grin, at least great-great-grandmama'd had good taste.

And then, saturated with thoughts of ancestors long dead, another realization hit him like a ton of bricks. It had to do with the people in the dream and was something so shocking that no sex on earth could make his heart pound as wildly as it did in that moment. The man involved was the man that was him, but wasn't him. And the woman was Tess...but she wasn't her either.

The biggest shock to his system, though, had no direct connection to the people at all. Somehow, he knew—just as sure as he knew he'd crushed out his last cigarette—that the toe-curling sex he'd witnessed in the dream had not only taken place in real life but had taken place in this very room and in this very bed. What disturbed him the most was the fact that he'd just witnessed a repeat performance of something that had happened...geeze...it made his skin crawl just to think of it...more than a hundred years ago.

"You've gotta be *shittin'* me!" Luke was so surprised that he'd almost screamed the words, and I jumped at the sound of his voice rising to that volume. "Oh, geeze..." he muttered. Now he was visibly upset, rocking back and forth in his chair and raking his fingers through his hair. "Geeze...geeze..." He paused to catch his breath and ran his fingers through his hair again. "Oh, *geeze!*"

I looked at him in amazement. I'd never seen a grown man act like this—especially not over something as simple as a link in a family tree.

"What the hell is *wrong* with you?!" It was more of a statement than a question and delivered with the same tone of voice as a mother who'd just discovered her child pulling the dog's fur right out by the roots. And just like that hypothetical mother, I didn't bother to wait for the answer. "All Chloe did was tell you that your great-great-grandmother might be the Lucinda I'm looking for, and now you act like you might be in the throes of cardiac arrest!" I'd tried to keep my voice even but failed miserably. When I realized that the color in his face was alternating between being white as a sheet and red as a beet though, I finally added, "You're not...are you?"

"Not what?" he asked shakily.

"In the throes of cardiac arrest."

"No." His skin tone had returned to normal and so had his voice. He looked at me as if I were the only person in the room. "There are some things I've got to tell you...some things I've just figured out...but honest to God, Tess...I'm going to have to digest all this first. And right now," he said, glancing at his watch, "I've got to go to work."

He set his coffee cup in the sink. "Are you going to be around later?"

"Sure," I said.

"Great. We can talk about this then."

Finally, he looked in Chloe's direction and actually managed a smile. "Great job, Short Cut—I can tell we're going to have an excellent working relationship."

He walked out of the kitchen without another word. And just when I thought he might leave without saying goodbye, he turned on his heel and came back, completely enveloping me in his arms and kissing me with such passion, I thought I might melt right into the floor. Then holding me at arm's length and staring at me as if he'd just seen me for the first time, he mouthed, "I love you." And without another word, he was gone.

"And wrapping up this hour," Rob Malloy announced, his voice issuing from Luke's radio, "*Fleetwood Mac* with 'Rhiannon.' Coming up next hour..."

What the *fuck?!* Luke turned off the ignition and just sat in the parking lot for a minute. He had to get his shit together, he thought, rubbing his temples in desperation as if the very act might somehow clear his mind. *Fat chance*, spoke the voice in his head. *Besides...did you get a load of that last song?*

"Yeah, yeah...I heard it. Every fucking word," he replied to the voice that no one else could hear. "But I *am* going to win. No matter what you say."

He tried to convince himself that it would all be fine. It was just a matter of needing to get back to his regular routine. Once he got back to business and immersed himself in work again, everything would settle back down and be normal. At least, that's what he told himself.

He was wrong.

And the message awaiting his arrival to the office was proof enough.

Now, normal would have been a while-you-were-out message, a Post-it note message or maybe even a message left on the answering machine. But it was none of those. No siree, Bob. It was the fucking radio again. And this time, it came through loud and clear by way of *Santana's* "Black Magic Woman."

That's *it*, he thought wildly. He was already at the end of his rope and that prick, Rob Malloy, seemed hell bent to cut him loose and send him free-falling right into oblivion. Well, it wasn't going to happen. Not now. Not tomorrow. Not ever, he thought as he snatched up the phone and started to dial.

"Good morning, this is..."

Rob's pleasant greeting was cut short by the angry caller on the other end of the line. A pissed off man who literally spat out the words, "What the *FUCK* do you think you're *doing*, Malloy?!"

Chloe and I were both in shock. So much so in fact, that we just stared at each other with wide eyes and said nothing for a while.

Finally, she broke the silence. "What the hell was *that* all about?!"

"Got me," I said thoughtfully. "I just can't imagine why he's so upset." I reached over and topped off our nearly full coffee cups. "He was acting a little weird on the way home this morning," I added, "but he didn't seem upset. It was more like he had something on his mind. And I thought it had to do with work."

"Well, maybe it's nothing. Besides," she said, her eyes regaining their normal mischievous sparkle, "he was at least pleased with the job *I* did. And that's something!"

"Yeah," I replied. I was still thinking about the last thing I'd thought he'd said—or mouthed—to me before he'd walked out the door. Surely I was mistaken. There was no way he could've said that to me—especially not after only a couple of days.

"...like to do that! So, what d'ya say, Tess? Do you think we can?" Chloe was obviously excited about something, and I hadn't even been listening.

"Hunh?" I responded, jolting myself back into the present.

"Does this mean I've gotta go through all this stuff *again*?!" she whined.

"Yeah, I'm afraid so," I said, trying to smile. "And this time, I promise to give you my complete and undivided attention."

"Well, well..." Liza began cattily, "so not only did you remember that you've got a newspaper to publish...you even remembered where the office was." She knew she was being a bitch but didn't care. She was still mad at him. And if the next sentence was delivered with just the right mix of venom and sarcasm, royal bitch status might be just around the corner. "How re*spon*sible of you!" she spat with a vicious half-grin, slamming her purse on the counter for good measure and searching his face for any clue that she'd hit her mark.

"Not now, Liza," he replied, drawing a ragged breath.

"Not good enough, Brother dear. I want to talk about this—and I want to talk about it *now*!"

He tried to be calm. "Look," he started, "I didn't get much sleep last night, and I've already had a really shitty morning. I..."

"Well, maybe if you weren't staying up half the night screwing your brains out..."

"Now wait just a goddamned minute..." His interruption fell on deaf ears. She went right on with her tirade, never missing a beat.

"That's what happens when you've got two heads and only one brain to go around," she exclaimed. "One head misses out. And in *your* case...it's the one between your ears!"

Luke closed his eyes and rubbed his forehead, willing this mess with Liza to go away. But when he opened them again and saw her still standing there—waiting expectantly for a response—he knew it wasn't going to happen. Not until he dealt with it.

"Okay, Liza," he said with a calm he hadn't known he could muster. "I could tell you to fuck off and die—which, personally, is precisely what I'd like to do—but that would only exacerbate things. Instead, let's call a truce. *Okay*?!" He looked at her to make sure he was getting through. And when the expression on her face changed from livid to utter amazement, he went on.

"It's been a crappy morning. Lately, I *haven't* been sleeping well, but it's not due to 'screwing my brains out,'" he said sarcastically. "I'm not just having weird dreams, Liza—I'm having the mother of them all—and it's making me crazy. So crazy, in fact, that I've already managed to make a complete ass of myself this morning - and with none other than Rob Malloy!"

"*What*?!" If she hadn't been properly shocked by the fuck-off-and-die remark, the last one had definitely done the job. "What on earth could that sweet, lovable guy have possibly done to..."

"That's just it, Liza. He didn't do a fucking thing. And I was such an ass, I'm lucky not to be in jail. Hell...I'm lucky not to be in the loony bin."

"Oh, Luke...I..."

"Wait. There's more." Might as well get this out too, he thought, looking her directly in the eye. "I am madly, passionately and maybe even eternally in love with Tess Logan, and..."

Her right eyebrow shot up, and she looked at him with disbelief as she let out a heavy breath. "Now, Luke, you can't possibly..."

He put up his hand to cut her off. "And," he continued, "I intend to marry her."

"*What*?!*" She couldn't believe what she'd just heard. The hell with Rob Malloy's decision not to follow through with calling the cops and the guys in the little white coats. If Luke kept this up, she might just have him committed herself. "*Surely* you're not *serious*!*"

"As a heart attack, Sister dear. And you need to get used to the idea. Moreover..."

"A few dozen roses and some flying pigs are one thing, Luke," she sputtered, "and she may be a terrific woman, but..."

"Moreover," he continued, "you need to understand that this is *not* lust, and *not* infatuation. And don't even *start* on me about the midlife crisis thing. It's not that either.

"And...while you're getting used to that idea, mix this in with it. Tess has no idea that's what I'm planning."

Well, at least that was something, Liza thought. The last thing she wanted was some gold-digging bimbo roping her brother into a lifetime of hell. But whether or not Tess fit that bill was still under debate.

"Don't you think *she* might have something to say about all this?"

"Absolutely," he said, relieved at finally feeling a grin crawl across his face, "as soon as I ask her. But I'm not ready to do that. And I probably won't for several months."

"But..."

"Subject closed," he said with finality. "However, there are some things I need to talk to you about—things that have to do with the dreams I'm having—but I haven't figured out..."

Luke never got to finish, for just at that moment the door burst open, admitting a yapping Yorkshire terrier on a rhinestone leash accompanied by a cloying cloud of Arpége. Apparently, Miss Ada Thompson, queen of the Sikeston Charities Guild, was here for their morning meeting.

What a morning it had been! Chloe and I had spent a good part of it discussing the vision in the library, her dream and the reasons she wanted to visit the cemetery on Luke's property—the first and foremost, of course, being that she might indeed, be the reincarnation of Nellie McGee. This time I'd listened carefully. I'd even gone so far as to play devil's advocate and suggested making an appointment for past-life regression therapy with Sally Nicewander. That way, I explained, time spent on a wild goose chase would be minimal if she happened to be looking in the wrong direction. I truly didn't think she was off the mark at all, but I didn't say so just then. There was no point in feeding any pre-conceived ideas—especially not any of this magnitude—until we had some facts. And since we both knew that Sally might be able to provide those, Chloe called her and scheduled an appointment for later that afternoon.

Of course, I also had an ulterior motive for wanting some verification. After the crazy way Luke had acted this morning, I certainly didn't want him upset further or unduly. And the last thing I wanted was to chance Chloe being the culprit. Waiting for facts would hold Chloe at bay, give Luke time to calm down and give me—if necessary—time to figure out the best way to handle things. It seemed like a good plan, and I hoped I was right.

In the meantime, I still had some things to figure out where Luke's newfound insanity was concerned. First and foremost was what had prompted it and why. Until I knew that, there wasn't a whole lot I could do. But maybe—just maybe—I thought as I lit a cigarette and considered things more carefully, I could get to the bottom of it when we talked this afternoon. And if things went as well as I hoped they would, I'd have plenty of opportunities to check out the clearing behind the house.

I was still kicking myself for not asking about it last night. He'd been in a great mood, and my chances of seeing that place had been good, if not excellent. But we'd been having such fun that I hadn't wanted to screw things up. I'd reasoned that the very mention of the clearing might take him right back to the horror of his dream, and I just hadn't wanted to go there. Besides, I really wanted to check out the place all by myself without any distraction. And I certainly couldn't do that with Luke around, I thought, crushing out my cigarette and lighting another.

I grabbed the sheaf of papers Chloe'd brought over and flipped through them. Obviously, I was missing something. While the Barnes mystery seemed to have unraveled itself—at least on the surface—other things were also at play. Things I didn't understand. Things that were making us all crazy. And those things had taken shape by way of the troubling dreams and visions effortlessly parted out to everyone even remotely involved. I couldn't help feeling like the bigger mystery—the one involving just exactly who might be buried in Lucinda's grave—was also in the works here and doing its damnedest to unfold. All it needed was a little help, but at this point, I had no idea what that help might be.

I crushed out my cigarette and tried to clear my mind. Surely a solution would present itself. It *had* to, I thought impatiently. Otherwise, we'd all go crazy, and that just wasn't an option. At least not in this lifetime. All of us still had too much left to do. And we sure as hell couldn't manage it as drooling, blubbering fools locked away in some insane asylum, I thought angrily.

Now emotion not only has a way of fueling magic, it's the catalyst that sends it soaring right into the universe. But there was no way, I told myself as I tried to calm down, it would ever bring any sort of solution.

I was wrong.

For just at that moment—as pictures of the people in our dreams formed a slide show in my mind's eye—a solution did indeed, arrive. It was so simple, so basic, so unbelievably mundane that it hadn't even occurred to me. And it had to do with Luke's family history, as well as any pictures or renderings of its members. The history, of course, was more important, for it might very well tell the story of what had really happened to Lucinda. But the pictures, I thought, could be very interesting too. I couldn't help but wonder if Jonah Barnes truly *had* shared Luke's face. And if so, what the implications might be.

If that weren't enough to consider, there was more. And it came in the form of questions prompted by a more careful look at the census reports.

According to the information, the Barneses had not only lived at the McGee plantation for the duration of their marriage, but Jonah had continued to reside there—even after Nellie'd taken ownership—until his death. If that was the case, then why wasn't Jonah buried on the property? More to the point though, why wasn't *Lucinda?!*

Apparently, work was just what he'd needed, Luke thought as he refilled his coffee cup and walked back to his office. Even the meeting with Miss Ada hadn't gone too badly, although it would've been nice if she'd left that prissy little yapper at home. He didn't know why it annoyed him so much. Maybe it was the rhinestone leash. Maybe it was the way Miss Ada interrupted everything he had to say by asking the dog what *she* thought. Hell, maybe it was just the fact that the dog didn't even seem like a real dog but more like a rat with long hair.

But then, lots of things had annoyed him this morning—not the least of which had been the goings on at the radio station. He still couldn't believe he'd been such a jerk. Especially after Rob had so patiently explained that he really had nothing to do with the music that hit the airwaves—that things weren't like they used to be—and that music selections now played only according to the computer program installed on the clocks. He'd further explained that the only reason he was in the deejay booth at all these days was just to announce what songs had been played, to make sure that the news and weather reports didn't run over the time limit and to keep a close eye on things so they didn't run amuck.

Geeze, Luke wondered, who'd have thought that radio had become so advanced over the years? Crazy as it sounded though, he still had that niggling feeling that the song of the day—at least lately—was somehow sending him personal messages. And then as if in confirmation, the first strains of today's damnable selection started up right on cue.

Here we go again, Luke thought as he tried to convince himself that this whole notion was absolutely ridiculous. He was well-educated. His IQ was above average. And even a small child would have better sense than to actually believe such crap. In fact, the very idea of such a thing conjured up a vision that made him laugh out loud. It was that select group of idiots who honestly believed that the fillings in their teeth served as transmitters—transmitters by which they frequently received all sort of strange signals and messages from extra-terrestrials. And if he let this go much further, there was a damned good possibility that he might join their folly, he thought with a grin.

With that in mind, he flipped off the radio and checked his day planner. Only one more appointment and he was done for the day. At the office anyway. He still owed Tess the explanation he'd promised and wasn't really sure he had one. But he guessed that didn't matter. He could at least apologize for his absurd behavior this morning, tell her about the dream he'd had last night and ask her about the eerie stuff with the music. And maybe, just maybe, they might be able to sort through things together and come up with an explanation. Damn, he hoped so. One thing was for sure. He couldn't keep going on this way and still hang onto the two things most important to him right now: Tess and his sanity. And there was no way in hell he intended to lose either.

Just as he picked up the phone to call her though, something else surfaced and wandered across his mind. And since it had to do with the nonsense over the song of the day, he did his best to dismiss it. Unfortunately, his best wasn't good enough. The errant wanderer was a simple term—black magic—that kept playing over and over in his head. And as he hastily punched Tess' number into the dialing pad, he prayed more fervently for two things than he'd ever prayed for anything else in his life: first, that she was home; and second, but perhaps even more important, that he was wrong.

Sally Nicewander had just had the strangest experience of her life. Not that it couldn't happen—or probably didn't—it just hadn't ever happened to her. Not in all her years as a hypnotherapist.

She rewound the tape and played it again, certain that she must be mistaken.

"All right, Chloe," her voice on the tape began, "I want you to relax. Start with your head...your neck...your shoulders...feel the tension move out of your arms...your hands...and let it flow out from your fingertips into nothingness..."

That much was fine. She listened as her voice walked Chloe through the rest of the relaxation exercise and had her count back from ten. A fine subject, Chloe had easily moved back through this life, past her birth, the time in the womb and out into the void again. There was no trauma, no pain, no discomfort. It had all gone off like clockwork.

And even when Chloe had been birthed into the past life and moved through her childhood, everything had gone fine. Oh sure, there was the trauma of the small child when losing her father and dealing with an especially nasty grandmother, but all that was normal stuff in this business—and she'd certainly heard worse.

It wasn't until she'd moved through the adolescent years that things had gotten sketchy and weird. And none of that was directly related to Chloe's responses at all. It had, instead, been directly related to *her*.

There it was, she thought as the strange dialect brought her back to reality. She hit rewind and turned up the volume, listening intently.

"Wha's you talkin' 'bout, Chile? Wha's you *mean*, she be's workin' black magic on yo' Mama?"

"That's just *it*, Mattie! She keeps giving Mama this tea—and it's making Mama sicker and sicker. And the baby..."

"Ain't no sense in thankin' thangs iz what dey ain't. Yo' Mama jes' be sick. Dat's all."

"But *Mattie*," she wailed, "she *hates* Mama and always has. And now she's trying to kill her *and* the baby! We can't just stand by and let it happen. You've got to *do* something!"

"An' jes' wha's you suggestin', Miz Nellie?"

"Well, you know how to work magic, Mattie. You've got some kind of magic bag for this. I just *know* you do!"

"Now you jes' cawm y'sef, Chile," came the reply. "Ain't no sense in gettin' awl worked up. No'm, sho' aint. If'n you do, I be havin' t'fix you up a mojo bag of yo' own. An' I don' wan t'be a'doin' dat. No'm, sho' don't."

And then, everything went back to normal.

How could this happen? How on earth could a session with someone else trigger a past life of her own? It just didn't seem possible, she thought, doing her best to ground and center. Maybe she was just letting her imagination run away with her. Maybe she'd just gotten caught up in the moment. Maybe...

Well, life was full of maybes, all right, Sally thought in exasperation as she searched the cabinet for valerian and filled the teapot. But this didn't seem like one of them. No'm, sho' di'nt, she thought sarcastically as she packed the tea ball firmly with the herb, dropped it in her cup and waited for the pot to boil.

She needed answers and she wanted them now. Otherwise, her practice was in danger—and she just couldn't have that. With that thought pushing her forward, she pulled the St. Louis phone book from its place on the corner shelf. And in no time at all, she had a professor on the phone—not just any professor, mind you, but the head of the Past Life Regressions Department at the Missouri Hypnotherapy Institute.

I'd thought the morning had been tense, but obviously I hadn't seen anything yet. This afternoon had been fraught with all sorts of chaos—admittedly, a lot of it was my own doing—but it was chaos, nonetheless.

It started off with a call from the Parks and Recreation Department regarding the replacement monument I'd agreed to purchase for Lucinda. And when I'd heard the reason for the call, I'd assumed that the monument company had been able to duplicate the structure and that it was all ready for installation. I was right—sort of—but it was the "sort of" that posed the problem.

Apparently, the duplication process had gone off without a hitch—the guy at Parks and Rec said it was the most gorgeous thing he'd ever seen—and it had, indeed, been installation ready. However, there had been some sort of problem when they loaded it, and...you guessed it...the marker fell to the ground and broke. Worst of all, they couldn't tell me how long it might take to work up a new one.

While this aggravated me to no end—I knew damned good and well that the problem involved was incompetence—I held my temper and said nothing. Part of it was the fear that I might just chew this guy up and spit him out, and it really wasn't his fault. But the main reason I said nothing was because I was too shocked to say a word. You see, he'd said that the monument hadn't just broken—it had broken into four pieces—and with that knowledge, memories of the four women from my dream resurfaced.

Maybe it was for the best, I thought as I listened to him ramble. I still wasn't sure exactly *who* was buried in the grave. And what if it *wasn't* Lucinda? It wouldn't do to have the wrong name on the marker, I reasoned.

With that in mind, I asked him to reorder the monument and have it finished except for the name. I could tell he thought I'd lost my mind, but that was all right. I'd been thinking the same thing all day.

The rest of the afternoon followed suit. Nothing was working right and nothing was going right. Hell, "right" just didn't seem to be a part of the universal vocabulary today. So, rather than hitting my head against brick walls, I opted to rack my brain. And the racking that ensued directly involved the best way to handle things with Luke.

I played the on-one-hand-this-on-the-other-hand-that game until I was nearly crazy. And I still didn't have a good answer. Yes, searching through his family history and pictures was definitely a good idea—and one I planned to act on—but not right now. Chloe'd just dropped the bombshell about her past-life session with Sally; while I certainly didn't intend to hide that from him, given this morning's behavior, I had no idea how he might react. There just wasn't any point in going there at this juncture. And somehow I knew that a better opportunity would present itself later.

I was also going to have to tell him about my dreams and admit to sharing the one related to the murder. Damn it! I knew I should have told him right away, but the time just never seemed right. Besides, I'd had no earthly idea that I was dealing with his ancestors here. I'd just thought they were some family who'd lived in Sikeston during the Civil War. And finding out that he was related to them had become very uncomfortable for both of us.

I guessed the best solution was just to tell him all of it upfront and get it done, regardless of what might happen. One thing was for sure. No matter whether I scattered the information over time or told him all at once, his reaction wasn't likely to be pleasant *or* calm. And looking at it from that angle, it was probably best to get the whole thing out in the open once and for all.

It wasn't like I had a lot of time to plot my options anyway. Luke was due here in a few minutes, and no matter how much I liked him, this was one visit I really wasn't looking forward to. The only saving grace was that he'd sounded much better when he'd called.

I could only pray that his good humor would last. And that he'd had a much better day than I.

CHAPTER 8

Luke looked at me with adoring eyes and took my hands in his. "What I'm trying to tell you is that...well..." he floundered pitifully, "I'm madly in love with you."

I nearly choked on my coffee. This was not at *all* what I had expected. And just what the hell was I supposed to say to something like that?! I love you *too?!*

Holy shit, I thought, trying to keep from looking shocked. It was way too early for this sort of thing. It was way over the top. And no matter how much I liked him—or how strong the attraction between us— I certainly wasn't prepared to return his declaration of love. I hardly even *knew* the man!

To say I was uncomfortable would have been putting it mildly; I was right on the edge of a nervous twitch. Still, I took a deep breath and tried to keep my voice even. "But you *can't* be. Not yet. It's way too..."

"Aw, c'mon, Tess. Please don't go there," he pleaded. "I've already had this conversation once today, and I really don't want to repeat it.

"Besides...I'm not asking you to say anything you don't mean. Hell, I'm not asking you to say anything at all. I just wanted you to know how I felt." His voice was soft and gentle, with no twinge of rejection. And I was as grateful for that as I was for his clarification.

"All right," I said, not sure where to go with this without giving him the wrong idea. "I'll admit that I like you a lot." So far, so good. "And right now, I can't imagine my life without you in it." That was true as well. "But at the same time," I continued, "I'm not sure..."

"That's good enough," he said, cutting me off with a soft smile. "I..."

"Wait a minute, Luke," I said. "There's more. Because so much weird stuff has happened lately, I'm beginning to wonder if," I continued, doing my best to choose the words carefully, "there's not something bigger than both of us at work here."

"What do you mean?" He cocked his head to the side and waited expectantly.

"Well, I'm not sure exactly how to put this...I'm afraid you'll think I'm crazy...but..."

"But what?" he asked, the smile still playing on his lips.

"I'm afraid that we may very well be the victims of...well...a spell." There. I'd finally gotten it out. Now it was my turn to wait expectantly.

The grin on his face widened. Then he burst right into laughter. I'm not sure what I'd expected really, but it certainly hadn't been *that*.

"You've got to be kidding," he exclaimed between chuckles, trying to reclaim his composure.

I looked him right in the eye. "Not at all," I said. My voice was grim, flat and totally without humor. This was serious business, and I hoped he got the message. "In fact, I'm afraid that it may involve something called hoodoo—a form of magic commonly used by the enslaved in and around Louisiana—and that the spell in question could very well be over a hundred years old."

His smile faded slowly and traces of disbelief took its place. "You're serious, aren't you."

"Yeah...I'm afraid I am."

"Now let me get this straight," he said, pausing to light a cigarette, inhaling deeply and finally releasing a thin stream of smoke into the air. "You're telling me that I may not really be in love with you at all—and that what I'm feeling could actually be the result of some *spell*? A spell cast in the *1800's*?!"

"Yeah. That's exactly what I'm saying."

"Well, even if I believed that—and I'm certainly not sure I do—there's a big flaw in that theory."

"And what would *that* be?" I asked, trying hard not to let my frustration show.

"You're talking about some kind of magic in Louisiana. And we're here in Missouri. There's a lot of distance between..."

I cut him off with a wave of my hand. "For starters, geographic location has nothing to do with reincarnation *or* magic. At least not in the present."

He opened his mouth to say something, but I ignored it and went right on.

"What I'm telling you is that the soul of a person who lived in Mobile, Alabama could very well wind up reincarnated in Calcutta. Or Athens. Or Rome, for that matter. Are you with me so far?"

A nod of his head assured me that he was. "Magic," I continued, "knows no boundaries. It can reach to the ends of the earth. However, I have reason to believe that the spell in question was not only cast in

Missouri but right here in the area. And because of that, the source of its power was more likely hoodoo than Gullah or some other sort of magic commonly practiced by the black population during that time period."

"I'm not sure I understand." He crushed out his cigarette, got up and paced around the room. "I don't see..."

"Okay. Let's go back to Civil War history and the role that Missouri played in the slave trade," I said. "You know as well as I do that folks in this state normally bought second-hand slaves. Slaves who'd been sold to slave traders by their previous owners then transported here by way of the Mississippi River..."

"Where they were sold again," he said as he stopped pacing and sat down.

"Exactly. And since they were brought here by way of the river—and there wasn't any other clear shipping route to this area—it only stands to reason that most of them were shipped here from Louisiana."

I searched his face to see if I was getting through. And when it appeared that things might finally be sinking in, I continued. "Hoodoo practices often involve particular types of magical bindings. The magic is 'fixed' or 'set,' rather than charged."

"What does *that* mean?" Luke asked anxiously.

"The vernacular isn't important," I said, waving it away as insignificant. "What I'm saying is that while I'm not familiar with the processes themselves, I do know that this sort of magic can outlast the magician. And there's no reason to believe that it can't work beyond the grave.

"Let's look at this hypothetically," I went on. "Let's say that, for whatever reason, a practitioner bound two people together for eternity. That magic would not only last through their current lifetime but would also bind them together through every reincarnative life thereafter."

"Okay," he said. "I'm still not sure that I buy all this. But even if I did, I don't understand why it's such a big deal. You're a Witch, Tess. Just fix it."

"That's the problem, Luke. I'm not sure I can."

He looked as if he couldn't believe his ears. "What do you *mean*, you're not sure you can? Didn't you ever learn how to break hexes and stuff? I mean...geeze, Tess...surely..."

"Of course, I did," I said, trying to be patient and reminding myself that Luke knew little or nothing about magic. I was going to have to put this in terms he'd understand. "But this is different. I know as much about hoodoo practices as you do about magical theory. And that's little or nothing.

"Let me put it this way. If you were having trouble with an algebra problem, it's not likely that you could solve it by way of geometry, trig or physics—no matter how well-versed you were in those subjects. Instead, you'd need to talk to a teacher, a tutor or someone who understood algebra better than you did.

"The same is true of magical practices. If I'm going to be able to break this thing—provided it even exists—I'm going to have to find a Root Doctor, a Conjure Woman or someone who understands this sort of magic inside and out," I stated flatly. "And I don't have a clue where to look!"

"Well," he replied, "maybe we're jumping the gun here. Maybe there is no binding. Maybe I'm not 'bewitched.' And maybe," he said with a wink, "I'm just madly in love with you! End of story."

I squelched the urge to roll my eyes heavenward. "Maybe," I said tentatively. "But I think there's more to it than you'd like to believe. In fact, I'm sure of it. And when you hear everything I've got say, I think you'll see it that way too."

Okay, here goes nothing, I thought grimly. The time had come to toss it all on the table and let him have a look. But whether he chewed and swallowed—or ran retching to the bathroom—still remained to be seen.

"Have you lost your fucking *mind*?!" Brian thundered as he stomped through the living room. He'd always loved that part of Chloe who saw things that other people didn't—that part that set her aside from everyone else—that part that might even be considered as somewhat eccentric. But *this*?! This wasn't just different. It was the craziest thing he'd ever heard.

"No," she replied calmly.

"Well, apparently you have," he retorted, throwing his arms in the air and pacing back and forth like a caged animal. "What you're proposing isn't just crazy, Chloe. It's illegal. Or have you forgotten about that too?"

"I thought that maybe..."

"You thought. You *thought*?! Jesus God in heaven, Gal...that's just it...you didn't think at all! You can't just go barging onto somebody's property without their permission. In case you've forgotten, that's called trespassing. And *that* will get you *arrested*!" His voice had been picking up speed and volume during the tirade, and he bellowed the last word so loudly it nearly rattled the windows. Then acting as if the whole episode had totally exhausted him, he sighed in exasperation and plopped down in the recliner to stew.

Chloe looked at him in disbelief. His face was red, his eyes were bulging, and the veins in his neck were actually pulsating. She'd never seen him so mad. He wasn't just pissed, he wasn't just livid, he was downright furious. So much so in fact, that she thought he might actually have a stroke.

"Come on, Bri'," she said in that soft, silvery voice that always made him melt. She moved across the room toward him and settled into his lap, putting her arms around his neck. "I really didn't mean to upset you. It was just an idea...all right, a *bad* idea," she soothed, running her fingers through his hair, "and certainly not something I intend to put into action."

"Well, I sure as hell hope not," he retorted, somewhat calmer but obviously still annoyed. "Because if I get a fucking call about a trespasser at the McGee plantation, and I have to wind up arresting my own *wife*...well, let's just say you'd fare much better with the devil himself. I *mean* it, Chloe. Don't even think that I won't...I swear to God..."

"Not to worry, Darlin'," she said softly. But the wheels in her head were already spinning. She had to figure out a way to investigate Nellie's grave without any outside interference. And asking Luke's permission would only give him an opportunity to hang over her shoulder and expel his energy into the atmosphere. It wasn't something she was willing to chance. Somehow, some way, she was going to get what she was after. And if Brian didn't like it? Well that was just a chance she'd have to take.

Brian glanced down at his wife of umpteen years. They'd been together so long he could almost read her mind and hear the thoughts as they popped into her head. Almost was the key word though, he thought with a grin, and at times like these, he was very grateful he couldn't. Still, one thing was for sure. Chloe was sitting there scheming—devising some harebrained plan to get what she wanted—and she wasn't likely to give a rat's ass who she pissed off in the process. The only way to stop her—and avoid any embarrassing surprises—was to get personally involved. So against his better judgment, he did just that.

"Come on, Gal, let's go for a ride," he said, shifting her from his lap and fishing in his pocket for the car keys. "I've got an idea. And if we play our cards just right, it might even work."

Sally Nicewander paced when she was nervous. And she'd never been more nervous in her whole life than she was right at this minute. Even worse, her mind was spinning at least as fast as her feet. "If only I hadn't called the professor," she whined aloud. "If only I'd left well enough alone. Of course, there was no well enough to leave alone. Not after I insisted on listening to that frigging tape!"

Back and forth. Back and forth. Her feet marched and pivoted across the same patch of floor. When Sally finally realized that she was actually wearing a rut in the carpet, she settled into the recliner where the offenders couldn't do any more damage. But that didn't help either. With nowhere else to go, the excess nervous energy now traveled onward and took up residence in her hands.

"*DAMN IT!*" The words rushed from Sally's mouth with such force, she almost scared herself. But at least, the hand-wringing had stopped. And to keep it from resuming, she firmly placed a hand on each armrest where the two weren't likely to meet again.

Life was full of what-ifs. But the what-if she was hoping most to confirm by talking to Professor McElroy was still the biggest what-if of all. He'd not only never heard of a regressionist's past-life experiences coming out in connection with a client's but didn't think it was likely. Not that he'd said it was impossible. He hadn't. It was just that he thought she was mistaken—and didn't have a problem saying so. By the time they hung up, she'd felt worse than ever. In fact, she wished she'd never bothered to call him at all.

The worst of it was that she absolutely, positively *knew* that the voice on the tape was hers from a previous life. But there was just no way to confirm it.

Oh, sure...there were other regressionists. And she could make an appointment with one. But they really weren't as good—or as careful—as she was when it came to things like that. And the last thing she needed was to wind up stuck somewhere in a past life with no hope of getting back. It simply wasn't high on her priority list of fun things to do.

"So...now what?!" she muttered. "Do I just sit here and do *nothing*?"

Doing nothing certainly wasn't Sally's forte. What's more, she wasn't any good at it. So, instead of just sitting quietly and trying to clear her mind, she wiggled around in her chair until she looked like a human pretzel and then racked her brain for a solution.

Of course, a solution wasn't going to present itself—of that, she was sure—and still, there was that niggling feeling that one was right around the corner just waiting for discovery. It was only a matter of uncovering it.

Well, that may be, she thought as she drummed her nails on the table. But enough was enough. She'd wasted the whole day with this mess, and there certainly wasn't any sense in wasting the whole night on it as well.

Looking for something to take her mind off things, she eventually opted for the radio. And after flipping through stations one after the other, she finally found what she was looking for: the St. Louis station that played nothing but big band music.

"...That was Nat King Cole with 'Unforgettable,'" soothed the mellow voice coming from the box beside the chair. "And after station identification, we'll be back with Ol' Blue Eyes and his rendition of..."

Sally eased back into the chair, flipped the lever and put up her feet. She felt better already. How could she not? There was nothing like the sound of Sinatra's voice to transport her into another dimension—that place where life was easy, love was the answer and complications simply didn't exist.

As if on cue, the first strains of the music started. Frank's voice filled the room. What's more, he seemed to be singing just to her—a personal sort of serenade—and she snuggled down into chair allowing him to captivate her being with every silken note. This is the most peaceful I've felt all day, she thought as she closed her eyes dreamily.

It wasn't until the last stanza of the song that she realized something was amiss. Badly amiss. So amiss, in fact, that it sent her jolting right out of the chair.

"Oh, *SHIT!!*" she screamed, flipping off the radio in horror. Even so, Frank Sinatra wasn't to be silenced. He continued to enchant the rest of the St. Louis listening area with his rich, mellow voice and his beguiling rendition of "Witchcraft."

And once again, her feet—the very ones she'd tried so hard to keep still earlier—went right back to pace mode as she frantically jabbed at the portable phone.

She was talking so fast I couldn't understand a word she said. Well, that wasn't exactly so. The words, "Witchcraft," "Sinatra," and "Chloe" had come through loud and clear but not much of anything else. I was having lots of trouble drawing a connection and even more difficulty getting a word in edgewise.

"What?! Sally...Sally...WHOA!" I'd damned near screamed the last word, but it was the only thing I could think of to make her stop for a second.

"Now, just tell me what happened...Yes, from the beginning. And could you do it slowly? Step by step?" I took great pains to be calm and hoped it would be contagious—at least to the party on the other end of the line.

Thankfully, my wish was granted. And once I'd assured her that I wouldn't think she was crazy, Sally managed to explain the situation and the reason for her call.

"Are you *sure*?!" I wanted to slap myself as soon as the words issued from my mouth. "Of course, you are," I muttered apologetically. "Yes...I know...otherwise, you wouldn't have called." Phone tucked between my ear and shoulder, I fumbled around for my cigarettes and was just getting ready to light up when she got around to the real point of her call.

"But, I don't know if...Sally...*wait!*"

It was too late. The only response to my protest was the dial tone on the other end of the line. Sally Nicewander was on her way over, and that was that. Even worse, she thought I had some ungodly sort of power—the sort that could fix this mess and get her life back to normal—and she'd insisted that I conjure it up and use it. Not tomorrow. Not the next day. But right now—this very minute.

I wanted to scream. But instead, I let out a long breath and glanced at Luke, who was still sitting on the couch with that dreamy look on his face. It was going to be an interesting night all right, I thought as I lit my cigarette and took a deep drag. And the Gods only knew just how much more interesting it might get before the Sun finally saw fit to peek over the horizon again.

"God*damn* it!" Liza growled and fiddled with the car radio in search of another station. "It's the jillionth time she's played 'That Old Black Magic.' Doesn't she have any other records at that goddamned station?"

Her growing aggravation was replaced by a half-grin as a push of the last button brought the last few bars of "Proud Mary." Now we're getting somewhere, she thought, as she turned left on Malone and headed toward Matthews Avenue with no particular destination in mind.

She'd tried to sleep, but worry over Luke had stopped that short. Her brother was losing his mind—that much was obvious—and she simply couldn't let it happen. If he kept on like this, he was going to lose everything that was important to them: their friends, the newspaper and maybe even the plantation. He didn't seem to care about anything anymore. At least, nothing except Tess.

Didn't he understand that something was dreadfully wrong there? That there was no way he could possibly be in love with someone he'd only known for a few days? That it took time to build the kind of relationship that was solid enough to stand firm in the face of whatever crossed your path? Didn't he understand...

Her thoughts were interrupted yet again by Frank Sinatra and his melodious acceptance of black magic and well-woven spells.

"Jesus fucking *GOD*!" Liza screamed it at the top of her lungs and banged the steering wheel as an underscore. "What *is* it with this song? It's got to be at least *forty years old*! And *now* it's getting all this play?!"

She snapped off the radio before it could offend her any further and looked for a good spot to turn around. She needed a good stiff drink, she thought. A good hot toddy to take the edge off. And tomorrow, she'd find some time to talk to Luke.

Yeah, right, said the voice in her head. *Like he's really going to make time for that. You're one funny lady!*

"Well, of course, he will. I'm his sis...Oh, shit! Now *I'm* the crazy one. I'm actually talking to a *friggin' voice in my head*!"

Hardly able to believe she'd done that, Liza shook her head slowly then flipped the radio back on and headed for town. And as if on cue, Frank's voice joined her for the ride. Only this time he was singing about the spine-tingling chill of bewitchment every time he gazed into his lover's eyes.

"Oh...my...God." Liza pulled the car over to the shoulder and put her head against the steering wheel. It was "That Old Black Magic" again. The same damned song. And now—finally—she got it. "*That's* what's wrong with Luke! Well, no time like the present to get to the source of the problem," she said, "and we *know* who *that* is!" Then she pulled out on the road again—this time heading directly for Tess' before she could talk herself out of it.

"What are you *doing*?!" Chloe screeched as Brian turned into the driveway. "We can't just barge in there. Besides, Luke's car is parked..."

Brian grinned at her. "Of course we can, Gal. *You* barge in on her all the time. And at least this time, we know she's awake!"

"But what if they're..."

"With company?" he quipped, pointing to the Buick Century parked just in front of them. "I doubt it. If I was a bettin' man in fact, my money'd say they both have their clothes on. Now, get outa the car and let's go see!"

"But they have company, and we can't just..."

It was too late for further protests. Brian was already out of the car, holding her door and extending his hand. There was nothing left to do but walk up the steps and ring the bell.

She shrugged off his hand and got out. "Well," she said with a heavy sigh, "I just want to go on record as saying that I don't like this one bit. Not one *bit*, Brian Dawson!"

She was still chewing him out when Tess opened the door.

"You can't be *SERIOUS*!" The voice belonged to Luke, and for a moment, he looked as if he might have a seizure. But then, he started to laugh. "It's a joke, right?" he chuckled. "A joke just to fuck with me. Well...joke away! I'm not playing."

A quick scan of the faces around the table answered his question even if their silence did not. At a loss for words, Luke ambled over to the counter and topped off his coffee. Then he sat back down and lit a cigarette.

"Look, Luke," Brian started, tactfully breaking the silence and hoping to break the tension as well. "It's not that farfetched. We all know..."

"But what you're talking about is...is...*reincarnation*!"

"Yep...that's exactly what we're talking about."

I thought we'd gotten the reincarnation thing straightened out earlier, but apparently, I'd been mistaken. Thank the Gods for Brian, I thought, as I watched him handle the situation. He was talking to Luke as if they were the only two people in the room. That course he'd taken in police negotiation was paying off—and right here in my kitchen—even though Luke certainly wasn't a criminal. At least, not in this lifetime.

"O-okay," Luke stammered, "but I'm having a little trouble wrapping myself around this one. What you're saying here is that all of us except for you...every other person at this table...have shared some sort of relationship in a previous life? And that the people they once were in a past life were either my ancestors or," he said, glancing at Sally and stubbing out his cigarette, "had some connection to them?"

I opened my mouth to answer, but Brian cut me off with a look.

"That's right," Brian answered evenly. "And to my knowledge, the only one missing from the batch right now is Liza."

"Oh, geeze...Liza," Luke said, pausing to light up again. "She's just going to *love* this! She already thinks I'm crazy. And if I lay this story on her...well...she's going to have me fucking committed! Even if I believed this—and I'm not sure I do—I don't know how in the hell I'm going to explain this to..."

"No need to, my friend," Brian said, clapping Luke on the back with a grin. "Just let me handle it. I did, after all, handle it pretty well with you!"

"Yeah, but you don't know how she can be...you don't know how she can..."

"C'mon now, Luke! She's your twin sister. She can't be much more of a hard case than you."

Brian was still grinning, but I had a feeling that his grin was short-lived. Liza was a hard case, all right. The hardest of the hard. And it wasn't going to be long before he found out just how inflexible she could be.

A quick glance at the kitchen clock confirmed that the night was moving toward its end. But somehow I knew it still had plenty of surprises left in store. And I, for one, wasn't looking forward to any of them.

"Just who the hell does she think she *is*?! The very fucking idea, using *black magic* on *my* brother!" Liza talked out loud to herself upon occasion—especially when she was upset—and this was one of those occasions. Problem was, this time she had interference. And the voice in her head was the culprit.

Black magic, indeed! Do you know how ridiculous that sounds? The voice guffawed, then chuckled and finally broke into full blown laughter. *And you,* it managed between giggles, *think you brother is fit for the loony bin. Have you listened to yourself lately?*

"Oh, shut up," she responded tersely. "What do you know anyway? If you'd had any sense, you'd have figured things out hours ago."

Not my fault, it shot back. *I only think when you do. And in this case, you were really stupid! Or deaf!* The chuckles resumed.

"That's *it*!" she screamed. "I've had enough out of you. Now go back wherever you came from and leave me the fuck alone!"

Careful, the voice admonished as Liza pulled to a stop in front of Tess' house. *Don't do anything you'll regret later.*

"Regret? A little late for that, dear voice. I'm going to kill her with my bare hands," she muttered under her breath. "That's what I'm going to do!" And in a matter of seconds, she'd sprinted across the yard and run up the steps.

And then who's going to remove the curse? The girls on

'Charmed?!' it giggled.

But the questions came too late. So late, that Liza didn't even hear them. By the time the last word was uttered, in fact, she'd already darted through the front door—and slammed her fist right between Tess' eyes.

Holy shit, I thought as I started to fall. She really is the Gestapo! I reached back with my hand to break the fall but was a fraction of a second too late. A connection with the television was inevitable, and I connected perfectly with the corner of the device being introduced in a less than friendly manner to the back of my head.

Now it's a well-known fact that I wasn't the most graceful of my mother's children. Or the quietest either. And when personal clumsiness saw fit to pay a call—which was frequently—it always came with enough embarrassing clatter to make the whole neighborhood take notice. This time though, it paid off in spades. It had brought the others in a dead run from the kitchen. And even better, Brian had gotten Liza in tow before she could land another punch.

"Just what the fuck is going on here?" Brian demanded, as Liza squirmed and fumed.

Liza was so out of breath, she could hardly speak. But that didn't stop her from trying. "She cast a spell...black magic...Luke..." she panted.

"What the hell are you *talking* about?" Luke sputtered angrily. "And what the hell are you *doing* here?" He suddenly turned and looked at me, realization creeping across his face. "Oh, geeze...Tess! Oh, geeze..." he whined as he moved to help me.

But one look from Chloe told him to back off. She'd already examined my head, helped me up and sent Sally to the kitchen for an ice pack.

And that one look was all he needed. He turned on his sister with a raging fury none of us knew he possessed. "What the *hell* are you doing here?" he spat between his teeth, grabbing her by the shoulders and shaking her like a rag doll. "And who the hell do you think you are? You can't just go barging into someone's house..."

"Now let's just all calm down here." Brian delivered the

command with a heavy sigh then looked in my direction. "You okay?"

"Yeah."

"Wanna press charges?"

"*Charges?!*" squealed Liza. "But she..."

"Don't wanna hear it, little lady," Brian shot back. "In case you've forgotten, *you* walked into *her* house without an invite. Then to compound matters, you had the balls to assault her. I really don't think you wanna be in any more trouble than you already are..."

"But you don't under..."

"And if you keep talking, that's exactly where you'll be. One more word outa you, little lady, and I'll file charges myself. Are we clear?"

Brian turned his attention to me. "Charges or not?"

Other than being much more pissed off than I should've been, I really was okay. My vision was fine and I hadn't even cut my head. The only malady was a slight headache, and that was something a couple of aspirin could handle. Still, I was having some real trouble calming my inner bitch at this point, so I decided to give it a go and just let her loose.

"Well...I don't know," I replied coolly, looking pointedly at Liza, as I prepared to tick off the charges. "Being on the property without my permission...that's trespassing. Walking in the house without being invited. I believe that's breaking and entering. And smacking me in the face? Well, if I'm not mistaken, that's assault with intent to do bodily harm. And if she keeps talking," I added sarcastically, cocking my eyebrow and pausing to light a cigarette, "I suppose we could add 'interfering with a police investigation' to the fray. Want to go there, Liza?" I exhaled smoke in her direction to underscore my sarcasm. "Or do you just want to shut...the...fuck...up?"

I was a little surprised when Brian choked back a chuckle and turned away to hide his amusement. But Liza was a different story. No surprise there at all. In fact, she'd behaved just as I'd planned: wordlessly.

"No charges, Bri'," I said with a grin. "Now, suppose you show Liza to the kitchen and get her a cup of coffee. We've still got lots of things to discuss, and now it looks like she's got something to add to the mix too."

CHAPTER 9

I sat at the kitchen table with a cigarette in one hand, a coffee cup in the other and a mind full of thoughts. It had been an interesting few days, all right. In fact, I was beginning to feel a bit like Alice, for things in my world just kept getting curiouser and curiouser.

Once Liza finally settled down—due, no doubt, to the healthy shot of whiskey that Brian added to her coffee—we all began to compare notes. And the more we talked, the more certain I was that magic and reincarnation were both at play. While I couldn't do anything about the reincarnation factor, Sally could. And because investigating that angle might shed some light on what was really going on, it didn't take long for her to convince everyone there to undergo a past-life regression. She also brought up the need to look at the old family paintings, photos, daguerreotypes and other renderings and put Luke in charge of gathering them up. We agreed to meet at the plantation over the weekend and spend an entire day going through them.

With that out of the way, they tossed the magical problem right in my lap. It didn't matter that I didn't know how to fix it. It didn't matter that I didn't know someone who could. Hell, it didn't even matter that a part of Luke still seemed to think that the trick I kept talking about was all bullshit. All that mattered to them was that I had more magical experience than anyone else in the room. And the five pairs of eyes that stared at me from across the table drove that point home with steadfast assurance. So like it or not, I'd finally agreed to do a little research and find somebody to get us out of this mess. I just hoped I could.

But as anxious as I was about that, it didn't even begin to compare with the angst I felt over my relationship with Luke. As much as I couldn't bear the idea that we'd fallen victim to some sort of deliberate magic, I couldn't help but agonize over what might happen when the trick was broken. There was a distinct possibility that any attraction we felt would just disappear into thin air. That we might not even like each other. Even worse, that the dislike might be so strong that we couldn't even stand to be in the same room with each other. And I just didn't think I could handle that.

I wasn't so sure that Luke could either. It was in his eyes when he begged to spend the night. It was in his voice when we talked on the phone. Yeah, it was even in the way that he held me as if someone might rip me away from him at any moment. And even though he was now convinced that we were the reincarnation of his great-great grandparents, he was obviously humoring me over the magic involved and still didn't want to believe it was real. But what was going to happen when he was forced to face the truth...when reality reared its ugly head and smacked him right between the eyes? I couldn't even bring myself to think about it.

Whether I wanted to admit it or not—and I hadn't up to this point, not even to myself—I wasn't just falling head over heels in love with Luke, I was already there. Just the sound of his voice made my heart race. The sight of him made my knees buckle. And when he kissed me? Well...I melted into a useless puddle of mush. It was love, all right, and the possibility of not having him in my life was already tearing the heart right out of my chest.

Blinking back tears, I reached for my cigarette, only to find a filter full of lifeless cinders. I lit another, refilled my coffee cup and reminded myself not to borrow trouble. There was always plenty of that to go around. Worrying about stuff before it happened was just plain crazy. Things never worked out as planned anyway, and there was no way to fix something that hadn't even happened yet. Best to shift the focus elsewhere. And today's events were a pretty good starting point, I rationalized, trying to push my fears out of the way.

I dragged deeply on my cigarette and exhaled a series of perfectly formed smoke rings. Despite my worries over Luke—and the shades of lavender creeping across the bridge of my nose and feathering out onto my eyelids—it had been a very productive day. In fact, I could hardly believe my luck. I'd actually found a Conjure Woman. And a highly recommended one at that.

Not that the search had been easy. In fact, finding a needle in a haystack would've been less taxing. It had involved research, phone calls and countless dead ends. There were small fibs, white lies and every other form of human manipulation I could think of. But I'd finally gotten a break. And it came in the form of getting in touch with the author of a book on South Carolinian Gullah magic. Not that I thought it would do me much good—at least not at first—but I'd wound up hitting pay dirt. He'd referred me to a Root Doctor in Hilton Head, who'd sent me directly to one of Dr. Buzzard's descendants—a man by the name of Arthur Coleman. And that's where things got interesting.

First, there was my peculiar reaction to actually having contact information for a descendant of the legendary Root Doctor. I just couldn't bring myself to call. In fact, I must've stared at his phone number for more than an hour. I tried to justify my lack of motivation by telling myself that the man couldn't really help me. After all, it wasn't a Gullah practitioner I needed; I had to find someone well-versed in Louisiana hoodoo—and nothing else would do. When that didn't work, I went a step further. I tried to convince myself that there might not even be a trick at play at all. And to bother the man with something that might not even exist would be absolutely unconscionable. But deep down inside, I knew the real reason for dragging my heels. I was in complete awe of his family, his lineage and his heritage. I didn't want him to think I was an idiot and was afraid that I might just come across as one. Still, I needed help in the worst way, and there was nowhere else to turn. So, swallowing back a severe case of the nerves, I finally picked up the phone and began to dial.

I certainly wasn't prepared for what awaited me on the other end of the line though. Arthur Coleman's voice was rich and friendly and had a sort of homey quality that put me right at ease. By the time I'd introduced myself, I felt like I'd known the man forever. But that wasn't the interesting part. He knew who I was and he knew why I'd called. And while that could have been chalked up to nothing more than the referring party having called ahead, this couldn't: Arthur Coleman not only knew the exact nature of the trick in question but insisted that there were two tricks involved rather than one.

There was more. He'd already called his niece, Calliope Jones— a woman who'd grown up in the hoodoo practices of New Orleans—and let her know that I'd be getting in touch. And if that weren't enough, he'd ended the conversation by saying, "Now don't you be as scared to call Cal as you were to call me. I mean it. And Ms. Logan?"

"Y...yes?" I'd stammered.

"Don't tarry. You do it right this minute...while you've still got some gumption left. She's the best there is. And," he added with a chuckle, "she's your only ticket out of this mess." Then he'd hung up without another word—not even so much as a goodbye—and left me staring at the receiver in my hand. If I'd been in awe of the man before...well...it was nothing compared to what I'd thought of him after. He was utterly amazing. And if his niece was half as perceptive as he, I could hardly wait to speak with her. I'd hastily stabbed Cal's number into the pad—and the rest, as they say, was history.

"Ladies and Gentlemen, we are now beginning our final descent into St. Louis. Please return to your seats and make sure..."

Calliope Jones, better known as Cal to her friends and business associates, didn't need to hear the rest. She knew the drill. Smoothing her grey Armani suit, she tightened her seat belt and shoved the budget reports haphazardly back into the folder. They weren't important anyway and had only served as a preventative measure against the most common plague known to airline passengers: those meaningless and often ridiculous conversations folks feel compelled to strike up with anyone unfortunate enough to be seated next to them. And the ruse had worked better than any vaccine she could've whipped up. Some might even have called it magic, she thought with a grin.

While the nosiness of the other passengers normally didn't bother her, today was different. There were other things on her mind. More important things. Things that just didn't seem to know how to sit tight and be still. One of them was the phone conversation she'd had with Tess Logan—a woman she'd never met but had agreed to see while on this trip. Another was the reason for that conversation; more specifically, a plea for help with breaking a trick that was supposedly fixed over a hundred years ago. But even more important, there were those dreams of her grandmother—an accomplished Conjure Woman in her own right— which had come three days before the phone call and hadn't let up since.

Still deep in thought, Cal grabbed her briefcase and disembarked. Problem was, she wasn't sure she even believed in magic anymore. Not with all the trouble in the world. Even America, its richest nation, was filled to the brim with the homeless, the hungry and the downtrodden. Murder and suicide and hopelessness as far as you could see. And for every criminal taken off the street, there were twenty more in the making. Magic? Well, she thought, grabbing her bag from the carousel and heading for the rental car shuttle, if there ever was such a thing, it had certainly died in the United States a long time ago. And that was exactly what she intended to tell Tess Logan.

You ain't gonna tell that white woman anything of the kind, Little Missy! It was the voice in her head again—her grandmother's voice—the one that had suddenly begun to interrupt her thoughts at the most inopportune times. It was a strong voice. An insistent voice. A voice that simply refused to pay heed to any of the measures Cal had taken to shut it out. Instead, it just grew louder and sassier and gathered momentum. *You know better than that. I taught you better myself. What's wrong with you?! I...*

"Not now, MawMaw," Cal muttered under her breath.

Not now? Then when? When you make a complete fool of yourself? Magic ain't dead and you know that. Only the art that's dead, 'cept in those who know better. And I...

Cal rolled her eyes heavenward, stepped off the shuttle and yet again made a silent plea for her grandmother to hush. No such luck. MawMaw just kept right on.

Don't you cut them eyes around at me, Little Missy. Just 'cause you don't wanna hear it, don't make it not so. Just 'cause you been to school don't make it not so. If I had the power, I'd cut me a switch and...

Cal tried hard not to listen to the goings-on in her head, smiled at the rental agent and produced her confirmation number and credit card.

...give you a lickin' you'd never forget! I'd switch you so hard...

With the rental agreement signed, Cal tapped her manicured nail impatiently on the counter as she waited for the keys. There was no way to stop MawMaw's incessant chatter, and the best she could hope for was the safety of the rental car before she inadvertently responded aloud to the voice no one else could hear.

...your bottom be red as a fox's. Couldn't sit down for a week. Just who do you think you is? No magic! I ain't never heard of such foolishness in all my...

Finally, the woman behind the counter returned, jingled the keys with a flourish and handed them to Cal. "Can I help you any further?" she asked pleasantly. "Maps? Directions? Anything?"

"No, that's all I need. Unless you have something really strong for a splitting headache caused by a grandmother who won't quit," she responded. They shared a knowing chuckle, and Cal grabbed her bag and started for the door.

What you mean, won't quit? retorted MawMaw, obviously oblivious to any other voice but Cal's. *Don't you sass me, Little Missy. Your mama didn't sass me but once, and...*

"*ENOUGH* already, MawMaw!" she finally responded, tossing her bag in the car and starting the engine. "I need to think now. So please...*PLEASE*...hush!"

Ain't no need to be thinkin' about nothin' 'cept how to break them tricks. Yes'm. That should be the only thing on your mind...

"But what if there *is* no trick, MawMaw? What then?"

Oh, there be's tricks all right, Little Missy. And good'uns too. Tougher and stouter than you ever seen. And all I want to know is this: Just what's you gonna do to make 'em go away? Eh, Little Missy? Just what's you gonna do?

"So when does she get here?" Chloe asked, settling into her seat at the table and lighting up.

"Sometime tomorrow. She's lecturing in St. Louis and said she'd call when she's through. But I'm thinking mid-afternoon."

"Lecturing? About what?"

"I don't know."

"What do you mean, you don't know!"

"Just that, Chloe," I said, heading toward the oven. "I didn't ask and she didn't say."

I'd just told a half-truth and couldn't help but feel a little guilty. While I didn't know *exactly* what she was lecturing about, I did know that Calliope Jones was a cultural anthropologist. And I was willing to bet that she was also an artifact specialist of some sort. But at this point, I simply couldn't say that to Chloe. Admitting as much would've opened a whole new realm to my inquisitive friend. And the last thing I needed was for Chloe to bombard the woman with anthropological questions when I needed to discuss magic. It just wouldn't do. But knowing that didn't make me feel any better.

Chloe watched me retrieve the last pan of cookies and didn't bother to speak again until they'd taken up residence on the cooling rack. "Need help with those?"

I grinned. "Little late in asking, aren't you? Especially now that I'm already done!"

"Well...some of them *do* look a tad burnt," she said, craning her neck to peer at the rack, "and there's no way you'd ever serve those to a guest." She put out her cigarette in the ashtray and sauntered over to have a better look. "Not a *real* one anyway. You'd be mortified. So," she said, peeking over my shoulder, "I was just thinking that you might need some help disposing of those."

Her tone was serious enough for me to take a look. I gazed at the cookies in horror. The last thing I wanted to do was bake another batch, but if they were scorched...well...I couldn't very well serve them to Ms. Jones. Sighing heavily, I bent forward to examine them more closely.

Now, cookies are either burned or they're not, and you don't have to put them under a microscope to tell. So by the time I'd decided to flip one over, I realized I'd been taken.

"Where?" I demanded playfully.

Chloe didn't say a word. She just stared at me with wide eyes.

"Just exactly where are they burnt?!" I put my hands on my hips for effect and tried to keep from laughing.

"Right here!" Chloe said. She grabbed the cookie, took a bite and moaned in delight.

Giggling at her tactics and seeing an opportunity to assuage my guilt, I put a half dozen cookies on a plate and handed them to her.

"So, what's she like?"

"Who?"

She rolled her eyes. "Calliope Jones, silly."

"Nice enough, and friendly."

"C'mon, Tess...that's no answer," she said between bites. "You could say that about the dog down the street. You could even say that about your crazy neighbor." She looked at me expectantly.

"Well...I only talked to her for a few minutes," I said, taking the seat across from her. "But I get the feeling that something's bothering her about this."

"Well, *duh*! It's bothering *all* of us. If it weren't, we wouldn't have even *bothered* to..."

"No, it's something more than that. Something not quite right. Something I can't quite put my finger on." I lit a cigarette, drew deeply and studied the tendrils of smoke twirling through the air. "And I'll be damned if I can figure out what it is."

"What the hell do you *mean*?! And just what the fuck did you think you were *doing*, barging in like that?" Had Luke's voice been venom, he'd have poisoned the whole planet. He'd promised himself that he wasn't going to bring any of this up. He'd promised himself that he wouldn't speak to his sister at all. In fact, he'd promised himself that he'd just pretend she didn't exist. And he'd kept that promise for the last two days. But this was too much. Way too much. And he simply wasn't going to let her by with it.

"And if that weren't bad enough, you thought you had the right to punch her in the *face*?!" He plopped down in the chair and rubbed his chin. "There's something wrong with you, Liza...bad wrong. And the worst of it," he said, looking her directly in the eye, "is that you don't even know it."

"I d-don't understand," she stammered. "I don't think I...I don't see what you're..."

"Exactly my point, dear sister! You don't think. You don't see. The big picture doesn't matter to you at all. You just run off half-cocked, saying and doing whatever you please, and it's supposed to be all right. Well, it's *not* all right! Geeze, Liza...it's not even *normal*!" He spat the last word with enough force to surprise both of them.

She'd never seen Luke so mad. Her chin dimpled up, a sure sign that she was going to cry, so she tilted her head back slightly to keep the tears from escaping. After a deep breath, she lowered her head again, fixed her gaze on Luke and commanded her voice to stay on an even keel.

"Normal? You think *any* of this is normal? Hell, Luke...I'm beginning to think we're living an episode of the 'Twilight Zone.'" She managed a weak smile then continued. "Your girlfriend is a Witch. And to her credit, even *she* admits that you're under some sort of spell. So if those are the facts, just tell me...what's so abnormal about thinking that *she* might have put the spell on you, herself? I don't think it's that far out of line, Luke."

"That's the most *ridiculous* thing I've ever heard come out of your mouth!" His voice was calmer now but still underscored with complete exasperation. "Have you *looked* at her, Liza? *Really* looked at her? She's beyond gorgeous." His face softened as he thought about Tess and brought her image to mind. "And if you'd taken the time to get to know her," he continued, "even a little bit...you'd have discovered that she's also smart and funny. She's perfection personified, Liza. She could have any man she wanted. And she certainly doesn't need love spells for that.

"But you can't stand that, can you?! You can't deal with the fact that, after all these years, I've not only *found* the perfect woman but intend to spend the rest of my life with her. And even worse, you can't deal with the fact that I've somehow managed it all without the help of supernatural forces.

"So, what do you *do* about all this? You charge in like Rambo and try to beat the shit out of her." He tapped a cigarette from the pack in front of him and lit up before continuing. "Damn it, Liza," he said, pausing to inhale, "you're lucky not to be in jail. Damned lucky. And in case you've forgotten, it's only by Tess' good graces that you're not."

He was right on the last part, and Liza knew it. Tess definitely could have had her thrown in jail and would've been more than justified in doing that. But for whatever reason, she hadn't chosen that route. Of course, having your lover's sister tossed in the pokey probably wouldn't be conducive to a very happy relationship. Yet, she had the feeling that it truly hadn't been a deciding factor in Tess' choice. Tess Logan had, after all, stood up to her that night and didn't seem to care what anybody, including Luke, had thought of it. She'd let everybody there know that she was in charge of the situation, that she didn't need anyone's help in assessing it and that her word on the matter was final. And as much as Liza was concerned over Tess' relationship with her brother, she couldn't help but admire that mix of independence and grace under fire.

But what about that little voice in her head? Could it just be a load of crap and something she should learn to ignore? Doubtful, since someone always got screwed every time she did that. But maybe she'd missed the point this time. Maybe it had just been a warning of those old spells Tess had talked about. Maybe...

"Anything you want to say?" Luke asked, interrupting her thoughts. "Or is this conversation over?"

"Okay," Liza said. "You're right. I acted like an ass, and I'm sorry."

"And?"

She hated it when Luke prompted her like she was a three-year-old but took her cue anyway. "And," she sighed, "I'm sorry that I knocked Tess on her ass. That was wrong too."

"Then I think you need to tell her that." His tone was now completely devoid of all emotion, and Liza knew he meant business.

"You're not going to speak to me again until I do, are you?"

"Not likely," he said, tapping another cigarette from the pack on his desk.

She opened her mouth to respond but realized it was futile. He'd already gone back to the business of sorting through the papers on his desk. And back to the business of ignoring her.

Lecture notes in hand, Cal sat cross-legged on the bed and leaned back against the pillows. At least the bed was comfortable, and that usually couldn't be said for hotel beds in this day and time. In fact, she mused, a block of Styrofoam was more conducive to a good night's sleep than most of those she'd slept in lately.

But back to matters at hand, she thought, making a concerted effort to force all errant thoughts from her mind. Tomorrow's lecture wasn't just any old lecture. It was probably the most important one she'd ever been asked to present. Everyone who was anyone in the industry would be there, and that demanded a flawless delivery while maintaining the folksy, down-to-earth style and grace for which she was known. She couldn't afford to stutter. She couldn't afford to lose her place. And she damned sure couldn't afford to get off track. The only way to keep any of that from happening was to know this lecture so well that it was as much a part of her as her own shadow.

And what about those tricks, Little Missy? What's you gonna do about them?

The voice didn't belong to MawMaw this time. It was only a culmination of thoughts born of their earlier conversation.

I'll figure it out later, Cal answered silently.

No time like the present, it shot back.

Go *away,* she demanded, forcibly pushing the thought from her mind and returning to her notes.

But all she got for her trouble was a snort, a giggle and further insistence.

"Look," she said angrily in her out loud voice. "There's nothing I can do about it right now. I don't even have the particulars. I don't even know..."

Ask MawMaw, it teased.

"Oh, all *right!*" she responded, slamming her notes on the bed in aggravation. She closed her eyes, took a deep breath and turned her focus toward peace and tranquility. And as the exercise evened her breathing patterns and brought her into a state of calm serenity, she called her grandmother's image to mind and set about the business of summoning her.

"Okay, MawMaw...I'm ready to talk." She listened closely, straining to hear. But not a single sound issued forth. There was nothing at all. Not even so much as a sigh.

Cal tried over and over, but to no avail. MawMaw apparently wasn't in the mood to talk just now. She'd always had a stubborn streak—a streak that obviously hadn't improved with time or in death.

"Damn it!" She jumped from the bed and threw her arms in the air with disgust. "What the hell *is* it with you anyway, MawMaw? First, you won't shut up. You just rattle on like the balls in a bingo cage until I'm right on the brink of insanity. And when I really need answers...what do you do? You run off somewhere and leave me sitting here to wring my hands and twiddle my thumbs in worry. What kind of grandmother *are* you *anyway*?!"

She stopped to listen again, hoping that her sassy little tirade might provoke MawMaw enough to come forth. When nothing happened, she tried again, this time using a different tactic.

"Come on, MawMaw," she begged in earnest. "*Please* help me! *Please*?! You know that I don't have a clue how to fix this mess. These tricks are over a hundred years old, and I'll never find the packets." She paused just long enough to wipe the errant tear rolling down her cheek with the back of her sleeve before continuing. "You *know* they've got to be rotted by now. You *know* I can't undo this unless I've got the packets.

"Please, MawMaw...*please*!" she implored, her voice cracking and tears streaming down her cheeks. The last few words of her soliloquy were completely unintelligible as she threw herself face down in the pillow and cried herself to sleep.

"Damn, I've missed you." His voice was like smooth-sipping whiskey, just begging to be sampled.

"I missed you too," I purred before I could stop myself. Damn it! I'd promised to put some space between Luke and me—at least until we were sure that our feelings were real—and I wanted to slap myself for responding as I had. I didn't want him to have this effect on me. I didn't want to melt every time I heard his voice. I didn't want...

"So...how did it go today? Any luck with solving our problem?"

"Good," I said, trying to keep my emotions in check. "And as a matter of fact, I did. In fact, our Conjure Woman arrives tomorrow." That was better. I'd actually managed to respond without sounding like a lovelorn pup. I just hoped I could get through the rest of the conversation with the same tone.

"Well, I made some progress too."

"You did? With what?"

"Lots of things," he replied. "And if you could see your way fit to opening the front door," he added with a chuckle, "I'll tell you all about them."

"*What?!*"

"That's right...I'm sitting in your driveway. So, what do you say, Gorgeous? You gonna let me in...or do I have to sit out here all night?"

"Well...I don't know," I deadpanned. "What's it *worth* to you, Handsome?" That flirty lilt had crept back into my voice, a sure sign that my heart had once again taken the lead and overridden all common sense. But what the hell, I rationalized, whipping the door open and peering outside. There'd be plenty of time to see where we really stood once the tricks were broken.

"Just let me in...and you'll see!" he countered playfully, waving at me from the car.

An armful of flowers, a bottle of champagne and fifteen minutes later, I did. And my better judgment? Well...it definitely wished I hadn't.

CHAPTER 10

"To be perfectly honest, Ms. Logan, I'm not sure I can help you." She studied her coffee cup as if the cream she'd just added might somehow produce the answers I needed. Finally, she shrugged her shoulders and looked at me expectantly.

"To start with, Cal..." I said setting the carafe in the middle of the table, "I thought we'd gotten that 'Ms. Logan' thing out of the way. Every time I hear that phrase, one of two things happens: Either I revert to the mindset of a five-year-old and think I'm in serious trouble, or...I start looking around for my ex-mother-in-law. And the latter makes me *really* nervous!" I chuckled and so did she.

She rolled her eyes and grinned knowingly. "I have one of those too."

"More importantly though, I have complete faith in you *and* your abilities. I have to, Cal," I said, making direct eye contact with her. "You're the only chance we have."

"So much for weaseling out of this, hunh?!" She sighed and smiled and shook her head from side to side. "I just wish you *didn't* have so much faith in me. It would make what I have to say to you *so* much easier."

"What do you mean?"

"Well, I'm going to level with you, Tess," Cal said, peering over the cup in her hand. "To break a trick, you have to locate it. And no matter how much faith you have in me, locating a trick that's over a hundred years old is going to be next to impossible." Her voice had taken on a matter-of-fact tone; the same sort of tone a professor might use when explaining an exact science with no allowance for possibility. "What I'm saying," she continued evenly, "is that even if I could determine the exact trick location, the packet in question would be rotted...so rotted, in fact, that by now the earth itself would have swallowed it whole like a hungry child."

I refilled our cups and let her words sink in. I hadn't even considered this problem, so I asked for clarification.

"So, you'd need to have the complete trick at your disposal...with all the components tied up together in one neat little package then? And just finding bits and pieces of it probably wouldn't work?"

She bit into a cookie and considered the question while she chewed. "I honestly don't know, Tess. I've never tried to break a trick without having the whole packet."

"But you don't know that it won't work either."

"No," she responded with a sigh. While she obviously wasn't at all comfortable with the idea, she hadn't discounted it entirely either. And that, in itself, was good news. At least it was to me.

"Okay," I said thoughtfully, "I won't even pretend to understand your magical system...I know it's much different from mine...but at its very basis, magic is magic. Provided that the tricks were fixed in the ground and not in running water, I'm not sure that having the whole packet is necessary. Even if it disintegrated and became a part of the earth itself...the components would still be a part of the soil. And if you're able to find the exact location where the tricks were originally fixed, it seems to me that you could use a sample of the soil from that specific spot to break them."

"Well...that *sounds* logical." She looked at me and grinned. "But we both know that magic and logic seldom make for cooperative partners. If they did, there would be little point for extensive magical study. Again, I'm not saying that it won't work. But I'm just not sure that it will."

I liked Calliope Jones, I thought, watching her from across the table. But then, what wasn't to like? She had a no-nonsense sort of style coupled with that old school Southern charm I'd grown up with, and that made me comfortable. She was knowledgeable, honorable and seemed honest to a fault. My instincts said that she wasn't likely to lead anyone down the path of quick fixes, and I liked that too. Fact was, I found myself trusting and respecting her, neither of which I did easily. And that made my next question even harder to pose.

"Okay." I paused to sip my coffee as I struggled for words. "Is there anyone who might know? The last thing I want to do is insult you, so please don't take this the wrong way...but is there anyone you could ask? A teacher? A relative? Anybody?" I searched her eyes, hoping that I hadn't screwed this up.

Her laughter set me at ease again. "Don't be so worried, Tess," she said between chuckles. "Offending me takes more than a few questions. So if that's your aim, Honey...you need practice. A lot of it!

"But back to the subject at hand. Yes...there is someone I could ask. But whether or not I can locate her is another story." She winked.

"She's a little like a cat. She seldom answers when called and only responds when she feels like it. Still," she added, "I'll see what I can do.

"Even if your theory is workable," she continued, "there's something else you should know...something I've debated on telling you since we first spoke...something that may have a bearing on whether you even *want* my help." She arched an eyebrow, a gesture that always seemed to accompany her most serious tone. "Were I in your shoes, it would definitely be a deciding factor for me."

If she'd been trying to get my attention, she'd done just fine. Goosebumps popped up on my arms and the hairs on the back of my neck stood up. Whatever was coming next, one thing was for sure. I wasn't going to like it. Not even a little.

"Well, that doesn't sound promising at all," I said, trying to lighten things up. My eyes and lips caught the cue immediately, managing to spread a warm smile across my face. But the tingle crawling up and down my spine didn't respond as planned. Instead, it slithered all the way up to my head. I looked at her expectantly and hoped that this wasn't going to be as bad as I thought.

"The truth of the matter, Tess," she began, "is that I'm not even sure I *believe* in magic anymore. And we both know that without belief..."

"B-but your uncle said..." I blurted, unable to contain my objection.

She waved me off with a hand and continued as if I hadn't interrupted. "... there *is* no magic."

I felt like I'd just been kicked in the gut. "Then why on earth..."

"Because I promised I'd come," she answered, picking up on my thoughts. "And I always keep my promises."

I took a deep breath, toyed with the pack of cigarettes in front of me and tried to steady the wave of emotions churning up inside of me.

"It's not a problem," she said, gesturing toward the pack. "I indulge upon occasion too. In fact, we could both probably use a smoke about now." A quick search through her purse produced a cigarette case and lighter. And I shot her a thin smile as we both lit up.

"I guess I just don't understand," I said, exhaling heavily. "Don't you believe anything I've told you?"

"Of course I do. It's not a matter of believing *you*." She paused to twirl the end of her cigarette around the rim of the ashtray and then looked at me pointedly. "It's a matter of whether or not I believe that *I* can fix your problem."

"Look, Cal," I countered. "Maybe you're just having a 'dark night of the soul.' Maybe you're just not sure what to believe in anymore. Maybe you're just confused."

"Maybe." She studied the length of her cigarette, then took another drag. "But what really bears consideration here is something only you can decide: Knowing what you do, do you really trust in my ability to break these tricks? And if so..." She paused to double the butt into the ashtray and crush out its life. "...Do you have enough belief for *both* of us?"

I exhaled slowly and wondered if I did.

While the meeting with Cal hadn't exactly gone according to plan, she had agreed to meet with us at the plantation, check things out there and do what she could to help. It was the best she could offer—she said that she wasn't about to promise something she couldn't deliver—and I guessed I should be grateful for that. Cal did, after all, have knowledge that I didn't. And even if she couldn't break the tricks, having access to that knowledge might give us an advantage toward finding another solution. It definitely couldn't hurt.

Rationalization, I thought with a chuckle. It was something I'd definitely gotten good at lately. Hell...I seemed to be able to justify *everything* these days...even those things with hardly a shred of rhyme or reason. I shook my head in wonder at how I, such a balanced and grounded person, could ever have come to this point.

There was one thing that I couldn't rationalize away though. And it had to do with three carats worth of diamonds in an antique platinum setting. The same diamonds that flashed brilliantly from the ring finger of my left hand. And no matter how hard I tried, there was no explanation at all for that. Or for how it had come to be there.

Luke's proposal had been more than perfect. Our glasses filled with vintage Dom Pérignon, he'd gotten down on one knee, taken my hands in his and looked into my eyes. Then he'd delivered the most beautiful soliloquy I'd ever heard; so beautiful, in fact, that I'd committed every single word to memory and had no trouble at all conjuring them up as I called the event to mind once more.

"My whole life has been spent searching for something that, up until a few weeks ago, had completely eluded me. It was of course, that one simple but magical reason for my existence. I never thought I'd find it, but the search continued anyway, with the hope that someday I might.

"Then one day, you walked into my office. And I came away from that off-chance, unscheduled meeting knowing that my quest was over. That in *you* were my hopes, my dreams and all that I could ever wish. Just your smile brought light to the shadows of my soul, and your laughter, fresh life to my entire being.

"You are the love of my life...that rare and perfect treasure that makes me whole. And as long as the tides roll out to sea...as long as breath and life endure...I will cherish you beyond measure.

"What I'm trying to say is that I love you with all my heart...with all that I am, and all that I'll ever be..." His eyes still locked on mine, he paused for a second, reached into his pocket and retrieved a tiny box. "And," he continued, "there's nothing in this world or any other that can ever change that."

He placed the box in my hand and covered it with his own. Then pausing again to blink back tears, the question foremost in his mind finally issued forth. "Will you marry me?" he whispered.

I was stunned. I didn't know what to say. And the fact that my heart and better judgment picked that exact moment to wage war certainly didn't help matters.

Say yes, Heart commanded. *He loves you more than life itself...and always will!*

You can't be serious, Better Judgment countered. *Broken tricks. Broken engagement. Broken heart. You wanna go there?!*

You're gonna lose the best thing that ever happened to you, Tess Logan, Heart snorted. *You wanna go* there?!

The truth of the matter was that I didn't want to go either place. I couldn't bear the thought of losing Luke. I didn't just love him, I absolutely adored him. But there was no way I could promise to marry him. Not right then. And certainly not before we had some answers.

Fortunately, this stance satisfied both Heart and Better Judgement, and they quickly retreated to separate corners and returned to the matter of minding their own business.

With them out of the way, I wrapped my arms around Luke's neck and engaged him in a long, slow kiss.

"Is that a 'yes,' Ms. Logan?" He looked at me expectantly with twinkling eyes.

"Well..." I said carefully, taking his hand in mine and searching his eyes, "it's certainly not a 'no.' But I'd like to hold off on the engagement for a little while. Just until we clear up the possibility of magical interference." So far, so good. His face hadn't fallen, and the twinkle in his eyes was still intact. Relieved, I continued, "And once that's done...if we still feel the same way about each other...there's nothing I'd rather do than marry you."

"But how do you *know* there's nothing you'd rather do?!" he teased. "You haven't even looked at the ring yet! Don't you want to see if I can *afford* you?!" His brows shot up over wide eyes, and I giggled at his antics. It was obvious that he was very pleased with the ring selection and couldn't wait for me to see it.

"Oh...I don't think that's an issue." I pretended indifference, still holding the unopened box in my hand.

"Not even one little peek?" He looked at me in disbelief.

"Oh, all right," I replied, rolling my eyes and feigning disdain. "Let's see what you came up with, Mr. Benson." We both burst into laughter, but mine was cut short when I opened the box. I was absolutely stunned for the second time that day.

"Oh...my...God," I breathed. It was the most beautiful ring I'd ever seen. Sprinkled with diamonds, the platinum setting was fashioned in antique filigree. The band had been carved into a delicate feather pattern. And situated right in the center was an enormous perfectly symmetrical square-cut solitaire.

My breath caught and a tear made its way down my cheek. "Where on earth did you..."

"Does that mean you like it?"

Swallowing back tears and doing my best to control the sudden dance of butterflies in my stomach, I nodded. "But where..."

"I had it made for you," he said happily. "The setting is an exact duplicate of..."

"Lucinda's ring," I said, finishing his sentence.

"Yeah," he answered, an odd look creeping across his face. "But how could you possibly know..."

"I don't know." I was just as baffled by my response as he but did my damnedest to toss it aside. I didn't want to spoil the moment. And I knew if the conversation veered off in that direction, that's exactly what would happen. "I just knew. That's all." I lightened things up with a smile and even managed a chuckle.

"So...you like the ring, you think I can afford you and you've sort of promised to marry me later. But there's still one question that remains unanswered," he said playfully.

"And what would *that* be?" Surely he didn't have any *more* surprises for me. How many times, after all, could a girl handle being stunned all in the same day?

"Well...we still don't know if the ring fits. And I need to know just in case you eventually do better than 'sort of' agreeing to marry me!" He'd been holding back his laughter for a good while now but simply couldn't manage it anymore. And once let loose, it took off like a contagion, infecting us both with the absurdity of my maybe-maybe-not answer; so much so in fact, that it took a few seconds to get ourselves back under control. "So..." he continued, trying to catch his breath, "would you do me the honor?"

Still giggling, I held out my hand, and he slipped the ring on my finger. "Perfect fit," I said, holding my hand up to the light and admiring the setting.

So how many times in one day could a girl deal with being stunned? Apparently, at least once more. For as the diamond flashed its brilliant fire, other flashes came too. Flashes of Luke and me in another time. Flashes of Luke and me in a meadow. Flashes of our wedding day...my pregnancy...a little girl...the two black women from my dream. On and on they came, one right after another, as if they were part of some endless slide show run amuck. I was caught in the vortex of a life gone mad, its pictorial fragments spinning me round and round, faster and faster, with the express purpose of absorbing every shred of my being into its funnel. I couldn't get my bearings or catch my breath. Beads of cold sweat chilled me to the bone, and I was dizzy to the point of nausea.

Then somewhere from the edge of consciousness, I felt my spirit disengaging itself from my body, and one thing was certain: This wasn't just a simple out of body experience. I was being forced into another world—a world from which there was no return—a greedy sort of world designed to snuff out my life force and everything in it. And that's exactly what it intended to do. *This can't be happening,* I thought, slamming my eyes shut and struggling to stay in my body. I would *not* go out this way. Not today. Not tomorrow. Not ever. *Turn me loose,* I screamed in terror, *and stay the hell away from my life!*

And whether it was by the command that echoed only in my mind, from Luke's frenzy to shake me back to consciousness—or a little of both—I finally felt my life force settle in once again and firmly reattach itself to its physical boundaries.

"Are you *all right*?!" Luke's face was lined with concern, and he quickly scooped me into his arms.

"Yeah," I lied, leaning into him and taking a deep breath. "I've just been feeling a little out of sorts today." I drew in another deep breath, then reached for the glass of champagne on the table and drained it. "See? Better already," I fibbed again.

Luke obviously wasn't buying it. "You scared the shit out of me! Geeze, Tess...you were hardly *breathing*! You..."

"Really, I'm fine." I managed a smile to underscore my words.

"I thought you were gonna have a *stroke*! I really think a trip to the emergency room..."

Admitting that I'd come to nearly the same conclusion wasn't going to fix things...and neither was a doctor. The best solution here was to diffuse the situation and move on. And I did my best to do just that.

"A *stroke*?! That's the most *ridiculous* thing I've ever heard. You wouldn't even know a stroke if it slapped you in the face!" I laughed for good measure.

"I still think..."

"C'mon, Luke...I'm fine! How could I not be fine?" I asked, grinning up at him. "I do, after all, have *you*!"

"Okay...if you're sure," he said skeptically.

"Now then," I said, changing the subject and winking, "since the ring fits, suppose you hang on to it until we're ready to make this official. It's so gorgeous, I'd just die if anything happened to it, and you *know* how things tend to get swallowed up in this house!"

"That's probably a good idea." Diffusion process complete, I thought. Not only was he smiling again but actually skimming the brink of laughter. Of course, the memory of his disappearing car keys was still fresh in his mind. The same keys that had been on a three-day sabbatical before turning up, despite the fact that he'd specifically remembered hanging them on the rack by the door.

Thrilled that he wasn't giving me any hassle over this, I reached over to remove the ring and put it in his waiting hand. But within seconds, I realized that removal was not an option. The ring wouldn't budge. Not even a little. It wasn't a tight fit, and I'd only been wearing it for a few minutes. My fingers weren't swollen at all; in fact, the ring was actually loose enough to twirl around on its own with nothing more than a simple shake of the wrist. The only thing impeding progress was its absolute refusal to slip back over my knuckle.

Way past the stunned point now, I was well on my way to the panic attack from hell. I would not—could not—have a repeat episode of that topsy-turvy world that had damned near taken my life. Just the very thought of that brought a pounding to my chest and a need to gulp huge quantities of air. It was all I could do not to scream. I wanted that ring off my finger and in short order. It needed to be back in its box and back in Luke's possession before something else happened. That ring had to come off—and right this instant.

Just calm yourself. The interjection was Better Judgment taking over again, and this time it was right. I took a deep breath and worked at the ring some more. Unfortunately, it refused to cooperate.

"Shit!" I muttered under my breath.

"Need some help with that?"

"Yes!" I practically shouted.

And so the process began. We tugged and we pulled. We tried cold water to shrink my finger and hot water to expand the band. We tried soap...petroleum jelly...vegetable oil...and any other slippery substance we could think of. But all to no avail. The only thing I got for our trouble was a red, sore and over-worked finger. More specifically, a red, sore, over-worked finger upon which a gorgeous diamond ring twirled round and round. A diamond ring with absolutely no desire to relinquish claim on its squatting rights.

Finally, Luke got tickled with the whole episode—it had after all, gotten past the point of the ridiculous—and began to laugh. I, on the other hand, couldn't find any humor in it at all. He hadn't seen what I'd seen. He hadn't felt what I'd felt. And since it was obvious that he wasn't even convinced of the tricks at play, I wasn't about to tell him.

"Oh, c'mon, Tess...don't be so upset," he soothed. "Don't you *get* it?" His smile indicated some sort of joke that I, in my consternation, had obviously missed.

"Get *what*?!" I snapped in dismay.

"Honey...we've been working our asses off. And all for nothing. The ring's not going anywhere. The house isn't going to swallow it up. The ring's safe and sound and *happy*..." His voice trailed off as he tried desperately to smother an escaping chuckle before continuing, "right where it is!

"And as long as you marry me...at least, sort of," he chortled, "I won't have to cut your finger off to get it *back*!"

Recounting the event in my mind, I did have to admit that the lengths to which we went in trying to remove that ring—and the antics that resulted because of them—were enough to make Ma and Pa Kettle laugh out loud. Truth be told, any team of comedy writers in the country might have paid handsomely for the material.

But the events leading up to it held an entirely different flavor—something terrible that smacked of greed and despair with a bittersweet edge. And the one thing I knew was this: No matter how well presented or skillfully served, nothing in this world would ever make it taste any better.

Magic, however, was a sweet dessert, I thought, glancing at the ring that had so stubbornly staked its claim. The ritual I'd performed had completely obliterated yesterday's apprehensions as well as whatever power the object had held over my life. And while I'd been very careful not to destroy the ring's visionary magic, I was absolutely certain that nothing associated with it could ever put me in harm's way again.

Just the same, I made one more attempt to dislodge it from its resting place. There was even more play in the band than yesterday, and yet, it still wouldn't budge. It simply didn't make sense. Unless of course, there was some reason that my connection with it was important. But even if I was a reincarnated version of Lucinda—and I didn't know that yet for certain—that didn't make sense either. This ring had never belonged to her. It only was a replica, so there was no way that the energy of the piece could have been directly connected to her.

Still, I studied the ring, paying close attention to its band, its markings and the placement of its stones. It wasn't until I got around to examining the center stone that the one thing that had escaped my grasp finally became apparent. And as usual, it was the one thing that should've been clear all along. The setting itself was completely irrelevant, and so were the diamond embellishments. It was that flawless, perfectly symmetrical square cut diamond that had wielded all the magic. And as silly as it sounds, I also knew that removing the stone would release it from my finger.

Had the realization come yesterday, I'd have insisted on an immediate trip to the jeweler. But there was no point in that now. Doing so would only destroy a beautiful piece of jewelry, and I wasn't prepared to do that. Better to just let it be and enjoy it for a while, I thought. The worst case scenario was that we'd eventually have to have it cut off. And that was, I thought with a chuckle, a much better scenario than Luke had proposed!

Just the same, I couldn't help but wonder where Luke had gotten the stone, why it seemed so connected to me and what could possibly have caused its past-life images. But if my luck held out—and so far, it had—I had no doubt that the answer to the first would bring clues to the second and third. And if I was really lucky, it might even solve the riddle entirely.

Fool!

Well, isn't this an unexpected pleasure, Cal thought sarcastically, as she pulled out into the flow of traffic on Highway 61. In all actuality, MawMaw's timing couldn't have been better. Cal was on her way to the plantation to do a little poking around, and any help she could get from her grandmother would definitely be welcome. Still, she couldn't help lashing out at MawMaw over her blatant refusal to come when called.

"Oh, that's just *great*, MawMaw. You finally decide to drag your happy ass away from whatever it is you do...never when I need you of course, but only when you feel like it...and then it's only to insult me. Well, to tell you the truth, I've had about all the fun I can stand out of you!"

Mmm-mmm-mmm...You ain't just a fool, you a damn fool! I can't believe...

"You can't believe *what*, MawMaw? That I'm more than just a mite pissed at you? Well, *believe* it. You hung me out to dry and left me blowing in the wind with my skirt up around my neck. And now, you have the nerve..."

...what you done gone and told that white woman! Ain't you got a lick of sense in that book-schooled brain?! Or do them graduatin' papers just be's for show?

"Don't you *dare* to go there with me, MawMaw! I was honest and forthright, and refused to promise something I wasn't sure I could deliver. I never said that magic didn't exist. I just said that *I* wasn't sure I believed in it anymore."

I ain't never heard such foolishness in all my life! What was you thinkin', Little Missy? Answer me that. Or was you thinkin' a'tall?

"Foolishness? Did you say *foolishness*?! Just what the hell would you have had me do? *Lie* to the woman?"

I taught you better than that, Little Missy. They's times to talk and times to hush. And you, of all people, knows the difference.

"Okay, MawMaw," she said, changing her tone. She really needed her grandmother's help and was smart enough to know that pressing the argument wasn't going to get her anywhere. "I'm sorry. And you're right. I screwed up," she said contritely. "Look...could we just call a truce? I really could use your help just now."

And just what makes you think I can he'p you? Just what makes you think that?

"Oh, come on, MawMaw," Cal begged. "You know everything there is to know about hoodoo. You're the expert, not me. I've never even tried to break a trick without the packets. And we both know that's exactly what this is going to involve."

She glanced at the directions in her hand, made a left and headed up the plantation drive.

Maybe. And maybe not.

"What do you mean?!"

Just what I said. You got a problem with them ears, Gal?

"No, MawMaw...but I don't think you understand. They're asking me to break tricks that were laid over a hundred years ago. And we both know that those packets have already rotted into nothingness. I need..."

You don't need nothin' but a lot of gumption, Little Missy. And, it's you who don't understand. You got a personal stake in this'un and there ain't nothin' I can do about it.

"A personal stake? What on earth are you *talking* about?"

Just what I said. I can't say no more, so pay heed, you hear? You already got all you need to break them tricks. Just use what you got, Little Missy. And use what you have.

For the love of the ancestors! She was almost there, and this was no time to talk in riddles. And yet, MawMaw had chosen to do just that.

"MawMaw, *please*!" Cal's voice cracked, and her eyes filled with tears. "I don't know what you mean. Can't you..."

What's wrong with you, chile? Ain't you paying me no mind a'tall? I done told you to put them book smarts to work. I done told you to use what be's yours. Now I can't say no more. They ain't gonna let me.

"What the hell am I going to do?" Cal asked in earnest.

You can start by wipin' that sniffledy nose, Little Missy. You got hankies in that purse?

"Yes Ma'am." Cal smiled in spite of herself and dug dutifully through her bag. She retrieved a tissue and swiped at her nose before balling it up into the litter bag.

"MawMaw?"

Hunh?

"If you can't help me...then who *can*?"

You got questions, ask that white woman. She be's smart as a whip and knows more than she be's sayin'. Ain't no sense in bein' scairt now. Just heed what I be's tellin' you. Do 'zactly what I say. And them tricks be's better than broke...they be's broke up fine as hairs on a frog's back.

CHAPTER 11

My heart pounded in my chest and echoed in my ears. The dream was back...the cemetery dream...but this time it was different. I fumbled for the pad and pen by the bed and began to scribble furiously. Oh Goddess, please let me remember it all, I prayed. Never in my whole life had I prayed as fervently as I did now. But never in my whole life had anything seemed this important.

My ghostly visitors had brought answers this time, each stepping from the grave with advice. It didn't matter that the sum of their words formed a riddle. I'd heard every word. And if I could just remember it all, there was no doubt in my mind that we could solve the riddle and break the tricks.

"Come on," I pled, "Come *on*!" All I needed now was the last line...the line that posed the riddle...and for the life of me, I couldn't bring it to mind.

"Damn it!" Pen still in hand, I reached over and flipped on the light, then took a look at what I'd written. It looked like hen-scratching all right, but I knew I could decipher it—as long as I did it immediately. So, ripping the page from the pad, I began to copy what I'd written. And I hoped against hope that in doing that, the last line would pop back into my head.

As I wrote, I realized that something else was different about this dream too. It had to do with the order in which the women had stepped from the grave. This time, the young white woman had emerged first and was followed by the middle-aged black woman. The young black woman stepped forth next. And the older white woman brought up the rear. After, they had again taken their original places in the four corners of the plot, with black across from black, and white across from white.

I lit a cigarette and pondered possible significance. Other than the balance of age frames and skin color—something that had been present in the original dream—I simply wasn't sure. What if it was something else entirely though? What if their positions had nothing to do with balance at all? Maybe instead of taking stations *across* from each other, they were actually posed *against* each other, indicating some sort of feud in which each pair had engaged. I just didn't know. But as everything seemed important right now, I flipped to a fresh page in the notepad, jotted down my thoughts and added a diagram of their positions.

Taking a deep drag from my cigarette, I set it in the ashtray and went back to translating the scribbled mess in front of me. I was almost done when something else came to mind, and that was the matter of which specific advice had come from whom. So I added that too and finished with the copy job.

Crushing out the cigarette, I settled back into my pillows to look at what I'd written. It was verse. The wording was simple. In fact, the whole damned thing was written in couplets, and couplets were my specialty. So why the hell couldn't I remember the last line?

"Come on, Tess," I chided myself out loud. "Any idiot should be able to figure this one out!" I knew it was something about destiny, but that didn't seem to help. Fact was that the line I needed ended with a word that rhymed with *tricks*, and there just wasn't a synonym for destiny that fit the bill. Finally, I read aloud the last line I'd written:

"But heed my warning of these tricks..."

What the hell could it be? Maybe I was going about this the wrong way. Maybe I should just jot down words that rhymed with *tricks*, and go from there. Sometimes that worked and sometimes it didn't, but with nothing to lose, I set the pen to paper again.

Hmmm...picks, sticks, kicks...no, none of that was right. Ticks, wicks, mix, flicks. I sighed heavily, knowing that those weren't right either. "Come on, Tess...you can do this," I prodded myself on, idly rubbing my temple as if the friction might actually produce coherent thought. That I was looking for a one-syllable word was apparent from the rest of my notes. But just how many were there? And why couldn't I come up with the right one? Maybe I was looking for a derivative. Something close to rhyming, but not exact. Maybe...

Too tired to think anymore, I put down my pen and glanced at the clock. "Almost time to get up anyway," I muttered to myself, turning off the alarm and hitting the switch on the coffeemaker. "If I'd fixed that coffee an hour ago, maybe..." My voiced trailed off in sudden realization. "Holy *shit*!" I yelled, grabbing my pen and getting back to work.

This just proved that my theory was right all along. Coffee was, indeed, one of the most magical tools known to humankind. And after this, no one would ever be able to convince me otherwise.

Cal stared at the notes in front of her and exhaled slowly. Then she read them again, this time paying careful attention to every word so nothing would escape her.

Three together, two as twins
Two as lovers, held by pins
Bound together are these three
As they travel through eternity
*

At the crossroads, clear the gate
Open all to hands of fate
Pray the saints to come to you
And bring help in what you need to do
*

With firm belief and open heart
Command the spirits in their part
Demand that you not be denied
Of entrance to the other side
*

Bring the bag to break trick one
Find the pins, trick two's undone
But heed my warning of these tricks:
What's laced with destiny must stay fixed

Could MawMaw have been right? Could Tess Logan—the Witch who'd begged for help—really have all the answers already? And if so, what did all this have to do with her? What sort of personal stake could she possibly have in this?

Not ready yet to give voice to her inner questions, she turned her attention to Tess.

"You got all this from a *dream*?!" Cal exclaimed.

"Yeah," I responded. "But I don't know if it's going to help us or not." I tapped the ashes from my cigarette into the ashtray and sipped my coffee before going on. "I mean, how the hell could we possibly know what's destined and what isn't? And what does that mean, 'bring the bag'?"

"I don't know." She rubbed the back of her neck thoughtfully. "Do you have some sort of amulet bag you normally use in ritual?"

I shook my head. "Nothing like that. In fact, I usually work on the fly these days," I admitted sheepishly. "And that's become so much my style of late that...well, I'm almost embarrassed to tell you this...but I haven't even bothered to hunt down my box of ritual tools since I moved here."

She picked up the pages and nodded knowingly. "I know the feeling. It's been years since I've felt the need to set up any altar other than the one for the ancestors. Sometimes, all that stuff just seems to get in the way.

"But did you ever?" she asked pointedly, her eyes meeting mine.

"Ever what?"

"Have an amulet bag that you used specifically in ritual?"

I shook my head again and fingered the handle of the cup in front of me as I searched my brain.

"Nice ring," she said, leaning over to peer at my hand. "That's gorgeous...and look at the fire in that stone! Is it an antique?"

"No...but it's got some connection to all this. And I just can't figure out what it is."

I pushed back my chair, put on a fresh pot of coffee and filled her in while we waited for it to brew.

"Amazing," she said when I'd finished. "Could I have a closer look?"

"Sure." I extended my hand.

"Well," she said as she examined the ring, "replica or not, the center stone is definitely an antique. If I had a jeweler's loupe I could probably pinpoint an exact date. But without one, I feel safe in saying circa eighteen-forty or fifty."

I was incredulous. "You've gotta be shitting me, Cal! How can you tell?"

"It's in the cut," she explained matter-of-factly. "They haven't cut stones like this in a hundred and fifty years or so. Just a second and I'll show you what I mean." She fished through her purse and retrieved a mechanical pencil. Then clicking it once and using the lead as a pointer, she held my hand to the light and gestured toward the stone.

"See these points?" she asked, moving the pencil toward an outer corner of the stone.

"Yeah."

"If you look closely, you'll see eight points per corner, forming perfect octagons at each angle of the square. Now, look at this," she said, pointing to a set of sharply beveled edges at the top. "Although this sort of cut allows for more fire, it's not done anymore either."

"Why not?"

"Because fewer cuts at both the corners and edges," she said, releasing my hand, "makes for a stronger stone. One that's less likely to shatter. Nowadays, the radiance of a diamond mostly comes from the under cuts, or those made to the bottom of the stone."

She sipped her coffee as if pondering her own words and then looked up at me. "Where did Luke get this stone?"

"I don't know."

"Well, in view of its age...and the way it affected you, we need to find out." She drummed her nails on the table. "Do you think he'd tell?"

I laughed at the question. "Why wouldn't he? It's not like we're asking what he paid for it or anything! Besides," I added, "he loves old stuff. And once he finds out that the stone is an antique, he'll be itching to talk to whoever sold it to him."

Cal made a note on the back of the pages. "The other thing I'm curious about," she continued, "is whether you've had any more flashes since you cleansed the ring?"

"Yeah," I answered. "As a matter of fact, I have."

"But they're all visions from a past life, aren't they? The same past life you experienced when Luke slipped the ring on your finger?"

"How did you..."

"Know?" she asked, finishing my question. "I didn't...it was just an educated guess. But knowing that may actually help us with your problem." Obviously feeling at home now, she paused to top off our cups then continued, "It might be possible to use the stone as a scrying device of sorts and perhaps..."

"Find out what really happened so we don't walk into this thing blind!" I interjected excitedly. Why the hell hadn't I thought of that? "Oh, Cal...you're a *genius*! Do you think we oughta try it *now*?!"

Waiting for her answer was a moot point, as a quick glance at the clock had already done the job. The others would be here any minute. And as if on cue, the first of a series of knocks sounded from the front door.

Liza had arrived with a huge basket of gourmet coffees, and once the introductions were made, Cal excused herself and walked outside. Her reasoning was twofold. For one thing, the basket was obviously a peace offering—and since anything even remotely resembling good will between Tess and Liza had been, up to this point, tenuous at best—a bit of privacy was a necessary component to the task at hand. But even more important than that, Cal needed to think. And she couldn't do that unless she had a few minutes to herself.

Her thoughts traveled back to her last conversation with MawMaw; more specifically what she'd said about Tess Logan, and she'd certainly been right there. There *was* more to the woman than met the eye—a lot more—and she suddenly wished that she could get inside her head. Of course, she knew full well that Tess would answer whatever questions she asked. It wasn't that. It was that she just didn't know what the questions were at this point, and that was a problem. Even worse, she had this niggling feeling that time was of the essence here. And if that was so, she might not have the time to figure them out.

The niggle had first breathed life when she'd stood in the crossroads between the two cemeteries at the plantation and had gained strength with the appearance of her own visions. She'd seen a woman face down in the dirt—right in the center of the intersecting paths—the axe blade buried deep in her back. But as awful as that was, what disturbed her even more was the bloody red felt bag that lay just beyond the woman's reach and the teen-aged girl who'd bent down to retrieve it.

Just who was that girl? And what had she done with the bag? Had she buried it with the woman? Tossed it in the creek? Maybe put it some place for safe-keeping? What?!

Now you be's getting somewhere, Little Missy...

After yesterday's conversation, MawMaw was the last person she'd expected to pipe up, and the sudden interjection startled Cal enough to jump.

"I-I am?"

Yes'm, sho' is. You just keep a'studyin' on that.

"Studying on what, MawMaw? All I've got is questions, and..."

Lawd Gawd, chile, what be's the matter with you? Questions got answers. And you studies them questions hard enough, them answers be's...

"...poppin' up like corn on the fire," Cal finished, lapsing into the Southern drawl she'd worked so hard to erase. "I understand all that, MawMaw. But I don't think I've got much time here. Something tells me that these tricks..."

Just think hard on that chile and that bag, Little Missy. What be's familiar and what don't. What you seen and what you ain't. And Little Missy?

"Yes ma'am?"

You remembers what I told you. Just use what you got and use what you have.

"But.." It was too late. MawMaw had gone as quickly as she'd come, something she'd mastered in life and only seemed to have improved upon in death.

Cal sat down on the porch swing and tapped a cigarette from the pack in her hand. She rocked back and forth in an easy rhythm and pondered the possibilities. Then conjuring up the vision at the crossroads again in her mind's eye, she suddenly realized several things that hadn't even occurred to her. It was in the girl's face. It was in the construction of that bag. But more than anything else, it was in the fact that MawMaw hadn't sashayed back into her life to tease her, insult her or make her feel stupid. No, not at all. MawMaw's reappearance had a purpose—she really *had* come back to help—and paying attention to her impromptu messages, no matter how cryptic, was the only way to solve this thing.

Still deep in thought, Cal exhaled a stream of smoke and watched it fade into the air. The girl. The bag. They really did look familiar. But why? She knew full well that she'd never seen them before. Or had she? And if so, how? Or where? Or why?

The thought that she was starting to sound like a newspaper reporter hot on the trail of some big story made her laugh. And as she flicked the burning coal from her cigarette, an entirely different vision came to mind. A vision of Great Aunt Marguerite, her most opinionated relative, who'd always talked ninety-to-nothing, smoked like there was no tomorrow and had possessed a laugh more infectious than any contagion known to humankind. Watching the coal burn out in the flower bed, she remembered the day that Auntie M had gotten on a tangent about only smoking cigarettes half-way down and how those who didn't subscribe to that method were just asking for trouble. Her stance hadn't had anything to do with good health. No, it was a matter of reverence to the ancestors, of giving them the comfort of a good smoke too. And as a result, Auntie had always kept a cut glass ashtray on her altar, relighting the half-smoked butts to burn there as an offering to be enjoyed by the ancestors after their evening meal.

Thinking back on that, Cal smiled and tucked the butt back into her pack. After all, what could it hurt? And if it helped, so much the better. It was always good to keep the ancestors happy, and doing so might even coerce them to come to her aid—and MawMaw's.

Letting her mind wander elsewhere, even for a few minutes, had been a welcome respite. In fact, Cal wished she could stay outside and reminisce about Auntie M forever. She'd been a wonderful, bubbly sort of woman, the most fun-loving of all MawMaw's sisters, the one with the most magical ability, the one who had...

For the love of the ancestors! The realization hit Cal like a ton of bricks. Could it be?! Surely not. And, yet...there it was...screaming in her mind, insisting on total recall and demanding that she refuel her memory banks and produce the pictorial evidence it required.

Slamming her eyes shut, she brought the vision to mind, then shaking her head in disbelief, expelled a heavy sigh. Absolutely unbelievable! Never in a million years would it have occurred to her. Not in her wildest imagination would she have dreamed it. Still, it was as tangible as the clothes on her back and just as well within her reach.

"No half-smoked cigarette for you tonight, Auntie M," Cal whispered gratefully. "You deserve better than that. A lot better. Keep this up, and I might just buy you a whole damned pack!"

No sooner than she'd made a mental note to pick up a pack of her aunt's favorite brand at the corner store, the bargain was struck. But as is often the way of the ancestors, Marguerite's acceptance didn't come by way of words. Or pictures. Or even thoughts meandering through Cal's head. Instead, it came by way of warm, infectious laughter. That delightfully glorious laughter that no one had heard in at least twenty years.

"Yeah...I see it, Boss. Gimme just a minute." Hector Thibodeaux peered at the strip of duct tape under Cal's desk from his position on the floor and wondered if he could reach it without hitting his head. Always in a hurry and inherently accident-prone, his vast assortments of bumps, bruises and abrasions no longer concerned those who knew him well. They were simply a part of his life, a part of who he was—Murphy's Law in the flesh—something so apparent to Cal, she'd affectionately nicknamed him "Hex" on the very first day he'd been in her employ.

While this sort of clumsiness might have posed a problem for any other anthropologist, especially one who specialized in cultural artifacts and the religious antiquities of long dead civilizations, it wasn't for Cal. She knew value when she saw it, and his came in the ability to handle even the most difficult tasks with ease. Hex was efficient, organized and so detail-oriented that nothing—not once in all the ten years they'd been together—had ever escaped his discerning eye. The key was not to let him touch anything of value; or better yet, nothing but pens and papers.

Cradling the phone between his ear and shoulder, Hex rolled over on his back, scraped the tape loose with his fingernail and freed the key.

"Got it, Boss. Now what?"

"Watch your head!" Cal teased and waited for the inevitable crack of wood against skull.

"Yeah, yeah..." He chuckled as he scooted out from under the desk. Then still lying on his back—there was no way he was going to let her *hear* him hit his head, especially after her admonishment—he repeated the question.

"The package is under my bed, about center of the headboard. Just pack it up for overnight delivery. And be sure you send it out today, okay?"

"Okay, Boss. Anything more?"

"Yeah, Hex."

"What?"

"Don't touch anything else while you're there," she quipped affectionately.

Hex was still laughing when the pile of folders on the edge of the desk inched forward and spilled their contents all over his head.

Sally was already passing out sets of type-written notes by the time Cal made her way back to the kitchen, and once I'd made the introductions, she got right down to business.

"What I've just handed out," she began, "are brief recaps of all of our regression sessions tied up into one neat little package. The only one missing..." she said, pausing to sigh and roll her eyes in my direction, "...belongs to Tess, who so far, hasn't seen fit to grace my couch."

"B-but with everything else going on I..."

She cut me off with a wave of her hand, chuckled and took the rest of the group along for the ride. "I know you haven't, Dear. But I just couldn't resist." The twinkle in her eyes eased my angst, and I began to smile in spite of myself.

"However, we need to get that taken care of as soon as humanly possible, okay?"

I nodded and she went on. "There aren't many real surprises here. In fact, since most of this pretty much just confirms what we'd already guessed, there's no point in rehashing it all right now. Instead, it's probably better for everybody to read the notes at their leisure before our next meeting, which is tomorrow afternoon at the plantation.

"But," she continued after a sip of coffee, "a couple of interesting things did crop up. For one thing, we now have a name for Liza's previous incarnation—her name was Belle—and we also have some interesting information about her death. It seems that Jonah Barnes..."

At this point, Luke turned pale and clutched my hand. It was obvious that he didn't want to hear this. He didn't want it brought up. But more important, he didn't want to have to relive it. Especially not in front of everybody at the table.

"...did *not* kill Belle. In fact..."

"W-what?!" Luke was incredulous. "But I...I saw...I mean...I..." he stammered, rising from his chair.

"Oh, for pity's sake, Luke," Sally exclaimed with a chuckle, "calm down...I'm getting to that!" And then, looking over at me and pointing an accusatory finger, she announced that trying to keep up with my coffee-drinking habit was obviously turning our normally laid-back friend into someone she no longer recognized—and that it was my responsibility to either curb his caffeine intake or cut it off entirely. When that brought a round of laughter that included Luke, I wanted to kiss her on the spot. Instead though, I just settled for an appreciative wink in her direction and called it good.

"Now that Luke is breathing again," she continued, "one of our sessions confirmed that although Jonah Barnes probably went to his grave believing that he was a vicious murderer, that was more than likely not the case. It seems that someone else—a slave named Carl—murdered Belle for reasons of his own...reasons that aren't clear as of yet. But we do know..."

I watched Brian squirm in his chair while Sally talked, adjusting his weight this way and that. He pulled his chair up to the table and back again, then finally got up and walked over to the kitchen sink. His face was red as a beet, and I was just about to ask if he wanted a glass of water when he turned on the tap and helped himself.

Luke leaned forward. "Reasons that aren't clear? What does that mean?"

"It means," Brian answered shakily, still leaning on the sink with his back to the group, "that I have to undergo at least one more session to find out." Then without another word, he set his glass in the sink and stomped out of the room.

"Holy shit! What the hell was *that* all about?" Luke finally broke the silence, and I was glad he had. To say that we were shocked at Brian's reaction was putting it mildly. And after Chloe had rushed off after him, we'd just stared at each other in amazement, our mouths hanging open. Still, no one answered.

Luke tried again. "Do you think we oughta go see about him? See if we can help?"

"Maybe we should give him some time," I answered, pausing to light a cigarette. "If anyone can get to the bottom of this, it's Chloe. And I think our appearance right now may be seen as more of an intrusion than anything else.

"So," I said, looking directly at Sally, "let's get down to business. I'll update Chloe and Brian later."

Sally looked at me in disbelief. It was obvious that she either didn't agree with me or thought she'd misunderstood. Either way, it didn't matter. Regardless of how her findings had affected Brian, we still had work to do and time was short. A nod of my head prompted her onward. Expelling a heavy sigh, she went on.

"Okay," she began, "If you'll look at the first page of my notes, you'll see what I've come up with as far as who we were in the past life in question. There's a section listing our names in this life along with those in the eighteen-sixties and a brief summary of who those people were. The next few pages summarize our regressions, but..."

Cal scanned the list, flipped through the rest of the pages, then scanned the list again. Obviously, she was searching for something—something that wasn't there—and the peculiar look on her face was enough to stop Sally in mid-sentence.

"Something wrong?" she asked.

"Are you sure this is a complete list?"

"Well," Sally said, "I *think* it is. Why do you ask?

"Because I was under the impression that someone else was involved...a teenaged girl..."

"The only one who fits the bill—at least, the only one I'm sure of—would be Nellie. We went through various stages of her life during Chloe's regression, and..."

Cal shook her head, that peculiar look still on her face. "No, the person I'm looking for couldn't be Nellie," she said, "since she's black."

Liza looked at her with wide eyes and leaned across the table. "Do you know something that we *don't*?"

"Not really," Cal countered. Then turning her attention to Sally again, she said, "Sorry for the interruption. Now what were you saying about the hand-outs?"

"No problem," Sally said. "The pages that follow are probably the most important though, as they summarize our past- life connections and our interacting roles—at least, from what I could gather..."

But Cal didn't hear a word she was saying. She was still considering the teenaged girl she'd seen in her vision. Who was she? Why had she grabbed the bag? And what was her connection to all of this? There was more to this than met the eye, all right. A lot more. And a quick glance at Liza proved that she thought so too.

"Oh my God, Bri'...what on Earth is the mat..."

"Not now, Chloe," Brian snapped, leaning over the tailgate and gripping it for leverage. His stomach churned, his knees were weak, and beads of cold sweat bathed his body. He thought he might faint or vomit, or both. It was definitely not a good time to have this conversation. Truth be told, he didn't want to have it at all. Not now. Not later. Not ever.

He'd spent his whole life—at least this one—fiercely protecting the masses. On more than one occasion, he'd put his own life on the line to shield them from harm. He'd prided himself on delivering them safely from horrors only visible from his side of the badge—horrors devised and perpetuated by greed and hatred and all the other components that fed the malevolence in this world. And now to find out that he was part of that evil? Well, it was too much to bear. It made a mockery of his life...

"Bri'?"

...that's what it did. How could a spirit who could murder so easily and so viciously ever truly protect anyone? How could he ever—even for an instant—have thought that he, of all people...

"*Bri'?!*"

...could ever save the world? He wasn't part of the solution...he was part of the problem. A real part. Hell...maybe he and others like him were the whole problem.

"Are you all *right*?!"

All right? Now, that was a stupid question—even for someone as naïve as Chloe. Of course, he wasn't all right. But the problem had nothing to do with the shortness of breath, the numbness crawling up his arm, or even the fire that seemed to take on a life of its own and was burning his chest into ashes. That was all secondary. It was the fact that he was a failure—didn't Chloe get it at all?—and he intended to tell her exactly that.

The panicked look on Chloe's face was the last thing he saw before falling into the void. Somewhere in the distance, her scream—a sad reminder of the evil that he was and always would be—pierced the shadows. But it was too late to come back now. The darkness was courting him with all the flirtatious intrigue it could muster, and he embraced it as if tomorrow might never dawn. And for Brian Dawson, the absence of tomorrow was a distinct possibility.

CHAPTER 12

Cal plumped the pillows behind her, eased back into them and eyed the bottle of Rhum Barbancourt on the nightstand. Yeah...it was usually reserved for the Ancestors, but surely she, too, deserved the best that money could buy. Didn't she? After all, she'd be an Ancestor as well someday, and it was certainly better to enjoy that heavenly nectar while she could savor it fully. Smiling at her suddenly skewed logic—practicality did have its limits—and at how quickly she'd been able to justify the treat, she poured three fingers of the Haitian delicacy into a glass and took a sip.

It had certainly been an interesting few days, she thought, swilling the warm liquid about in her mouth. First, there was the trip out to the plantation cemetery, the details of which she hadn't bothered to share with anyone—not even Tess. Truthfully, except for the vision of the girl, there wasn't much to share. It was set up like most of the other plantation cemeteries she'd visited over the years, with a makeshift crossroads separating those who'd owned their bodies from those who hadn't. Judging from the tingle that began at the crown of her head and traveled swiftly down her spine as she stood in its center though, one thing was certain: This particular crossroads had served as more than just an ordinary pathway or a simple division of the classes. It was not only a place where magic had been defined and performed and loosed into the world, but sacred ground as well. It was a place of religious ritual, where Voudon met Catholicism, where the saints and lwas had connected and interacted in perfect harmony.

Another item of interest had to do with the actual intersection of the crossroads. It wasn't in the center of the grounds at all. Instead, it was located toward the front edge of the plot in close proximity to a body of water: a creek that bent its head toward the section reserved for the enslaved and then doubled back to flow on to parts unknown. The setting and location had definitely peaked Cal's interest, as it would have that of any other seasoned cultural anthropologist, for it provided insight into those who had used the cemetery for purposes other than burying their dead.

Since all hard labor fell under their domain, it was a given that the enslaved had formed the crossroads themselves. But because water is seen as a power source of great magnitude by both practitioners of hoodoo and the Afro-Caribbean religions, chances were that they'd also personally chosen the location. As the creek was literally only a stone's throw away, such a spot gave them ready access to the water and its power for fixing tricks and discharging their magic, as well as for breaking them later if necessary. In addition, a thick line of oaks, cedars and cottonwoods hid the creek from view, giving it a feeling of seclusion and secured the site from prying eyes—all of which made it the perfect spot for magical work.

Now, she wished she'd had a chance to really explore the cemetery itself. But with the sun going down and no flashlight in hand, there hadn't been any time for that. Still, it was certainly worth checking out. And making a mental note to do just that, she took another sip from her glass and moved her thoughts toward today's events, the information they'd brought and the questions they'd raised.

It had all started with Tess' dream, its set of clues and the antique diamond with visionary abilities. And while she was still mulling over the dream-channeled poem and its meaning, at least Luke had been able to shed some light on the origin of stone. Apparently handed down through his family, he'd found it in the safe deposit box. And when he realized that it was the same center stone from the ring depicted on Lucinda's hand in an old portrait, he'd had it set identically for Tess. Of course, he had no idea what had happened to the original setting or where or from whom the stone was initially purchased.

But chances were good that none of that really mattered. Fact was, the stone itself, had belonged to Lucinda; and as a result, it had not only picked up her personal energies but quite possibly, had recorded certain events in her life. Stranger things had been known to happen, and if the stone's recent foray into Lucinda's life was any indication of its power, it might prove very useful in resolving some of the mysteries at hand.

But that wasn't all the day had brought. There was the strange vision of the girl who'd made off with the mojo bag and the visit from Auntie M. Well...there was the visit from MawMaw too...but since she'd been popping in more and more frequently of late, that could hardly be considered intriguing anymore, she thought with a chuckle.

The most interesting part of the day, though, had to do with Brian Dawson's strange reaction to his past-life regression. She'd never known anyone to respond so strongly to that sort of thing—especially not when it involved details more than a hundred years old. He'd been so upset, in fact, that he'd actually worked himself right into a stroke. And if they'd been any slower about getting him to the emergency room, his immediate sleeping arrangements might have involved a metal gurney at the morgue instead of a one-night stay at the hospital. Brian Dawson was a fortunate man indeed.

Cal took another sip and stretched as she felt the rich liquid slide down her throat and warm her from the inside out. Then setting the glass on the nightstand, she moved to the makeshift altar on the round table by the window and lit another cigarette for Auntie M.

"So...are you going to tell me just how we wound up with that bag or what?"

She didn't really expect an answer, but out of respect, she waited a few seconds for one just the same.

"Maybe you could just tell me who the girl is and how she's connected to us, Auntie," Cal finally continued pleasantly. "I kept my end of the bargain, you know. You got your pack of cigarettes. God knows you've been chain-smoking them ever since I got here," she said with a chuckle. "And I'd think that the least you could do is to..."

The answer didn't come in words. There wasn't even a sound. And yet, there it was, as Sally's handout fluttered to the floor at her feet.

Oh, all *right!*" Cal, whose mood had now changed from playful to mildly frustrated, snatched the sheets from the floor and wondered if all Ancestors were as aggravating as hers. Didn't *any* of Them ever offer a straight answer? Or was the speaking-in-riddles thing just part of the fun of being an Ancestor? Maybe screwing with folks on the physical plane was one of the perks. They should, after all, have *some* fun, she thought. Even if it *was* at her expense.

"I know...I know..." she responded, shaking her head sideways and rolling her eyes toward the ceiling. "'Use what you've got and use what you have.' And for all practical purposes, this is it," she said, gesturing with the handout, "isn't it?!"

The coal on the end of the cigarette in the ashtray brightened in response, a signal that she'd finally understood. There wouldn't be any more help from the Ancestors on this one. Not any direct help anyway. She was going to have to figure it out for herself. And no amount of Barbancourt, cigarettes or Godiva truffles was going to change that.

Resignedly, Cal positioned herself against the pillows again and scanned the list of people involved and their reincarnations. There really weren't any surprises. Luke had been Jonah Barnes, Chloe had been

Nellie McGee, and even though it hadn't been proven yet, everything pointed to the fact that Tess had been Lucinda. The other key players were the slaves involved. And since Cal knew less about them than the others, she flipped through the pages to their stories.

Sally Nicewander's incarnation—a woman named Mattie— headed the list. Cal lit a cigarette, inhaled deeply and poured herself another drink. Then she set about the business of making Mattie's acquaintance.

Brian Dawson eyed the apparatus with distaste. It looked like a goddamned coffin...that's what...and if they thought he was climbing in that thing, they were crazy as hell. He'd seen pet crates bigger than that, and he wasn't about to climb into one of those either.

Looking much like a caged animal, his eyes darted this way and that but finally found their focus on Chloe. "Now let me get this straight," he said with as much calm as he could muster. "You want me to lie down in there...in that little bitty tube...and while I'm in there, you want me to be still. I can't move or wiggle or even scratch my nose."

Chloe sighed heavily and braced herself. For all of Brian's tough guy act, he was scared shitless of tight spaces. So scared, in fact, that closets, sheds and enclosed stairwells were iffy at best. And elevators? Well...you could just forget about them.

Damn it! Why hadn't she thought of this? Why hadn't she just asked the doctor to give him a sedative before bringing him down here? It would've been so easy to avoid all this. But it was too late for that now, she thought, running her fingers through her hair and trying to figure out how to calm the storm that he'd put on to brew.

"But that's not all," he continued with gathering momentum. "No siree, Bob! You actually have the *balls* to expect me to re*lax* in that goddamned thing! Have you lost your fucking *mind*?!"

She looked at her husband with amazing calm and smiled sweetly. "Come on, Bri'," she said softly. "It's not going to be that bad. They'll just give you a sedative..."

"Not that bad?! How the hell could *you* know? You're not the one with claustrophobia. You're not the one who feels..." His voice trailed off and he looked like he might cry.

Chloe put her arms around him and looked into his eyes with adoration. "Look, Darlin'...I love you and want you to be around for a while. If I didn't, this wouldn't matter so much," she said gently. "We just need to make sure that everything's okay. And running this CAT scan is the best way to do that."

"The doctors think I'm fine," he retorted, looking at the machine fearfully as all common sense irrevocably took flight. "If they didn't, I wouldn't be going home today. So, why the hell are you insisting on this fucking CAT scan? Do you just *enjoy* the thought of me being tortured? Is that it?" He knew he was being unreasonable. Hell, he knew he was being a regular ass. But at this point, he just couldn't help himself. He was not climbing into that motorized coffin, and there was nothing they could do to make him. "Well," he continued sarcastically, "I don't care what you might or might not enjoy. I'm not having this test run and that's that."

This was too much, even for Chloe. The CAT scan was important, and Brian was going through with it, no matter what. And if calmness didn't work, she thought squaring her shoulders and clearing her throat, she'd just have to try another tack.

"Don't you *dare* to pull that shit on me, Brian Dawson!" she thundered with enough venom to make Brian jump. "You are *not* a child. You're a *man*. And you're *going* to have that CAT scan...even if it kills us *both*!"

"You're right," he retorted. "I'm a man...a grown man...and *I* can decide what I'll do and what I won't. And I'm *not*..."

She cut him off with a wave of her hand. "Please don't make them restrain you, Bri'..."

"*Restrain* me?! That'll be a cold day in hell," he snorted. "I'm a fucking deputy sheriff. Or have you forgotten that too?"

Mattie's story had proven good reading and not only offered some insight into the problems at hand, but into the life of a very interesting woman. The mother of Carl, she'd also been the property of Etta Blodgett McGee until her death. After that, she'd belonged to Lucinda Barnes but only for a short while. It seemed that Lucinda had given all the slaves freedom with the announcement of the Emancipation

Proclamation, even though Missouri state residents weren't bound to do so. Still, Mattie had stayed on out of loyalty—loyalty that was born of the fact that Lucinda had literally saved her life when she'd come under suspicion for Etta's murder.

Mattie also had a real sense of loyalty when it came to the rest of the slave community. Fact was, only they knew what it was like to be property. Only they knew what it was like to be treated unfairly or blamed for actions beyond their control. And for all practical purposes, Mattie was the glue that held them together as family.

That's why it was so hard to stand up against Belle and her plans. She knew what Belle had gone through. She knew what Belle was feeling. And she knew that all of them—Belle included—deserved a better life than they had. Even so, she also knew the difference between right and wrong. And the scheme that Belle had cooked up? Well, not even the trimmings were edible.

The gist of the story was that Mattie had, indeed, laid a trick to bind Jonah and Lucinda together for eternity. But the decision had neither been easy, taken lightly, nor made for the reasons one might think. Fact was, it had nothing to do with ensuring that the couple didn't fall out of love; instead, it was all about keeping Nellie from harm at Belle's hands. Interestingly enough, it never occurred to Mattie that Nellie might not be saddled with Belle as her new stepmother. And knowing that Belle would never stand for anyone sharing Jonah's attention—or money—and would do whatever it took to have both all for herself, it only stood to reason that Nellie's best chance for a reasonably happy life hinged on Lucinda and Jonah staying together.

The other, more important thing that didn't occur to Mattie was that the trick she laid wouldn't keep Belle from killing Lucinda. She thought that binding the couple together would make separation of any sort totally impossible, something that even death itself couldn't manage. Thus, she not only saw this trick as a way to ensure a good life for Nellie, but also as a way to save Lucinda's life and repay the debt owed to the woman who'd saved hers. Best of all, it was something she could do in good conscience. By figuring a way around working magic against Belle, she also kept loyalties intact. And that meant she could sleep at night.

Unfortunately, things hadn't panned out quite as she'd expected. And Mattie had gone to her grave thinking she was a failure: both as a Conjure Woman and as a human being.

Cal finished the last of her drink, tapped out a cigarette and lit up. Poor Mattie. How awful to give so much and get so little. How awful to live with such a conflicting sense of ethics and struggle so hard to find equitable solutions. And then to still die thinking she was a failure? Well...that was the most awful of all. Especially since she really *had* accomplished her prime objective: Nellie's life had worked out just fine; in fact, it couldn't have worked any better if she'd planned it herself.

Inadvertently, Mattie had also accomplished something else. And that something was even more important in the here and now. She'd managed to unravel one of those elusive poetic clues: There was no reason in the world to keep Luke and Tess joined by the bonds of magic. No reason at all.

Or was there?

A satisfied smile played on Chloe's lips. Cold day in hell or not, Brian Dawson was strapped to the table inside the imaging tube and the CAT scan was now in full swing. Yes, getting him there had been a pain in the ass but not nearly the pain she'd first imagined. He hadn't stomped out. He hadn't torn the place apart. He hadn't even thrown a hand or threatened a life. Of course, it had taken some creative problem solving. But since creative problem solving was definitely her forte, she'd certainly been up to the task.

Still, she didn't like telling bald-faced lies. Stretching the truth was one thing. Omitting a few facts to get what she wanted was okay too. But telling Brian that the Versed injection—the one that had gotten him on the table—was nothing more than a sedative to keep him from having another stroke? Well, that was another story.

True enough, Versed *was* a sedative. Brian *had* worked himself up into a wall-eyed fit, so it did stand to reason that his blood pressure was high. And everybody, including Brian, knew that high blood pressure was the chief culprit when it came to stroke and heart attack.

Chloe crossed her legs, tapped her fingers nervously on the arm of the chair and tried to convince herself that the lie she'd told was okay—at least in this particular case. She had, after all, done what was necessary for Brian's health. Hadn't she? And that's what was important. Wasn't it? No one could fault her for seeing to it that Brian followed the doctor's orders, especially when the orders in question were in his best interest. But the way she'd gone about it really bothered her. She didn't want to be a liar. And as of thirty-one minutes ago, that's exactly what she was.

Damn it, she thought, why hadn't she just told him that the injection was to lower his blood pressure?

Because, answered the voice in her head, *that's not the truth either, and you know it. You know damned good and well why you told that lie. Besides...Brian Dawson doesn't give a shit about his blood pressure. But he damned sure doesn't want to have another stroke.*

But she should've thought of something else...

And what good would that have done? What else would've gotten him on that table? The truth? Just answer me that, it snorted. And then, that little voice in her head—the one that had always been so good at easing her conscience and rationalizing her actions—did something it had never done. It screamed, *"Liar! Liar! Liar!"* at the top of its lungs.

Chloe shook her head in disbelief. "What on earth is *wrong* with you?" she muttered under her breath. "You're supposed to make me feel better, not worse."

I don't have time for liars, it announced calmly. *Especially not those who lie to themselves. And I don't know anyone else who does either,* it added with a snort.

Chloe opened her mouth to respond, but it was too late. That little voice in her head—the one that had always helped her justify her every action—was gone. And now there was nothing left to do but keep company with her guilt, stare at the clock and listen to the incessant thunk, clang and whir of the imaging machine.

Hex breathed a sigh of relief and started his car. Getting that package for Cal hadn't been as easy as he'd thought. The truth of the matter was that he'd never been inside her house alone. And although he'd always liked the place and felt comfortable there, such was no longer the case. In fact, it was now quite obvious that the house really didn't like him. Not one little bit.

It was one of those gorgeous monstrosities in the Garden District: a house that causes drool to slip from the mouth of the most discriminating tourist and kindles an unbridled craving in those residents with enough money to own the city. It hadn't started out that way though. Cal had gotten the thing at auction for a wish and a prayer. And back then, it was in such a state of disrepair that no one—not even a bum off the street—would've dreamt of darkening its doors; in fact, it looked worse than anything the Addams Family could've concocted, had they drawn up the plans themselves. But Cal was not to be deterred. Little by little, she'd renovated that architectural horror and transformed it into one of the most stunning buildings in the whole neighborhood.

Who'd have ever thought it would've made the cover of *Southern Living*? But it had. And when the reporter asked what part of the renovations had been most difficult—there were many, including leveling the whole mess so it wouldn't sink into the ground or fall over into the street onto somebody's sister—she'd dismissed the question with a wave of her hand and that contagious laughter, which only she could spout. "Just needed a little love," she'd said between chuckles, "and a good dusting off to clear its pores."

Well, one thing was for sure, Hex thought as he rubbed the sore spots on his head and gave the house one last glance. It had pores, all right. And skin too. That thing was a living, breathing entity with a gazillion eyes and ears and the strength of a small army of mad women. He'd been kicked and bitten and scratched. He'd been thrown against the wall and knocked off his feet. And when he'd persisted in retrieving the package Cal had asked for? Well, that damned bed of hers had nearly snatched him bald and then popped him on the head a few times for good measure.

A quick glance in the rearview mirror confirmed his worst fear. He looked like he'd been in a fight with a buzz saw. His eye was swollen, his face was scratched, and the bumps on his head were beginning to take on a life of their own. Just exactly how was he going to be able to explain *this* when he got back to the office? Who'd believe that a house was responsible for putting him in this shape? Nobody, that's who. Not even Cal herself.

As he put the car in reverse and backed down the driveway, he decided it was best to keep his mouth shut and not say anything at all about the episode. That way, they'd all just worry about the state of his health without a single thought as to the state of his mind.

But Cal was another story. He wasn't just going to tell her about that man-hating house of hers, he was going to paint the story in full, vivid, living Technicolor, so there was no doubt of her getting the picture. And if she thought he was crazy? Well, so be it. She'd dealt with his clumsiness, and she'd just have to deal with this too.

Then as he turned left on Canal and entered the fringe of the Quarter traffic, he made another decision. Boss or no boss, he was never going back in that house again. Not for love nor money, nor an abundance of both. Not even if Cal was there. And if that pissed her off? Well, she'd just have to get over it. His mind was made up, and there wasn't anything that the incomparable Ms. Jones—or anybody else—could do about it.

So, if there wasn't any reason to not break the trick that connected Tess and Luke, why wouldn't that niggle at the base of Cal's skull—the one that always alerted her to things gone awry—go away? Something still wasn't right, she thought, lighting another cigarette and releasing a cloud of smoke into the air. Had she missed something? Or was it just that the other possibility—the possibility that Jonah and Belle might really belong together—seemed so outrageous?

Maybe the real answer didn't lay in any of the above, she reasoned, taking another drag. Maybe it was something else entirely. Something she hadn't thought of. Could it be that neither trick should be broken? Could it be as simple as that?

The unmistakable snort that answered her last question belonged to MawMaw. Cal let out a tired sigh and tossed the sheaf of papers aside. "So, you *are* still around," she said, taking one last drag and crushing out the cigarette butt. "Got anything else for me?" she asked pointedly. "Or are you just hanging around to watch me make a fool of myself?"

A second snort filled the air and then, there was nothing.

"Well," Cal answered disgustedly, turning off the light and staring through the darkness at what might be the ceiling when her eyes adjusted, "there's a fool born every day. And I certainly hope that your response is in no way an indication that you've raised one."

Desiree stared at her mother with wide amber eyes. "What you talkin' 'bout, Mama?" She was fourteen, pretty, and she bore her mother's smooth caramel skin. She had sense enough to know that white men in the South never married black women. If they had, most of the pickininnies she knew wouldn't be running around without daddies right now. And that was a fact.

Her mother looked at her worried face and laughed. "You knows what I be's talkin' 'bout. I's talkin' 'bout gittin' us some proppity. An' when I's done...

"But Mama! It ain't right! You cain't be goin' 'round an' stealin' other wimmen's...

"Wha's you mean, stealin'? Wha's you mean, ain't right? I'll show you what ain't right," she screeched, her eyes catching fire as she pulled her nightgown over her head and threw it on the floor. "Dis!" she thundered, turning around to expose the scars on her back. They were large and deep with keloid tissue so tough they looked like long blisters on the surrounding flesh. "Take you a good look, heah? Dis be's what happen t'us f'jus' breathin' de air, less'n we got some white man t'take keer a us. You want dat t'happen t'you?!

"Stealin'?" Her voice rose an octave, though it didn't seem possible. "I ain't stole nuthin'! It's dat white bitch in de big house who done all de stealin'. He be's mine b'fore she come along, a'wringin' dem hands an' a'battin' dem eyes an' a'blubberin' 'bout cain't make do. I ain't stealin' nuthin'," she spat, getting right in her daughter's face and lowering her voice to a stage whisper. "I jes' be takin' back wha's mine!"

As Belle tossed the gown back over her head, Desiree shifted in her chair and blinked back tears, not knowing whether to speak or not. She didn't want to make her mother any madder than she already was. She didn't want to seem disrespectful or sassy—a whipping was sure to follow if her mother even thought she might have been—and at the same time, questions burned in her mind. Questions that would never be answered if she just sat there like a bump on a log. Curiosity overtaking good sense, she finally found the courage to open her mouth.

"Mama?" she began timidly.

"Hunh?"

"Jes' how's you 'spect t'do dat?"

Belle fingered the bag around her neck and grinned a sly and evil grin. "I still be's studyin' on dat, Chile" she said, taking her

daughter's face in her hands. "But I kin tell you dis much. I be's gettin'
back wha's mine. Yes'm...I sho' nuf will. Eben if it mean slittin' her
throat like de pig she is an' puttin' her in de groun' myse'f!"

Cal sat straight up in the bed, fighting for air and her heart
pounding like no tomorrow. "Oh my *God*!" she gasped. The nations sack
that Hex was shipping wasn't a nation's sack at all. It was a trick—the
very trick that had fixed Jonah and Belle together for eternity—and it had
been handed down through her family. Did that mean that she herself
was descended from Belle and her daughter, Desiree? Did that mean...

A shrill cackle resounded through the room, causing Cal to jump
again, and this time, nearly out of her skin. "MawMaw?" she whispered.

Now then, Little Missy...I b'lieve you be's cookin' with gas!

Liza was in a foul mood and had been ever since she'd gotten up
that morning. Truth be told though, that wasn't exactly so. Oh, she was
in a foul mood all right—there was no question about that—but it had
started at yesterday's meeting.

Why was everything always about Tess? It was Tess this and
Tess that, and nobody else seemed to matter. Didn't anybody care that
she was the victim of a spell too? Of course not! Didn't anybody
understand that if it hadn't been for her and her good sense, Luke might
not have ever even gotten to know that woman? Not likely! Didn't they
realize the trouble that she'd gone to for her brother and all she'd
sacrificed to keep him out of trouble and on the straight and narrow? And
how, if it hadn't been for her, the family business would have gone right
to hell in a hand basket? Absolutely not.

Fact was, nobody in her world seemed to give a shit about
anything anymore *but* Tess. If they had, they'd have told her to back off
when she'd offered to file those charges. But nobody'd done that. It
hadn't even occurred to them that *she* was Luke's *sister* and as such, she
might be more than a little upset at the thought of him being victimized
by that Witch! No...that hadn't occurred to them at all. The only thing on
their minds was their precious little Tess, her precious little rights and
her precious little property. And she, for one, was sick to death of it.

The worst offender of all, was her very own brother. They'd
always had a special bond and had always been the best of friends.

Maybe it was because they were twins. Maybe it wasn't. But whatever the case, he'd always treated her as if she were the most important thing in his world. At least until Tess had come along. And now, he couldn't even be bothered to give her the time of day.

Come to think of it, it had been weeks since they'd had lunch together or so much as shared a cup of coffee. They didn't even talk at the office anymore unless they absolutely had to. Even after she'd done everything he'd asked her to, he was still treating her like some insignificant wad of paper. What kind of crap was that?!

And what kind of crap, for that matter, were their living arrangements? Why the hell had *he* inherited the plantation while she'd only gotten some money? Why the hell was *he* living in the big house scot-free while she was paying rent on an apartment. You'd have thought he'd have done more than just offer her a room there. You'd have thought that, at the very least, he'd have *insisted* upon it. Hell...if he'd given a damn about her at all, he'd have just signed over the deed and given her that place free and clear.

But no...not her loving brother! Greedy is what he was. And now he was going to marry that bitch, Tess, and she was not only going to move right into the big house but own the goddamned thing as well. A house that should've been rightfully hers. And all that plantation property that should've been hers too.

A cruel smile played across Liza's lips as she thumbed hastily through her Rolodex. "Well, we'll just see about that, darling Brother," she said, stabbing her attorney's number into the keypad on the phone. "We'll just see about that, indeed."

CHAPTER 13

"**Y**ou want me to do *what*?!"

Hearing Cal's voice on the other end of the line was surprise enough without this; enough so that Chloe wasn't sure she'd heard correctly.

"I'd like for you to go back through the census records at the library, and see if you can track some of the people that the Barnes family enslaved," she repeated nonchalantly. "I know it's not going to be easy, but..."

"I'm not even sure it can be done, Cal," Chloe said with a sigh. "You know that slaves often came and went without recorded bills of sale—especially in this area. There were no certificates of record at all for them. Not for birth or marriage or death. I'd have better luck trying to track down the Barnes family livestock," she said, tapping a cigarette against the table and lighting it, "than I would tracking these people."

Cal didn't miss a beat. Already having figured out that Chloe was susceptible to praise, she laid it on thick. "But Luke says you're the best when it comes to this sort of thing. In fact, I think the word he used was 'amazing.' He says if you can't find what I'm looking for, no one can, and..."

"Well, I don't know. I've just gotten Brian home from the hospital, and..."

Knowing Chloe was also susceptible to money—and never seemed to have enough to cover her on-going shopping sprees—Cal quickly added, "Of course, I wouldn't expect you to do this for nothing, Chloe. I'd be more than happy to pay you for your efforts...and quite handsomely too." There...she'd played her trump card and played it in spades. She only hoped it would work as well as she'd planned.

"Oh, all right," Chloe said, sighing like a little girl who feels put upon. "But I can't promise you anything. And I don't want you to be upset if nothing turns up."

"Not a problem," Cal said, a wide grin working its way across her face as she closed her eyes and silently thanked the Ancestors for finally coming through. "Now here's where I want you to start..."

"Wha's you mean, I gots t'lissen to Miz Nellie?" Mattie spat, hands on her hips. "Wha's you sayin', boy? You sayin' dat Miz Nellie gots mo' sense den yo' Mama? You sayin' dat..."

"No'm. A'int sayin' dat a'tall," Carl cut her off sheepishly but lifted his eyes from the floor to meet her gaze. She obviously wasn't in a good mood, and he didn't want to make matters worse. Still, this was important—important enough that every life on the plantation might depend on it—and he couldn't back down now, no matter how much his good sense argued otherwise. "It's jes' dat Miz Nellie be's right 'bout Belle. She be's tryin' to kill Miz Cinda and dat chile. She's..."

"Wha's got into you? You knows dat ain't so. You tole me so yo'sef. You knows..."

"Yessum...but dat was befo'," he said with conviction. "And dis is now."

Mattie threw her hands in the air and huffed through her ample cheeks. "Befo' what?!" she demanded.

"Befo' she tell me so h'sef, Mama. An' we cain't let her do dat, cuz you knows what happen nex'. Dey skin her 'live, Mama!" The words came out in a whisper, and his bottom lip began to quiver. "Dey skin her 'live!" A single tear slipped from the corner of his eye and crept down his cheek.

And from that space of fitful sleep that feeds all nightmares, a single tear traveled down Brian Dawson's cheek as well.

I tossed my book aside, squirmed around in the chair and tried to relax. Knowing that the latter was an effort in futility didn't help matters a bit. I'd been wiggling around in that chair all morning trying to assuage my guilt, and that wasn't happening either. Oh, the wiggling around was coming along just fine; it was that assuaging part I couldn't seem to master. Still, a good friend—or so my mother said—dropped everything and came running when someone they loved was sick. And for what it was worth, that's exactly what I'd done. Though whether I was a good friend or not was definitely up for debate.

A good friend wouldn't have just let Brian stomp out like that. A good friend wouldn't have let Chloe try to handle the situation alone.

And a good friend certainly wouldn't have put her own interests at the forefront, with little or no thought whatsoever to anyone else's. But unfortunately, that's exactly what I'd done, and it was something I was going to have to live with.

For the life of me, I couldn't understand why that session had hit Brian so hard. Even if he *had* murdered someone in a former life—and I still wasn't sure that was the case—he'd damned sure made up for it in this one. Just thinking of how he always made everyone around him feel safe and secure was enough to make me smile. He'd given his whole life to law enforcement and then some. Then in spite of myself and that damnable guilt, I felt a chuckle rise from my throat. It was that "and then some" thing that caused most of his problems. If he'd spent less time with the law and more time with Chloe, she wouldn't have had so much time to spend money. So, I guess that just went to prove that Brian Dawson—as wonderful a human being as he'd become—still had a few lessons to learn this time around too!

I got up, stretched and walked down the hall to look in on him. He was still sleeping. It was a side-effect of the Versed, something that was completely normal. Or so the doctors said. But on her way out to the library, Chloe had mentioned that he'd already been asleep for ten hours—something quite unusual for someone who usually only slept for six—and according to my calculations, it had now been thirteen. Versed or no Versed, I didn't think *that* was normal at all. At least not for Brian. And if he didn't wake up in an hour or two, I was going to see to it that he did.

I strolled back down the hall and into the kitchen to search for coffee but came up empty-handed. All I could find was that nasty instant stuff, and there was no way to even doctor it enough to make it passable. Still, I put on the kettle and made a mental note to bring my own coffee if I wound up with Brian duty again tomorrow. Another day of drinking this vile concoction might actually kill me—provided, of course, it didn't do the job today.

As I shook my head in disgust and reached for a mug, the ring on my hand sparkled in the sunlight and caught my attention. The magical part of me still couldn't believe that anyone would have such a stone reset without knowing its history. And then, to have it reset as an engagement ring? To do such a thing was just asking for trouble.

The rational part of me insisted that Luke couldn't have known its history, and there was no one still living he could've asked. It also

reminded me that people bought diamonds and had
them set all the time. They didn't know how the jeweler wound up with
them or what sort of pain and suffering was associated with them. And
those very same people lived happily ever after without any of the
previous energy affecting them at all.

Even so, that rational, practical, common sense part of my brain
didn't get very far in silencing its magical counterpart. It didn't even
come close. But since that damned ring had almost killed me—and still
didn't have any intention of budging from my finger—I guess that was
understandable.

Fortunately, the opposing parties did eventually call a truce and
manage to agree on one thing: The stone in question wasn't just any
stone. Luke had found it in a safe deposit box while looking for some
family documents. As near as he could figure, it was the very same stone
that had once been the center of the ring he'd duplicated: Lucinda's ring.
And if that was the case, then whatever energy it had accumulated during
the time she'd worn it not only lived on but had been passed along to me,
its new recipient. Had the energy been light-hearted or fun-loving or
even remotely pleasant, that might not have presented a problem. But
since it was none of those things, it had definitely caused one for me—
and I wasn't one bit happy about it.

The whistle of the kettle brought me back to the matters at hand.
And against my better judgment, I spooned some coffee crystals into my
mug, topped them with off with boiling water and gave the whole mess a
quick stir. The diamond flashed again, sending its sparkling rainbow
across my line of vision and reflecting off the kitchen wall. It was almost
as if it had a life of its own. A life that demanded complete and
undivided attention. Not from just anyone, mind you, but from me.

"What!" I snapped under my breath. I couldn't believe I was
actually talking to a stone and was damned glad that no one was around
to witness it. Of course, it didn't answer. But I wouldn't have heard it if
it had—not over the blood-curdling scream that filled the house.

"You gots t'stop dis, Belle," he pleaded, "b'fo' it be's too late!"
"Stop dis?" she retorted. "Is you a fool?"
"Please, Belle," he implored. "Don' you know what dey do

t'you ? I cain't stand to be's thinkin'..."

"*You cain't stand to be's thinkin' what?! Dat I might be's gettin'
sumpin' bettah den you? Dat I might be's makin' myse'f a bettah life den
dis?" she raged, dragging him to the window where they could see the
slaves fetching and carrying and loaded down like a herd of human pack
mules. "Jes' what cain't you stand to be's thinkin', Cawl," she asked,
looking him in the eye. "I tell you what it be's. You cain't stand to be's
thinkin' dat I might axshly own you 'fore long. Dat's what!"*

"*But when dey find out...*"

"*And how's dey gonna do dat, Cawl? Jes' answer me dat!*"

"*Dey be's knowin' sumpin' ain't right when Miz Cinda drop
dead, dat's what. Dey be's knowin'...*"

"*Dey ain't be's knowin' nuthin. An' eben if dey did, wha's dey
gonna do? Whup me?" she quipped. "Ain't likely...not wit' me beddin'
the massuh. And dat bitch—and dat baby—still be's jes' as dead!*"

Carl looked at her aghast. There had to be some way to make
her understand. Didn't she realize that she was putting them all in
danger? Didn't she care?

"*Now you lissen t'me, Gal," he thundered. "Ain't jes' you I's
worried 'bout. Miz Cinda drop dead an' dey whup us all—ev'ry las' one
a'us—an' dat's jes' de beginnin'. Don' you keer 'bout nobody but
y'se'f?!*

"*No!" she snapped.*

"*Den let's talk 'bout what dey be's doin' t'you." She opened her
mouth to interrupt but shut it again at the hardness in his eyes. "Dey
be's stripping yo' hide off a piece at a time while you be's screamin' fo'
muhcy. Dat's what dey be's doin'. Dey be's skinnin' you 'live, Gal...an'
dey ain't nuthin' any a'us kin do 'bout it!*"

"*Ain't gonna happen," she said with more confidence than she
felt. Surely Jonah wouldn't let that happen to her. Would he? She knew
he loved her, and that meant doing everything in his power to protect
her. Didn't it? Besides, all she was doing was setting things right
again—the same things that were right before Lucinda had come along.
And nothing was going to stop her now.

"*You know what yo' problem is, Cawl?" she said with a sneer.
"You ain't got no sense. You ain't got no gumpshun. An' if'n you don' git
outa dis house and leave me alone 'bout dis, I make you a promise. It
be's yo' hide stripped off little by little—an' yo' mama's too! I be's
seein' t'dat m'se'f. Now git out!" she yelled*

"What do you mean, you absolutely refuse?" Cal wasn't used to taking no for an answer, and she certainly wasn't used to that response coming from Hex.

"Just that. I'm *not* going back inside that house," Hex answered firmly, not feeling as certain about it as he sounded. He didn't know what was wrong with him. He'd rehearsed this speech a jillion times, but once he'd actually had Cal's ear, it seemed downright silly—even to him. Still, there was no going back now. So no matter how ridiculous the whole thing sounded, he was going to have to stand his ground. And that's exactly what he intended to do. "No way. No how," he continued. "Not even torture could make me change my mind!"

"Oh, c'mon, Hex," she coaxed. "It couldn't have been that bad. It's a house for God's sake...not a monster!"

"Well, you could've fooled *me*!" he quipped. He'd already broken out into a cold sweat at the very thought of returning to that torture chamber of hers, and now he was starting to shiver. "You weren't there, Cal. You didn't see the stuff I did. You didn't experience the stuff I did. Hell...I was glad to get out of there with my life. And the next time, I might not be so lucky!"

"It's just a *Bible*, Hex. All I need is the family Bible, and it's right on top of the..."

"*NO!*" he shrieked into the phone.

"Do you mean to tell me that I'm going to have to spend somewhere in the neighborhood of three hundred dollars to fly all the way *back* there to pick up something I *need*? Something that can be shipped for less than *ten*?" When her voice rose with the last word's enunciation, he could tell she was getting pissed. But he didn't care. Not much, anyway. He couldn't go back in that house, not ever again. He just couldn't.

"No. I'm not saying that. Not at all," he answered as calmly as he could. "All I'm saying is that you'll have to find someone *else* to do it. And that's that."

Cal rubbed the back of her neck and sighed heavily, seeming to exhale enough air to fill a small bag of birthday balloons. Finally, she said, "I'm not even believing this, Hex. You're a grown man. A man who not only struggled through a difficult childhood but one so difficult that most folks couldn't have even survived it. And now...after all that...you're telling me that you're afraid of a *house*?!"

There it was again. That raised note at the end of her sentence. And if it happened one more time, he was likely to get fired. Still, he decided it was better to take his chances with the unemployment ranks than to ever have to walk inside that place again.

"That's *exactly* what I'm saying, Boss!" Hex stood there holding the phone, trying to still his shaking knees and waiting for the axe to fall. Time seemed to stand still as the worst case scenarios played out in his mind. *Please don't let her fire me,* he prayed in silent desperation. *Please, please, please! I need this job, but I can't...I just can't.*

And then, after what seemed a lifetime, Cal finally spoke again. "Okay," she said, chuckling to herself and shaking her head in bewilderment. "If you won't do it, then put me through to Lysette. Maybe she has more balls than you do."

Tears streamed down his face as he sharpened the axe. This wasn't what he'd had in mind at all. He'd thought Mama could fix it—she'd always been able to fix everything else when it came to protecting their own—but this time, Belle had gone too far. And Mama said there was only one way to save their lives. He tried not to think about it since it only made him cry harder. But knowing what he had to do, it was hard to think of anything else.

Sacrificing one for the good of all only made sense. And getting rid of the problem guaranteed the safety of every other family on the plantation. Yeah...one little girl might be heartbroken...that was a fact...but none of the other pickininnies would be left without mamas or daddies or someone to take care of them. And that was important. Or so he tried to convince himself.

But how was he going to be able to make himself do this? If she just hadn't been so bull-headed. If she'd only listened when he'd tried to tell her. If he didn't love her so much, maybe it wouldn't be so hard. Maybe he wouldn't care if they tortured her. But he did. And it was. And "if" was a mighty big word.

"Ain't no other way," he muttered, wiping his tears on the back of his arm. "Ain't no other way a'tall." He took a deep breath, stepped

from the shed and tried to prepare himself for what he had to do. And as he made his way to the clearing, the axe blade glittered in the moonlight as if guiding the way to the deed before him.

Whether or not Brian's scream really was loud enough to wake the dead is hard to say, but it accomplished something nearly as remarkable: It jolted me back to life, both immediately and expediently. And the anguished wail that followed sent me flying down the hall. What really did me in, though, was what I saw when I got to the bedroom.

Brian—that self-assured, confident man I knew and loved—had lost all sense of composure. There he sat, rocking back and forth, tearing at his hair and muttering to himself. Then eyes wild and wet with tears, he began to sob.

"It was just a nightmare, Darlin'," I soothed, cradling his head on my shoulder. "The doctor said you'd probably..."

"BULL*SHIT*!" he screamed, pushing me away. "It wasn't just a nightmare. You don't know what the hell you're talking about! You don't have any idea what this..."

"All right," I said as calmly as possible. Moving off the bed, I settled rigidly into the chair across from it and gazed into those wild eyes that didn't seem to belong to him. "Then what was it exactly?"

"It was a fuckin' vision, that's what it was. A fuckin'..."

"A vision of what, Bri'?"

"The most hellish thing you can imagine. I...I..." His voice broke off into nothingness, and then he began to cry again.

I sat in the chair, wanting to do something for him but not sure what. Fact was, Brian Dawson didn't cry. Not ever. And I just couldn't bear seeing him like this. Still, gathering him in my arms hadn't been a good idea the first time—being pushed aside was evidence of that—and I doubted it would work now. I opted to keep him talking instead and hoped that would do the trick.

"You did what, Bri'?" I asked gently.

He looked up at me with wide red eyes. "I...I...I killed the person I loved most in my life. I..."

I breathed a sigh of relief. It *had* been a nightmare, and this I could fix. "No, you didn't, Darlin'. Chloe's just gone to the library. In fact, she should be back just about..."

"Not Chloe," he said, looking at me as if I were stupid. "I killed Belle. And worst of all," he sniffled, "I did it on purpose. I loved her so much that I...I...loved her to death!"

With Lysette on her way to retrieve the Bible and few hours left until FedEx could possibly deliver her package, Cal eased herself back into the recliner, lit a cigarette and wondered if Chloe'd been able to turn up anything on the Barnes slaves. Part of her wanted to go over to the library and urge things along. But the more sensible side of her said to leave well enough alone, and let Chloe do what she did best: delve into the stuff she didn't have the time or patience for. Wasn't that, after all, why she was paying her?

Besides, Cal still had work to do—she had yet to read Belle's story—and there wasn't any point in getting ahead of herself. But for some reason, she wasn't quite ready to do that. And she had no idea why.

Was it because she knew there was some personal connection between herself and Belle, and she was afraid to know exactly what it was? That if she did, she'd somehow think less of herself and her family? Or maybe that the knowing, itself, would spoil everything and answer the questions that had provided her with countless hours of enjoyable speculation?

"Ridiculous," she breathed, crushing out her cigarette and eyeing the stack of papers on the table. Utterly ridiculous. That's what it was.

Then what are you waiting for, the voice in her head teased. *Why not take a look and see exactly what the connection is?*

Because I'm not ready, she responded silently.

What a load of crap, it countered. *You're just scared. That's what it is. You're just scared of what you might find.*

Am not.

Are too.

You know, she replied silently, drumming her nails on the arm of the chair, *I've had just about enough of you and your silly-ass shit.*

Then quit fooling around and prove me wrong! Or don't you have any gumption?

Gumption? No gumption? That voice was getting as sassy as

MawMaw, she thought with a grin. And despite the intimidating effect she seemed to have on people in the real world—the ones that were still alive, anyway—there didn't seem to be a damned thing she could do about either one of them. "Oh, all right," she muttered under her breath and grabbed the papers from the table. If there was one thing she couldn't stand, it was letting that sassy voice get the better of her.

Where the hell was Chloe? Surely, she hadn't been at the library all this time. I'd already left forty jillion messages on her car phone, but to no avail. And I was just getting ready to call her again when Luke banged on the door.

"What the fuck's gotten into her?" he bellowed as he marched into the living room. "She's not acting right...not right at all...and she wanted to have *me* committed to the insane asylum! She's lost her fucking mind, that's what!" He was tossing his arms up and down in the air and looked so much like a bantam rooster, it was all I could do not to laugh. I finally grabbed his hands to make him stop.

"It's not funny, Tess," he growled, wrenching his hands away and crossing his arms across his chest.

"The hell it's not," I said, looking up at him with a grin. "You come in dancing and prancing and making more commotion than a rooster shut out of the hen house—without so much as a 'hello, how are you'—and you think there's nothing funny about *that*?" The sparkle was gone from my smile, an arched eyebrow having made it gone flat. "You also seem to expect me to know just exactly who you're upset with and why. And then...if that weren't enough...you also have the audacity to growl at me. Hmmm..." I sighed, pretending to weigh the situation and consider the next step. "Maybe we should just start over from the 'knock-knock' part, and proceed with 'who's-there.'"

"I'm sorry," he sighed, gathering me into his arms. "It's Liza. She's lost her fucking mind. And if this shit keeps up," he said, tossing a sheaf of papers on the end table, "I'm going to lose more than mine. I'm going to lose my home too!"

While Belle's story was much the same as thousands of other enslaved women who'd lived during her time, there were a few exceptions. And it was those exceptions that made her story as interesting as the woman living it. For one thing, Jonah Barnes had given Belle her freedom long before the Emancipation Proclamation came into play. He couldn't afford to give her property—he didn't have any other than the tiny house he'd inherited from his parents—and he couldn't afford to give her money. All he could really afford to do was feed her, house her and clothe her. And because of that, Belle opted to stay rather than take her chances in a racially prejudiced world.

But Belle was smart enough not to come right out and say that. She'd had something more in mind. So to that end, she'd laid on the guilt as thick as molasses. She'd wrung her hands and begged Jonah not to turn her out. She'd told him that she had nowhere to go, that she needed him and that it was his duty to take care of her.

Yes, she'd used every trick in the book to make him feel manly, strong and necessary—and she'd done a damned fine job of it. Had she lived a hundred years later, Cal thought wryly, she might have even managed what she'd set out to accomplish.

Fact was, Belle had fallen in love with Jonah and expected him to marry her. Not that Jonah had ever given her the slightest indication that it might happen or that his intentions might ever waiver in that direction. So rather than fact or promise or declarations of undying love, her expectations were born of something much simpler: a headstrong heart unwilling to listen to reason—that same stubbornness with which most human hearts is afflicted—and a strong belief in possibility.

But there was more to the story. A determined sort, Belle refused to wind up like her mother or grandmother before her: all used up with nothing to show for her trouble but a scarred back and a broken spirit. Fact was, she'd already managed to set herself apart from most of the others in her predicament. She'd not only learned to read and write, but to add, subtract, multiply and divide as well. And because of the times, that did, indeed, make her special. It meant that she could be assured a place inside any household without the slightest worry of hard labor.

Being the enterprising woman that she was though, that wasn't enough for Belle. She wanted property. Yes, it would've been nice to have her own piece of land to do with as she pleased, but there was more to it than that. A lot more. Property meant status. Status meant power. And power was something that she intended to have—no matter what it cost or how long it took.

Although Jonah's decision to marry Lucinda was definitely a shock to her system, Belle soon saw that the marriage could very well aid her plans rather than hinder them. And that was because of the property involved. It was common knowledge that the bride's property became the husband's after marriage—and with Jonah taking ownership of the plantation, he'd be able to give her the piece of land she so desperately wanted. The only reason he was getting married anyway, was to get the plantation; otherwise, he'd never have bothered. Or at least, that's what she'd told herself.

But then, life as Belle knew it went awry. First, the property didn't fall into Jonah's hands. It was, instead, deeded to Nellie. And that didn't set well with Belle at all.

The second thing, though, was what really pushed Belle over the edge. Lucinda got pregnant with Jonah's baby. And while that normally might have been excused as an error in judgment, that which followed couldn't. Jonah was absolutely beside himself with joy. He wanted this baby. He wanted to be an integral part of the child's life. He was more excited about this than she'd ever seen him about anything. And even worse, he was now doting on Lucinda like never before: hanging onto her every word and indulging her every whim. It was more than Belle could stand. And that was when the real trouble began.

Now William Congreve once wrote that "Hell hath no fury like a woman scorned," and whether she'd been truly scorned or not, that was certainly the case with Belle. In fact, fury didn't even begin to describe the boiling well of emotion that bubbled up inside her. And with no available escape route, it finally settled into the only thing it could: a bitter, cold, rage as unyielding as it was deadly.

So with that force driving her on, Belle had taken action. Yes, there was the matter of getting rid of Lucinda and the baby. But that was nothing that adding a little something to her food here and there wouldn't handle. The biggest problem was winning Jonah's heart again. And for that, she needed help. Help beyond the normal scope of her resources. For that, she needed the help of the spirits—and a well-laid trick.

Cal finished skimming the notes and tossed them aside. Then she got up to put on a fresh pot of coffee. Drumming her nails on the counter, she thought about Belle's story. As hideous as it was, she understood why Belle saw the need to remove Lucinda and the baby from the picture. What she didn't understand was why she hadn't gone after Nellie too, since for all practical purposes, Nellie owned the plantation. It only stood to reason that the best way for Belle to get her hands on that property was to make sure that the only person left to inherit was Jonah. If you're already planning to kill two people to get what you want, why not kill the third and clear the path entirely? It just didn't make sense.

To Belle's credit, the trick she devised to win Jonah back might have worked well if she hadn't been murdered in the process of fixing it. And Cal couldn't help but wonder how her own life might have turned out if Belle had lived to see things through. Would she be standing here today—an educated black woman with her own business, her own home and the world by the tail? Or would she have, instead, been tossed into that huge vat of unskilled labor, forced to clean and scrub rooms like the very one in which she stood?

Well, she thought as she poured the fresh brew into her cup, one thing was certain: Belle—who'd been willing to do anything for a better life—would definitely be proud of her now. And if she was right about her hunches, what Belle would have thought was going to matter a great deal. Yes ma'am. It sure was.

CHAPTER 14

I couldn't believe what I was seeing. "This is a joke, right?" I asked, never taking my eyes off the document.

"Only wish it were," Luke sighed.

"But she doesn't have a case...she couldn't...not after all this time. I mean, your parents died several years ago. And if she didn't contest the will then, how on earth could she possibly hope to..."

"I don't know," Luke said. "My attorney's looking into it. But since the money Liza inherited didn't even come close to the value of the house and property, I might have to sell the place to make up the difference."

"Oh, Luke! You can't do that! That property's been in your family for..."

"Yeah, I know. And the worst of it is," he said, pausing to light a cigarette, "she doesn't even want the money. That isn't what this is all about. She wants the actual property itself."

I wanted to ask why but knew I wouldn't get an answer. Luke didn't know why anymore than I did, and even if he had, knowing what was rolling around in Liza's head certainly wasn't going to fix things.

"Okay," I said, topping off our cups, "What's the worst case scenario? You sell her the property for...I don't know...say, two-thirds of the value, and..."

"But you don't understand! I've offered to let her live there. More times than I can count. And she didn't want to do that. Said she'd rather have her own place.

"And now...this! With us getting married and all, where the hell does she think *we're* going to live?! We can't all live there together after the wed..."

The look on my face cut him short. "If, after all of this is said and done, the wedding still takes place," I said carefully, "you can always move in with me."

"Well...I don't *want* to sell the plantation," he said, snatching the document from my hand and stabbing the center with his finger. "I've lived there all my life. Goddamn it, Tess...it's my fucking home, and I..."

"And you think a piece of property is more important than continuing a relationship with your twin sister? Is that it?"

I wanted to bite my tongue in half the second I'd said it. But it was too late. He was already glowering at me, and with good reason.

"I'm sorry. I didn't mean that the way it sounded. It's just that..."

"Just that what?" he retorted. "You don't think I *care* about Liza? You think I'm putting more importance on the plantation than on my own sister? Is that it? Damn it, Tess," he said, fishing around in his pocket for another cigarette and coming up empty, "you must think I'm a real asshole!"

"Of course, I don't. That's not it at all," I responded quietly. I handed him one from my pack and watched as he lit it from the one in his hand. He was chain smoking again and so upset I doubted he even realized it.

"Then what is it?!" he asked, crushing the stub into the ashtray on the end table, blowing smoke through his nostrils and pacing around the room. "Just tell me that!"

"Okay," I said, taking a deep breath. "Maybe you should just talk to her...find out what's going on, and see if you can fix things."

"Like that's going to do any good! If she'd wanted to talk, she'd have done it before she filed those papers."

"Maybe not." I settled into the chair again and lit a cigarette of my own. "Maybe," I said, dragging deeply, "she thought you were too tied up with me and the rest of this mess to even care about what's going on with her. Maybe she just misses you and wants some attention."

"*Attention*?!" he spat. "I'll give her some fucking attention!"

What was it with me and my choice of words today? No matter what I said, it was wrong. I watched Luke as he paced. He only paused long enough to crush out his current cigarette, and then he was off again. Hair mussed up and tie askew, he looked like he was running a foot race against some deadly and invisible opponent. I wondered what had happened to that cool, calm and collected man I'd fallen in love with? The one who'd won my heart with flying pigs and always seemed to make me laugh?

"You did," said the little voice in my head—the one that always came to torment me at the worst possible moment. *"He wasn't like this before you came along. Not ever. It's all your.."*

"Oh, *stuff it!*" My command was silent but effective. Certainly more effective than anything that had managed to roll off my tongue in the last few hours. Nonetheless, Luke's pacing was making me crazy. And before I could stop myself, that thing that kept getting me into trouble—that hyperactive tongue with a mind of its own and no common sense whatsoever—sprang to life once more.

"Just *stop* it!" Much to my dismay, the exclamation came out with more volume and force than I'd ever intended, but it did, at least, hit its mark. Luke stopped dead in his tracks and looked at me.

"Hunh?!"

"Stop it." To my relief, the reiteration was much more gentle. "You're making me crazy with all that pacing stuff. And if you don't stop, I'll be forced to found the International Newspaper Publishers' Pacing Contest and tell all the bookies in Vegas that you're a shoo-in." One corner of his mouth turned up in a slight grin, so I continued. "I don't know though, Mr. Benson," I said, giving him the once over. "You've got some pretty good legs on you there. Maybe I'll just enter you in that International Mule Jumping Contest they hold up at Altenburg every year. You're certainly stubborn enough, and if I could teach you how to jump...maybe you'd have a shot at that too!"

That did it. His face crinkled into a smile. And then, much to my surprise, he actually laughed out loud. "Okay...*okay*! I'll give Liza a call. Better yet, I'll run by and see her. And," he said with a quick hug and kiss, "I'll see *you* at seven!"

Cal watched Liza from across the small table in her hotel room. She'd shown up unannounced, then breezed in, claimed a chair and started an endless rant about all sorts of personal things—none of which had anything to do with Cal nor frankly, none in which she'd have chosen to become involved had she been given the choice. To complicate matters, none of these things—the unfairness of the Benson family inheritance, Luke's selfish nature and how Liza was finally going to get some justice—were even any of her business. And as Cal did her best to listen politely, she couldn't help but wonder what had possessed the woman to expose the family's personal affairs to a complete and utter stranger. But that wasn't the only question in her mind at that point. A great many had risen to the surface. And most of them began with "why."

First of all, why had *she* been chosen to witness this tirade? There were lots of people with whom Liza could have discussed this—at least Cal assumed that was the case—people who might have had a better

understanding of what was going on. The only reason to go to a complete
stranger with something like this was to get an objective opinion. And
from the sound of things, that wasn't at all what Liza wanted. No, she
wanted someone to commiserate with her, tell her that she was right and
help her obtain what she wanted. Which were all things that only a good
friend or family member might do.

Further, why had Liza waited so long to contest the will?
Especially if the terms hadn't suited her at the onset? It seemed that the
time for a successful protest would have been during the probate and
execution of the document instead of several years after everything was
said and done. Of course, "successful" was the key word here. But that
brought up another why.

If Liza didn't truly hope to win, why had she even filed the
papers at all? If she'd wanted to disengage herself from her brother,
surely there were easier and less expensive ways to accomplish that,
none of which required the court system.

"...talked him into this. Daddy would never have given the
plantation to Luke. Not of his own free will anyway. That's because
Daddy *knew* that women needed property. That they were *nothing*
without it. That the only way to keep a man from screwing them over
was if they owned *everything*...lock, stock and barrel! Yeah...this was
Mama's doing, all right. She..."

Keeping eye contact and nodding her head in the appropriate
places, Cal watched Liza's body language as she talked and tried to get a
grasp of what was really going on. For all practical purposes, it appeared
that Liza truly thought her scheme would work. More to the point, she
intended for it to work. But something in the way she held her head and
the way she gestured with her hands wasn't right. Even the rhythm of her
speech patterns was somewhat off kilter. Obviously, Cal was missing
something. She knew she was. But what on earth was it?

Not knowing Liza very well didn't help at all. They'd never
shared any of the things—laughter or tears, successes or
disappointments—that give one person insight into another. So, there
was little or no way to honestly gauge whether Liza's actions or reactions
were appropriate to her personality. And yet, something was definitely
wrong here. Even worse, there was something vaguely familiar about all
of it. Something that Cal couldn't quite put her finger on, but familiar all
the same.

"...because property brings status. Status brings power. And that's one thing I intend to have, even if I *do* live in this one horse town!"

"What?!"

"Weren't you listening at all?" Liza quipped. "I said that owning the plantation will bring me what I want: the power to do as I please, regardless of what..."

Her words hit Cal like a ton of bricks. This couldn't be happening. It wasn't possible. And yet, the dread rising from her belly told her otherwise.

"...other people think I should do. Before it's said and done, I promise you this: I'll own those little peons...the ones who think they're so important. And I'll make their lives just as miserable as they've made mine!"

Trying to keep her face as expressionless as possible, Cal managed a slow nod and gestured toward the coffee pot. Then getting an affirmative nod from Liza, she crossed the room to the tiny kitchenette. Her hands shook. Her heart pounded. She didn't really want coffee. What she wanted was to run screaming from the room, and scream one scream after another until someone came to take her away. She told herself it couldn't be. And yet, the thought at the forefront of her mind—the thought that Liza had somehow managed to flip back into her previous life as Belle—simply refused to go away. And the question of how to handle it, if by some remote possibility she actually had, was even stronger.

Wha's you waitin' on? Cat got your tongue?

"I can't ask her if she's reliving the past, MawMaw. She'll think I've lost my mind," Cal responded silently. *"I can't even ask her why she's doing this. It's none of my business, and I..."*

None of yo' bizness, my foot! She done made it yo' bizness. And if you ain't even got enough gumption to ask, you goin' t'mess this up good. Real good. You goin' to...

"Oh, all right!" Cal snapped in her head.

Liza was still ranting, and since Cal needed a minute to calm down and get her thoughts in order, that was probably a good thing. She filled the filter cup, poured the water through the top of the coffeemaker and flipped the switch. Opening the cabinet and grabbing two mugs, she wondered just how she could ask the questions MawMaw thought were so necessary; more to the point though, how could she ask them casually or with any measure of diplomacy.

Realizing there was no way to manage either, she formulated

another question instead, one that she hoped would bring about the same results. And since Liza took a breath just about that time, Cal spit it out before she could change her mind.

"But why now? Why after all these years?"

"Because it should've been mine in the first place. And it would've been...if Luke hadn't decided to marry that woman! I'll be damned and go to hell," Liza spat, "before I let her steal it from me again...along with everything else that's rightfully mine."

"Everything else?"

Liza just nodded as if the gesture, in and of itself, should explain it all.

"I see," said Cal carefully, placing a steaming mug in front of Liza. "And you're telling me all of this why?"

"Because *you're* going to keep it from happening."

"I'm not sure I understand," Cal lied. Fact was, she understood all too well, and the gleam in Liza's eyes told the story.

"Of course you do," Liza retorted condescendingly. "You're only going to break *one* trick...the one that binds Luke and Tess together...and you're going to leave the other one alone."

"And if I break both?" Cal asked pointedly.

A sickening smile played across Liza's lips, laced with the sort of evil one might expect to find on an executioner's face were it visible behind the mask. She held Cal's gaze as she downed the rest of her coffee then rose from the table. "Oh, you won't," she said, setting down her mug and leaning in close to Cal's face. "If, that is," she whispered, "you know what's *good* for you!"

And without another word, she crossed the room and let herself out.

Chloe's search had turned up very little; so little, in fact, that she was almost embarrassed to take her findings to Cal. She'd spent hours at the library—several more than she'd intended—and still, all she could come up with were the names of the people who'd worked for the Barneses. There were only two items of interest, and they were both found in addendums to the census reports she'd already searched.

First, those who'd previously been listed simply as "slave" now had names and were categorized as household employees. And since they were listed as people of color, this meant that they'd been given their freedom and were being paid for their work. That, in itself, was noteworthy because even though the information came from an 1864 census report, Missouri hadn't been bound by the Emancipation Proclamation. So for whatever reason, the Barneses had obviously taken it upon themselves to free their slaves and offer them wages and living space. Initially, this discovery gave Chloe some semblance of hope, for when slaves were freed, there was paperwork involved—some sort of legal document—if only in the form of a handwritten note to that effect. It was common knowledge that there was paperwork for everything involving the enslaved; they couldn't even leave the plantation without a pass from their owners, lest they were picked up as run-aways. And free people of color? Well, it was common practice for them to carry a copy of their documentation at all times to avoid the same dilemma.

Unfortunately, since most folks of that time period felt that people of color—free or not—deserved fewer rights than the average plantation dog, those in charge of handling such paperwork seldom found those sorts of documents worthy of filing at all. And so the chances of locating them was slim to none. Still, Chloe had thought it was worth a shot.

It wasn't.

After searching the library, she'd even gone as far as to make a trip to the courthouse. But she'd come up empty-handed there too—at least as far as the household employees went. She did, however, manage to find a marriage certificate for Jonah and Lucinda. But further search for records of Lucinda's previous marriage was fruitless, as was a search for her death certificate.

So much for good-ol'-boy towns, she thought as she unlocked her car and got in. It never failed to amaze her how any person could live and die—or even worse, be purchased and freed—without any records whatsoever. They were human beings, for the sake of the Gods! How anyone could view *any* human life as that insignificant was beyond her.

Turning left on Malone and heading for the house, she pondered how she'd spent the day. She really hadn't accomplished anything at all, except to spin her wheels. The day had been a complete wash. A total waste of time. And even worse, it had kept her from what she really should've been doing: staying at home and taking care of Brian, which was the whole reason that Luke had given her time off. She was still feeling guilty about the way she'd handled his ordeal with the CAT scan, and guilt wasn't something she was used to dealing with.

Still thinking about her day, she turned right and headed down Route AA. She had nothing to give Cal at all, other than the news about the freed slaves and the other little tidbit that didn't amount to a row of pins. Sadly enough, it only involved a new name appearing among the household employees in an 1865 census report—a fourteen-year-old girl named Desiree—a name that didn't appear on any report thereafter. And that wasn't going to be any help at all.

Sighing heavily, she pulled into the driveway, cut the engine and headed for the front door.

Luke leaned back in his office chair, tossed his feet on the desk and stabbed at the numerical phone pad one more time. The trip to Liza's apartment had proven fruitless, and a part of him was truly glad she hadn't been home. He was confused and pissed off by her behavior, but more than that, he felt betrayed. And since none of those things was conducive to satisfactory resolution, he knew that a face-to-face chat was likely to make things even worse.

Truth be told, he didn't want to talk to Liza right now at all, and at this point, he might never want to again. Still, he'd promised Tess that he'd do it, and he was determined to make good on that—or at least make the necessary effort. So, he listened to the obligatory four-ring transmission and waited for the answering machine to pick up. This time, he didn't bother to leave a message. He figured that if the first three he'd left didn't prompt her to return his calls, one more plea wasn't going to make any difference.

Opening his desk drawer, he reached for his fourth pack of cigarettes of the day and idly switched on the radio. What the hell was wrong with her anyway? She'd never been upset about the will before. Hell, she'd never acted like this before. And she knew good and well that as long as their family had owned it, the plantation had always been passed down to the eldest son if there was one. It was part of their heritage, the way things had always been done. Besides, he thought, ripping the cellophane away from the pack and tapping out a cigarette, she'd never given a rat's ass about the house or the property. In fact, he remembered a conversation they'd had shortly after their parents' funeral in which she admitted that she was delighted she didn't have to fool with any of it. She'd said that the last thing she wanted to do was deal with the day-to-day maintenance of something as old and decrepit as that house...money pit was the actual term she'd used...and had then gone on to tease him about the fact that he'd be old and gray by the time he ever hoped to enjoy a social life. And, of course, she'd added gleefully, that by then it would not only be too late to enjoy one, but he'd be way too broke.

That conversation seemed a lifetime ago, he thought, as he tapped the business end of the cigarette on the desktop and lit it. So, what could have caused Liza's change of heart? And why now? Could Tess have been right? Could Liza actually be jealous of the time he was spending with her and feel left out? No, that couldn't be it. Liza had always wanted him to have a social life and find that special someone. In fact, she'd chided him about it constantly.

Luke watched his cigarette smoke curl into misty tendrils and wished he didn't give a damn about what Liza was doing or why. But he did. And if he kept playing in that stream of why's and what's and how's floating through his head, one thing was certain: He was going to drive himself crazy with this. Hell, he already was.

"Fuck it!" he barked to the empty office, as if that was going to squelch the questions running through his mind. And for a moment or two, it did.

He quickly scanned his desk for pressing matters and finding none, checked his calendar for the following day. The evening edition of the paper had already gone to print, so there was nothing left to do. Except, of course, to pick up Tess. And if he hurried, he could manage to get there right on time.

As he flipped off the lights, Bette Midler's voice came through the speakers serenading him with the first few bars of "I Put A Spell On You." "Yeah, yeah, yeah," he responded sarcastically. "Suppose you tell me something that I don't know!" Then he walked out, locked the door and shaking his head, he strode out to the parking lot.

Cal studied the items spread out across the coffee table as if they were the most precious artifacts she'd ever seen. In a way they were. They were a part of her. A part of her heritage. Pieces of a family puzzle thought to be lost forever, but like all other precious artifacts, simply hidden from view until the precise moment in time arrived and connected with the person who could most appreciate their value. Who'd have thought she'd been in possession of them the whole time? And without having a clue as to what they were or who they'd belonged to!

For Cal, this was the discovery of a lifetime but not just because these things provided a missing link into the blood that ran through her veins. It was also proof positive that magic—that thing she'd been raised to embrace but had scorned as totally non-existent only a few days before—did, in fact, live and breathe, regardless of what the scientific side of her brain wanted to believe. But that wasn't all. It also disproved the theory that magic couldn't affect the person who didn't believe in it. It could and did. And the proof was right there on the table, and in the chaos, those seemingly insignificant items had created for at least three non-believers caught in their web. What's more, it had for the last hundred years.

Even more amazing to Cal was that her very own family was not only involved in this problem, but one of its members had actually started the whole mess. The family Bible confirmed that an ancestor named Belle had, indeed, borne a child named Desiree—a child who had grown up to become her great-grandmother. And while Chloe's census research didn't actually connect Belle to Desiree, there was a girl of the same name listed on that report. A girl who would have been about the same age as the one in her dream. The girl whose face she could still see vividly in her mind's eye.

Cal idly tapped out a cigarette and lit up as she gave the matter some thought. Breaking Belle's trick might not be so difficult after all. Not only did she have the parcel in hand but was a direct descendant of its creator. The real problem, she thought, was going to be Liza. And if this afternoon's conversation with her was any indication of what lay ahead in that department, she was going to be a real handful.

The good news was that Liza didn't have any magical training, so any trouble or interference she doled out was likely to be mundane in nature. Still, if she was indeed, the reincarnation of her great-great-grandmother—and Cal had no reason at this point to believe otherwise—residual knowledge from the prior lives could come into play. It was a fact that spirits didn't forget; it was just a matter of whether or not they chose to remember.

Cal exhaled fully, filling the room around her with a wispy veil of smoke—a veil that MawMaw obviously saw as a formal invitation.

Ain't got no time for speculatin' on what might *be's, Little Missy...only what be's.*

"But preparation's everything, MawMaw...you taught me that yourself. If I'm not prepared for what could happen, this whole thing could backfire. And we can't afford for that to happen again!"

But while you be's speculatin' on might be's and could be's, time's a-wastin...and you be's the one a-wastin' it.

Damn it, thought Cal. How could anybody be so frustrating when they were dead? MawMaw's death hadn't brought peace at all...not to anybody...she jabbered more now than she ever had when she was alive. But the worst of it was that death had taught her a new trick: She'd learned to talk in riddles.

Ain't got time for no sassy talk either. 'Specially when I only be's tryin' to he'p you. And don't you be's drawin' no long breath or cuttin' them eyes around at me, Little Missy, or I be's...

Cal was just about to sigh and roll her eyes heavenward but immediately thought better of it. She couldn't have MawMaw leaving her in the lurch now. Not when she needed some real information and direction.

"I don't understand," she said. "If I'm not prepared for whatever happens...for the worst case scenario...then how can I..."

Ain't you payin' me no mind a'tall? Just do what I be's telling you. Use what you got and use what you have. You already gots more of that than you did, Little Missy. Lots more.

"But MawMaw, I don't..."

Somethin' wrong with that head of yours? Or do it just be's sittin' on them shoulders for looks? All that schoolin' and not one lick of common sense. A fool be's what I raised...sure 'nough did...a goddamned fool what can't even...

Cal was now past the point of frustration, past the point of utter annoyance and with MawMaw's last remark, was well on the way to being downright pissed. No matter how much she needed her grandmother's help, this snarking had to stop—and in short order—or the work at hand would have to take a back seat to figuring out how to get her insurance company to pay for insanity leave.

"There's no call for that," she said curtly. "Just because you insist on speaking in riddles doesn't mean I'm stupid. It means that you're not explaining yourself well. If you'd simply speak in plain

English, maybe we could get this resolved. And then, I could go back to work and..."

Lawd A'mighty, Chile...ain't you hearin' what I be's sayin'? MawMaw's tone was much softer now and almost pleading. *Use that head and them book smarts of yours...and use that white woman's too. Then stir them thoughts up real good with what you got and what you have, and what you* know *be's risin' up like bread in the pan.*

Cal sighed in relief. At last, there seemed to be light at the end of the tunnel. She just hoped that nothing else would block it from view.

"So, you're saying that if Tess Logan and I put our heads together, combine information and stick to the facts, we should be able to break these tricks easily and put this whole thing to rest."

Ain't nothin' easy about workin' them knots loose, Little Missy...'specially when the magic be's stuck like glue.

"I understand that. But about the rest of it..."

MawMaw let out an exasperated breath. *Just do what I say. And, Little Missy?*

"Ma'am?"

Ain't no more time to lose. The clock be's tickin' off seconds quicker than you can bat them eyes. So don't go a'wastin' what little be's left.

"Okay, MawMaw...but what's the rush? These tricks have been around for a hundred years or better, so I don't understand why I'm so short of time. It seems to me that another day or two really isn't going to make..."

'Cause lives be's dependin' on it, Chile. Real lives. And this time, one of them lives could be's your very own!

CHAPTER 15

I didn't feel good about this at all. And the farther we got from town, the more I wanted to kick myself. I should've known it was a trick. I should've known that Luke would never have sent Liza to pick me up, especially not after that stunt with the lawsuit she'd pulled this morning. Still, her explanation of how they'd talked things through had sounded plausible. And because it was important to me that they resolve their differences, I certainly hadn't wanted to be the wedge that drove them apart. So, here I was—barreling down the road with Luke's sister behind the wheel—watching helplessly as the odometer ticked off the miles, and we sped farther and farther toward what I could only assume was the middle of nowhere. So much for trying to be nice.

There wasn't any point in asking Liza where we were going. I'd already tried that. And all I'd gotten for my trouble was a smirk. There wasn't any point in trying to make small talk either, as my feeble attempt at that had been answered in much the same way. The only difference was that she'd punctuated the latter with a roll of her eyes and a sigh of complete and utter disgust. She obviously wasn't in the mood to talk, so with little else to do, I spent most of the time pretending to look straight ahead while making mental notes of the landmarks along the way.

Stealing a glance, I studied Liza from the corner of my eye. While she didn't appear to be dangerous, the mentally ill seldom did. Fact was, I'd had a similar situation with my ex-husband many years before, and I'd been lucky to escape with my life.

It had all started out innocently enough as a spur-of-the-moment weekend trip into the city. But the innocent part had come to a screeching halt about twenty miles outside of town, when he pulled over unexpectedly and backhanded me with enough force to make me see stars. Then before I could even catch my breath, he'd grabbed me by the neck, yanked me from the car, and dragged me across the interstate, where he'd had every intention of tossing me over the guard rail into oncoming traffic.

Now, coming to the conclusion that your life is hanging by a thread held in the hands of a crazy person has a way of invoking that fight or flight phenomena, and for all practical purposes, I'm a fighter. But a smart fighter knows her limitations. More importantly though, she weighs her odds before taking action—and at that time, mine were downright bleak. I was being wrangled about by a professional bodybuilder who not only outweighed me by a hundred pounds but was a seasoned street fighter. Still, I'd had a shot. I was smarter than he was. I was more level-headed. And that flapping appendage of mine—the tongue that was usually responsible for most of my troubles—had been known to turn to purest silver in dire circumstances.

Fortunately, the latter hadn't let me down. It had worked its alchemy well enough to talk my way back into the car, back to civilization, and straight into my attorney's office, where I'd filed for a divorce and a restraining order.

With that in mind, I took stock of my current situation. Liza obviously wasn't playing with a full deck. That was a given, as I was in her car under false pretenses, and she was quickly whisking me away from any sign of human habitation. And while I doubted that her original intention had actually been to injure me, I wasn't sure what might happen if her plans went awry. Even a good-natured dog can turn ugly when backed into a corner—and from what I'd seen, Liza's nature had never been exactly pleasant.

In any case, I couldn't just sit there and do nothing. So, I prayed for my tongue to work its magic one more time and set about shifting the odds in my favor. I only hoped it would work.

"You know, Liza," I started tentatively, "Luke's going to be frantic when I'm not at home." I watched her face for a reaction. There wasn't any. So I went a step further. "He's even likely to call the police."

Fire lit her eyes as she turned to look at me. "And why would he do *that*?" she sneered. "Do you really think he *cares* about you?" A smug grin crossed her face, and she turned her eyes back to the road. "You really *are* an idiot!"

Now we were getting somewhere. Hurt feelings were at the root of this problem—her caustic remarks had proved that—so soothing them was likely to get me out of this mess. But there was time for that later. Right now, I had a chance to hedge my bets. And it wasn't a chance I was willing to pass up.

"Maybe I should just call him and let him know I'm all right," I said, gesturing at the car phone settled between our seats. "That way, he won't call the police and..."

"You don't *get* it, do you?" she snapped, whipping the car sharply to the left and turning onto a nearly invisible trail in a heavily wooded area. "He doesn't want *you*. He wants the *plantation*. And you're the easiest way to get it!"

Now, *that* was a reaction. It just wasn't the one I'd expected.

"What do you *mean*, she's not *there*?!"

Luke was more upset than Chloe had ever heard him, and she couldn't understand why. "Just that, Luke," Chloe answered breezily. "She left here a couple of hours ago, and..."

"Did she say what her plans were? Where she was going? Any mention of stopping off somewhere? For God's sake, Chloe...I've got to find her!"

Being upset was one thing, but this was ridiculous. Luke was ticking off questions faster than she could think. And why? Because Tess wasn't right under his thumb where he could watch her every move. Instead of a concerned lover, this man was starting to sound like a stalker—and Tess had already had one too many of those in her life.

"What's the big deal, Luke? All upset because you don't know what she's doing every second? Well, I've got news for you, Mister. Tess Logan is a grown woman. She can go where she pleases. Do what she pleases. And she damned sure doesn't need your permission to..."

"Oh, geeze, Chloe...oh, geeze...you don't understand..."

"Oh, I think I do. I think I understand perfect..."

"No!" he screamed into the mouthpiece. And then to the dead silence that answered, he whispered, "You don't!"

Had Brian Dawson custom ordered something to get him out of bed and back on track, it couldn't have worked its magic any quicker than the news that Tess was missing. In fact, he was already dressed and standing at the door with keys in hand by the time Chloe hung up the phone.

"What's the story?" he asked. "Other than the fact that she's disappeared?"

Chloe exhaled fully and raked shaky fingers through her hair while she decided what to do. Brian was supposed to be in bed. He wasn't supposed to get upset. And while she might eventually be able to talk him back into bed, there was no way he was going to be happy about it—or stay there. She knew he'd be up and gone just as soon as she turned her back, and there was nothing she could do to stop him.

Resignedly, her eyes met his. "We don't know that she's even missing," she said carefully. "She wasn't home when Luke went by to pick her up...this was the night we were all supposed to meet at the plantation...but it could be that..."

"Jesus God in heaven, Gal...she's missing all right," he retorted. "And you can bet your bottom dollar that Liza Benson has something to do with it."

She looked at him aghast, hardly able to believe her ears. That was exactly what Luke had said. And hearing it now from Brian—who couldn't possibly have overheard Luke's part of the conversation—sent cold chills soaring up her spine. "You can't know that," she said, hoping she sounded calmer than she felt.

"Well, I do." Then looking her straight in the eye, he added, "And so do you."

I couldn't believe this was happening. I kept hoping it was just a bad dream—the sort that I'd wake up from any minute and eventually be able to laugh about. But it wasn't. Any fantasy I might've entertained was cut short by the burning in my wrists as I struggled against the ropes. And if that didn't do the trick, well...the throbbing in the back of my head and the blood streaming into my eyes provided an additional dose of reality.

There was no point in chastising myself over how stupid I'd been, but I couldn't help reflecting on that whenever my most recent plans of action proved futile. I thought I'd been so smart. I'd actually managed to convince Liza to let me call Luke. Of course, it had never occurred to me that she'd coldcock me just as soon as my head was bent over the console. I'd come to with my arms splayed over my head, my wrists bound tightly to a tree branch, and my feet chained and shackled and anchored to the ground.

Poetic justice, Liza had said, for a slave owner.

Those words had brought me to a chilling realization. Liza Benson's actions had nothing at all to do with mental illness. In fact, she'd probably never been more sane. The problem was that she'd recovered memories of a former life—a life in which she'd been severely mistreated—which by some strange phenomenon, had slipped to the forefront and obliterated most recollection of her current one. That being the case, this was her opportunity to exact revenge. And judging from the bullwhip she'd brandished, that was something she certainly intended to do.

The thought of being whipped, in and of itself, was terrifying enough—especially with Liza wielding the tool—but I knew my problems weren't going to end there. The gleam in her eyes told me that she had more in mind. A lot more. And if I didn't manage to get loose before she got back, there was a good chance I might not even survive the other horrors she'd dreamed up.

Trying not to think about what they might be, I went back to work on the ropes. But nothing I tried made the slightest difference; moreover, my every effort seemed to have the opposite effect of its intention. With the ropes getting tighter instead of looser, all I managed were a pair of raw, swollen wrists and a panic attack.

"Fuck me," I muttered. The sun was already sinking low on the horizon, and the best I could hope for was another thirty minutes of daylight. After that, I knew that my odds of escape were slim to none because even if I could manage to work my way free, finding my way back to the road in the dark would be damned near impossible. And the last thing I needed was to inadvertently bump into Liza again.

Just the thought of that pushed me back into action. I examined the knots from every angle, giving major consideration to the points of least resistance. Then I bit back the pain and tried one more time, working more feverishly than I'd ever thought possible. And when that effort proved futile as well, I embarked upon a new course of action, a course of action I'd been saving if all else failed. I let loose a string of expletives laced with enough filth to embarrass a drill sergeant. And then I closed my eyes and cried.

Regardless of country or region, small towns all have one thing in common: They are never short on gossip. Word spreads quicker than melted butter while the truth twists about as easily as pretzel dough. Things rise way out of proportion. And before it's baked and done, the final product bears no resemblance whatsoever to the original news tidbit; in fact, the two generally don't even share the same flavor.

Sikeston was no exception.

Tonight, time was a precious commodity. And because Brian Dawson knew that, he damned sure wasn't going to waste a single minute of it trying to set things straight. So, he did what any other seasoned law enforcement officer would do in this situation. He grabbed some insurance in the form of that universal small town utensil—the one that slices and dices like no other can—the one we all know as "stature." And with a family like the Bensons involved, the tool had plenty of power to handle the job. He just hoped he wouldn't need it.

Truth be told, Brian's reasons for wanting to work on the sly had very little to do with the gossip factor. It was the media he was trying to avoid. The last thing he needed right now was a bunch of gung-ho reporters and newscasters from St. Louis following him around. Since every last one of them was filled with bright ideas and silly notions about Pulitzer Prizes, they shot film and asked questions at the most inappropriate times, misinterpreted the facts and just generally got in the way. The last time he'd had to deal with them, they'd nearly gotten someone killed. And because of their First Amendment rights, charges of interfering in a police investigation wouldn't stick.

As far as he was concerned, the media was an unnecessary evil, and he didn't have time to fool with them. Besides, he owed Tess and Liza better than that. Everything within him screamed that their very lives depended on it. And this time—no matter what it took—he was hell bent to save them both.

For that reason, it didn't take Brian long to get things organized. He'd had Luke change the meeting place from the plantation to Tess' house and used Chloe's spare key to let them in. Then, he'd begun to pass out jobs. Sally Nicewander was to man the phone at the house and pass messages along as necessary. Luke had a hunch about where Liza might've gone, so he was riding with Brian. That only left Cal and Chloe. And while he was sure that Cal knew better than to get in the way, his wife was another story. She had a way of being in exactly the wrong place at the right time, and he couldn't chance that tonight. He was going to have to come up with something to keep her busy, and that was going to be a problem.

He'd no sooner thought it than Cal spoke up. "Chloe's going with me," she said matter-of-factly.

Her intuitiveness was uncanny, but Brian managed to keep the surprise from his face. "And where would that be?" he asked pointedly.

"Okay...there's something you don't know," she began, directing her remarks to Brian. "Well, maybe you do or you wouldn't have already decided to start this search. But Liza isn't in her right mind. I have reason to believe that she's reverted back to the memories of a previous life and blames Tess for all her hardships. That's why she's suing you for the plantation, Luke," she added, looking at him.

"You know about..."

She waved him off with a hand. "It doesn't matter. Not right now. The only thing that *does* matter is that I break those tricks *immediately*. I don't have time to go into a lengthy explanation. Suffice it to say that it's the only thing that's going to make Liza snap out of this and bring her back to the present.

"So," she continued hastily, "I'm heading out to the plantation cemetery to get to work. And Chloe's the only one with enough training here to help me get this done."

Chloe's eyes widened in horror. "But I can't do that!" she exclaimed. "I don't know *anything* about breaking tricks. I don't know anything about *hoodoo*. I can't...I don't...I'm not capable...I'm just a..."

"Yeah, I know...just a 'wish,'" Cal said with a grin. "Tess told me.

"All that's necessary is that you love your friend. And since that's already obvious," she said, squeezing Chloe's shoulder, "you'll do just fine."

Having gotten Chloe in hand and in a hurry to be on her way, she turned to Brian. "I'll need somebody's car phone," she said, "just in case I need to call in."

"Take mine," Sally offered. "Car's unlocked."

"Thanks!" Cal said appreciatively then turned to Chloe. "Ready?"

Chloe nodded and they were out the door. Just as Cal was getting into the car, Luke appeared at her side. He extracted a plain brown envelope from his jacket pocket and handed it to her. "I've got a feeling you might need this," he said hesitantly, "but you're the only one who's going to know."

"What's..."

"Never mind. Just promise me you'll open it before you do anything, okay?"

I had no idea how long I'd been asleep or what exactly woke me. Since the autumn night had turned cold enough to make my teeth chatter, it may have been the change in temperature. The dampness from the blankets of fog didn't help either nor did the breeze that kicked up and blew its watery contents across my bare skin. But more than likely, it was the searing pain in my wrists, courtesy of the full body weight straining against them.

I was chilled to the bone, scared to death, and I hurt like hell. I was well past any point of understanding. I didn't care why Liza had pulled this stunt. I didn't give a rat's ass about her mental state or her problems with slipping in and out of realities. I didn't even care what had caused it. All I cared about was getting out of here before Death came to claim me. And at this point, whether pneumonia ratted me out, or Liza did the deed, didn't make much difference. Dead was dead, and I certainly wasn't in any hurry to add a journey to the Summerland to my repertoire of experiences.

Come to think of it, where the hell was the Goddess? And what sort of Mother was She, anyway? I was Her child. I was in the worst mess I'd ever managed to stumble into. And mothers didn't just leave their children hanging by their wrists like this. At least, not good ones. *Careful*, the voice in my head—the one belonging to Good Sense— whispered, *or you'll go too far.*

Bullshit, Irrationality countered. *If She hasn't noticed her by now, you think a little disrespect is going to do the trick?*

They volleyed back and forth until I thought I'd scream. And finally, I did—so loudly, in fact, that I wasn't even sure the voice was my own. It cut through the fog, echoed through the woods and, I hoped, right into the range of celestial hearing.

Whether the Goddess heard me or not was a matter of debate. But one thing was not. I'd screwed up again. And the proof was in the guttural snort that shot through the fog just before Liza's face appeared two inches from mine.

"Do that again, Bitch," she spat, "and by the time I'm done with you, you'll be begging me to kill you."

I summoned my courage and shot her a glare. "Oh come on, Liza," I said, hoping I sounded braver than I felt, "that's what you've got in mind anyway...well, isn't it?"

The blank look on her face urged me on. I just hoped that in my effort to force her back to reality, I wouldn't go too far. "A little torture between friends?" I quipped, leaning forward to within a scant inch of her nose. "A little something to work up the courage necessary to commit murder?

"Well, if that's what you've got in mind, Liza, then let's get it done. I'm tired. And I'm cold. And I'm sick of your shit."

She tilted her head to the side. A strange look crossed her face. And then, a flicker of recognition. It was almost as if she was seeing me for the first time. Finally, her eyes lit up and actually twinkled. "As you wish," she said with glee.

And then she held the branding iron right up to my face where I could get a real good look.

Avoiding the media came with its own set of problems, the largest of which was no all-points bulletin. That meant fewer sets of eyes on the lookout, and little or no backup. But since Brian had no intention of alerting his superior officers at the sheriff's department—he simply couldn't take the chance—he guessed it was a moot point anyway.

Luke was incredulous. "But don't you think we oughta tell *someone* where we're going? Geeze, Brian...what if we get into trouble? What if we need help? What if..."

"Do you *want* those idiots from St. Louis to get a hold of this? Is that it?" Brian quipped.

"Well, no...but..."

"That's what I thought. If Liza *is* involved, they'll have a field day with this. They'll chew her up and spit her out. And neither of your lives will ever be the same again," he said, turning left onto I-55.

"And what about Tess?" he growled. "Do you want to ruin her life too?"

Luke understood the problem, but he didn't like this one bit. If

Cal was right about this...if Liza *had* absconded with Tess...if Liza *wasn't* herself...he wasn't sure they could handle her on their own. At least not without hurting her. And he didn't even want to think about that.

"No," he answered, the resignation apparent in his voice. "But isn't there anyone at the sheriff's department you can trust? I mean...those guys cover your back. You trust them with your life. You depend on them every single day. And now you mean to tell me that you can't trust a single one of them enough to keep their mouths shut? Geeze, Brian...if that's the way things are, I'm sure glad I'm not a cop."

As much as Brian hated to admit it, Luke's words made a lot of sense. And yet, every cell in his brain still screamed with the need for secrecy. So, what was it, really? Was it that he *couldn't* trust his fellow officers? Or was it that he'd been given a second chance to do this right, and his need to excel this time was overpowering his good judgment? He just wasn't sure.

There was someone he could call. They'd grown up together and shared each other's deepest secrets. They'd even joined the Marines together. And when they'd gotten out, they'd both gone into law enforcement. There was nothing they wouldn't do for each other—no questions asked—even if it meant hiding a body.

Without saying a word, Brian punched in a number on the car phone beside him and hit the speaker button. Much to his relief, the call was answered on the second ring.

"Hey, Griz...it's Brian. Listen...I've got a situation here..."

Chloe had been uncharacteristically quiet on the ride out to the plantation. It wasn't worry that stilled her tongue—that always made her yammer ninety-to-nothing. Instead, it was abject fear. Fear of an unknown area of the Craft. Fear of not knowing what she was doing. Fear of screwing something up. But the thing she was most afraid of— the thing that really scared her shitless—was the thought of inadvertently doing something that might cut short the life of her best friend. And although Cal had assured her repeatedly that such wasn't even within the realm of possibility, the fear associated with that notion was eating her alive.

Cal had been rather quiet too, but not for the same reasons. She'd been putting her efforts toward contacting MawMaw. Not that it had done any good of course. MawMaw seemed hell bent on forcing Cal's hand. On making her take a chance that whatever she came up with would work. On believing that no matter which route she took with breaking the tricks, everyone involved would be so much the better for it. Her stubborn silence was proof of that. And Cal wished she was as sure of imminent success as her grandmother seemed to be.

Cal pulled in as close to the cemetery as possible, cut the engine and rested her head on the steering wheel. Although she already had a vague idea of what needed to be done, she still didn't have a firm plan. And she'd never done this sort of thing without one. Working magic on the fly could be a dangerous business, especially when involving tricks this powerful. But all the worry in the world wasn't going to fix it. There wasn't time for worry anyway—it had run out just like MawMaw said it would—and like it or not, she was on her own. She made a mental note to give Chloe some additional protection, then raised her head and turned in the seat.

Chloe looked at her expectantly, the fear on her face more apparent than ever. "Are you all right?" she asked.

"No," Cal sighed. "And you aren't either...are you?"

The answer came in the shake of her head, punctuated by tear-filled eyes.

"Well, at least we're in agreement on something," Cal said with a half-hearted chuckle, "and if we can both stay on the same pages until we see this through...well...I have a feeling we're going to do just fine."

She touched a button under the dash and the trunk flew open. Then she grabbed Luke's envelope from the seat beside her and reaching for the door handle said, "Come on, 'Wish.' We've got work to do. And there's no time like the present!"

Chloe waited just outside the cemetery grounds while Cal finished with the preparations. She'd been visiting cemeteries all her life, and this was the first time she'd ever heard that there was a proper way to enter one. Or that entering in any other way was not only insulting to the residents, but to Oya, the Goddess Who carried the spirits of the dead through the veil. Looking back on her gross disrespect—no matter how unintentional—it was a wonder that the ground hadn't simply swallowed her alive.

Maybe Oya excused ignorant white girls, Chloe mused, or maybe it was something else entirely. It might just be that once insulted, Oya ignored impertinent offenders and refused them passage when the time came. And that was a scary thought. Either way, she had a lot to make up for, and now that she'd been fully apprised of good cemetery manners, she wasn't likely to forget them.

Cal stepped back and checked her work. Chloe's forehead had been anointed with red wine, and her hair was completely covered with a long white scarf that been twisted and securely wrapped around her head. She had an offering in her right hand—a vial containing nine pennies and a small amount of red wine.

Satisfied, she went over the instructions one more time. "I'll ask Oya's permission to enter, but even if I go on ahead of you, wait until She gives you a personal okay."

"But what if She doesn't?" Chloe wailed, her concern apparent.

"Don't worry. She will." Cal's smile was nearly imperceptible but there all the same. "Just remember that She's the Queen of the Cemeteries. And queens are used to doing things in their own time."

Chloe nodded.

"Then what?" Cal asked.

"Once I get permission, I cross into the cemetery and thank Oya by pouring the pennies and wine on the ground in libation to Her."

Cal nodded in approval. "Exactly," she said. "Are you ready?"

"As ready as I'll ever be."

"Then let's do it!"

And without saying another word, they gathered the bags of ritual supplies scattered at their feet, hoisted them over their shoulders and made their way toward the edge of the cemetery.

How Liza had ever managed to get a fire going in that dampness was beyond me, but since I could smell smoke and hear the crackle of wood, I knew she had. Drizzle had replaced the night's pea soup, and I was beginning to think that my best bet was to pray for a good old-fashioned rainstorm. Yeah...I could get struck by lightning, but I seriously doubted that could be much worse than my current state of affairs. At least there was a slim possibility of immediate death by lightning, and I couldn't say the same for branding. If I'd had to choose between the two, there would've been no contest.

I had to wonder just what I'd done to piss off the Ancients, but I guessed even They had Their limits. Maybe all that smart-alecky talk about going to lunch and staying for dessert had finally caught up with me. Maybe the Good Sense voice in my head had been right. I'd finally gone too far. I'd made my bed. And now, I was being forced to lie in it.

But for whatever reason, be it wishful thinking or outright stupidity, I just didn't buy it. The Ancients—the Mother Goddess, in particular—had never ignored me like this. They'd never failed to come to my rescue, and this was damned sure no time to start. So, what the hell was the deal?

There's nothing quite like helplessness to breed anger and resentment, and by now, I'd had time to breed a bunch of each. In fact, I'd turned the corner on hurt feelings hours ago and was firmly on the road to livid pissed. Just Who the hell did They think They were? Just what the hell did They think They were doing? I was a Witch, goddamn it! A *Witch*! And a damned good one at that. I was one of Their own. And now They had the nerve to...

If I could've mustered the strength to laugh at my mental outburst, I would have. But at that point, I was way too weak to even crack a smile. Still, I knew that one day I'd laugh about this realization—and the preposterous way that the Ancients had engineered it.

Yes, indeed...I *was* a Witch, goddamn it. And as such, I was going to do more than just survive this mess. I was going to get myself out of it. It was only a matter of using the basics. My most valuable resources.

With that in mind, I took three deep breaths and plunged right in. "Oh, Mighty Element of Water," I whispered softly as I visualized its magical symbol. "You Who present us with the gifts of power and life, moisture and chill, shrinkage and contraction...I conjure, call and stir Ye up..."

CHAPTER 16

Cal had sure been right about one thing: Oya definitely took her time. In fact, Chloe was beginning to wonder whether she was ever going to gain entrance. She found herself begging silently, apologizing profusely for past transgressions and pleading ignorance. But nothing seemed to work. She glanced helplessly at Cal who, holding up a hand to stay her, waited patiently on the other side.

Chloe took a deep breath, then tried again, this time in a whisper. "Come on, Oya...I didn't know. How could I? I didn't even know about You. Not until just a few minutes ago. So how could I possibly know that You're in charge of the cemeteries? Please, please, *please* let me in! I promise never to insult You again. Honest!"

She waited a few heartbeats. But still, there was no answer. *Oh, horse shit! I don't have time for this crap,* Chloe thought. *Not right now! I need...*

Chloe clapped her hand to her forehead. How could she have been so stupid? Thinking that sort of shit in Oya's direction sure wasn't going help matters. Not at all. Especially not after having just promised never to insult Her again. In fact at this rate, she'd be out here all night. If she'd only heard what Cal had said, maybe she'd know what to do. But she hadn't. And because she and Cal weren't supposed to speak to each other again until they were both inside the cemetery, it was too late to find out.

"Oh, give me a break," she muttered in desperation. While she'd been careful to avoid any expletives that normally would have accompanied that request, she doubted that it mattered. Not at this point. She'd already screwed up more royally than she ever dreamed possible, and Cal might just have to go ahead without her. In fact, that was probably what needed to happen. Besides, if she couldn't even manage something as simple as gaining a cemetery permission's slip, there was no telling what else she might fuck up before the night was done.

With that in mind, she gestured to Cal to go on. And just at that moment, it happened. She got the break she'd asked for—and it came in unexpected words that flew through her mind with so much solidity, she might have been reading them from a book.

Oya, of the Winds of Change
I come before You to arrange

My passage into Your domain
This sacred place where You do reign
I pay You homage as its Queen
And come before You scarved and clean
Anointed with a wine of red
To aid with magic of the dead
And protect the lives of others who
Aren't ready to be ruled by You
I have a gift for You in hand
Which I shall give you once I stand
Within Your realm beside my friend
Oh, Oya! Your permission, please extend!

The cackle, which surprised Chloe enough to jump a good three inches, came out of nowhere and everywhere all at the same time. But even more unsettling was the voice that followed—a voice rich with the melodious accents of the South—a voice that many would never have associated with a Goddess.

"A present? You got me a *present*? Well...what's you *waitin'* on, Girl?" Oya demanded. "Get your scrawny ass in here and lemme see!"

The reaction was so unexpected that it was all Chloe could do not to laugh out loud. And the only way she managed to cross the boundary in silence was to clasp one hand firmly across her mouth. But once she drained the vial, heard the pennies clink to the ground, and said her thank-you's, she lost it. She burst into such a fit of laughter that it almost took her breath, for Oya—that great Queen of Cemeteries Who'd refused to hear her pleas—was now literally purring over those wine-soaked pennies with a mixture of feminine ecstasy and child-like pleasure.

"I suppose I should have warned you," Cal said with a smile. "She takes some getting used to."

"Not at all. Any Goddess Who likes presents *that* much is all right with me," Chloe panted, still trying to catch her breath. "And if all your deities are this much fun, well...what's not to love?!"

Cal cocked an eyebrow at Chloe's last remark but didn't say a word. She couldn't help but wonder, how her new friend would react to Papa Legba, the Keeper of the Gates. Now *that* was going to be interesting.

It seemed like they'd been on the road forever. They'd already left Cape Girardeau, Jackson and Fruitland in the dust and were now headed toward Perryville. "Jesus God in heaven, Luke...how far are we going?" Brian asked. "All the way to St. Louis?"

"No. It's right off Sixty-One between St. Mary, and Ste. Gen'," he said. "Out in the middle of nowhere."

Out in the middle of nowhere was right, Brian thought irritably. He wished they'd known sooner. He wished Liza had picked some place closer. And damn it to hell...he wished Tess had had better sense than to get in the car with her. "Wish in one hand and shit in the other," he muttered.

"Hunh?"

"Nothing," he replied. "You sure you can find this place?"

"Yeah," Luke said. "My folks owned it for years. Even thought about building a place there. Then Dad got sick and all those plans went to hell in a hand basket. They sold it just before they both got killed in that car wreck."

"So, what makes you think Liza might've gone there?"

"She loved the place. Even talked about buying it back for a while. Not sure what happened with that though," he said. "Guess the owners just weren't interested in selling."

Brian's ears perked up. If somebody lived on the property, maybe there was a way to get a jump on this situation after all. "Owners?" he questioned. "They *live* there?"

Luke shook his head. "Somewhere down south, last I heard. Florida, maybe. But I don't think they've even seen the land in years. Just pay the taxes every year."

Brian grunted. If Luke was right...if Liza really had absconded with Tess...if she really had lost her fucking mind...well...what they needed was a miracle. And as if in answer, a brown sign appeared on the side of the highway.

"Ever heard of that place?" Brian asked, gesturing toward the side of the road.

He'd been a kid the last time he was there. It was one of those places parents took kids whether they wanted to go or not—especially when they were acting up and it was time to scare the snot out of them. He remembered that visit like it was yesterday. And the way his mother had tried to snatch him back to the straight and narrow with her scare tactics:

What on earth would the Blessed Mother say about this?! I'll bet She's very disappointed in your behavior, Brian John Dawson," she'd preached, *"very disappointed, indeed. So disappointed, you've probably made Her cry. In fact, I'll bet She's talking to Jesus about you right now. And you know He's not going to be very happy at all if you've made His mother cry...*

Hell...he couldn't even remember now what he'd done that was bad enough to warrant that speech. But he did remember feeling terrible about making someone as nice as the Blessed Mother cry. And he also remembered doing his best to be good for some time after that, just so he wouldn't upset Her again. Brian smiled at the memory in spite of himself.

"The Shrine of Our Lady of the Miraculous Medal? Yeah, I've heard of it," Luke said.

"So...you believe in miracles?"

"I don't know," he said truthfully. "But some people seem to think that's the place to get one if you need it."

"Well, my friend," Brian said, glancing over at him, "that's what we need right now. A real, live, bona fide miracle. So, if you know any prayers that might bring one about, I suggest you get busy. Otherwise..."

Brian's voice trailed off. And Luke didn't prompt him to continue. Neither wanted to think about the alternative possibilities.

Liza added some more leaves and poked at the fire with branding iron. At this rate, it might be daylight before it was hot enough. The leaves she'd crammed under the fresh wood hadn't caught. And the only indication they were there at all came from the clouds of smoke that billowed up in her face and stung her eyes. She used the iron for leverage, lifted a log to let in some air and was rewarded by a tiny flame that licked at the wood and danced along its belly. Continuing to hold the log aloft, she watched the flame grow and smiled a satisfied smile.

Even though she loved the woods and enjoyed their beauty,

she'd never been much good at this outdoor stuff. But give her a cook stove or a fireplace, and she could build a fire so hot it would run you right out of the house. Maybe she should have paid more attention in Girl Scouts.

Girl Scouts? What were Girl Scouts? Puzzlement clouded her face as she considered the phrase. She was certain she'd never heard it before, but if that was so, why had it filtered through her brain and surfaced? She searched her memory banks and came up empty. A lot of that had happened lately. Terms completely foreign to her—terms that had nothing at all to do with her or her life—kept cropping up here and there. It was more than disconcerting. It was enough to make a perfectly sane person think they were crazy.

Well, Liza thought, removing the iron and letting the log fall into place again, I'm not crazy. In fact, the only crazy thing I ever did was to let this go on. I should have tended to it the minute he decided to marry her.

Well, none of that matters. Not really, she thought, watching the flames spread rapidly through the pile of wood in front of her. *I'm tending to it now, and that's what counts.*

The fire crackled in agreement, and sparks lit the night as she added another log.

"North to South," she intoned, swigging from the Barbancourt bottle and spitting rum forward and backward. "And East to West." She swigged again and shot the mouthful of alcohol from side to side before continuing. "As I stand in this cross, heed my request."

Motioning to Chloe to hand her the lit cigar, she turned the glowing end toward her mouth and inserted it, holding it firmly between clenched teeth. She drew in a mouthful of smoke and blew it out toward the north, repeating the process for the other three directions.

Removing the cigar from her mouth and holding it in her hand, she continued with the incantation. "Papa Legba, fling the gates forth now! Open them wide and do allow my passage through them with great haste. Remove all obstacles that are placed within my way from each direction; dissolve them all without objection.

"And for these tokens of our affection," Cal continued, grabbing the liquor bottle with her free hand and raising both arms above her head, "grant us Your power of protection." She brought the bottle to her lips, swilled the liquor in her mouth and spit it between her feet. Then inserting the inverted cigar between her teeth and drawing deeply, she exhaled the smoke in the very same spot and waited for the gates to open.

After waiting for a minute or two with no results, Cal handed both the bottle and the cigar to Chloe. "Sheer stubbornness," she said in a confidential tone. "He enjoys His fun and likes to screw with people. Sometimes, it takes Him awhile."

"But weren't you supposed to call on the saints?"

"What?"

Chloe shrugged her shoulders. "The *saints*," she repeated. "The stuff Tess got from that dream said to call on the saints."

Truth be told, Cal had been so concerned about handling the tricks properly that she'd completely forgotten. But now, it all made sense. Tricks fixed that long ago would not have been laid using the actual names of the deities—especially not by those who'd come from New Orleans—because of a Louisiana law of the time regarding the enslaved. To comply with the law, owners were bound to have their charges baptized in the Catholic church. It was the state's way of stamping out the practice of Afro-Caribbean religions while removing the very last freedom from those who had little or none.

But that hadn't stopped the enslaved; they'd just figured a way around it. In studying the lives of the saints, they'd found counterparts for their own deities. And by exchanging one name for another, they'd not only been able to continue their religious practices and worship as they pleased, but managed to do so while cloaked under the cover of Catholicism and in compliance with the law.

"I don't suppose you've got a copy of..."

"Already way ahead of you," Chloe said, grinning from ear to ear. She dug through one of her bags, produced a file folder and thrust it toward Cal. "I found this tonight on Tess' kitchen table and grabbed it just in case."

"Well, well, Ms. Wish," Cal said, flipping through the pages and extracting what she needed, "when we get through this, I'm going to personally recommend your promotion to full-fledge Witch!"

Scanning the notes carefully, she drew in a deep breath and exhaled fully. "Okay, Papa," she called out, "let's try it this way!"

Sally Nicewander had never felt so guilty in her life. It wasn't really her fault. She hadn't been the one who'd decided to unearth all those past lives. But that didn't make it any better. *She* had been the one who'd done those regressions. *She* had been the one who'd turned over the reports. And *she* had been the one who'd played with the missing pieces until they all fit together in one nice, neat little package.

Like it or not, she was responsible.

Maybe if she hadn't regressed Liza, she wouldn't have flipped out. And maybe Tess would be sitting here right now—lounging around in her satin pajamas and guzzling coffee in a cloud of cigarette smoke—instead of Gods knew where with a crazy person. Maybe if she hadn't regressed Brian, he wouldn't have had a stroke. Thank the Gods she hadn't regressed Tess. Heaven only knew what might have happened if she had.

Like it could get any worse, she thought, shaking her head irritably. She got up again and paced the floor. If only she could do something other than sit by the phone. If...if...if...

Well, "if" was the biggest word in the English language. And all the "if's" in the world, no matter how she sliced them, stretched them or put them back together again, weren't going to fix this. The only thing that would was bringing Liza back to reality. And that wasn't going to happen unless—no, until—Cal was able to break those tricks.

Sally wondered how Cal was faring with that. Although she'd put on a good front, she hadn't looked too good when she'd left. She'd looked as worried as Chloe—and that was worried as hell. Cal had seemed so frazzled, in fact, that if Sally hadn't known better, she'd have thought that Cal had never handled this sort of thing before.

Dat's cuz she ain't! It was that voice again. The one that had plagued her ever since she'd regressed Chloe. The one belonging to Mattie.

"What do you mean, she's hasn't? She came highly recommended," Sally retorted, glad there was no one to hear her talking out loud to the voice in her head. "She's the best there is. She..."

Oh, I s'pect she done broke a plenty, all right. But she ain't never seen no tricks like dese. Sho' ain't.

"That's okay. She's smart. She'll figure it out. She'll have those tricks broken in no time."

No'm. Not dese tricks. Not lessen she be's gettin' some he'p.
"But she's got Chloe. She..."
Melodious laughter caught her off in mid-sentence. *Lawd have mercy, you be's a funny lady! Dat chile ain't no he'p a'tall. Not for dese tricks. She be's needin' Mistuh Will. Dat's who she be's needin'.*
"Mister Will?"
Unh-hunh.
"Who's that?"
Well, sit down in dat chair right dere, an' lemme r'fresh yo' mem'ry...

With Chloe's help, Cal repeated the gate-opening process, complete with the rum and cigar offerings. Only this time, the incantation was different. Much different. So different that Chloe actually cringed at its tone from the very first words.

"Open the gates! Open them *now!*" Cal called, her voice both insistent and unyielding. "I *won't* be denied or be disallowed!"

Instead of a request to the Gods, Chloe thought, this sounded more like a mother demanding appropriate behavior from a spoiled child. And even though she'd often heard Tess doing much the same thing, it was something she'd never gotten used to. In fact, it scared her shitless.

"I'm Calliope Jones, the daughter of Jeanne, granddaughter of Sadie who passed through Irene, descended of Buzzard, and John, and Marie. I call to all saints that You hearken to me: St. Peter! St. Peter! You hold the key! St. Peter! St. Peter! St. Peter, come forth—and open the gates from East, South, West and North!"

And no sooner had Cal flung the last word from her tongue, something astonishing happened. Electrical charges streaked brightly around Cal, lighting up the night and dancing across the ground in all four directions. Chloe flew back in terror, certain that her most secret fear—that of being struck by lightning—was sure to be realized.

Cal, though, breathed a sigh of relief. "Nothing to worry about," she said nonchalantly. "Papa's element is fire, and it often accompanies the gate opening in some form."

Chloe wasn't a bit happy about the fiery exhibition and when she spoke, her voice was laced with sarcasm. "Well," she said, "maybe you should've warned me about *that* too!"

No matter how indifferent Cal seemed to Papa's display, such truly wasn't the case. The gates had flown open with such speed and force that Cal had never seen its like. The process had never failed to amaze her, but this time it was downright unsettling. It was almost as if Papa Legba, or St. Peter as the case may be, had taken some sort of special interest. As if He'd made it His personal business to watch and wait in anticipation of her arrival. Although she wasn't complaining about the way He'd expedited matters, the whole thing left her feeling very ill at ease.

Trying to shake it off, she patted the ground and motioned for Chloe to sit. Then she fished in her bag for the envelope Luke had given her. Ripping it open, she said, "Maybe we'd better check this out before we go any further."

"What's in there," Chloe asked, craning for a better look.

"Looks like old photographs. Well, actually, a collection of daguerreotypes and tintypes," Cal answered, looking at a few she'd already pulled out. "Luke said I needed to look at these before we did anything about the tricks." She started to dump the entire contents out in her lap but thought better of it. Instead, she retrieved a cloth from the bag, spread it in front of them and went about the business of laying the pictures out one by one.

"Good Goddess!" Chloe exclaimed. Goosebumps, courtesy of the images on the cloth, had already formed on her arms and were making their way up her spine. She could hardly believe that she was really seeing this and gave her eyes a quick rubbing just to make sure. "Just look at them," she gasped. "Do you see it too? Oh, Cal...*please* tell me that you do...and that I haven't lost my mind!"

At a loss for words, Cal merely nodded. She'd never seen anything like this in her entire life. In fact, she'd never even dreamt it was possible. Could magic really cause something like this? Well, apparently it could, she thought to herself, because it had.

There was no other explanation for the current changes in the old images spread before her, for one by one, each was taking on a life of its own. A personal animation of sorts. Eyes blinked, moved and followed. Lips smiled and frowned. Facial muscles twitched. They were alive, all right. And if that wasn't disconcerting enough, they seemed to be evaluating the two women sitting in front of them.

"Okay," Cal said, trying to keep her voice calm and looking

directly at Chloe, "they don't seem dangerous...it's just that neither of us is used to magic manifesting in this form. But since it has, these have to be pictures of the people connected with the tricks."

Chloe nodded.

"So, I want you to do me a favor. Close your eyes and take deep breaths." When Chloe complied, Cal slowly counted to ten. "Now," she said, "open your eyes and tell me which image you noticed first."

"This one," Chloe answered, pointing to the tintype image of a young man. He looked vaguely familiar and yet, she was sure she'd never seen him before.

"Great!" Cal carefully placed the rest of the pictures back into the envelope and handed Chloe the one she had chosen. "Just hang on to this," she said, gathering the rest of their things. "I've got a hunch."

Chloe's eyes were still wide and disbelieving. And by the way she was holding that picture by one corner, it was obvious that she'd rather be handling a poisonous snake. "What sort of hunch?" she asked cautiously.

Cal's smile came easily for the first time since they'd left Sikeston. "I've got a feeling that the spirit of the guy in that tintype is going to be our salvation tonight. So, come on, Ms. Wish," she said, gesturing for Chloe to get up, "let's go see if we can find him!"

"God-*DAMN* it!" Sally screamed at the top of her lungs. She'd already tried the car phone three times without any luck. Surely Cal and Chloe had it with them in the cemetery. Otherwise, there wouldn't have been any reason to take it at all.

She went through all the reasons that they might not be answering the phone. The battery pack? No. She'd just replaced that the other day, so they'd have plenty of juice. Out of range? Doubtful. Her service was so good, she could probably talk to the Dalai Lama. So, why weren't they picking up? This was important, damn it! And there wasn't a minute to lose!

She left another message then sat down in the chair to think. Mattie's story had been intriguing, to say the least. And the gist of it was that Cal needed to visit a specific grave in that cemetery—the grave of Sergeant Will McGee, CSA. Lucinda's first husband and Nellie's father, he'd been slain on a Confederate battlefield in 1864. And for whatever reason, Mattie felt sure that his spirit could still be contacted; moreover, she felt such contact was imperative.

The gist of it was that the help had to come from someone who'd truly loved Lucinda, someone who'd always done whatever it took to make her happy, even if it meant extreme personal sacrifice. But that wasn't the only reason that contacting Will's spirit was important. Chivalry and good manners had always been a big deal to him; so much so, in fact, that his pet peeve had been men who were too cowardly to defend their women. And with Tess missing and in possible danger, she damned sure needed defending. Sally couldn't imagine a more appropriate spirit to conjure than Will's, or a better time to do it. In all actuality, she thought, it might be the only thing that stopped Liza in her tracks long enough for Cal to break those tricks.

At this point, she decided that placing another call was a moot point. They weren't answering and that was that. Still, there had to be another way to get in touch with them. She couldn't leave the house— that was a given—and because of the need for secrecy, she didn't dare send one of the neighbors to the plantation with a message. Besides, sending a message would call for an explanation, and she simply wasn't up to concocting one. Who, after all, would believe the truth even if she told it?

There was a way, but Sally wasn't sure she was up to that either. It involved mental telepathy, and that was something she'd only played with occasionally. Since she wasn't close to Cal, establishing a connection was iffy at best. And even if she succeeded, the chances of conveying a *clear* message were even worse.

Den try Miz Nellie.

"What?!"

Lawd, Chile! Do I gots t'tell you everything? Mistuh Will be's her daddy, an'...

But Sally wasn't listening anymore. She was already working her way through the mental checklist for contact. Counting breaths, she grounded herself. Then visualizing a thin gold wire attaching her thoughts to Chloe's mind, she set up the line of communication and prepared for the test.

"Chloe!" Even though Sally's lips were pressed together and she hadn't uttered a word, the name went screaming through the ether. She counted to five and tried again. *"Chloe, answer me!"*

Ten seconds went by with no response. Even so, Sally had the feeling that she was getting through loud and clear. The problem wasn't that Chloe couldn't hear her; it was that Chloe was ignoring her. And she just didn't have time for that shit. None of them did.

"DAMN IT, Chloe," she yelled, "I'm *talking* to you! So, whatever you're doing, just stop it right now. This is fucking important! And I don't have time to play games with..."

Sally involuntarily clapped her hands over her mouth in horror, and her face flushed red. She couldn't believe she'd said that word, aloud or not, regardless of her level of aggravation or how badly she wanted to get Chloe's attention. It simply wasn't in her vocabulary. It was a good thing her mother wasn't around to witness that crude remark; otherwise, she'd have died of embarrassment at having raised such an ill-mannered and...

"What?!"

Sally stifled a chuckle. No matter how common the word, she'd damned sure gotten Chloe's attention. And at this point, that was all that mattered.

CHAPTER 17

"Are you all right?!"

Chloe didn't say a word. She just stood there under the gigantic oak, her face a complete blank with eyes devoid of all expression. The moonlight peeking through the mossy branches illuminated her such that she looked more like a marble statue than a living, breathing human being.

"Chloe?"

Her answer didn't come in words, but in the simple gesture of throwing up one hand. With her fingers splayed outward, that one motion probably did more to convey its message than any words she might have spoken. It not only let Cal know she was fine but made her hush. And the latter was much more important right now.

She tilted her head to the side for a moment and opened her mouth as if she might say something. But she closed it again and simply nodded. Then suddenly, her eyes came to life again and focused on Cal.

"This way," she said, gesturing to the right with her thumb.

"What?"

"This way," Chloe repeated, quickly rounding the corner. "I know where we're going, and I know who we're looking for. And if we don't get there in a hurry," she called over her shoulder, "we may all be screwed!"

The last word was barely out of her mouth before she took off down the path in a dead run. And by the time Cal caught up with her, she was already standing at a gravesite, tintype crushed to her breast and in the process of initiating a conversation.

"Sergeant McGee," she began, "my name is Chloe Dawson. You might not recognize me...I'm sure that my voice and body aren't the same as you remember...but we used to know each other very well. There was a time that you'd have done anything for me, or for my mama. And that's because you...well...because...you were once my father. And I..."

"Nellie?!"

The voice reverberated through the cemetery with such force that it shook Cal right to her very core. She'd had lots of conversations with spirits in her lifetime but never anything like this. Spirits spoke to the mind, integrating their messages with personal thought patterns, so it was often difficult for the inexperienced communicator to separate the two.

She'd never before experienced a spirit who'd been able to talk right out loud. She didn't even know it was possible.

Chloe's eyes were wide with confusion. And from the helpless shrug of her shoulders, it was apparent that she'd never experienced anything like this either.

"Don't stop now, Chloe," Cal whispered with a reassuring pat on the shoulder. "You're doing fine."

Chloe took a deep breath. "Y-yes, Daddy," she stammered. "The reason I'm here is because Mama...well, the woman who used to be Mama—her name is Tess Logan now—needs your help. We all need your help. You see, there are these magic spells, and...gee, Daddy...you can fix anything!"

Now, Chloe was more confused than ever. That wasn't what she'd wanted to say. It wasn't even close. She'd already formed the whole speech in her mind, and the words were right on the tip of her tongue. No matter what she did though, she couldn't seem to loosen them from her mouth. Suddenly, everything that rolled off her tongue resembled the fearful ramblings of a small child rather than the intelligent pleas of a grown woman.

She shook her head and tried again. "I'm not explaining this too good, Daddy...I..."

Visions of a little girl with auburn curls floated through her mind's eye. She was all smiles, sitting on the sergeant's knee as he read to her from a book of fairy tales. She was swinging from the rope swing tied to the old oak. She was running through the cotton fields, playing a game of chase with the other kids. She was...

Damn it, Chloe, she thought, you've got to get a grip! He's not your daddy...not anymore! Holding on to that thought for dear life, she visualized herself as the person she was today. Blonde. Blue-eyed. Middle-aged. But even that didn't stop the images. They just kept swirling about in her mind's eye as if trapped in some ancient kaleidoscope from which there was no release.

But her distress—no matter how vast—didn't even come close to the icy horror that dug its tentacles deeply into the pit of Cal's stomach as she watched Chloe slip into little girl mode right in front of her eyes. This couldn't be happening. Not right now. She couldn't be slipping into a past life just as Liza had. And yet, she was. Hell, she already had!

Her speech patterns had become child-like. Her face had already begun to undergo a soft metamorphosis. Even her hands had gotten pudgy. And if she didn't find a way to ground her immediately...

Grab a'hold of that chile, Little Missy, and don't you tarry, MawMaw shrieked. *Snatch her up like a duck on a june bug! And don't you be's turnin' her loose. Not 'til she be's done. Y'hear?!*

Cal sprang into action, throwing both arms around Chloe and crossing them in front of her to hold her tight. She just hoped it wasn't too late.

"Daddy...can you fix this? I mean...it's a real big mess...the biggest...and I..."

Quickly changing positions, Cal jerked Chloe's body back against hers so that her head rested on her shoulder. Then securing her with one arm, she firmly placed her free hand across Chloe's forehead and prayed for results.

"...the reason I came here was to ask that you defend our names and defend our honor. In fact, Sergeant McGee, our very lives lay right in your hands."

Cal's knees nearly buckled from relief. Chloe's voice was back. Her sense of reasoning was back. Her face and hands had returned to normal. And there was nothing to indicate that a change had ever occurred. Now, all she had to do was keep it that way.

"On my honah as a Suhthun gentleman, Ah've nevah refused a lady in distress," the spirit answered, *"and Ah'm not likely to staht now. So, if you'll just tell me how Ah may be of suhvice...we'll get this wah undahway!"*

I wiggled my left foot around in the shackle but couldn't quite free my heel. There was no need to worry though. I'd already managed to gain the freedom of my right wrist and foot by breathing Water into my pores, a little exercise that applied properly caused minor shrinkage in the body. And with those results in hand, I knew that by concentrating all efforts toward the left side of my body, I could free the remaining foot as well.

My only enemy was time. I had no idea when Liza would return. And I damned sure needed to be out of there before she did.

Gauging by my progress, I thought another ten breaths or so should do it. I opened my pores again and inhaled deeply, feeling the cooling vapors permeate my left foot. Repeating the process again and again brought a tingling sensation and finally, the partial numbness that indicated complete saturation. I grabbed the branch with both hands for support and stood on my toes. Then using my free foot as leverage, I pushed down on the shackle and maneuvered it carefully around my heel and over my instep until it finally slipped from my toes.

Ah, the wonders of pore-breathing! It had to be the best invention since milk chocolate, I thought as I quickly exhaled the liquid and flexed my toes. Part of me could hardly believe I hadn't thought of this earlier. But the other part knew why.

You see, my initial experiences with the exercise had left much to be desired, especially when practiced in conjunction with the Element of Water. In fact, I'd nearly managed to flood all thirty-eight floors of a posh California hotel right in the middle of Hollywood.

It had been one of those sleepless nights. The sort where your brain won't shut down, and no matter how you toss and turn, you can't get comfortable. I'd tried reading. I'd tried counting. I'd even gotten up and taken a warm shower. But it was no use. My brain simply wouldn't cooperate.

Finally, I'd decided to work on my pore-breathing exercises. They were simple enough, and best of all, I could do them in bed. All I had to do was visualize every pore in my body flying open and accepting a small amount of my Element of choice as I inhaled. That night, I chose Water and my objective was ten breaths.

Within the span of twenty minutes or so, I'd met the goal. And since I still wasn't sleepy, I decided to push the envelope a bit. But instead of adding a breath at a time—something I'd been specifically instructed to do—I got cocky. I added five. And the truth of the matter was...well...I lost control.

It started with a gurgling racket in the bathroom. The toilet overflowed and water rushed into the bathtub with such force, it sounded like Niagara Falls. The next thing I knew, water was spilling from the sink spigot and the showerhead.

Now, practicality would dictate that I just shut off the water valve. Easy enough, I thought, so I tried that. When that didn't work, I did what any good Witch would do: I expelled all the water from my pores. That didn't work either. In fact, the problem just got worse and worse.

The final straw was when the hotel room sprinkler system

initiated as I was frantically calling the front desk for help. And that was when I discovered that the whole building was awash.

Looking back on that fiasco, it was understandable that a repeat performance wasn't high on my priority list of fun things to do. But tonight was a different story, I thought, working rapidly to unknot the rope on my remaining wrist. If I was going to escape that branding iron, I needed Water and a lot of it. And if, in the final analysis, I had to swim my way out of here? Well, all I could say was...so mote it be!

"Are you sure about this?" Cal asked. They'd been on their hands and knees for the last twenty minutes, digging up dirt from Mattie's gravesite and still had nothing to show for their efforts.

"You heard him as well as I did," Chloe said. "So, they've got to be here. Unless you think he was lying or something..."

"No. It's not that," Cal said, putting down her stick and scooping away the loose soil with her hands. "Even though spirits don't have to tell the truth, I think he was probably as honest as they come. It's just that I'm beginning to wonder if he was mistaken."

"Well, I say we keep digging. Unless, of course, you have a better idea!"

Cal had to admit that she didn't. And according to Sergeant McGee, she couldn't break one trick without the other.

He'd also told them that the pins from the trick binding Lucinda and Jonah were not only still intact, but were resting comfortably in this plot of ground. It seemed that the trick—a pair of poppets pinned together—had been sewn to the underside of Mattie's cemetery quilt, the quilt that had covered her grave when she'd been laid to rest. And since by tradition these were never removed, it stood to reason that bits of the fabric should still exist under the ground. What they didn't know was how much dirt, leaf matter and debris might have fallen on top of that coverlet in the last hundred years. So, they had no reference point as to depth.

Cal thought about the poppets and still wondered if the sergeant might have been mistaken. He'd actually called them dolls, but she knew what he meant. The fact of the matter was that even though poppets were often attributed to the practice of Voudon, their roots were actually buried in Witchcraft. So the notion that Mattie would have utilized them in any sort of trick—even this one—came as a surprise. Still, anything was possible. Magical systems seldom existed in their original states for any length of time. Practitioners had always picked up bits and pieces along the way and added them to the personal mix. So it stood to reason that Mattie had done the same thing. And even if the use of poppets did seem odd in this case, there was no way to tell what Mattie might have learned over the years, or from whom.

"Just a second," Chloe said, motioning her out of the way. Picking up a fallen limb and using it to carefully scrape the loose dirt toward the foot of the grave, she shined the flashlight across the cleared portion. Not so much as a thread caught her eye.

"That's about five inches," she said, surveying their work. "I figure we've got at least two more to go."

Cal sat back on her heels and looked at the shallow trough. She momentarily wished for a shovel but then thought better of it. They were looking for pins—the proverbial needles in the haystack—and for this sort of work, hands were much better.

"Okay...let's change our course," she said, giving birth to an idea. "If the sergeant was right...if the poppets were, indeed, sewn to the underside of the quilt...I'm willing to bet that they were attached right in the center. So..."

"We'll stop digging everywhere else except the middle," Chloe said, finishing the thought for her.

"Exactly!" Cal exclaimed. "If we come up empty, we can always expand the search. After all," she added, "you've already bought us some time by sending the sergeant to protect Tess." Lord knows, she thought with a sigh, if he can't protect her from Liza, no one can.

Then without another word, she dug both hands into the center of the grave and resumed her work.

Sometimes, what appears to be a good idea at the onset and what actually constitutes one are two entirely different things. Developing the downpour of the century when it had first occurred to me would have qualified, since Liza's chances of starting a fire would have been slim to none. And while she still might have used the iron as a weapon, the possibility of having the flesh scorched from my bones would have been the least of my worries. Taking a good look at my surroundings might've been a good idea too; I'd have been better equipped to plan my escape route.

But I was far too worried about freeing myself to bother with either of those. In fact, it was all I could think about.

So once I'd gotten loose, I hadn't wasted a second on anything else. I crept into the cover of the woods and putting one foot in front of the other, headed in what I thought was the direction of the road. Inching my way through that dense thicket seemed to take forever. And it probably did, since I knew that the slightest noise might alert Liza— something I had to avoid at all costs—and stepping on a stick, jostling a branch or stumbling over my own two feet could very well sound the alarm. To compound matters, my body ached all over and didn't want to cooperate. My head, wrists and ankles throbbed. My joints and muscles screamed for rest and recuperation, respite and regeneration. So it was only by force and the sheer will to live that I was able to propel myself onward and keep moving.

Just when I thought I couldn't take another step, I came to a clearing. But as I peered through the scrub brush to survey my surroundings, a sudden realization brought my heart to my throat. That patch of woods I'd thought was so deep was nothing more than a long, semi-circular grove, and even after all my efforts, I'd only managed to travel a few yards from my starting point. Even worse was the other sight that awaited my arrival: There stood Liza, branding iron in hand, busily stirring the fire.

In retrospect, I probably should've just worked my way to the back edge of the grove, climbed up in a tree and stayed put. Instead, I thought my best bet was to double back through the woods and sneak out behind her. But because hindsight is always 20/20, and the wicked always seems to grow eyes in the back of their heads, that decision proved to be as faulty as all the rest.

While I did manage to pick my way to the other end of the grove without noise or incident, my reward was not escape. Instead, I came face to face with a furious Liza.

Under normal circumstances, I doubted she could've kicked her way out of a wet paper sack. But these circumstances weren't normal. Not by a long shot. The reversion back into that past life seemed to have given her an inordinate amount of strength, and even though I got in a few rabbit punches and at least one sound round-house kick—Gods only knew how I'd managed that—they didn't even slow her down. And when I finally landed a punch right in the middle of her face, the sight of her own blood only served one purpose: which was, of course, to piss her off even further.

Considering the errors in judgment I'd made over the past several hours, now was not the time to make another. So when faced again with the fight or flight options, I didn't think twice. I ran—not just as fast as my legs would carry me or faster than I'd ever thought possible—I ran like there was no tomorrow. Because there was one thing of which I was absolutely certain: If I didn't, there might not be—at least not for me.

"It's right up here," Luke said, gesturing toward the left. "Between those two trees."

"You *sure*?! That's not even a *road*," Brian said in disbelief. "I'm not even sure it could pass for one in a pinch. Hell, Luke...that looks more like a cattle trail than anything else. Surely..."

Luke nodded his head. "No, that's it. I'm positive. Just pull in on the left."

Brian turned the wheel and carefully maneuvered the car into the tight space Luke had indicated. "Now what?"

"Well, normally," Luke said, trying to peer through the steadily moving windshield wipers, "I'd say to drive on back. But maybe we should just park here and walk. Looks pretty muddy and..."

"Yeah," Brian said, cutting the lights and shutting off the engine. "I'd hate to waste a perfectly good miracle on a stuck car. Probably be better off saving it for later," he added with a wink.

He breathed a sigh of relief as his poor attempt at humor elicited a nervous chuckle from Luke. The man had been wound up like a nine-day clock all night, and that sort of tension, left unchecked, often overrode good sense. And Brian knew that before this was over, they were going to need every single shred they possessed.

Waiting for the rain to slack up would have been optimal, but it was a moot point. They couldn't afford that luxury and they knew it. So, braced for the chill of the autumn rain, they got out of the car and sloshed through the narrow pass.

The bright glare of the flashlight revealed remnants of tire tracks, and even though the rain had obscured all but the faintest trace, following them wasn't a problem. Woods bordered both sides of the grassy strip, and there was no other way to drive in. Someone had been here, all right, Brian thought. He just hoped it *was* Liza, and they hadn't spent all this time on a wild goose chase. Otherwise...well...he wasn't even going to think about that.

Brian glanced at Luke. He looked like he'd aged a hundred years in the last few hours. His face was grim and haggard, and his mouth, nothing more than a tight line. But the renewed look of determination in his eyes said it all. He was a man on a mission, and come what may, he intended to see it through.

They'd walked about a quarter mile when the rain stopped. But the sticky clay-based mud left in its wake brought its own set of problems. It grabbed and snatched at their shoes, sucking them down and impeding their progress like a demi-demon short on souls and hell bent on making his monthly quota. At this rate, they were going to be worn to a frazzle before they even got there. But Brian tried not to think about that either. Instead, he opted to break the silence between them.

"How much farther?" he asked.

"Depends on where she decided to park," Luke said. "Probably another half mile or so."

Even though they'd spoken in near whispers, their words seemed to echo in the night. It was quiet. Too quiet. After the rain, the tree frogs should have been singing. The wildlife should have been moving. And yet, the only sound that broke the stillness was the slurping of their feet in the mud.

What bothered Brian the most, though, was that the crickets weren't chirping. And every seasoned woodsman knew that could only mean one thing: danger.

"C'mon," he said, trying to keep his voice even. "We're going to have to step it up and get a move on. Time's running out and there's no time to lose." No time at all, he thought to himself as they broke into a trot. Not a single second.

Cal and Chloe stood at the crossroads by the creek, gazing into the rushing water and caught in its spell. Filled to the brim by the sudden shower, its contents swirled and twirled with a life of its own, leaping over rocks and fallen limbs, insistent on moving debris out of the way as if to clear the path for something new. A thousand voices, young and old and in-between, seemed to speak in its lofty gurgle, each pleading for some sort of action before it was too late.

A minute or two passed before Cal spoke. "I don't know about this," she said, her eyes never leaving the water.

"Well, you're just going to have to trust me," Chloe said with a confidence she didn't really feel. "I haven't steered you wrong yet, have I?"

Cal had to admit that much was true. Chloe had led them straight to the sergeant's grave. She'd communicated with his spirit and gotten the information they needed. She'd been right about continuing to dig for the trick parcel too. It had been exactly where the sergeant said it would be, and they'd found it still attached to a tiny remnant of rotted cloth.

And the poppets? Well, surprisingly enough, they'd found those also. But even more surprising was that they were found nearly intact in their original forms. And that meant that they weren't made of cotton, the substance that would have been the main crop on the plantation at that time. Instead, they'd been constructed of a much more durable fiber—a fiber that Cal could only assume was hemp—as if they'd been meant to stand the test of time.

Yes, Chloe had been right about everything so far. But *this*?! Some poem that Tess had scribbled on the back of her dream notes? She just didn't know.

True enough, it *did* look like an incantation. But if Tess Logan had had the solution all along, why was she still here? She could have just given Tess the trick parcel she already had, and with Chloe's help, they could have found the poppets and taken care of everything else themselves. It just didn't make sense.

Besides, Tess' poem—this poem that Chloe insisted was an incantation—didn't even vaguely resemble what she'd planned on using to break these tricks. She needed to blow this magic wide open. Blast it into smithereens. And she just wasn't sure this was going to do the job.

"*Well*?!" Chloe demanded. "Are we going to stand here all night or what?"

Cal looked up and let out a heavy breath. "I'm just not sure this will work," she said gently. "I think we'd be better off sticking to the original plan."

Chloe was incredulous. "Original plan? You're kidding, right? Back at the car, you admitted to being as scared as I was," she said indignantly. "And that tells me that you probably didn't even have a firm plan in mind.

"Besides," she continued, "if Tess wrote this down—especially on these particular pages—it's got to be important. It's what we've got. It's what we have. And if you want to add some..."

"*What* did you just say?!"

"I said, it's what we've got and what we have. And if..."

MawMaw's cackle echoed through her brain, its melody filling every nook and cranny in her head. And it was all the confirmation that Cal needed.

"All right," she said, suppressing a chuckle of her own. "Let's get this show on the road!"

They smelled the smoke before they saw it and headed in that direction. The fire, unattended and reduced to coals, glowed with heat just a few yards from Liza's car—a sight that rendered both men speechless. Although the soggy ground and remaining puddles of water confirmed that no fire could have survived the recent downpour, blue and yellow flames licked at the coals in contradiction, insisting that the fire had been started hours ago. So did the myriad of puddled, tennis-shoed footprints around the ring of stones that encased it.

The prints all belonged to the same pair of shoes, and squatting down for a closer look, Brian gauged them at somewhere around a seven or seven and a half.

"Liza wear about a seven and a half?"

There was no response, and Brian looked up to find Luke nowhere in sight. "Just fuckin' ducky," he muttered disgustedly, scanning the area. "Like I've really got time to hunt for you too..."

His voice trailed off as he glanced quickly at the open space ahead. And when that didn't produce Luke, he set off following the tree line at the edge of the grove and found him a few steps later, just around the bend.

"Luke," he called in a stage whisper. "Come on!"

But Luke wasn't listening. He stood stock still, eyes wide and fixed, staring intently on something in front of him.

"We don't have time for this," Brian said, making no attempt to hide his aggravation and clearing the space between them with a step or two. "Come on!" he said, grabbing Luke's arm and jerking him around. "We've gotta stick to..."

The rest of the words stuck on Brian's tongue as he took in the scene and swept it with his flashlight. Shackles tethered to the ground with chains and railroad spikes. A stout length of rope, looped ends knotted securely to a tree branch, fibers and bark dark with that rich, jewel-toned crimson only known to blood.

"Oh, geeze...oh, *geeze*..." Luke breathed, rocking back and forth anxiously as his brain finally registered the full impact of the sight before him. "You don't think she's..."

"No." Brian hoped he'd replied confidently enough to wipe that thought right out of Luke's mind. "Not enough blood. And the wrist restraints are still intact. My gut says she got loose. But how the hell she managed that, I don't know."

He aimed the flashlight at the ground, checking the damp dirt around the shackles. A hasty examination revealed more footprints; and while some of them obviously belonged to the same person who'd built the fire, he was most interested in the others, the ones made by bare feet that trailed into the grove.

"That way," he said, nodding toward the woods. *Damn it, Gal,* he thought as if wishing it would make it true, *I hope like hell you used your head, found a hiding place and just stayed put!* But deep down, he knew better. And if he'd been in her shoes, he wouldn't have done that either. He'd have been on the move, trying to get the hell out of there— and since he and Tess were often on the same page when it came to strategy, he was willing to bet hard money that that was what she had done too. This time though, Brian just hoped she'd been smarter than he.

The answer came in the blood-curdling scream that pierced the night and stopped both men in their tracks. Tess Logan and Brian Dawson were still on the same page, all right. And their brain cell counts? Well...those seemed to be identical, as well.

CHAPTER 18

I'd run until I thought my legs wouldn't carry me any farther. And then, I'd run some more. Mind over matter was the only thing that kept me moving. I'd even been able to ignore the burning sensation in my muscles and the horrendous aches in my over-taxed body by insisting to my brain that they weren't really there and were only a figment of my imagination.

But my lungs were another story. I'd always had some inexplicable fear of not being able to breathe. At first, I'd made myself believe that it wasn't so bad, that the slow burn in my chest was manageable. It was only when my lungs felt as if they'd actually caught fire and might explode that the tricks I'd played on my brain ran out; it simply wouldn't listen anymore. I was forced to stop for a few seconds and catch my breath. And that was my undoing.

I'd taken cover behind an old oak tree, wrapping both arms around the trunk for support. My body screamed for rest, insisting that I sit down, lie down or do anything other than stay on my feet, but I didn't dare. Instead, my intention was to climb up into the branches, consider my options and hope for the best.

Unfortunately, I'd never gotten that far.

Liza's whip had come out of nowhere, its sharp leather strap cutting through my shoulders and back and knocking me off my feet. And before I could scramble up again, she'd secured me with a well placed kick to the ribs and heavy foot right in the small of my back.

"Going somewhere?" she asked sarcastically. Her satisfied grin was already enough to scare me shitless, but that's not what evoked the primal scream that issued from the very depths of my belly. It was the branding iron—still red hot and smoking—that she held in her hand.

Whether it was from seeing Tess in such a vulnerable position at Liza's hands, from the shock of the transformation Liza had undergone, or a little of both, Luke ignored Brian's demands to stay back and let him handle the situation. Instead, he raced across the clearing and got right up in Liza's face.

"God damn it, Liza! Just what the hell do you think you're *doing*?!" Luke screeched.

"Just taking care of something you should've taken care of a long time ago. And isn't that just like you," she spat, "to choose her over me? Little Miss Perfect, who never does anything wrong? Even when she steals my man *and* my property? Even when..."

"*W-what*?!"

"Put it *down*, Liza. *Now!*" Brian had stepped out into the open and had his .357 trained on her, hammer cocked back and ready to fire. He just prayed he wouldn't have to use it.

She turned in Brian's direction. "And isn't that just like you too," she hissed, "to take her side over mine? Wasn't it enough to murder me the *first* time? The axe wasn't *good* enough? Now, you're going to shoot me and make sure the job sticks?"

Brian took another step forward and tried to ignore the impact of her words. He couldn't afford the guilt. Not right now. He reminded himself that this was 1994, that he was Brian Dawson, and that he was a deputy sheriff whose only job was to protect the innocent.

He forced himself to smile at her while taking a couple more steps in her direction. "Well," he said with a calmness he didn't feel, "that sure isn't the plan. I'd much rather no one get hurt this..."

"Really?!" She laughed as if that was the funniest thing she'd ever heard then shifted her full weight to the foot on my back. "Same old coward," she said thoughtfully, shaking her head in mock sadness. "Only this time you'll have to *face* me while you do your dirty work. And to be perfectly honest, Mr. Big Bad Deputy Sheriff...I just don't think you've got the guts!"

Even though I was still pinned to the ground and hurt like hell, the burning in my lungs had subsided and I could breathe again. Of course, as my fate still hung in the balance, I didn't know how long that would last. I desperately needed Luke to stay out of this and let Brian handle it, but since I could only see his feet from my position, catching his attention was a moot point.

I'd had the strangest feeling that someone was watching me

since before I'd managed to escape Liza's initial restraints. But once
Luke and Brian had shown up, I figured it was just my subconscious
letting me know that they were on the way. They were here now though,
and the feeling still persisted. Even stranger was the fact that the
presence, whatever it was, was vaguely familiar. Almost like a partially
forgotten memory that nags at the corner of the brain, just begging to be
remembered and acknowledged.

Well, I thought disgustedly, whether it was a presence or simply
my imagination, it certainly hadn't done me any good. Liza had still
found me. She was still as crazy as ever. She was still holding me
captive. And the two men who'd come to rescue me didn't seem to be
making any progress; instead, they seemed to have initiated some sort of
Mexican standoff. I was no better off than I'd been before. Except now,
there were three people at risk instead of one—and I couldn't even move.

I was starting to get pissed again, which was probably a good
thing since it put the enormity of my current situation back at the
forefront and kicked my brain into gear. While my hands were free, they
were positioned under my body, and I didn't think I could slide them
loose without alerting Liza. Even if I could, I wasn't sure I could reach
her foot and grab it with enough force to throw her off balance. But
assuming that was possible, yet another problem reared its head. As far
as I knew, she still had that branding iron in hand. And the Gods only
knew where it might land or how hot it still was.

Yeah, I thought, wouldn't that just be a perfect end...to knock
Liza off her feet and gain my freedom...only to die of a brain hemorrhage
from being conked on the head with a fucking branding iron? Under
other circumstances—a Laurel and Hardy movie or maybe an episode of
The Three Stooges—it might have been laughable. But this was real life,
and it just wasn't a workable solution.

My brain ticked off questions, answers and possibilities as fast as
I could process them, but nothing seemed plausible. In fact, the only
thing I managed was a splitting headache.

For the umpteenth time since this had all begun—since I'd been
stupid enough to get in the car with Liza—I prayed that this whole mess
was nothing more than the mother of all nightmares. That eventually I'd
wake up and everything would be fine, that life as I'd known it would
resume. But the aching of my body, the constant pressure on my back
and the words flung back and forth between Liza and Brian reminded me
again that it simply wasn't so.

I closed my eyes and fought back tears. My only hope at this point was Brian. And as much as I hated anyone else being in control of my life, two things were abundantly clear: that there was nothing for me to do but accept my current lack of power, and that Brian—who *was* in control now, whether I liked it or not—was one of the few people I trusted enough to handle the job.

Living Water, intervene: break this trick and wash it clean of malice and of ill intent...

Where the hell had that come from? The words that echoed through my brain were mine—I'd written them a few days before—but the voice was Chloe's. What on earth was she doing with them? Surely, she hadn't taken it upon herself...

Break the chains it represents—separate the ties that bind—uncross their magic and unwind the lives it's held for all these years...

For the love of the Gods, I thought, hearing Cal's voice take over. They were breaking the tricks. They were doing it together. And best of all, they were doing it *now*!

Hurry, I prayed, hoping they could hear me. For Gods' sake, hurry!

"Come on, Liza," Brian said patiently. His voice had taken on a charming, soothing quality I'd never heard. And if I hadn't known better, I'd have thought he was trying to coax a kitten from a tree. "Just hand the branding iron to Luke, and..."

"And you'll do what?! You'll shoot me...that's what!"

"Now, Liza," he said with a slight chuckle, "you know better than that. If I'd wanted to shoot you, I'd have already done it.

"Give Luke that branding iron and I'll make you a deal."

"What?"

"I'll put my gun back in the holster, and we'll call it a day."

Her eyes darted from Luke to Brian, and a look of uncertainty crossed her face. Then her mouth tightened, and she glared at Brian with cold, hard, calculating eyes. "I don't think so," she said. "I've got something you want, and you're not likely to shoot me to get it. So...it seems that I've got all the bargaining power here, and..."

"What do you want, Liza?" The smooth, relaxed tone in Brian's voice had been replaced by utter disgust.

"What I've always wanted," she said as casually as if she'd ordered a cup of tea. "The deed to the plantation. Signed. Sealed. And delivered."

The wind, which had died with the earlier rainstorm, suddenly rebirthed itself as she spoke. And by the time she'd uttered the last word, it was literally howling with a raw sort of power and had transformed itself into a zephyr of gale force proportions.

Just lovely, I thought. As if I didn't have enough to worry about already, the Gods had decided to add a tornado to the mix.

Holding the red felt bag in her left hand, Cal reached inside with her right and pulled out the last object. It looked like a fingernail clipping, and she couldn't help but wonder if it had belonged to Belle. Surely it had. She thought about how old it was, how long Belle had been gone and yet, how this tiny piece of her had still managed to survive. Part of her thought it was a shame to toss this relic into the rushing water where it would be lost forever. And yet...

"So they move forward without fear." Chloe paused and shot Cal a look to prompt her along. And then as if to punctuate the message, she added a jab with her elbow.

Cal sighed, tossed the fingernail into the water and turned toward the paper Chloe held in her hands. "The past is past, it's washed away," she read aloud. "Its power's gone and cannot prey upon the living here and now!" She balled up the bag in her hand and threw it into the water as well, watching as it twirled away and was quickly sucked down into the belly of the creek.

"But Living Water, do allow the purest form of love to live," she continued, "the sort that freely takes and gives...the sort that aids and adds support...the sort that magic can't distort..."

There was a sudden change in the atmosphere as Cal's words trailed off. It was almost as if the plot of ground on which they were standing had breathed an initial sigh of relief, but the spirits who inhabited it were waiting for something more.

Cal and Chloe exchanged a puzzled look. "Go on," Cal mouthed.

Chloe's voice rang out loud and clear. "That love ingrained in humankind...that love that doesn't tie or bind," she called out with joy. "That love that lives without provision, without manipulation or condition...that love inherent in each soul, that dries the tears and aids the goal!

"The love of friends and family," she continued softly, her voice cracking as a tear rolled down her cheek, "without which we could not be the human race we've come to know." Then pausing to swipe at the errant tear, she took a deep breath and spoke the final words. "As I will, it shall be so!"

The change was immediate, but felt rather than seen. It was a shift in the energies—a healing sort of shift—as if the land and its spirits had suddenly been cured of some dastardly disease that before, had no remedy.

For the first time that night, spontaneous laughter—the sort born of pure, unadulterated joy—bubbled up from inside both Cal and Chloe and spilled forth into the atmosphere. They hugged each other excitedly, squealing in delight and jumping up and down like schoolgirls, for they'd accomplished something they'd never truly thought possible: They'd not only unraveled the magic that had held lives in the balance for more than a hundred years—quite a feat in itself—but had also managed, even if unwittingly, to bring a sense of peace to the cemetery and rest to its residents.

Don't be's countin' them chickens a'fore they hatch, Little Missy! You still gots work to do!

"Come on, Chloe," Cal said with a grin. "Give me that other trick, and let's get this finished up!"

"No...Noooooo...NOOOOOOOOOOOOOOOOOOOOO!"
The anguished protests seemed to go on forever, but in all actuality, it was probably only a few minutes. That awful, wailing racket that reverberated through the atmosphere didn't have one damned thing to do with the wind. It wasn't the result of a force of nature at all. Rather, it was the result of a supernatural force—a spirit of some kind—and it was mad as hell! And by the timing of the outburst, it was obvious that its angst had something to do with Liza's demand of the plantation deed.

What happened next was even more unsettling. You see, Liza

wasn't just knocked off her feet. She didn't just lose her balance or her footing. Instead, she was literally lifted into the air, transported across the clearing and dropped—rather unceremoniously—right at Brian's feet.

But even then, the spirit wasn't done. *"Mah daddy built that house and worked that land,"* he thundered, *"and it was mine by right. I fought that wah and gave mah life to protect it and keep it safe for mah family."*

He paused for a moment as if waiting for his words to sink in before continuing, *"And Ah'll be damned and go to hell—and tangle with Ol' Scratch, himself—before Ah* evah *see it belong to anyone not of mah own choosin'. Or mah name,"* he added, *"isn't William Cyrus McGee!"*

I don't think any of us so much as breathed for a minute or two. We just stared at each other with wide eyes.

Finally, Brian broke the silence. "Holy Mother of God," he whispered, crossing himself.

Brian had asked for a miracle, all right. But never in his wildest imagination did he dream he'd get one—certainly not like this—and especially not in the off-handed way he'd asked for it.

After a silent but fervent prayer of thanks to the Virgin, as well as a personal promise, he holstered his weapon and reached for his cuffs. While Liza was unconscious, there wasn't any point in taking chances. Not now. Not after what he'd just witnessed. So, rolling her over on her stomach, he snapped the cuffs on her wrists and secured them behind her back.

By the time Liza was cuffed, Luke had already stripped down to his jeans and had me dressed in his shirt and jacket. I hurt so bad, I could hardly move. My back was killing me, my ribs hurt like hell, and every muscle in my body throbbed. In fact, it was probably safe to say that the only thing that *didn't* hurt at that juncture was my hair. But that didn't stop Luke from scooping me up and smothering me with kisses.

"Yow!" I screeched, unable to stop myself.

"Oh, geeze, Babe," he said apologetically, his eyes filled with concern, "I'm sorry...I didn't mean to...I'm just so glad to...oh, geeze..."

The man was so obviously undone at the thought of having injured me further, I thought he might actually cry. And if he did, I was afraid that I might too. So I mustered a sort of half grin—it was the best I could do at that point—looked him straight in the eye and said, "Well, Ollie...'tis certainly a fine mess I've gotten us into. But just this once," I added playfully, "please don't slap me around with your cane!"

Liza groaned and turned over on her side. It wasn't an easy process. Her shoulders and arms ached, and her hands seemed to be caught on something—something hard and sharp that bit into her wrists with even the slightest movement. From that lucid space between sleep and wakefulness, she wondered what was wrong with them. Had she injured herself in the night? Surely not.

With a great deal of effort, she finally managed to roll over on her back. That made things even worse. Now, those useless limbs were pinned beneath her, their muscles straining under the weight of her body, and she couldn't move them at all.

Something's wrong, she thought. Dreadfully wrong. The panic stirring in her belly sent her heart racing, and her eyes flew open in terror.

What the hell?! She was outside—on the cold, damp ground, no less—and from the looks of the sky, it was nearly dawn. She tried to sit up and get her bearings, but without the use of her hands and arms for leverage, she only managed to strain her stomach muscles. Easing back down on her side, she looked around. Oh, my God, she thought. She was out in the middle of nowhere. She racked her brain, desperately searching for some clue as to where she was, how she might have gotten there, and of course, what the hell was wrong with her arms.

"Mornin'."

Liza wrenched her head around and looked up. Brian Dawson was standing over her.

"W-wh-wha..."

"Just calm down, Liza," he said, making a concerted effort to be pleasant. Deep down, he knew none of this was her fault—not really— but the pressures and anxiety of the night before still weighed heavily on his mind. Truth be told, he was downright pissed. But that was something he'd have to work through on his own. He also knew that letting that sort of anger seep through at this juncture was only going to make matters worse—matters that were already bad enough without any additional help. "Everything's going to be fine," he added, helping her into a sitting position. "Just fine."

"B-but my arms and hands..."

"Oh, that," he said, much more sarcastically than the situation warranted. He was being an ass and he knew it. If anger's not going to work, neither is a case of the smart mouth, he chided himself. Stop being a jackass and get on with it! The personal admonition seemed to do the trick, but he took a deep breath as reinforcement before continuing. "Nothing to be concerned about," he said, a bit surprised at how quickly his tone of voice had changed. "It's just a set of handcuffs, and..."

"*Handcuffs*?!" she screeched.

"Yeah. I'm afraid we had to restrain..."

"*Restrain* me?!" Her eyes went wild and she started to pant.

My God, Brian thought, this is the last thing we need. The woman was starting to hyperventilate, and if he didn't do something quick, she'd have a heart attack right on the spot. He hurriedly unsnapped the cuffs, brought her wrists in front of her and snapped them again. Then pushing her head between her knees, he said, "Slow, deep breaths, Liza. In through your nose and out through your mouth."

After a few seconds, her breathing steadied somewhat and she raised her head. "Thank you," she managed. "But I don't understand...I don't understand a lot of things," she blurted. "Like where I am...how I got here...what I'm doing here...and wh-why you saw the need to...to *restrain* me! I...I..." Unable to go on, she dropped her head in her hands and burst into tears.

"Well, to start with..." He paused to buy some time. How the hell was he going to rationally explain something so bizarre? The simple fact of the matter was that he couldn't. And coming to that realization brought another: He was going to have to stick to the facts and leave the rest to someone else.

"Well," he started again, "it seems that you kidnapped Tess Logan, and..."

"I couldn't have," she blurted. "I didn't even see her yester..."
Her voice broke off in mid-sentence as her eyes fixed on something off
to her right. "Oh...my...God!"

Oh my God is right, Brian thought, shaking his head. He could
only assume she'd just seen Tess.

Chloe was more excited than a kid with a ticket to the North Pole
at Christmastime. According to Sally, Brian and Luke had located Tess,
Liza was Liza again, and although Tess was a little banged up, it looked
like everybody was going to be just fine. And to top it all off, they'd
managed to break tricks that were over a hundred years old! How cool
was that?!

She wanted to dance. She wanted to sing. She wanted to jump up
and down like a six-year-old. Truth be told, she'd wanted to mambo out
of the cemetery, but when Cal had laughingly declined her offer, she
settled instead, for a hearty rendition of "When the Saints Go Marching
In" and talked Cal into singing backup.

At some point, Chloe changed the word "saints" to "Oya." And
singing and prancing like a member of a Dixieland parade, she
promenaded right up to the entrance, twirled with a flourish and danced
out backward. Cal laughed so hard she could hardly catch her breath.

"What?!" Chloe batted her blue eyes and shot Cal that look of
innocence that was hers alone. "I went out backward. I met protocol.
And I did it," she said, bursting into giggles, "in a way that even Oya
could appreciate!"

"Yes, you did," Cal said, still chuckling. "Hedging your bets for
the next time you encounter Her, hunh?"

"You betcha! After all," she said with a twinkle in her eyes,
"who has time to hang around all night while the Ancients make up Their
minds? Besides, it never hurts to flatter the Gods...no matter *Who* They
belong to!"

By the time they got back to the car, it was a little after six. The
sun had poked its nose over the horizon and painted the sky in vibrant
shades of orange, pink and cerise. It was going to be a beautiful day.

"So, how long before everybody gets back over to Tess'?" Cal
asked. She reached for her cigarettes and lit up before starting the car and

slipping it into reverse.

"At least a couple of hours," Chloe said, lighting up as well and drawing deeply on her smoke. "Damn, this tastes good!" She exhaled fully before continuing. "Sally said the guys were stopping by the doctor's office first, just to make sure Tess and Liza were okay."

"Doesn't sound like anyone was seriously injured then..."

"Well, I don't know," Chloe replied. "Sally didn't have much information, and..."

"But if they didn't call the paramedics, then it would stand to reason..."

"Not necessarily. Calling for an ambulance or going to the emergency room would mean answering a bunch of questions. And that's something Brian would jump through his ass to avoid. Especially with this situation. I mean, who's going to believe that someone flipped back into a previous lifetime? The whole bunch of them would wind up in the loony bin!"

Cal stopped at the end of the drive then turned south onto Highway 61. "Yeah," she said thoughtfully, exhaling smoke through her nostrils and crushing out her cigarette. "I see what you mean. But what do *you* think?"

"Well, my gut says it's nothing that a few days of pampering won't cure. But," she added, "the situation between Tess and Liza is another story. I'm not sure anything will ever cure that."

"I guess that just depends on how Tess and Luke feel about each other since we broke that trick."

Chloe nodded. "Yeah...I guess it does. Speaking of tricks," she said, "what are you going to do with those pins?"

"Well, I started to just toss them into the creek with the poppet remnants. But my *grandmother*..."

Chloe's eyebrows knitted together, and she looked at Cal questioningly.

"Don't ask!" Cal said, as if there was any need to after she'd rolled her eyes and chuckled. "Anyway," she continued, "MawMaw didn't seem to think that was quite right. So, I've decided to give Tess and Luke each one, and they can take it from there."

"Hmmm..." Chloe paused, seeming to consider the possibilities for a moment. "What do you think they'll do with them?" she finally asked.

"Honestly?" she said, glancing in Chloe's direction. "I don't know."

They were quiet for a few minutes, each lost in their own thoughts. It had been a long night filled with more unease than either of them had thought they could handle. And yet, they'd made it through just fine. The dawn had brought a brand new, beautiful day for all of them—a fresh, clean slate upon which their lives could be written and drawn and started anew in any way they pleased. All they had to do now...was start living it.

EPILOGUE

I sat at the kitchen table pouring over my notes, thinking about the events that had prompted them and wondering if turning them into a novel was really such a good idea. It was a great story, all right. And if I tweaked it a little here and there—and changed the names to protect those involved—nobody would ever guess it wasn't fiction.

I pushed the pile of papers aside and reached for the coffee carafe on the table. Then topping off my cup, I peered out the window. The twins were being twins: Lucy, busily picking pansies and lilies-of-the-valley from the flower beds—which, of course, meant she was pulling them up by the roots—and Logan, sitting beside her, completely engrossed in the examination of an earthworm he held between his chubby fingers. It was hard to believe they were almost three.

Momentarily caught up in the glint of the sunlight on their chestnut hair, my mind wandered back to the morning that Cal and Chloe had broken those tricks. Every year, I celebrated the day as fully as I did my own birthday, for it was just as important, if not more so. It was the day my life had been returned to me—the day I'd realized that life was so much more than simply existing day to day. It was a gift to be unwrapped with utter delight, explored to the fullest and cherished beyond measure. And while it was definitely a meal to be savored, it was also designed to be gobbled up hungrily so that nothing—not even the tiniest scrap—went to waste.

It was the day we'd all truly started living again.

I glanced at the rings on my finger and smiled. I'd known the very second that Luke and I had been unbound. It wasn't that anything changed between us. Far from it. We were as much in love as ever. It was that the ring—the one now accompanied by a diamond circlet—had nearly fallen off my finger.

I'd also known exactly when the magic holding Luke and Liza was severed. Liza had immediately zipped back into her present life, not only oblivious to Belle's actions but absolutely horrified to discover what she'd done to me in the process; so horrified, in fact, that she'd checked herself into a private facility for a complete psychiatric evaluation and refused to leave until she had a clean bill of mental health. Suffice it to say that I never filed charges. And whether because of that—or because of the absence of those tricks in our lives—the three of us had become much closer.

And Brian and Chloe? Well, they were still Brian and Chloe, with one of them—guess which?!—still shopping 'til she dropped and the other raising hell about it. I'd finally come to the conclusion that they actually *liked* to bicker, that it was part of the glue that held them together. Since the incident out in the woods though, Brian's hell-raising over Chloe's shopping trips was much less stringent. But whether that was due to the fact that he cared less about her spending sprees or to the fact that he'd run for sheriff and won was anybody's guess.

I glanced at the clock, put on a fresh pot of coffee and slipped the last two pans of cookies into the oven. Chloe was due in just a few minutes to help me go over my notes—and, of course, do her best to convince me that the pile of papers on the table really could be the novel of the century.

After checking on the kids one more time—they were playing with Cat, the stray kitten that had wandered up to the plantation and adopted us—I sat back down and lit a cigarette. Dragging deeply, I set it in the ashtray. Then picking up a pencil, I sorted through the papers again, scanning them as I went. If I was really going to write this book, I had to figure out what was still missing and what had to be established.

First, we'd never figured out exactly *who* was buried in that grave in the Sikeston cemetery. Of course, I had my suspicions. My heart told me that it wasn't Lucinda, but that wasn't something I could prove—at least, not yet. Chloe and I were still researching that, and eventually, I knew that we'd stumble upon the truth. In the meantime, I'd had the new grave marker inscribed exactly as the original. And while that certainly hadn't been my initial plan, it was the best I could do without all the facts.

Chloe and I were also still researching the lives of the enslaved who'd lived on the plantation. And even though that wasn't easy due to the lack of legal documentation, Cal had helped us more than we'd ever thought possible. Since she'd been related to some of people involved, she'd talked to her relatives about them and relayed the family stories they'd told. She'd also given us a list of folks to contact who might have additional information. But since life has a way of getting busy—and our lives were no exception—we hadn't gotten that far.

I reached for the cigarette that had all but burned up in the ashtray, took one last drag and crushed it out. It wouldn't do for the cookies to burn up too, I thought, getting up to see about them. Of course, perfectly browned or not, Chloe would still insist they were scorched, to justify stuffing a few more in her mouth. I grinned at the thought, removing the pans from the oven and scooping the cookies onto the cooling rack.

Meeeroooooooww!

The sound of Cat shrieking sent me racing out the back door. And as soon as I saw what was going on, I wanted to shriek too. Lucy wasn't just holding the kitten by his neck, she was swinging him over her head in delight.

"Laura Lucinda Benson," I said sternly, "you stop that this instant!"

She stopped in her tracks and looked at me with the innocence of a child being punished unjustly. "But Mama," she whined, "he likes..."

"But Mama, *nothing*!" I said, collecting the terrified kitten and holding him gently against my shoulder, well out of her reach. I took a deep breath and made a concerted effort to soften my tone. "He's just a baby, Lucy. And you need to be *gentle* with him. Okay?"

She nodded dutifully but didn't look one bit happy about it.

I opened the door and put the kitten inside. "There you go, Buddy," I whispered.

"But I'm not finished playing with him!" Lucy wailed insistently. "I still want to play..."

"Oh, yes...you are," I said, forcing a smile, "at least, for now. Babies need lots of sleep, Honey, and it's time for Cat to take a nap. So, let's let him sleep for a while. And later, when Daddy gets home, we'll all play with Cat together. Okay?"

"Okay, Mama." All smiles again, she grabbed her brother by the hand. "Come on, Logan," she said, "let's go swing."

Cat met me at the door, weaving in and out of my legs as if nothing had happened. Still, I scooped him up and checked him over. He was purring now and didn't seem any worse for the wear. But as the cold chills racing up and down my spine hadn't slowed down at all, I certainly wasn't going to take any chances. I closed Cat up in our bedroom—along with his food, water and litter box—where he'd be safe until Luke got home.

No sooner had I closed the door than the house resounded with the twins' joyous chorus of "Aunt Chloe's here, Aunt Chloe's here!"

"Mmmmm," I heard her say from the foyer, "smells like cookies. So...where's my cookie dough bowl?"

"In the dishwasher," Logan replied with a giggle. This was a game the three of them had played ever since the kids had begun to toddle, so they knew their lines well.

"In the *dishwasher*?!" she exclaimed in mock surprise.

"Yes ma'am!" Lucy said with wide eyes, trying to keep a straight face. "And somebody already licked it clean. Clean as a whistle!" She nodded her head in emphasis.

"Licked it?! Clean as a whistle? Who *did* that?!"

The kids barely maneuvered their token shrugs before breaking into giggles at the thought of what was coming next.

"I bet *you* did it!"

"NO!" they shrieked.

"Yes, you did!" Chloe exclaimed emphatically. "And now..." her eyes widened at this point, "I'm going to have to *tickle* the truth out of you!"

She flexed and wiggled her fingers in their direction, and shrieking and giggling, all three of them raced through the house and into the kitchen.

With the twins down for their afternoon naps, Chloe and I had gotten to work. I refilled our coffee cups and watched her scribbling on the legal pad in front of her. I'd never dreamed that my writing career would take off as it had, and certainly not to the point that I'd ever have been able to hire her. But it had, and I had, and I smiled at my good fortune.

Brushing her hair out of her eyes, she grabbed her coffee cup and looked up from the pad. "Okay," she said with a sigh, "there's nothing in here about the wedding, and..."

"Oh, I don't know if I oughta include..."

"Well, there's no way you can leave *that* out...not if you're going to do this book! Yeah," she said, pausing to reach for a cookie, "I know you're reluctant to write about something that personal. But my Gods, Tess! It was the event of the century..." Her words trailed off as she bit into the cookie.

I arched an eyebrow and shot her that look. The one that used to get her attention. Since she went right on, never missing a beat, I had to assume it had lost its effectiveness.

"Oh, come *on*! You on Brian's arm...coming down that mahogany staircase...a vision in all that gorgeous, antique ivory lace? Gods, Tess...it could be a book all on its own."

"Then suppose *you* write that one!" I teased.

She rolled her twinkling eyes heavenward and grinned at me, making a few more notes.

"Well...what about the pins? Don't you think folks should know what you did with them?" she asked, sipping her coffee and reaching for her cigarettes.

"Probably," I said, tapping out one of my own and lighting up. I leaned back in my chair and exhaled, remembering. It had taken us awhile to figure out what to do with them. Initially, Luke had wanted to keep his as a souvenir of sorts, but I'd managed to convince him otherwise. So, after a lot of research into the various hoodoo methods of breaking tricks and several conversations with Cal, we'd finally agreed to cut each pin in half and dispose of the pieces in four separate bodies of running water. That way, there was no chance of the pieces so much as ever touching each other again. It was the only way I could be absolutely sure that any magic they might have held over us was completely and utterly broken and that our love for each other could grow unencumbered.

"Well, look who's here!"

I'd been so wrapped up in my thoughts, I hadn't even heard Luke come in. "Hi, Handsome," I said, reaching up to kiss him hello. "What are you doing, sneaking in so early?"

He smiled that lopsided smile that always made me melt. "Just missed my best girl," he said, handing me the bouquet of flowers he'd been holding behind his back and scooping me up in his arms like he'd never let me go.

"Sounds like spring fever to me!" I said with a wink, giggling at him.

"So, where are the kids?"

"Down for naps. But," I added, glancing over my shoulder at the clock, "if we want them to sleep at *all* tonight, I probably oughta get them up."

"I'll do it," he said, "on one condition."

"What?"

He whispered in my ear.

"Well, I don't know, Mr. Benson," I teased, swatting him playfully with the bouquet. "I guess that all depends."

"On what?"

"On how much of that three-year-old energy you can exhaust in the next few hours!"

Hearing the water shut off from Luke's shower, I dished up the mashed potatoes and set them on the table with everything else. Perfect, I thought. And provided Luke didn't dilly-dally too long, things should still be hot by the time he sat down.

I was just on my way to call the kids in from the living room when Logan came running into the kitchen, his eyes wide and Lucy right on his tail. "Mama! Mama!" he shouted, his shrill voice echoing through the house as only a three-year-old's could.

"What, honey?" I said, smiling down at him. Logan was my serious child, the one who thought everything—from an untied shoe to a spilled drop of water—constituted an emergency.

"There's sumpin' wrong with Lucy's arm! It's..." Lucy shot him a glare that stopped him in mid-sentence.

"Let's see," I said, squatting down to take a look. Continuing to glower at her brother and huffing in disgust, she dutifully held out her arm.

"Oh, Lucy!" My eyes fixed on the long, bleeding cut that traveled from her elbow to her wrist. "What on earth happened?"

"Guess Cat scratched me."

"Cat couldn't have scratched you, Honey," I answered. "Cat's been..."

"Oh, *geeze*...oh, *GEEZE!! TESS! TESSSSS!!*"

Following Luke's screams, I raced down the hall and into the bedroom. There, lying in the middle of our bed, was a limp and lifeless Cat, his neck askew and blood trailing from his nose.

"Oh, geeze, Tess..." he whimpered, bending over the dead kitten and gently picking him up. "He's been...his neck...it's been...oh geeze...it's been broken!" The last word issued forth as a whisper, his voice cracking and tears rolling down his cheeks.

My heart pounded. My blood ran cold. And that horrible dream I'd had over three years ago came to life again in my mind's eye. This couldn't be happening! It couldn't, I thought, whirling around at the sudden noise behind me.

Lucy stood in the doorway and looked at me, a satisfied grin on her tiny, perfect face.

OTHER BOOKS FROM
E. M. A. MYSTERIES IMPRINT

The award winning **Rowan Gant Investigations**
occult suspense thriller series:

The RGI Series follows Rowan Gant, a practicing Witch, as he
aids the Saint Louis Police Major Case Squad in solving high
profile and often horrific serial homicides with occult overtones.

HARM NONE:
A Rowan Gant Investigation
By M. R. Sellars

EAN 978-0-9678221-0-5
$8.95 US

MURDEROUS SATAN WORSHIPPING WITCHES

NEVER BURN A WITCH:
A Rowan Gant Investigation
By M. R. Sellars

EAN 978-0-9678221-1-2
$8.95 US

THE RETURN OF THE BURNING TIMES

PERFECT TRUST:
A Rowan Gant Investigation
By M. R. Sellars

EAN 978-0-9678221-9-8
$8.95 US

P I C T U R E   P E R F E C T

THE LAW OF THREE:
A Rowan Gant Investigation
By M. R. Sellars

EAN 978-0-9678221-8-1
$14.95 US

LET THE BURNINGS BEGIN...

CRONE'S MOON:
A Rowan Gant Investigation
By M. R. Sellars

EAN 978-0-9678221-4-3
$14.95 US

WHEN THE DEAD SPEAK,
ROWAN GANT HEARS THEIR WHISPERS

LOVE IS THE BOND:
A Rowan Gant Investigation
By M. R. Sellars

EAN 978-0-9678221-2-9
$14.95 US

SHE LOVES THEM TO DEATH ...

BOOK ONE OF THE MIRANDA TRILOGY

ALL ACTS OF PLEASURE:
A Rowan Gant Investigation
By M. R. Sellars

EAN 978-0-9678221-3-6
$14.95 US

PLEASURE IS A RELATIVE CONCEPT...

BOOK TWO OF THE MIRANDA TRILOGY

THE END OF DESIRE:
A Rowan Gant Investigation
By M. R. Sellars

EAN 978-0-9678221-6-7
$14.95 US

EVIL HAS A NAME, AND IT IS MIRANDA...

BOOK THREE OF THE MIRANDA TRILOGY

BLOOD MOON:
A Rowan Gant Investigation
By M. R. Sellars

EAN 978-0-9678
$14.95 US

<u>**New Release**</u>

While consulting for the Greater Saint Louis Major Case Squad has become an almost full-time job for Rowan–as well as a deeply ingrained part of his life–his desire for a normal existence devoid of crime scenes and horrific visions fuels a deep reluctance to get involved. However, when a long time enemy within the police force and an insistent spirit both demand the benefits of Rowan's unique talents, he is thrust into a situation that leaves him no choice in the matter.

But as questions are answered, a thread of deception unravels in the encroaching darkness, leaving the unofficial Witch of the Major Case Squad to wonder who he can really trust.

Non–Fiction Titles

From WillowTree Press

CHASING THE RAINBOW:
Facilitating a Pagan Festival Without Losing Your Mind

By Tish Owen

EAN 978-0-9678221-5-0
$14.95 US

Chasing The Rainbow is destined to become the quintessential guide for facilitating Pagan festivals. Author, Tish Owen, draws from over a decade of experience running one of the Mid-south's largest alternative-spirituality gatherings. In her down to earth and often humorous style, she offers sound advice and common sense planning techniques that will help to make any festival coordinator's job a pleasure rather than a pain—be it a small celebration or a large event on a regional scale.

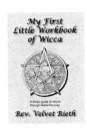

**MY FIRST LITTLE
WORKBOOK OF WICCA:
A Child's Guide to Wicca
Through Interactive Play**

By Reverend Velvet Rieth

EAN 978-0-9794533-0-4
$16.95 US

Containing general educational exercises blended with basic Pagan concepts and symbols, this workbook presents a wonderful introduction to Wicca for young children. Originally produced as a teaching aid for her grandchildren, Reverend Rieth's textbook grew into a project, which was home produced in limited quantities and sold at Pagan festivals nationwide by only a handful of vendors—it very quickly became one of their best-selling items.

Books by Dorothy Morrison
From WillowTree Press

UTTERLY WICKED:
Curses, Hexes, and Other Unsavory Notions
By Dorothy Morrison

EAN 978-0-9794533-1-1
$14.95 US
Non-Fiction

Hexes, curses and other unsavory notions. Most magical practitioners won't even discuss them. Why? Because they'd much rather find a positive solution that benefits all concerned...and, there's nothing wrong with that. Occasionally though, our problems are such that nothing in the positive solution arena will handle them. It's time to make a decision to stand tough, be strong, and take definitive action to defend ourselves. So, if you're ready to do that–*if you're ready to own that action and take responsibility for it*–then **Utterly Wicked** is the book for you!

Other Publishers Featuring Titles by **Dorothy Morrison**

Llewellyn Worldwide

New Page Books

US Games (Tarot Deck)

WillowTree Press Books
Are Available From
Independent and Chain Bookstores
Nationwide,
As Well As Through
Amazon.com
and Other Online Booksellers.

For Convenient Ordering
Via the
WillowTree Press Online Bookstore
Visit: www.willowtreepress.com

Dorothy Morrison

Dubbed by Publishers Weekly as "a witch to watch," Dorothy Morrison is the award-winning author of numerous books on the Ancient Arts and their application to modern life. She has won several awards for her writing and has become a favorite of readers and critics from all walks of life. Some say it's because of the easily appreciated conversational tone she applies to her work. Others say it's her down-to-earth and humorous approach to the subject matter. But regardless of the debate, all agree on one thing: Whether in her writing or her interaction with the public, it's Morrison's personal style that makes her memorable.

A practicing Witch since the early seventies, Morrison is an elder of the Georgian Tradition of Wicca, an initiate of the RavenMyst Circle Tradition, and a member of the Coven of the Raven in Flint, Michigan.

Morrison currently lives in Virginia with her husband, Mark, and their black lab, Sadie Mae. She handles a voracious tour schedule and travels the country giving lectures and teaching classes related to Witchcraft.

Printed in the United States
205803BV00001B/256-309/P